Barnstorm

Terrace Books, a division of the University of Wisconsin Press, takes its name from the Memorial Union Terrace, located at the University of Wisconsin–Madison. Since its inception in 1907, the Wisconsin Union has provided a venue for students, faculty, staff, and alumni to debate art, music, politics, and the issues of the day. It is a place where theater, music, drama, dance, outdoor activities, and major speakers are made available to the campus and the community. To learn more about the Union, visit www.union.wisc.edu.

Barnstorm

Contemporary
Wisconsin Fiction

Edited by
Raphael Kadushin

THE UNIVERSITY OF WISCONSIN PRESS
TERRACE BOOKS

The University of Wisconsin Press
1930 Monroe Street
Madison, Wisconsin 53711

www.wisc.edu/wisconsinpress/

3 Henrietta Street
London WC2E 8LU, England

5   4   3   2   1

Printed in the United States of America

Library of Congress Cataloging-in-Publication Data
Barnstorm: contemporary Wisconsin fiction / edited by Raphael Kadushin.
p.   cm.
ISBN 0-299-20854-0 (pbk.: alk. paper)
1. American fiction—Wisconsin.   2. Wisconsin—Social life and customs—Fiction.   3. Short stories, American—Wisconsin. I. Kadushin, Raphael.
PS571.W6B37   2005
813'.0108977506—dc22   2004024340

Contents

Acknowledgments   vii

Introduction   3
RAPHAEL KADUSHIN

Egyptian   9
MARGARET BENBOW

Brazil   19
JESSE LEE KERCHEVAL

Logjam   49
RON WALLACE

Touching Bottom   57
JOHN HILDEBRAND

Setting the Lawn on Fire   65
MACK FRIEDMAN

As It Is in Heaven   89
KELLY CHERRY

Mission Work   131
ANTHONY BUKOSKI

The Jewish Hunter   139
LORRIE MOORE

It's Freezing Here in Milwaukee   163
J. S. MARCUS

A Patch of Skin   171
TENAYA DARLINGTON

Contents

Unknown Donor   181
JUDITH CLAIRE MITCHELL

Dropping the Baby   205
ANN SHAFFER

The Short History of a Prince   231
JANE HAMILTON

The Green Suit   261
DWIGHT ALLEN

Happy   287
DEAN BAKOPOULOS

Contributors   319

Acknowledgments

I'd like to thank all of the contributors, for giving their stories so readily and freely (literally). And I'd like to acknowledge the work of my colleague Sheila Moermond, who was crucial to this project every step of the way—from its inception to its editing. This book would not exist without her wisdom, generosity, and devotion to words.

Barnstorm

Why Wisconsin? That's what most people outside the state (and maybe some inside its borders) will wonder and probably for good reason. Certainly Wisconsin doesn't spring to mind when people contemplate America's literary centers or even outposts. But then probably no place springs to collective mind—if the collective mind thinks much about literature anymore—except for New York, where the publishing industry is still largely concentrated.

To confuse publishing with literature, though, is a mistake. In fact, most of the country's truly singular writers live in the most unexpected places (and increasingly publish with the most unlikely houses) and every region boasts its own favorite literary sons and daughters. Wisconsin's roster of names is as impressive as any state's. Among our homegrown dairyland writers, and those passing through long enough to call the state at least a temporary home: Zona Gale; Ben Hecht; Ben Logan; Lorine Niedecker; Laura Ingalls Wilder; John Muir; Aldo Leopold; Hamlin Garland; Frederick Jackson Turner; Glenway Wescott; August Derleth; Edna Ferber; Carl Sandburg; Ellen Raskin; Eudora Welty; Felix Pollak; Yi-Fu Tuan; Joyce Carol Oates; Mona Simpson; and Wallace Stegner.

The list of writers currently living in Wisconsin is just as impressive, and a strong cross-section of that group is represented in the stories that follow. Why these particular stories? The simplest explanation is that they're all written by good writers, and that was my only criterion in selecting the pieces. And that's the reason the collection doesn't claim, like most literary collections, to represent the best or to be all-inclusive. There are many other volumes of good contemporary Wisconsin fiction that could and should be published, and certainly no one is single-handedly capable of judging the absolute best of anything. What I was looking for were simply the most powerful, homegrown, contemporary stories that I could find and that meant I approached the anthology with editorial blinders on, without trying to construct some statistical balance sheet based on any controlling factor (ethnicity, age, subject matter, local geography). I just chose stories that had their own voice and weren't derivative, and a lot of my selection process had to do with things I didn't want.

4

What I mostly didn't want was any of contemporary literature's popularized mono-voices. I didn't want any clones of Plum Sykes or Candace Bushnell, whose urbane humor is so childlike and witless it manages to make Manhattan look like the world's biggest hick town (when sophisticated humor has devolved into the world's longest-running gag—she loves Jimmy Choos; yes she does—and an ad for Bergdorf, it has more to do with catalog copy than comedy; the Algonquin Club is probably spinning in their graves, or maybe whirling around that hulking table). I wasn't looking for Bret Easton Ellis knockoffs, work that was already dated and inauthentic when it first appeared. And I didn't want any pomo stabs at fractured narratives that feel as avant-garde as Harvey Korman.

But mostly what I was avoiding, in selecting these stories, was the instinct to claim anything resembling a collection of intrinsically Wisconsin stories, or something pretending to capture a heartland voice. That instinct, of course, used to be the holy grail of regional collections, and maybe at one time—before our time, when America really was a patchwork of very different cultures—there was such a thing as a distinctly regional style. That era, though, is over, and only exists in the minds of people who've never actually been west of New Jersey, and nurse their old stereotypes because they're an easy form of condescension. Southern writers no longer write about church dinners in a hushpuppy voice, unless they're really bad ones, and Midwestern writers rarely wax lyrical about barn dances and bratwursts, unless they're joking. In fact, most of Wisconsin's contemporary writers, like all writers (except the Bushnell camp—probably the only truly provincial camp left) could be writing from anywhere and nowhere. They live in a global, contemporary world and what moves most of these stories is the fact that they are very centered in that world; every place is part of a bigger place now, every fear is a collective one, and most Wisconsinites are temporary natives, just arriving, just passing through, or just leaving. So anyone hoping for lots of down-home dairy farmers—most of whom have given way to corporate farmers in any case—or small town tragedies or main street comedies, or the quaint sense of place that regionalists used to cherish, should look for another book.

If there is one identifiable quality that does mark these stories as

Midwestern it may be their sense of autonomy—the fact that their authors have found their own place in that world—and their lack of pretension. All good writers eventually develop their own voice but any writer living in Wisconsin finds independence quickly, because there is no local culture club dictating style, and there is none of the intense literary rivalry that forces urban writers to keep looking over their shoulder for emerging fashions. Because they are living in a place that isn't consumed by trends or momentary culture-making— one of the reasons so many artists move here—heartland writers can soak in a quiet that lets them develop their own style. Don't mistake lack of pretension, though, for that butch, flat, faux Hemingway style that is a pretension in itself, or any kind of earthy, pioneering sensibility. In fact, a lot of these writers wouldn't know a cornfield from a wheat field. What an independent style really means is that you're writing a story guilelessly, so that your only impulse is to tell the story as truly as you can.

And that, in the end, is what all of these stories do, though many of the writers are tackling similar themes. In fact, the majority of the collection's pieces tell a form of romance. Take "The Jewish Hunter." Lorrie Moore is one of contemporary literature's most inimitable voices, and one of the very few writers who can balance tragedy and comedy so deftly that they ultimately merge. Her classic "Hunter" is a fractured romance, of course, like most contemporary romances, but it captures the ambiguity of love, the way it keeps reversing and revealing itself. Kelly Cherry, another writer who can do just about anything, locates the real magic in magic realism—itself a rarity—in her story "As It Is In Heaven," and composes a love poem that's part elegy and part sonnet to her standard of love, her parents' bond. Mack Friedman, on the other hand, in his "Setting the Lawn on Fire," focuses on first love, the kind of scorching love that is the template for every other lover, and he evokes the universal, primal whiff of infatuation, which may be the purest kind of love, because it's all passion and no brain. What Tenaya Darlington sees, instead, in her wrenching "A Patch of Skin," are the loveless, in their long night of the living dead, who can be the most passionate, because they know what they're missing.

Introduction

Where is the Midwest in all of this? It's nowhere and everywhere. For Moore it's the lover himself—half innocent and awkward, half wise and oddly beautiful. For Cherry it's a hopeful backdrop, the antidote to the musty, stultified, retirement home of an Old Country. For Friedman it's a purely erotic landscape, because it doesn't exist outside of his smoking brain, and in J. S. Marcus's "It's Freezing Here in Milwaukee," it's a place of defeat; his narrator's homecoming is a surrender and his home—a grim Milwaukee—is the realm of the quietly resigned. But then any place can be.

In other stories, though, Wisconsin is as much of a central character as anyone else and its soul is less of a metaphor than something concrete and indelible. And its beauty gets redeemed. Jane Hamilton perhaps evokes the heartland best, in the excerpt from *The Short History of a Prince,* one of the most humane and elegant novels to come out of anywhere in recent years. Hamilton sees Wisconsin as a place of homecoming too, a place to take stock, but it's also the land of second chances, with enough heart to match her Prince's own big heart. Leaving Manhattan and sitting in his white Adirondack chair, on the edge of Lake Margaret, wondering "where to live in the years before retirement," Walter, her protagonist, "smelled autumn . . . watched the chipmunks darting to the holes in the cracked seawall" and saw "all green things, the moss, the vines, the children at their desks . . . the fishermen holding their rods hour after hour in their metal boats . . . the cow pasture (and) . . . the water, where he sometimes saw his ghostly boyish form swim to the surface." This is the Midwest as a meditation, as something expansive and metaphysical, as something simultaneously singular and universal. In John Hildebrand's "Touching Bottom" it's a hunting ground, a territory of small murders and remorse, but also a wilderness of unadulterated beauty, a last frontier where the sky is a Delft blue and the river bottoms exude the rich smell of humus.

Surprisingly few of the stories really evoke the precise place—southern Wisconsin—where so many of the writers live. Certainly the whole state is represented in this anthology. Anthony Bukoski is based in Superior, Hildebrand in Eau Claire, Hamilton in Rochester, and of the writers no longer living in Wisconsin, two, Friedman and Marcus, are from Milwaukee, and return to the city in their stories. But the town that's most heavily represented here is Madison, and that's no accident, though it wasn't a conscious choice either. Certainly I didn't set out to seek Madison-based authors. But when I sat down with all of the contributed stories and made my final choices, without contemplating geography, I found that the Madison writers were hard to ignore, and there's a reason for that. What makes Madison Wisconsin's own contemporary literary epicenter is its university and its die-hard status as the state's soft-hearted, cultural capital. And that's only fitting. The job of the best universities—beyond launching students into the real world—is to help make culture, and conserve it. Their explicit mission is to generate knowledge for its own sake, and art for its own sake, and they are one of the few remaining American institutions dedicated simply to the brain, regardless of what the brain devises. For writers there are fewer and fewer refuges like this, and that makes the university in some ways the center of our national culture right now, and one of its only defenders.

Because every writer knows how fragile that culture and its books are these days, all of the contributors in this collection have given their work without accepting any royalties, so any profit can go back into the University of Wisconsin Press's regional fiction list. In the end, then, the anthology is a circular thing. Dedicated to the memory of Wisconsin's historic authors and representing the voices of its current ones, it is also a small way of assuring that there will be a corps of honest-speaking, clear-eyed Midwestern writers in our future as well.

I forget what moron it was who said we should fear no solitude, because there are angels in our midst.

Death changes everything. For example, Sam's and my big bed was no longer the conjugal couch but had become an ancient Egyptian cooling board, which I occupied alone. Night after night I lay awake as the embalmer, memory, practiced his craft. I lost my brains as surely as though he had drawn them out through my nostril with his little hook. My eyes and heart, lost earlier, waited separately on a platter for use in the afterlife.

I couldn't even write about it. There had never been anything, before, that I couldn't write about. Why, a whole genre existed of widows' memoirs and autobiographical novels in which the dead beloved rose again: to court and marry, to fight, eat vast pasta dinners, swim nude with the dusk on his skin, screw like a bandit, travel, sicken and then die in diamond-cut prose. The widows were not at a loss; they had kept extensive notebooks of their man's fits and starts while he was still breathing. I'd missed my opportunity. I'd lost words while Sam was sick, mislaid the vocabularies of the four languages I speak. The few words I still used during those months were not written down, they were always the same, and they were addressed only to the black beast living and waiting on our roof, his eyes bigger than his stomach: *"Are you really going to do this, you evil fuck, you evil motherfucker?"*

When Sam had been dead for a year, I tried clumsily to return to life. I still could not write, but I took walks, went to the store instead of having groceries delivered. My best friend, Sally, insisted that I had to. I even started dating. Once I embraced a man on the cooling board, trying to turn it into a bed again. I could not overcome a profound sense of strangeness. What was he doing there, where big Sam had held sway? I became a chaste moon maiden, discreetly shielding yawns, picking bits of mascara off my lashes. My silent apartment was enlivened by a furiously slammed door.

I didn't want him. I didn't want, period.

Now it had been two years. I couldn't write, I didn't date, and my friends had lost patience. Sally, a ferocious mother hen, accused me of wallowing in a rudimentary stage of grief, denial, when by her calculations I should long since have advanced to bargaining with fate. She watched me suspiciously, as though expecting me at any moment to emerge from my seclusion with a Victorian mourning brooch made of Sam's hair clapped to my bosom. Above all, she disapproved of a celibacy that she considered unseemly. "Two *years?*" she screamed. "It's indecent." In careful language, she pointed out that a passionate attachment to a dead man has no future.

My silence stretched on, became poisonous. Then I said, "You think I need a fuck."

Sally said, "It wouldn't hurt."

I said, "I'm old."

Sally replied loudly, as though she'd been waiting for this remark: "You are not old. You look ten years younger than your age. Why, the last time you and I went to Schuyler's—" Schuyler had a butcher shop in the next block, "—you were wearing that sky blue turtleneck, and I heard Schuyler say real low to Marty, 'I wouldn't mind a piece of that.'"

Well, this was just fucking great. My eighty-year-old butcher had said to his retarded shop assistant that he'd like a piece of me. I wondered which piece. I looked at my hand, small and white; my little left foot, which was beginning to get a bunion.

Sally's practical mind groped for solutions. After researching the topic, she gave me a well-reviewed book that was keyed to those who lack a partner with a beating heart. "Meg, you can't live with this tension," she said as she handed it to me.

The book warmly recommended certain implements, objects, and cruciferous vegetables. However, you could know Mr. Vibrator for ten thousand years and he would never bite your neck. Señor Broccoli will never pass you a cup of tea in bed on a cold morning.

Tension is fine. And I made a secret, revolutionary decision. I would have another human being, or nothing.

The new couple in the next apartment had no problems whatsoever experiencing sumptuous crises of desire. I had never seen them but already I knew that they were the busiest damned couple, desirewise, who ever existed behind a paper wall. I would be at my desk, correcting proofs from the novel I'd finished three years before. At any moment I expected their bed, a four-poster by the sound of it, to engine through the wall spraying plaster and lath and the thrashing manes of its oblivious occupants. I didn't mind the noise as such. It could just as easily have been traffic noise, a siren, a drill or wrecking ball.

It was fortunate I didn't mind it, because this couple had stamina. I imagined them powered by big lumberman breakfasts, stacks of smoking cakes, bloody steaks and six or eight fertilized eggs, washed down by Jolt Cola and half a dozen red poppers.

What disturbed me as I tried to work was not the noise, but the human voices, because this couple also talked a lot, and the things they said drew my attention. He had a deep, soft voice; hers was light and almost childish.

He was not exactly brutal, but took a firm, masterful tone. Once when she objected to something he wanted to do, he said, "I'm not the one you say no to. I'm the one you say yes to."

I'm not the one you say no to. I'm the one you say yes to. That was good; it was tough, meaty, to the point. I hesitated a minute, then reached for my pen. I wrote down what the man said. It was my first note since Sam died. In the next weeks there were many more. Sometimes I would record whole conversations.

The man liked overlord, warrior, and czar images for himself. In moments of highest favor, his girl became his "sweet little queen." It must be good to be king, a longhaired boss tiger prowling around. He said she made him feel as though he had a dozen different animals under his skin. I, scribbling madly to keep up, thought all these animals must be toothed and clawed. He himself was, judging from the sound of his stride, booted and perhaps spurred.

Once he dropped into a chair and said in his soft, coarse voice, "Come here. I'm going to crack you like a whip." The sound of a heavy body assaulting a slight one moved from chair to bed to—the top of the refrigerator? I took extensive notes that afternoon, blue strokes biting into the sheet, wondering all the time what I should do. But her shaken words of love matched his. I dutifully recorded them. I wondered how it could be that these primitive cave words, stark as a rock, could sound so poetic in the woman's small, pink, vaginal voice intertwining with the man's growling moan. I'd thought this was an anthropological experiment I was conducting, recording the life habits of a less evolved tribe. But how could they be less evolved, when they were having a better time than I had ever had? I'd never howled for joy. They did.

I didn't know what to think. I didn't know jack. I took notes.

It sometimes seemed to me that the wall between us was the thinnest of membranes through which I could distinguish splendid colors, reds and purples, swelling and waning. At other times the wall seemed like the steel plate door behind which the successful artist guards his perfect works of art.

Once he hit her. She hit him back. Had they reached a degree of intoxication in which anything given by the other's hand seemed good? He cried, and she cried, salt in their kisses. They always said freely what was in their hearts. Sometimes they did crack each other like whips, ending in a sad, plush luxury of sighs. High jinks shattered the light fixtures; she clawed the drapes.

I couldn't quite decide if they'd be together for sixty years, heavy with devotion and seniority, or if next week they'd be discovered by the howling of dogs, the reeling of odors, way past dead.

The night they hit each other, for the first time I read through all the pages of notes I'd been keeping—there were thirty, pretty closely written. Then, without thinking much about it, I reached for a pen and wrote a few paragraphs about a couple named Brett and Shelley. They were not having sex. They were preparing to go to the market. Afterward, they would go to a party. They were new; my new couple. I knew they were mine because I knew what they would do next. And not a thing was going to happen, not a goddamn thing, that I did not approve of.

In the next apartment, the man and woman ate a lot of fruit. He said that the skin of her breast was like translucent white plums, which he fed her. She squeezed ripe peaches in her hands, then worked the juice and pulp over his body. He told her to clean him "like a puppy," which she did. One afternoon there were adventures with other fruit.

They really made a lot of noise that afternoon, and to drown it out I laid down my pen and played some Beethoven on my stereo, rather loud. In an instant I heard his furious "Jesus Christ!" then her hesitant tap on the wall. "I'm sorry," she said in her tiny voice, "could you turn it down?" I turned it down.

When I put the record in its sleeve I read the album notes and saw that this was the piece, a late one, on which Beethoven had written, "Must it be so?" Beside this someone else had written, in a firm hand, "It must be."

That evening I wrote more about my new couple, Brett and Shelley. At first they did not do anything to anger or startle me. They went to a party. They had good hors d'oeuvres. Then they were dancing; Shelley was watching the pink-bronze sunset over Brett's shoulder, and suddenly out of the blue she saw and smelled black smoke. In the next instant a big gorgeous snake of blue flame crawled through the ceiling, and chunks of charred plaster began falling on the buffet table and in the punch bowl, bobbing beside rosebuds frozen in ice cubes.

I threw the pen down, and stared at my hand. It always frightens me when this happens; and besides, it had been so long since it had.

I got up and left the apartment. It was already dark, but I went to the park where I first met Sam. He had been a formidable sight to behold. He was a tall, burly man with shoulders straining his old leather jacket, hair halfway down his back, and at his side paced two ferocious-looking hounds.

We became engaged. I introduced him to Sally at lunch. She was aghast. "Meg," she said to me later, "you're a writer. You can't marry a man who holds his meat down with his thumb when he cuts it. I'm afraid to ask what he does for a living."

I looked at her silently. Sally owned many t-shirts that had barbarous but bracing slogans printed on them. Today she was wearing *Stop Sucking, Start Biting!*

"He works construction," I said.

"He . . . *works construction?*" she repeated, slowly and wonderingly, as if noting the gross preliterate fumblings of an ape man, a man of mud.

"We get on like a house afire," I said in a low voice. "He is it. And that is that."

Who would have guessed, when they saw him, that a gentle heart lived in that mighty house of bone? Or that in the end he would waste to ghost eyes and frog-legs? That in the last week, although he was so much taller than I, it was I who supported him everywhere he needed to go?

I stayed in the park very late, remembering all this. I stayed past the time when it was safe, so strong was my sense of his presence. I imagined so clearly his hawkish profile, that gladiator's walk of his, and the hounds who were tame to his hand as lambs.

I sat quietly, dreaming. The moon was behind a driving mass of cloud. Time spun itself out, so I don't know which moment it was that I saw a glitter, to my right. My mind moved slowly to comprehend this. When an object had no source of light, how could it shine? What glittered alone? And indeed the shine, whatever it was, disappeared.

But within a minute a voice spoke. It said, "Take off your coat." I looked around wonderingly. Surely this could not be directed to me?

A blurry-edged human shape walked slowly toward me from the darkness. "Take off your coat!" he said, this time in a hard, commanding voice. The blade in his hand had a pretty shine. Did he polish it?

Automatically I stood up and put my hands to my lapels, then paused. This man had the appearance of the dark real thing, the being and event that we are taught to fear all our lives. But I knew very well that the true dark real thing had happened two years before. This man was an imposter. Normally I'm a timid person, but now a rage began to burn in me, so heady and villainous I could hardly breathe.

For some reason I remembered the fierce slogans on Sally's T-shirts. Standing there, as the moon began to shift from behind the clouds, I quoted one to him. I said, *"You Must Be Mistaking Me For Someone Who Gives A Fuck."*

He stood silent and still, frozen. Then he raised his blade and started to walk toward me. I glanced wildly around me, scouring the ground for a weapon, and snatched up a jagged broken limb. I began walking toward him, the limb raised, chanting slogans: *"Better To Be Tried By Twelve Than Carried By Six."* I was not at all afraid. My blood seemed both molten and airy, dying to get at him. "*Stop Sucking, Start Biting!*" He backed, then stopped and began to raise the blade again, and it was then—"*Are We Having Fun Yet, Asshole?*"— that I aimed for his head like an ax going down on a chopping block. I put every ounce of power and fury I had into it, and missed him by six inches. I could barely see his stunned face in the darkness. He almost looked as though he were commiserating with me. I raised the tree limb, tried again and this time did manage to get a piece of his shoulder. He came up with an odd, almost girlish little scream, like a wounded rabbit. Now that I knew I could do it, I kept flailing away at him, sometimes hitting, more often missing, but trying my best. He seemed paralyzed with astonishment. There was the solid dead sound of the wood hitting his heavy winter coat. I'm convinced I would have stood there and belabored his sorry body with the hardwood until one of us caved in like an orange crate, except that after perhaps half a minute the limb was lifted out of my hands. It was taken from my clenched fists lightly, easily, as though by a giant or an angel. I almost fainted with shock. I flinched away, threw my arms up to protect myself, and saw a huge figure standing over me. In the dark I made out the lines of a massive shape, mighty-shouldered, clothed in a greatcoat. Long, rich hair flowed over these shoulders. *Sam's ghost?* I thought hysterically. Then the deep voice of my neighbor spoke. Apparently he'd been out for his evening stroll. "What do you plan to do, nudge him to death?" he said. "The dumb fuck isn't worth it. Go home."

I went home, shaking. Behind me I heard screams, none of them apparently my neighbor's. I did not turn to look.

That night Brett died in the fire. Shelley did everything she was supposed to do—*Stop, drop, and roll*—but she could save only herself, not him. Hysterically she threw the punch bowl with its icy roses in the direction of the flames, but that made it worse. She was scooped up by a monster in strange fetish regalia who turned out to be a fireman; she mightily fought him with head-butts and kicks of both arms and both legs, trying to stay where Brett was, but the fireman seemed to be a man without mercy. A woman who dies in a fire has very little pain at the end because the nerve endings are destroyed; yet the fireman insisted on saving Shelley and carried her out into the night in her smoldering chiffons.

At this point I laid my pen down. I remembered vowing to myself that nothing would happen to Shelley and Brett that I did not approve. Yet here they were, one dead against my will, one alive against my will; their every pore, tooth, and hair lit up in the conflagration of their story. *Story.* "Goddamn," I said aloud.

"I want you to try it. Please."

They were at it again, next door.

"No."

"Baby, please," he said." I've always loved cosmetics made from minerals, like the Egyptians used. Cleopatra was too much. Do it for me."

She said no. He said, "Did you know kohl is black powder made from lead ore? And they used to paint their lips with red ochre. I found a shop; I've got it here. Look what I got for you. Please."

She made some indistinct sounds, tears and words. I heard, "I'm not a doll," in a sob. I was trying to revise my new manuscript, and was annoyed.

He didn't hit her. He talked to her sweeter than I've ever heard a woman talked to, ever been talked to, in my life. And she cried harder than I've ever heard a woman cry. She cried so hard my hand hovered above 911. But what could I tell them? That he was committing abuse by cosmetics? And whom would they send? Firemen didn't seem right.

At last she said yes. He said, "Come over by the mirror. Start with the eyes. I love that elongation at the end of the eye. It should be shaped like a leaf. Smudge it a little. Then the mouth, outline it in red; it should look heavy and soft. I could go crazy for a woman with a mouth like that. A little gold on the lids. Nobody dares touch your gold but me. They want it, but they can't touch. The eyebrows should be heavy, black, and straight—" I heard a chair sway and creak. He was leaning back as he watched. He said, "Throw me one of those pears while you're at it." I heard the round smack of the pear hitting his palm. I pictured him, big-jointed, carnal-smelling, that rich hair down his back, his long fingers dripping with pears.

Oh, man, I thought. *Oh man alive.*

I wanted to see him. If possible to meet him. I listened to their preparations for departure, matched my step to theirs, burst out of my street door at the same instant they left theirs.

Anybody would have noticed her exceptional fairness and her beauty. She was ornately and seductively dressed, her bodice top full of flesh bloom as a rose is of petals. You would see also that she was a very large woman, a noble female vista. Her mane of chestnut hair fell over the mighty back and shoulders of an Amazon queen.

A dark man walked at her side. He was the most handsome man I had ever seen, in miniature. His head came to her heart. He made me think of a graceful Sherpa god, proudly flushed from scaling her thrilling gradients. I noticed that the woman's bloom was natural, accented by sweat on her brow and upper lip. He, however, had been exquisitely made up, the eyes lengthened with kohl, the red mouth heavy and soft.

But above all you would notice the tender accommodation each made to the other, so that although she was so large, and he so small, their bodies and postures dovetailed perfectly; they walked like twins.

Momentarily he turned his head when we passed. "Beautiful day, isn't it?" he said. I nodded, and as he smiled, his lids gleamed gold.

It is my birthday, my twentieth birthday, and I'm in the bar of one of the Art Deco hotels on the beach when I meet her. They are always using this hotel on *Miami Vice,* although they are careful to take tight shots of the pink front and not show the bums and junkies down the street, not until later in the episode, so it seems like they are miles away, in another Miami.

The bar is beautiful—*exquisite,* that's the word that comes to me—black and white and chrome. I feel odd here, like I'm watching myself on TV. I am with this guy, Roberto, who I met at Timmons College when I thought I'd made it out of Miami, had my ticket to the real America.

But I'd left Timmons after just one semester and gone back to working as a bellboy at the same hotel, the Royale Palms, where my mom and I used to live, where I worked in high school, a big 50s not 30s kind of place, not too far from the Fountainebleau but not nearly as nice. Roberto went on, building his grades, his sights on Harvard Law, while I got moved up from bellboy to parking attendant. That's how I ran into him again. I parked his BMW and I asked him about Maddy, who used to be my girlfriend before she decided to be Roberto's. He said she was fine, just fine, which is good because while I'm not mad at Roberto, I worry about Maddy. When he heard it was my birthday, he insisted, really insisted, we go out for a drink. So that's how I happen to be in this bar, which is very expensive, because Roberto brought me.

Roberto is Cuban, which I'm not, although everyone always says I look it. When I want to, I claim to be Brazilian, because my father is or was. I never met him, but we share the same name, *Paulo,* Paulo Silvas. Roberto is not only Cuban, he's Batista's grandson or great-nephew or something, and probably he will be the Republican governor of Florida someday. As soon as we sit down, some general disguised as a lawyer comes up and begins to talk the old politics. Even in a place like this, full of Yankee tourists, Roberto can't get away from Little Havana. When the white hair starts talking, Roberto shrugs, pats my shoulder. He buys a drink for me and I go sit at the bar, which is made of glass bricks and underlit so that all the people sitting at it look ghastly or exciting depending on your mood.

"I was born in Hungary," she says. "Buda."

"Budapest?" She shakes her head.

"Buda," she says. "The other side of the river, that is Pest."

"Like Miami and Miami Beach," I say, but she doesn't know about that.

We step out of the hotel and the hot August night air hits us. Claudia puts her hand around mine, and I notice that both our palms are sweating. We go for the car, which turns out to be a black BMW with Palm Beach County plates. BMWs are ugly cars really, very boxy looking, for all their expense. Their owners are crazy about them though. I backed one into a concrete piling in the parking garage, and the owner was really pissed. Luckily, the hotel garage has a big sign that says it doesn't take responsibility. Claudia gives me her keys, and I open the passenger door for her.

As soon as we are in the car, Claudia gets some coke out of the glove compartment—not a very safe place to keep it, any parking attendant could tell you—and hands it to me. In high school when I thought I'd be a lawyer someday, have to pass the bar and all, I practiced a lot of self-restraint. I was known for it really. But since I went to Timmons and came back the same year, it's been hard to see the point. Still, since I'm known for saying no, hardly anyone offers, and I am nervous as Claudia hands me a rolled bill, watches me set up, afraid of not getting it right. Then I do a line, get that chlorine feeling, like pool water up my nose. Immediately I feel a lot better, more cheerful. I do another. I can definitely see the appeal. I offer Claudia the last one, but she shakes her head, so I do that one too. It is my birthday.

"What now?" I ask. Since Claudia didn't touch the coke, I am guessing she usually does not do this sort of thing either. Maybe she thinks she is being the perfect hostess.

"I want you to drive," Claudia says. She unrolls the bill, holds it out, and I see it's a hundred, the kind of tip no one at the Royale Palms ever gives. I should be having doubts, I know, but by now I am feeling so cheerful I can't imagine what they could be. I take the money. I'll drive her around, catch a bus home.

"Yes, Ma'am," I say. If nothing else, working at a hotel teaches you to be polite. "Where?"

She shrugs. "All night."

I think about it a minute. Since we are on the beach, everything further east is water. West of Miami is the Everglades, and south is a dead end at Key West with no ferries to Cuba likely this century. So I head north, following the route the Greyhound bus took to get me to Timmons. Claudia turns the AC on high and puts a tape in the Blaupunkt, something African with a lot of drums. She turns it up until I can feel it like a fist in my chest. "To keep you awake, yes?" she says.

Claudia curls up on the seat, her head against the armrest, her stocking feet in my lap. For a while she moves her feet back and forth against the erection I can't help getting, but then she falls asleep. The headlights catch a turnoff, a green road sign, *Lantana— 38 miles,* the road I would take in the somewhat unlikely event that this were a trip to visit my mother. As soon as I pass it, I know I have driven farther than I ever have before. I think of my mother in her trailer surrounded by Spanish bayonets. Until my sixteenth birthday, my father sent two checks every month, one to my mother, one to Kirov for the suite. Even after the checks stopped coming, my mother waited three months, just in case, before she announced over breakfast that she was going to take a job assembling B-1 bomber sights in Lantana. An old friend from high school had put her name in for it. "And me?" I asked.

"Kirov will give you a job," she said. "After all these years, he owes us that."

I pop out the tape and put on the radio. The Blaupunkt has shortwave. I turn off the AC, roll down the window a crack and listen to Radio Havana. It's what drives the Cubans so crazy, makes them all stay in Miami. Humidity just like home and Havana close enough to hear, never touch. When Radio Havana fades out, I twist the dial around and hear all kinds of things, Chinese, Russian, maybe German. I try finding Radio Brazil, if there is such a thing, but I am not sure I would recognize Portuguese if I heard it.

After midnight, when it is no longer my birthday, I start noticing these odd signs on the side of the road, wooden letters mounted on cypress branches that say things like: *The World's Oldest Tourists Trap* and *Lady, If He Won't Stop, Hit Him!* Ten minutes later, I spot a low concrete building off to the left, catch a larger sign: *Cypress Knee Museum*. I wonder who stops at such places. Is this what people with cars do, people on vacation, people say on their way to the Royale Palms? Then the signs disappear from my side of the road, but a few minutes later I see one lit up by the headlights of a southbound car. From behind, the letters on the dead branch look like hieroglyphics: *!miH tiH, potS t'noW eH fI.*

By dawn, we are outside Orlando. Claudia sits up. She gazes out the window, yawning, though she is the one who has slept most of the night. I pull into a rest stop and get out, stretch. Claudia hands me a bottle with some foreign—French?—writing on it. "Vitamins," she says. The pills inside are blue and look too tiny to be seriously harmful. I take one. Claudia takes three. I ask to borrow some change for the phone and she says to get some out of her purse, which is on the back seat. Inside, there is a regular rat's nest of bills. I find a whole roll of quarters, hold it up to show her what I'm taking. She shakes her head like she's disappointed. "Take more," she says. "Buy some . . ." She pauses so I know what's coming—American slang. "Some snow," she closes her eyes, "or is it blow?" I take a couple of fifties.

Claudia goes off in search of tourist information. I call the Royale Palms long distance, ask for Freddie. "Hola," he says, picking up the phone on the first ring even though it is six in the morning. Like me, he has been up all night. I tell him I may not be in tomorrow, that my grandmother is sick. He laughs at this. When Dagoberto, the regular night desk clerk, wants time off he always calls in and says his grandmother died. But I say *sick* and not *dead* because I may, after all, have a living grandmother in Brazil, a superstitious sort of country, and I wouldn't want to wish anything too bad on her. "OK," Freddie says, still laughing. "I'll cover for you." August is the off-season, and he can afford to be easy. I tell him that if he needs my bed—I am living in one of the spare rooms—to lock my stuff in the linen closet.

"Thanks," I say.

"De nada," Freddie says. "Enjoy."

Inside, at the information desk, the clerk is recommending some fancy mall to Claudia, a place where she says there is a serious shopping mall. The girl and Claudia share a moment of bonding. "Rive Gauche?" Claudia asks.

"No shit," says the girl.

So we go shopping. There is a store full of Giorgio Armani. I feel the French amphetamine take hold and maybe Claudia does too. She trails her hand down a rack of suits. "For you, yes?" she says in a loud voice. After that the saleswoman, a short Italian woman dressed in shades of gray, sticks to Claudia like mildew on a shower curtain. Together, they pull things from the racks, from the stockroom, even off the male mannequin in the window who has only half a head that's as empty as a bowl. Claudia makes me try on everything, model it for her. The saleswoman hands the clothes over the dressing room door, then stands behind Claudia and watches me too. She and Claudia bend their heads together, talking very low, their accents melting into a general foreignness. Claudia makes no attempt to say that I am her son or anything, and I think the saleswoman is very excited by the idea that I may be Claudia's lover. She is older than Claudia, 50 or so, but I can see she is thinking—*why not?* Thinking maybe she'll find herself a pretty boy, someone who wants one of her suits and can no way afford one.

I turn my back on Claudia and look in the mirror. Each time I see myself, in black silk, in white linen, I keep having the same pair of thoughts. I think: *This guy looks great* and *who is he?* But each time the thoughts surprise me, like I am very stoned or dreaming. Claudia picks out a white linen suit, a pair of black jeans, two shirts, underwear, socks, a pair of shoes, and a suitcase to put it all in. More clothes than I own, worth more than everything I have ever owned, maybe, in my whole life. At least I'm getting a wardrobe out of this—the word *trousseau* pops into my mind. I decide to wear the white Armani suit over a yellow eighty-dollar t-shirt out of the store. I wonder what Maddy would think if she saw me.

"Come," Claudia says and pulls me down the mall and into a jewelry store. She points to a display of ear studs. "For you, yes?"

"For me, no," I say. Most of the guys who work at the Palms have gone through this. I mean, the whole question of which ear to get pierced. Does right mean you're gay and left straight, or will you move to Australia, find out that there you've got it backwards and get butt fucked? A salesgirl appears. She grins at me.

"We can do the piercing here," she says and shows Claudia what looks like one of those things that punch holes in paper. I keep shaking my head. Claudia moves toward me. I back up until I hit the glass counter. She moves in very close, rakes her fingers through my hair, pulling it back from my forehead. It is the first time she has really touched me, and I would jump if I weren't squeezed against the counter. Out of the corner of my eye, I see the girl behind the counter blush, look away.

"Paulo, Paulo," Claudia whispers. She pinches my right ear lobe between her fingertips. "A diamond?" Her eyes glitter as she says this.

"OK," I say. "If it's a diamond."

Before I can move, the salesgirl lifts her punch to my right ear lobe, and I close my eyes. I hear her breathing in my ear, and I think she is going to say something to relax me, like *this hurts me more than it does you,* but she doesn't. She just staples my ear. The pain makes my eyes water, and it occurs to me that this is something more permanent than a change of clothes. I take a deep breath, then with a click it is over. I imagine that Claudia is watching, but when I open my eyes she is inspecting her fingernails as if she is afraid she has broken one off in my hair. She pays cash for the hole and the diamond stud, and at the last minute she buys me a red Swatch watch, which is much too young for me. As we are leaving, the salesgirl says, "Remember to bathe that ear with alcohol. When it comes to your health," she glances sideways at Claudia, "you can't be too careful."

My ear throbs. As soon as we are out of there, Claudia puts her hand on the back of my neck. "Your head hurts, yes?"

"Yes."

"Poor Paulo," Claudia says, rubbing my neck. She sends me to the men's room to make a buy. I go, but I think she is crazy. This is Orlando. Home of Disney World, of M-I-C-K-E-Y M-O-U-S-E. But there is a tall black guy in a mall maintenance jump suit cleaning the urinal, and as soon as he sees me, he's selling. I give the guy what he asks for, not quibbling about the price which even I know is tourist high. "Have a good one," he says, stuffing the bills down the front of his coveralls.

Out in the parking lot, the car is like an oven but Claudia gets in anyway, kicks off her shoes, twists her feet up under her on the seat. "America," she says. I touch the hot steering wheel of the BMW, tap one of my new Italian shoes on the gas pedal.

"America?" I say, kidding. "Where?"

"You don't know, Paulo?" she says, serious. "Then we must find out." She waves her hand at the heat waves rising from the parking lot. "Is this America?"

"Malls are very American," I say, thinking maybe she is angling to take back my clothes.

"Malls, yes? And what else?" I rack my brain but can't think of anything.

She reaches under the seat and pulls out about fifty tourist brochures she must have gotten at the rest stop. She shows me one with a parrot peddling a bird-size unicycle on the cover. "America?" she says for the third time in less than a minute.

"Looks like it," I say, thinking maybe I should have woken her up for the Cypress Knee Museum.

"Paulo." Claudia touches a finger to my pocket, to the cocaine. The car is so hot now I can smell myself, like I'm in a sauna where what they throw on the rocks is sweat. I crouch down behind the wheel and do the coke while she reads names to me from the pamphlets. *Bible Land USA, Elvis-A-Rama, Confederama.* As soon as I finish, she pokes me hard, lays two pamphlets open on my lap. "We go to this one," she points to *Weeki Wachee, Spring of the Living Mermaids,* which a map on the back shows as somewhere near Tampa. "And this one," she points to a picture of a ceiling hung with department store mannequins to which someone has carefully added angelic wings. This is at *House on the Rock,* which is somewhere in Wisconsin.

"Why?" I say.

"Why not?" Claudia asks, and whether it is because of the coke or because I have slept so little, I cannot think of an answer.

Instead I ask, "How far is it?"

"To Weeki Wachee?"

"To Wisconsin."

She goes back under the seat and comes up with a road atlas. She checks the chart in the back. "24 hours driving." She pauses, reaching for the right word. "Max."

"Max?" I say.

"Max, yes?"

"Max. Yes," I echo. I imagine this going on and on, leaving us frozen in the doorway like those cartoon chipmunks—*After you. No, after you*—so I stop. I take the atlas from her, turn to the map of the whole United States. My heart is pounding so hard from the coke that the blue lines that are the interstates jump like veins. I know I should get on a bus and go back to Miami, but the longer I think about it, the less I can see myself back at the Royale Palms, breathing carbon monoxide for two dollar tips. Not yet. I think: *I am twenty years old and have never been out of Florida.*

I rub my hands over my face. Twenty-four hours. One day. I start the car. "OK," I say. "First stop Weeki Wachee," and as I pull out of the parking lot into traffic, it strikes me suddenly just how good it feels to be driving a BMW, like it is something I've missed for a long time without even knowing it.

By five, my usual dinner break time, we are sitting side by side in a mildewy auditorium while on the other side of a plate glass window girls wearing fish tails drink RC Colas underwater. The mermaids take occasional breaths from air hoses that bubble away like aquarium filters, and the water is so cold, their lips look blue in spite of their waterproof lipstick. The theme of the show is Carnival in Rio, and Claudia squeezes my hand as if she is afraid the sound of the samba is going to make me cry. At the end of the show, the mermaids wave a fond farewell, flippers flapping, as the PA system blares "We've Got the Whole World by the Tail." I lift Claudia's hand from mine and wave back.

Claudia pays to have a Polaroid taken of me with one of the mermaids, a blond freckled girl named Cindy from Fort Walton Beach, who is perched on a stool in the lobby for this purpose. Cindy smells so much like strawberry shampoo that my mouth waters. I am tempted to ask her if she goes to Timmons, see if she knows Maddy. But I am aware of Claudia watching me. She holds out the Polaroid for me to see, and an old man with a camcorder takes my place beside Cindy. I watch as two white blobs darken into smiling faces, and when I see mine, I am glad that I didn't say anything to Cindy. She looks wholesome in her green tail and modest bathing suit top, while the circles under my eyes are so deep and dark they look like anuses. My earring gleams.

Claudia takes my hair in both of her hands, pulls it back. "You should show off your cheek bones," she says. She borrows a rubber band from the girl at the ticket counter, fastens my hair in the shortest of pigtails. "Yes?" Claudia asks the girl at the ticket counter.

"Hot," the girl says, smiling at me. "Really."

About a week before I left Timmons, I walked in on Maddy cutting Roberto's hair, something she'd never so much as offered to do for me. He'd gotten a really bad cut somewhere, she explained, and she was trying to fix it. It didn't look to me like she was helping much. There was a towel draped around Roberto's bare shoulders and there was hair everywhere, on the towel, the carpet, on Maddy's T-shirt. They were laughing like crazy like they were in on some really big joke. "Oh, man," Roberto said, "what did I ever do to deserve a hair cut this bad?"

When we got back in the car, I ask Claudia, "What would you think if you walked in and found some woman cutting your husband's hair?"

"I'd assume he was paying her," she says.

"Not that they were sleeping together?"

"Either way," Claudia shrugs, "I'd assume he was paying her."

A couple of hours later we pass the *Welcome to Georgia* sign, but even though I am watching carefully, the only change I see is the color of the pavement. By ten we are in Macon. Claudia insists we stop at a drive-in, where, perhaps because it is so American, she actually eats a barbecue sandwich, the first non-pharmaceutical thing I have seen her put in her mouth. I am careful not to get any of the sticky red sauce on my Armani suit. After we eat, I go to the men's room to wash my hands. A guy, skinny and white this time, is upset because I don't want crack. He offers to trade me some for my watch. This is all beginning to strike me as funny, but when I laugh he gets nervous. So I buy some coke, do it in one of the stalls.

When I come out of the rest room, Claudia is bent over the atlas. "Seventeen hours," she says, without looking up.

"Max," I manage to say. It is twenty-four hours since we left Miami, and I haven't slept in maybe thirty-six. Out in the parking lot, Claudia takes a close look at me and offers to drive, but the coke has kicked in and I feel fine, ready to drive straight into the night, which we do, stopping only for gas near Nashville. I tell Claudia when we cross the border into Kentucky, but she doesn't seem interested. Her eyes are closed, and her lips are set in a line, a little gray. "Why don't you lie down?" I say finally and she does, this time with her head in my lap. This gives me an erection so hard it hurts, but she goes right to sleep.

I stay on I-65 and I don't stop, not even to piss, because although my bladder is full, Claudia is sleeping on that too, snoring slightly. Besides, there is something about the way my hands have locked onto the steering wheel, the fact that I cannot feel my toes or fingertips, that tells me to make time while I can before I come down, that the crash waiting for me will be worse than bad, unimaginable.

Claudia sleeps and sleeps. I make it to Indianapolis sometime after dawn, follow the interstate downtown. Downtown Indianapolis is dismal, hot, rain coming down passing steam going up. The buildings look rusty, vacant. We pass a convention center, windows dark, marquee empty, and I pull into the curved drive of the hotel attached to it. "I'm stopping," I announce to Claudia, but then I can't seem to get my foot off the gas and onto the brake in time. I end up back on the street, have to circle the block and try again. When I turn off the car, I just sit there, afraid I won't be able to stand. I'm so tired I could cry. Claudia sits up, yawns so wide her jaws crack. I tell her we are in Indiana, and she gives me this surprised look, as if maybe this whole trip is a joke one of us has taken too far. Then she shrugs, puts on lipstick. She leans across the seat and kisses me, slips her tongue between my lips. Surprised, I kiss back, and then I realize there is something bitter and hard in my mouth—one of her pills. I swallow, feel it burn all the way down. Claudia laughs.

A bellboy knocks on the window. "Sir?" he says, although not with any conviction. I give him the keys, watch as he gets the luggage out of the trunk, opens Claudia's door. He is blond, has no chin. Inside, Claudia registers for two rooms, like I am just her driver, just someone along for the ride. I don't know what to think, but mostly I am surprised by this. What about treating her like a war? Claudia yawns, stands closer to the bellboy than to me. So I let the bellboy carry the suitcases upstairs. Claudia slips him a twenty, but the bellboy shoots me a look behind her back. I think I know what is coming. He waits until he has opened her door and she has gone in, then he covers his mouth with his hand, and whispers, "Want to buy some pot? It's good shit, man." I almost laugh, start to say no, but then I stop. My hands are shaking, and I can feel Claudia's little blue pill. I need help coming down.

"Sure," I say. "Take my watch for it?" He throws in some papers. But after I've got it, I can't imagine smoking it. I lay down on my bed and wait for time to pass. I hear the TV come on in Claudia's room, the bathroom fan. I think about my father. The last time he came around I was two, and sometimes I think I can almost remember that. I have this memory of something white, like a terry cloth bathrobe, moving back and forth in front of the bars of my crib, sort of like the way they used to show Jesus in the old movies, all hem and no face.

After a while, it stops raining on Indianapolis. The sun comes out. I can see that much from where I'm lying on the bed. I think about getting up, but somehow I don't. Then it is dark, and I'm confused because I don't think I've been asleep. I call down to the desk and ask what time it is. "8:30," the girl says. "Probably you thought it was 9:30. Lots of people make that mistake because Indiana doesn't go on Daylight Savings. So in the summer, it's like we're on Central Time, and in the winter, like we're on Eastern. Really, we're on Indiana Time."

"8:30 *p.m.?*" I ask, and there's a pause at the end of the line as she realizes just how confused I am.

"Yes," she says. I give up trying to sound normal.

"And it's what day of the week?"

"Friday."

"Thanks," I say. "You've been a big help. Really."

32

I get up, and after I wash my face I knock on Claudia's door. "Claudia?"

"It's open, Paulo," she says. "I wouldn't lock you out." She is lying on the bed with her shoes off, drinking a Diet Coke and watching TV. I show her the pot. She looks in her purse. She pulls out a fistful of bills, the Polaroid of me at Weeki Wachee. "Maybe a lighter, yes?" she says and keeps digging. "Here," she pulls out another handful of stuff and hands me a gun, "hold this."

It's a small automatic. I know that much even though this is the first gun I've touched in my life. I'm surprised how heavy it is, as if Claudia has handed me a Bic Flic that weighs as much as a pipe wrench. I check to see that the safety is on. It's amazing what I've learned from watching TV all these years. I sight down the barrel at a lighted office I can see through the window. If I fired, would I hit someone? I look up to see Claudia smiling at me, a silver lighter open, flaming, in her hand. I can tell she is thinking how good I look with her gun, how experienced. "A nice toy for your line of work, yes?" she says, her excitement as strong as her accent. I remember who she thinks I am. "Was expensive."

I give her back the gun, sorry I know it exists; she puts it in her purse. I pick through the pot, roll a couple of lumpy joints, light one. We smoke half the dope, taking increasingly lopsided turns, two hits for me to her one. Then Claudia is standing by the door, her purse in her hand. "Come," she says. "I'm ravenous, yes?" We find an all night Zippy Mart, but before we go in, I make Claudia leave her gun in the glove compartment. Claudia wanders dazed down the aisle as if she has forgotten what is edible and what is not. I find a rack of health food munchies and in a fit of homesickness pick out a dozen little bags of dried papaya. We are obviously high but the checker, a women who must weigh three hundred pounds, barely glances at us, and we make it back to the hotel, Claudia's room, undetected. I rip open the bags, dump them out on the bed. But it is Claudia who hunts down and eats every pinkish orange cube, even the ones that are a little fuzzy from the bedspread, slapping my hand when I go for one.

We smoke the rest of the dope. While Claudia fills her lungs, I flip through the stations on the TV. We seem to be staying in the only major hotel in a major city that doesn't have cable. Indianapolis, my kinda town. I stumble across the opening credits of *Miami Vice*. Just seeing the blue shallows of Biscayne Bay makes me homesick. I groan. On TV, Miami looks better than real. Claudia pulls me back to the bed, puts the joint to my lips. "Shhh," she says, "shhh," kissing my shoulder, my neck. I think we are going to do something more but the bright colors of Miami pull us into the TV, and we watch hardly blinking as the boat Sonny is on undercover blows up. "Oooh," Claudia says as the black smoke and orange flames roll over the calm aqua water. When Sonny comes to, he's lost his memory, forgotten he's a cop. Everyone tells him he's a dealer, so he goes out to do a deal and ends up shooting a guy who is out to rip him off. He shoots him in the back, then once he has fallen, again in the head. Just like that, like pointing a finger. Claudia lets the joint go out. I relight it, burn my hand.

The show seems different stoned. The fast cutting, the coked-out pacing, is slowed way down so the whole thing just flows, as if when the boat blew up, Sonny went to the bottom of the bay and discovered some other liquid Miami. Sonny makes love to a woman, shoots a man at close range in a car. He's ordered to shoot Tubbs, his black partner, the only person—it seems obvious to me in that moment—who Sonny really loves. And he does shoot him, walks right by him without recognizing him and fires off two shots without flinching. I almost cry out, but luckily Tubbs is wearing a bulletproof vest and so is not dead.

Sonny sleeps with someone else, shoots someone else—another cop—but it seems to me that he is getting tired, as if this being someone else is losing its thrill. I want to tell him, *Hey, compadre, I know how you feel*. But suddenly the show is over—*to be continued*.

Claudia unzips my fly. On the T.V., a woman is dressing exotic birds in costumes fastened in the back by tiny Velcro tabs. I watch as she changes a green parrot into the Incredible Hulk, tiny padded muscles and all. Claudia has her mouth on my cock. I look down at her. I don't feel anything. Maybe it is the coke or the pot or maybe it is Claudia. Maddy used to do all right. Claudia is just sort of mouthing my penis, biting at it with her lips. Claudia lifts my hand and puts it between her legs, closes her thighs on my fingers. I rub Claudia's nylon crotch, but now that it has come down to it, I don't know how to treat her like a whore. I find myself thinking of my mother, so I close my eyes and try thinking of Maddy instead, of this certain smooth spot on her back, right at the base of her spine, where I always held onto her. I start to get hard. But then I remember that Maddy is with Roberto, who at this very moment may be touching her there. "Don't," I say before I think not to say it.

Claudia raises her head. She looks at my limp, wrinkled cock, then at me. Her eyes widen. She smiles, a strange knowing smile as if she is seeing me, really seeing me, for the first time.

"Claudia," I start, reaching for her. Her upper lip curls. Whatever she is seeing fills her with disgust. I don't know what is going on with her, but I don't like it. It is like she has switched channels in her head. One minute I'm a coke dealer and then . . .

"You do like women," she says slowly. "Yes?" I shake my head *yes, yes.* Then suddenly I remember the time Roberto and I got very drunk at his apartment and how he tried to choke me. I think by way of starting to have sex with me. But I didn't get hard then either. Really. Not at all. I threw up. I feel Claudia's eyes changing me into something I'm not. I am on my feet, backing across the room. "Stop it," I say. Her lips are pursed. Whatever she is about to say, I don't want to hear it. I reach for the doorknob, wrench the door open.

"Faggot!" she says, spitting. "Brazilian Faggot."

I am in the lobby, and then in the car. I drive without thinking, hit the bypass around the city, spin west. I enter a town, am out of it before I think to slow down. I think instead about stealing the BMW, driving south to see Maddy. *Brazilian Faggot.* What would Maddy say if I told her about Roberto? Would she believe me? Why should she? I'd walked in on Maddy and Roberto. I had opened Maddy's door slowly, so they wouldn't hear me. Never mind, I knew what I was going to find, had known since I'd seen Maddy cutting Roberto's hair. On Miami Vice when Tubbs knew from all the evidence that Sonny had turned, would shoot him dead as soon as not, he had to see it for himself. *Adios, compadre,* old friend. Still, it hurt. She was on top of Roberto, her head thrown back, a look on her face I had never seen. I turned on one heel and walked. On the way out of the dorm, I had punched in the glass door over the fire alarm. Let them run naked into the hall together, into the street.

Brazilian Faggot. My headlights flash on a road sign: *Brazil 3 miles.* For a second I feel like I have entered the Twilight Zone, then I realize it is just an Indiana town. Still, I start looking for a place to make a U-turn, but before I know it I am in Brazil. Storefronts close in on both sides. I hit the gas, trying to get through as quickly as possible, fast forward through this particular town. The downtown opens up and a car lot blurs by. Then, a second too late, I see the cruiser sitting in the corner of the lot, nose on the edge of the road. The cop turns on his light. I hit the brake the same second he hits the siren.

I pull over on the edge of town, behind the *Welcome to Brazil* sign. The cruiser pulls up behind me. The officer comes to the window, motions me out of the car. "Up early or out late?" he says. He takes my Florida driver's license without comment, calls that and the BMW in. Standing between the two cars, I can see he's not a highway patrolman but a Brazil cop, probably *the* Brazil cop. He comes back with my license. He is tapping a big silver flashlight against one leg. I feel totally straight now, as clearheaded as an Olympic diver about to go off the high board. I volunteer that the car belongs to my aunt. "We'll know all that soon enough, son. In the meantime, why don't you just stretch your legs." He shines his long silver flashlight down the edge of the road, along the white line he wants me to walk.

I can and I do. Just for good measure, the cop has me touch my index fingers to my nose with my eyes shut. "Fine, son," the officer says. His radio squeals, and he goes to answer it. When he comes back, he is frowning, tapping the flashlight against one leg. "Why don't you show me the registration for this car, son." I blink, start to shrug. "The glove compartment," he suggests. He turns on his flashlight. I get in the car, reach across the seat, and just as my fingers touch the latch, I remember with a flash of fear that goes through every cell of my body like some cocaine anti-high that the glove box is where I made Claudia put her gun. This is it, I think, the moment when amnesia turns serious, Sonny shoots Tubbs, this cop shoots me, but it is too late to stop. I open the glove box.

36

No gun. For a second I think I am going to be sick. Claudia must have put it back in her purse before we went up to the room. I grab the papers that are in the glove box, give them to the officer. "Your aunt . . ."

"Claudia," I say.

"Claudia Vanderhagen?" he asks. He shows me the registration. *William Vanderhagen.*

"Yes," I say. "But she's divorcing Uncle Bill. He drinks." The cop nods. "I'm not sure he knows that she's . . ."

"Listen," he says. "You're a DePauw kid, right?" He sees me hesitate, holds up his hand. "You're scared because one call to Dean Bunche and your butt is on the line." *DePauw.* A college or a prep school? "But I know how you boys are. Get your hands on a car— say your aunt brings you up to school, turns in early—and you just gotta blow off steam. No harm done, but listen," he puts his hand on my shoulder, "if you'd been drinking, I would have to call Dean Bunche, and she'd have to suspend you. Then what would you do? Where would you be if you weren't in college?" He gives my shoulder a squeeze. "Think about it." I nod, my mouth too dry to talk. He gives back my license, writes me a $60 speeding ticket. "You drive nice and slow back to the frat house," he says, "and tell the other boys all about this. Tell 'em I said to watch out when they drive through Brazil." He pronounces it *Braise-L.*

I watch as the cruiser makes a careful U-turn, heads back into town, leaving me standing on the outskirts of Brazil, in the middle of America. *Is this America, Paulo?* Claudia asked yesterday, almost too long ago to remember. Yes, I should have said, yes. This is America, a country where frat boys and parking attendants dress like Colombian coke dealers who dress like an actor on TV who used to date Barbara Streisand. I should have said that to her back in Orlando and then gotten out of her car and walked. I rest my head on the roof of Claudia's car.

I drive back to Indianapolis. When I hit the bypass, I think again about heading south, stealing the BMW and driving to Florida, not to see Maddy, but to go straight back to the Royale Palms, back to my job if I still have one, back to the life I was born into and been crazy to think I could ever escape. But I can see in my mind's eye how many police there are between Indianapolis and Florida, and I know in my heart they are not all like the cop in Brazil. I feel a profound awareness of having used up my luck. I will get my stuff, then take a bus.

The sun is creeping up gray and low over the convention center when I pull into the parking lot in front of the hotel, and it occurs to me that since I have been with Claudia I've seen the sun rise three days in a row, as many times as I have seen it before in my life. The lobby is empty, no one behind the desk, but when I step out of the elevator on my floor, I see the bellboy coming out of Claudia's room. His shirt is untucked, his sneakers untied. He sees me, and for a moment he starts the other way, but we can both see that there is nothing at the end of the corridor but a fire escape. He decides to brave it out, walks toward me smiling. He really has no chin. I hold the elevator door with one hand, then when he is inside, let it go. He opens his mouth, "She let me fuck her in the . . ." The closing doors cut him off.

As soon as I get in my room, I realize I am going to be sick. I make it to the bathroom, lean over the toilet, and when I straighten up, there are tiny pieces of rehydrated tropical fruit floating in the bowl. I go to the sink and rinse out my mouth. What I really want to do is brush my teeth, but one thing Claudia hasn't bought me is a toothbrush. I dump out the little wicker basket of stuff the hotel provided, but there is only complimentary shampoo and conditioner, a complimentary shoehorn with *Hotel America* in script on it. I wet the end of a washcloth, wrap it around one finger, and scrub at my teeth. I wash my face. I'll leave Claudia a note. *Dear Mrs. Vanderhagen.* Leave the note and her keys at the desk.

I go to the nightstand between the beds to get the complimentary pad, the complimentary pen. That's when I hear the crying. I stop, put my ear to the wall. Claudia is crying, not weeping quietly on her rented bed, but sobbing, big hard sobs. Crying like kids do, like I used to: *Nobody loves me. I wish I'd never been born.*

I can't stand it. I should be able to just pick up and go, after what happened, but I can't. I am not my father. I can't leave without a word. I sit down on the bed and pick up the phone. When Claudia answers I plan to be cool and correct and say, *Is this Mrs. Van-derhagen?* But what I say is, "Claudia, it's Paulo. Are you okay?"

"Oh, Paulo," she says. She sounds relieved, happy to hear my voice, happier than Maddy or even my mother would have been. "Can we talk, please?"

"Well," I say. I look around. Hotel rooms are by their nature mostly beds, and Hotel America doesn't even provide a decent chair.

"If you would be more comfortable, Paulo," she says, sitting on her own bed and seeing the twin of what I see, "we could talk in the lobby."

I pause, thinking about the bellboy. "No," I say, "you can come over here."

"Five minutes," she says, and hangs up.

Actually, it is closer to fifteen. She knocks on the door, three short raps, as if it were a signal. I open it, and she comes in. Her face is splotchy and the skin under her eyes is stained gray where her mascara ran when she was crying. "Paulo," she says. She touches my arm lightly, then backs off, sits on the edge of the bed. I sit on the other bed. "Just take me to House on the Rock," she says.

I start to shake my head. Enough with her mania for tourist attractions. "We should head home . . ."

"Please," Claudia says. She is crying again. "I don't want to be alone." She covers her face with her hands, so I can barely hear what she says next. *"I don't have a home."*

Home. *No home.* It isn't true that I left Timmons because I saw Maddy on top of Roberto, or not exactly. I walked out of the dorm after setting off the fire alarm, headed for the library, that's all. To study, catch a nap. It was finals and the stacks would be open all night.

But when I got to the quad, I stopped. The quad was my favorite spot at Timmons, four brick buildings facing each other across a slightly worn lawn, Harold Armstrong Timmons, or at least a bronze approximation of him, presiding over it all. Mock Harvard Yard, Maddy called it. But it seemed real to me, like the heart of something, a place where everything you needed to know to get ahead in this life was close enough to touch. The lights were on in all four buildings, the Library and the Student Union and the English and History

Halls, full of kids staying up studying or pretending to. But it was dark where I was, and looking up at the lighted windows, homesickness hit me like a fist. I'd never known what that word meant before, except in some sentimental Hallmark card sort of way. But this was pain in my chest, a pain maybe like when a man, say my father's age, is one minute feeling fine and the next can't breathe, is having a heart attack. I wanted to be somewhere else so strongly I would have run there, crawled there, hot wired a car and driven there as fast as I could even though I couldn't drive then. I wanted to be home.

But where was that? My mother's trailer? My father's apartment or tent or tree house for all I knew? Lantana? Miami? Brazil? I felt very clearly none of them would do. It was more like I wanted to curl up and squeeze back in the womb, not to be inside my mother, which was a pretty disgusting idea, but to get out of HERE and back to THERE. In that moment, standing on the brown grass of the quad, for the first time I understood why religions exist. Out there somewhere was where I'd come from and it had obviously been a far better place than where I was now. I was lost in the forest and the wolf was after me. I was tired and cold and I wanted to go home. I was willing to be dead, to kill myself, if that's what it took. I wished I had a gun. I even thought about who might have one and what I could say to get them to lend it to me.

That scared me, badly. I left the quad and Timmons and went straight to the Greyhound Station and got on the first southbound bus headed for Miami. If the Royale Palms wasn't home, it would have to do. But what had that gotten me?

"House on the Rock, yes?" Claudia is pleading. "We can finish what we started, yes? Yes?" She tears at her nails with her teeth.

I look at Claudia, her painted fingernails bitten to the bleeding quick. Why not? Why not finish what we started? The truth is, neither of us has any place else to go. "Okay, yes," I say, "House on the Rock."

Claudia checks us out. I carry my bag out to the BMW. Claudia comes out of the hotel, gets in on the passenger side, and I start the car. Through the glass doors, I can see the bellboy waiting for us to leave. I shift into first, pop the clutch. The tires squeal, although not as dramatically as I would have liked. I pull away from the Hotel America and out into traffic without even looking.

We go as far as the outskirts of Indianapolis, than Claudia makes me stop at a Waffle Hut. I think eating breakfast is her idea of what normal people do once the sun is up. We get a booth. "We need the big breakfast," she says, waving away the pair of menus the waitress holds out. The girl raises her eyebrows.

"Big or really big?"

Claudia opens her mouth, but I cut her off. "Just big will be fine."

"Two *Number 5 Farmers,* coming up," the waitress says, and turns sharply on one heel. She comes back with coffee, and again with the two eggs, sausage patties, bacon, hash browns, and toast.

"Thank you, Miss," Claudia says politely, on her best behavior. "This looks delicious." We ask simultaneously for refills on coffee, and seeing how much we need it, I think the waitress has us spotted as a couple of new members of AA.

I am hungry, but Claudia outdoes me. She starts on one side and works her way across, forking up whatever stands in her way, cleaning her plate, as they say, down to the shine. I leave half a piece of toast, a few shreds of potato on my plate.

"What's the matter, Paulo?" Claudia says. "Don't you feel well?" She leans across the table, puts her hand on my forehead acting like she is my mother, or at least like she thinks my mother would act. Then she uses the last of her coffee to wash down three of her pills. I shake my head.

The road through first Indiana and then Illinois runs as straight as a ruler, the land on either side flat to the horizon, flatter even than Florida, a state without a single decent hill. We pass nothing but miles of open fields with something low and green growing in them. Alfalfa? Soy beans? The farmers should put up signs, I think, for the benefit of bored travelers and tourists. Claudia stares out the window, hypnotized by the endless rows. What did the farmers do with all this mysterious green stuff. Eat it? Feed it to cows? If it was good with dressing, it was enough for a lifetime of salads.

"This would be better by train, yes?" Claudia says, staring out at the fields, which are now full of corn, a plant even I can identify.

"By train?" I say. It seems like something only a foreigner would say, or a very old person. "I've never even been on a train."

Claudia shakes her head. She wraps her arms around her as if she is cold, but she makes no move to turn down the air conditioning, which was pumping away on high as usual. "In Budapest," she says, "they have a special train, a train small enough to be run by children. Run by a kind of—I don't know what to call them—scouts, yes?"

Claudia pauses and I can tell she is looking at me. "On this train, children are the train drivers," Claudia says, "and the conductors, yes?, who take the tickets. They wear uniforms, dark blue, these train scouts, very neat. The conductors have little leather holsters for their silver ticket punchers." Claudia pats her waist, wearing her imaginary holster a little higher than a good gunslinger would.

I wait, but that is it. Claudia doesn't go on. "Sounds great," I say, imagining Sundays and school holidays, hordes of Hungarian parents taking their children on the special kid train, pretending it was a treat but all the while just waiting for the chance to point out the scouts as models, as children full of the terrible impulse to be good, to please the people who really made the trains run. Claudia stares out the window, her story over. I imagine her, a perfect tiny conductress taking a ticket held out to her by grossly oversized adult hands, and punching it just so. What had happened? Although Claudia did not say so, I am sure this is an old story, about a train that had run when she was a child. It might still be running, but it would be different. Everything would be. Her Hungary is as mythical as my Brazil. Driving past all those miles and miles of corn, I think maybe it's a good thing Claudia and I live in America, a country where everyone is from someplace else, and no one is going back there, not for real, not anytime soon. *America,* a whole country of people like us, homesick and homeless all at the same time. I think that, and also this: I would give a lot to see Claudia, happy for real, working on that pretend train.

When we cross into Wisconsin, the fields of corn give way to rolling grass-covered hills. And we start passing these billboards: *House on the Rock: You've Never Seen Anything Like It.* No pictures, just red gothic letters on black. House on the Rock, the last stop on our *See America First* tour. It is nearly two when we finally make it there. As soon as I get out of the car, I am stunned by how hot it is. I guess, Florida boy that I am, I always thought it got cooler as you went north. A load of senior citizens pour off a bus next to us. From the parking lot, I can't see any house, let alone the one on the brochure, a Chinese lantern set high above the surrounding dairy land. All I can see beyond the rows of cars with Illinois and Wisconsin license plates is a covered walkway leading to a ticket booth. "So Frank Lloyd Wright built this?" one of the senior citizens, a woman in a purple pantsuit, asks the slightly stooped woman walking beside her.

"No, Hildy, that's Taliesin," she says. "It's near here, but this is better, take my word for it."

"Frank Lloyd Wright," an old man in double hearing aids snorts. "That's a laugh."

"Who is Frank Lloyd Wright?" I whisper to Claudia. She shrugs. She doesn't know either.

"Are we ready, Paulo?" she says. I nod, and she takes my arm.

It costs ten bucks to get in, which seems steep to me, but Claudia pays without any objection, her mouth set in a thin line of determination. A plaque by the ticket booth explains that what we are about to see has been built entirely by a genius named Alex Jordan, who is still living and still adding more and more wonders to his House. *House on the Rock*, it says flatly. *More than a house*. And, I presume, more than a rock. We set out to see.

Inside, it is even hotter. After the ticket booth is some kind of tunnel, the floor, walls and the ceiling all lined with brown shag. A long row of box fans spin uselessly on the floor by one fuzzy wall. Clearly, there is no AC. The tunnel turns into stairs leading up. We pass under a sign that reads: "You are now entering the House" without which it would be hard to tell. The house itself winds around and crawls over outcroppings of rock, a living room here, a library there, all as dark as the tunnel. Stained glass lamps hang from the ceiling, stand on oddly shaped tables, and there are collections of bowls, paper weights, dolls, stuffed birds, skunks, frogs. It *is* more than a house; it's a house run amok.

The senior citizens grunt at what they see, at the steepness of the stairs. We pass a fireplace nook, complete with a shag carpet settee and a single burner hot plate. For hot cocoa? I try to imagine Jordan at home, snuggling there with a date. We climb up into the dining room, and see a violin playing itself. The bow and the strings on the neck are hooked up to heavy black rubber tubes that go whoosh-woof in time with a pneumatic pump. It isn't exactly state of the art electronics, but still it is eerie to see it sawing away without any help from human hands. "Remarkable," Claudia says. She puts her fingers in her ears.

"Wouldn't you like to have one?" the woman in the purple pant-suit says.

Finally, we reach the top of the house and enter what a sign says is *The Infinity Room,* a horizontal needle of glass and more carpet built out over the valley below. Trees stretch out on all sides as far as I can see. I can't help noticing that the glass panes that form the walls of The Infinity Room are put in haphazardly, not even puttied. A hot wind whistles through them, and I feel the floor move. I hope that Wisconsin has good building inspectors. As we walk, the room narrows, and Claudia moves close. I am dripping sweat by then. At the far end of the room, there is a porthole in the floor, just the kind they use in Florida glass-bottomed boats to reveal fish to tourists and tourists to fish. I look down. Below us, far below us, are rocks. Claudia takes my hand as we look down. In spite of the heat, her hand is cold as meat.

Beyond the porthole, in the very point of his space needle, Jordan has placed a dirty pink plush chair, a stuffed tiger, and a globe of the world. From where we stand, I can see the faded blue of Brazil. Maybe he is a genius, I find myself thinking, but this Jordan is one strange guy. "They say he's a recluse," one of the seniors behind me says, her voice a stage whisper. "They say he mingles with the tourists sometimes just to see what they think." Everyone looks at the person standing next to them, but unless Jordan is the old man with double hearing aids and plaid Bermuda shorts, or a woman or me, he isn't with us.

We go on. After the house come airplane hangar-size sheds full of stuff. The World's Largest Steam Locomotive, displays of hundreds of old-fashioned brass cash registers, and more antique dental equipment than anyone should own. Then an entire room full of violins and cellos sitting upright in plush chairs, playing themselves. The sign says the strings are playing the *Blue Danube,* but to me they sound tuneless. It's too hot for waltzes. By this time, Claudia is hanging on my arm, or I am hanging on hers. We've been walking for over an hour, and it is only getting hotter. I feel like we are in some sort of hell to which our lack of good taste and judgement has inexorably led us. But Claudia's lips are turned up slightly as if she us smiling, though I can't be sure in the shag-carpeted gloom. It is about this time that I, along with some of the frailer seniors, notice there seems to be no way out. No doors marked *Exit.* I pull Claudia past another musical tableau, kettle drums playing themselves to the tune of Kachaturian's *Saber Dance,* and into a black tunnel. "Where are you taking me, Paulo?" Claudia asks.

"To find the closest ex—. . ." I start to answer when we come out of the tunnel and into the room with the World's Largest Carousel. I am struck speechless. In the middle of the dark hangar, this *thing* is spinning, spinning like the wicked red heart of the universe. There are no people riding the carousel, it is roped off, but hundreds of mermaids and centaurs and beasts like impromptu genetic experiments fly by, so many they stretch out of sight, beyond imagining. My eyes roll up in my head, and then I see that the ceiling of the shed is hung, festooned, with hundreds of female department store mannequins like the ones in Claudia's brochure. They are draped in colored togas that carefully expose one breast apiece, and to these bland commercial breasts Jordan or someone has applied erect nipples the size of small flapjacks. Claudia looks up too. Her hand goes limp in mine.

Somewhere behind me, a man says, "What do you mean, we're not even half way?"

"This is it," Claudia says, and I look at her, uncertain whether she means that she has at last found the America she's been looking for, or that she wants out. She presses a finger into her chest, into some exact spot between her own breasts. Then her knees give way, and she falls. The old woman in the purple pantsuit appears from nowhere, is by her side in a second.

"Heart Attack!" she sings out. "Gang way!"

They put Claudia in a white helicopter with *Life Flight* in red on both sides, and I watch as it spins up into the hot cloudless sky. They are flying her to the University of Wisconsin Hospital, which is almost an hour away by car. One of the EMTs offers to ride with me to Madison, help me find the hospital. He is blond, a little older than me. When he sees the BMW, he whistles, "Nice." We get in, and a big man in a House on the Rock jumpsuit knocks on my window. I roll it down.

"Sorry, son," he says, leaning down to press a damp twenty dollar bill in my hand. Then he steps back. "Alex Jordan's money back guarantee."

"Was that Alex Jordan?" I ask.

"Who?" the EMT says.

The EMT gets turned around in Madison, and we wander past the same strip mall—Pet Land, Waterbed World, House of Dinettes—three times, until I am nearly frantic. Just then we pass the sign for the University of Wisconsin. "Now I know where I am," the EMT says. "The hospital's at the other end of campus." We pass rows of high-rise dorms, two student centers, the library. We pass the university dairy barn. The campus is huge. Like a dozen Hollins with half of downtown Miami thrown in for good measure. I try to imagine myself going to school here, just one more anonymous kid on his way to Chemistry lab. And the funny thing is, I can.

At last we reach the hospital, the emergency room. I go straight to the desk. "The woman who came in on Life Flight, is she . . .?"

The nurse frowns. "Mrs. Vanderhagen is in CCU. You'll have to check with the nurse there."

"Good luck," the EMT says, extending his hand. "Hope your mother's okay."

The sign in CCU says: *Welcome to the area's finest Coronary Care Unit. A Caring Place where there are no set visiting hours. Immediate Family* ONLY *are welcome in five-minute shifts anytime, day or night.* This does not seem to me like a good omen, that Claudia is in a place where life is measured in five minute shifts. I find the head nurse. "You'll have to wait," she says, in spite of the sign. "The doctor is with your mother now," she adds, making the same assumption as the EMT. I start to correct her, but catch myself. If I am not immediate family, then clearly I will be left standing outside the

CCU until the day after forever. "Have a seat," the nurse says. I sit down, rest my head in my hands.

The doctor bangs through the swinging door. I jump up. "Five minutes," she says, holding up that many fingers. "But first I want to talk to you about your mother, young man." It seems as soon as she gets better, Claudia needs to be transferred to their drug treatment unit. The doctor tells me this in a tone that does not allow for any ifs, ands or buts. And I am not about to make any.

Claudia is in one of the glass cubicles watched by a nurse near the door. She is resting, her eyes closed. Her hair is fanned out across her pillow, and she is breathing through a tube. She looks like one of the mermaids at Weeki Wachee. Her lips are the same shade of blue. The nurse nods for me to go in. I sit on the edge of Claudia's bed. Claudia opens her eyes. "Feeling better?" I ask. She tries to shake her head, but the tube in her nose stops her. She gives me her hand. She looks worse than I expected, really bad. She is hooked up to one of those machines that makes each heartbeat into a game of follow the bouncing ball. The rhythm is insistent, hypnotic. It starts *Brazil* running around and around in my head.

> The Brazil that I knew,
> where I wandered once with you,
> lives in my imagination.

Claudia's heart skips a beat, and the nurse at her desk looks up, concerned. My father, my mother, Maddy, one minute they were there and then the next, *nada*. I put my hand to my face and am surprised to find I am crying. "Damn it, Claudia," I say. "Don't you die on me."

"And leave you, Paulo?" Claudia whispers, her voice hoarse. "What kind of mother do you think I am?" Then she is crying too, stiff sobs that hurt, make her monitor jump, the nurse start from her desk toward our glass room. I hold on to Claudia's hand like our lives depend on it. Because, as it turns out, they do.

Logjam

Ron Wallace

It wasn't his fault. When they pulled into the campground, conditions were as bad as they could possibly be. The weather report called for high winds and hail. Four inches of rain had fallen in thirty minutes just sixty miles to the west of them, and the sky was an ominous shade of greenish-black. Mosquitoes hung like gauze in the heavy air. When he got out of the car to check the campsite, they shrouded him, and he danced like a marionette to their music. Yes, he thought, with his red hair and freckles and his stupid forced grin, he felt exactly like Howdy Doody dancing for the Peanut Gallery and selling Wonder Bread. Their ten-year-old daughter, Phoebe, was doing her best to be a Flub-a-Dub or Clarabelle, and his wife, Christine, glaring from the car, was grim as Phineas T. Bluster.

It dated him, he thought. No one under the age of forty (except Phoebe and Jennifer, perhaps, who had heard his stories of the fifties numerous times, told in the hyperbolic style he adopted to amuse them) would have made the comparison.

"It looks good," he shouted through the drone of mosquitoes and the Nova's closed windows.

Phoebe forced a smile, and Christine only glared.

It was the last day of their great Eastern car trip—something Christine had wanted to do for years. Jennifer, twelve and unwilling to leave the goats and chickens she raised on their recreational farm, had stayed home with Peterson's approval and to Christine's consternation. Christine's mother agreed to stay with her. Peterson, Christine, and Phoebe had driven 3,500 miles from Wisconsin to Cape Cod and then to Bar Harbor and Montreal, and were now in a Provincial Park in Canada. The park was called "The Chutes" because of the old wooden chutes that were designed to get logs past the small waterfall and through the rapids without jamming. The logging had denuded the countryside, and the whole area, all scrub pine and fir, even fifty years later seemed stunted or blighted.

"Get back in the car," Christine mouthed through the window.

They had followed Christine's plans exactly. In Cape Cod they stayed in Wellfleet, going to Provincetown only once to let Phoebe shop for an hour and take a whale-watching cruise. They had visited the beach once for two hours, slathered with the #45 sunblock Christine had brought, and spent the rest of the time hiking and bicycling in the National Seashore. Christine despised idleness. A vacation for her meant driving fourteen hours one day to get somewhere so you could hike fourteen hours the next.

They spent a day on an island off Bar Harbor, owned by one of Christine's uncles, hiking its seven-mile circumference through pine woods and over steep cliffs in the cold fog, and then a day driving to Quebec for a four-hour tour of the Old City before pushing to Toronto and beyond.

He would have preferred to sit on the beach or leisurely beach-comb, or spend a day poking around the Provincetown or Bar Harbor shops. But this was Christine's trip, and he was determined to be agreeable. He was, he admitted, even glad for her enthusiasms. If she hadn't pushed them over the years to go backpacking in the Rockies, rafting on the Colorado, tramping through the jungles of the Yucatan, and now driving through New England and Canada, they would never have left Wisconsin at all. He knew that it was good for them, and he was trying to be accommodating. If she wanted to camp, they'd camp, despite the abysmal conditions.

"Where's the mosquito repellent?" he asked from the front passenger's seat, as pleasantly as possible.

She fumbled around in the glove compartment, and then in her purse.

"I don't know what happened to it," she announced. "Maybe we don't have any. I can't think of everything."

He knew she knew he didn't want to camp, and it was making her surly. The more agreeable he was, the more she was sure of his insincerity. It had become a code between them. Whenever they were really angry or irritated, they would kill each other with kindness. It made it increasingly difficult *really* to be nice, when niceness itself was a weapon.

"Look," she said sweetly. "We don't have to camp if you don't want to."

"I want to," he assured her.

"Really, we could just stay in a motel."

"We do want to camp," Phoebe gamely piped up.

He marveled at how easy lying was for her. She could tell her mother anything she wanted to hear and make her believe it. Even he believed it this time, for a moment. It was enough to determine his resolve.

"Why don't you go into town," he offered, "and get some mosquito repellent. We'll set up the tent."

Thunder was rumbling all around them and the sky was blackening fast, but there wasn't a breath of wind. The mosquitoes whined like a bad connection.

"We'll use our machetes on them," he joked, sliding out of the car and motioning Phoebe to follow.

He and Phoebe set busily about the tent, while Christine slammed the Nova into gear, spun the tires, and drove off, faster than the narrow sandy park road quite allowed.

"I hate it when you guys do that," Phoebe frowned.

He was tempted to draw her out with a "Do what?" or a "So do I," but the mosquitoes whined insistently, and he knew he shouldn't martial his daughter's support in a conflict with her mother.

"Better stake it down good," he said. "The storm is coming." He separated the ridge poles from the side poles and began popping them into place.

How had they managed to live together for nearly twenty years, he wondered? When they were first married, it was different. Christine was sweet and reasonable, innocent and shy. She hadn't really dated anyone other than him and Frank, and, with her Scotch Presbyterian upbringing, had led a sheltered life. She seemed happy to keep house, cook, see her friends, and do her volunteer work. But soon she began to seem dissatisfied. Although she rarely complained directly about anything, she began to grow hard and testy. She debated him on insignificant issues just, he thought, out of irritability. He would mention some trivial problem at work, the kind of thing he didn't really want any more response to than a smile or a nod, and she'd find some way to argue an opposite side.

"The Dean's pushing us to publish again," he'd say. "What does he want from us anyway?"

"Well, he probably has a good reason for it," she'd say.

"Yeah, to make him look good."

"It's probably good for the whole college. He's probably just more ambitious than some of the faculty."

"You mean me."

"I'm not saying you should be more ambitious."

"What *are* you saying?"

"Oh, I'm just trying to understand why you're upset," she'd smile.

"I'm not all that upset."

"You seem pretty upset."

"I'm just telling you what happened today. I'm just letting off a little steam."

"Sounds like more than that to me."

"I don't want to talk about it," he'd say, and walk away.

"Why are you walking away from me? I thought we were having a conversation," she'd call, steely, after him.

"I don't want to argue."

"It's not an argument, it's a conversation. You think any time I don't agree with you, it's an argument. You want me to pretend to agree? You don't want my honest feelings?"

After a two-hour debate she'd seem rejuvenated, energized, and he'd be exhausted, depleted. She loved these discussions, said they were important to a healthy relationship. He hated them and thought they were symptoms of a disease. Her theory was that it was best to get it all out; confrontation therapy appealed to her. His theory was that it was better to keep it all in; to articulate a problem, where the merest shadow of one existed, was to give that shadow palpable shape and energy.

And so they argued. They argued about dependency. She insisted it was bad. The very word "dependency," she said, suggested weakness, addiction, and sickness, while "independence" suggested strength and self-reliance.

"Need is weakness," she'd say. "I don't want to be needy."

"But love is based on need," he'd counter. "If we don't need each other and depend on each other, why, what then?"

"What you mean," she'd reply, "is that you want everything your way. If we women are strong," she'd say, echoing her assertiveness training group, "you men think it weakens you."

So the power shifted from his benevolent monarchy to her reign of terror, her strong-arm dictatorship. She felt, it seemed, that she always had to be on her guard, lest he should wrest that power back. But he just gave it up to her. No contest. She decided what was best for Jennifer and Phoebe; she handled the money; she organized their social engagements and planned their elaborate trips.

She wanted to ensure that their daughters had the opportunities she felt she had never had. "I want the girls to know that they can be anything they want to be, do anything they want to do," she would say. By which she meant, he pointed out, anything that Christine approved of, anything politically correct and powerful. Jennifer and Phoebe could be doctors or lawyers or engineers. They couldn't be housewives, or maids, or bag ladies. And when Jennifer expressed a desire to do just that, or nothing, with her life, expressing her own independence, it drove Christine crazy. When he defended Jennifer's lack of appropriate "ambition," Christine merely countered, "You wouldn't say that if she were a boy." He wondered.

Inside the tent, dispatching the mosquitoes that had followed them, they rolled out the sleeping bags and arranged the packs.

"Why do you?" Phoebe asked.

"What?" he said.

"Do that."

She had raised such issues with disturbing frequency, and it placed him in a difficult position. If he supported Christine against his own judgment, he was being unfair to Phoebe. If he sympathized with Phoebe, following his natural inclinations, he was betraying Christine. He wanted Phoebe to know he respected and valued her feelings, even shared them, but he didn't want to martial her as an ally.

"We all get a little impatient sometimes," he replied. "I guess I do too."

From inside the tent they heard the sound of tires spinning on the sandy park road, a screech of brakes, and a crash of underbrush. Then there was the sound of a car backing up. It whined through the heavy air like a giant mosquito. Then silence, a door slamming, and footsteps.

Christine had been hurrying back with the mosquito repellent, he conjectured, she had run off the road, and it was his fault.

She slipped into the tent and zipped up the mosquito netting.

"Look," she said brightly, her face in a tight smile, her voice lilting. "Let's not camp."

He knew how mad she was by how extremely pleasant she was being.

"Neither of you really wants to camp," she continued, "and I'd be just as happy to go to a motel. I passed several nice ones in town with vacancies. It's going to rain and there are mosquitoes. Besides, we should have the headlight repaired."

The headlight? There was something ridiculously funny in all of this, he thought. He wondered if he just started laughing she would see the humor in it and they'd all start laughing, dismissing all the tension and hostility as their laughter rang out into the night over the drone of the boring mosquitoes and the impotent roar of the storm. He pictured the three of them for a moment, alone on this earth in their small warm place, their laughter sailing out into the universe.

Outside the wind whipped through the trees and the rain began in earnest. No. He wasn't about to let her outcharm him.

"Well," he smiled. "We've got the tent all set up and we all want to camp." Small hail began pelting the tent like popcorn, the taut nylon fabric snapping merrily. "The rain will probably pass, and the mosquitoes aren't that bad."

"Oh, but the weather report," Christine said. "And look at all those bites on poor Phoebe."

Phoebe was a large red welt in the corner of the tent, a flurry of itch.

"Phoebe's happy to stay here," he smiled.

"Phoebe would rather go to a motel," she smiled back.

"Phoebe . . ."

"Phoebe . . ."

Phoebe, propped in her dark corner, closed her eyes and squinched her face into a grotesque stiff grin. "Hey, kids!" she screamed, her voice all crackle and static, "What time is it?"

Outside, the storm howled and whistled. Inside, their smiles sluiced faster and faster through the dark, like logs slipping unimpeded down an ancient long chute.

The woman I've been seeing won't eat wild meat. Her ex-husband had been a hunter, and perhaps he'd been brutal in other ways or simply a bad cook, but his memory has tainted all wild game for her. This seemed a shame the first time I invited her for a duck dinner and she pushed aside the main course to concentrate on the acorn squash, brussel sprouts, and wild rice. She's a big-boned woman with a rope of wheat-colored hair down her back and vulnerable blue eyes. She's thinking, she says, of becoming a vegetarian.

I have noticed how often friends emerge from divorce only to immerse themselves in some new obsession. They drink too much or run marathons or give themselves over to a breathless fundamentalism. My friend and I pursue separate diets but share the same hunger. Obviously, she hasn't learned from her mistakes because I'm allowed to stay over on the nights before I go duck hunting.

4:30 in the morning. After batting the alarm clock off the nightstand, there is the heavy weight of inertia to deal with. Lately, I cannot so much as get out of bed without screening a private newsreel of the past that always ends with why I am sleeping in a strange bed. Also, there is this cat lodged between my legs.

Pulling myself from the warm covers, I dress quietly in the dark. The woman sighs, rolls over on her belly, and pretends to sleep. Outside the bedroom window, the streetlight illuminates a trapezoid of bare elms and sidewalk. The cat cries by the door. Boots in hand, I pick up my canvas coat and gun case in the hallway and slip out the door before the cat can make its getaway.

The highway flows through the October darkness, steeply banked with stubble fields and woodlots. Farmyards sail past in the circle of their arc lights. Fiddling with the radio, I dial through storms of static and settle finally upon a distant country station. "Heartaches Til Dawn" is the name of the show, and a plaintive, hillbilly voice solicits my phone-in requests.

At the Fox Coulee landing, duck hunters are already gathering in the pre-dawn gloom. Most of the pickup trucks have Minnesota plates, the hunters having crossed the state line to hunt the river bottoms with its Byzantine sloughs and tangled beaver canals. Waiting their turn at the boat launch, they hunch in heated cabs or stand outside playing flashlights over the swirling current. Every so often, someone asks what time it's getting to be.

Spotting Richard's blue station wagon, I slide in beside his retriever, a black Labrador with grinning white teeth and minstrel-show eyes. Richard passes me a cup of coffee from his thermos and a gooey breakfast roll and then proceeds to outline the situation. Heavy fall rains have raised the river too high to wade, so we'll need to beg a lift across the channel. Richard steps outside and hails a party of Minnesotans cozying into their camouflaged jon boat with its mesh blind and big Evinrude. Through the windshield, I watch him gesturing as he re-outlines the situation. The men in the boat have thick, bland faces and apparently no necks. They look at Richard and then follow his outstretched arm to the car where the dog and I are waiting. In a single motion, they shake their heads and roar down the river.

The woods on the far shore have begun to take shape in the silvery half-light when we finally convince a coon trapper to ferry us across the channel. He's been waiting for sunrise to legally make his sets along the riverbank and now decides there's sufficient daylight. We clamber aboard, the black Lab riding masthead on the bow, my boots resting against a tangle of traps and chains on the bottom of the boat. As the trapper ferries us across the misting, slightly stygian river, no one mentions how we are going to get back.

Ashore, we set off through the woods single file, the terrain presenting itself as a series of blowdowns and water hazards. Beavers have cut the willows into harp pungi sticks and moated the bottomlands with interconnecting canals and ponds so that every inch of land is an island within an island. Wading a beaver canal, the black water rising sharply to my waders, I nearly tumble over a sunken log. I wrench my foot loose and bubbles of methane gas break the surface with the pungency of rotten eggs.

Approaching the pond we plan to hunt, I can make out another party of hunters in silhouette, their anchored decoys riding high in the water. It's nearly dawn, so Richard and I split up on either side of an inlet, flickering our flashlights to keep from blasting each other in a crossfire. There's nothing much to do but wait. The sky turns a delft blue, and I busy myself leading blackbirds on the horizon. A breeze comes up and shifts the decoys around so they no longer appear to be on speaking terms.

From the distance comes the far-off thunder of shooting. High above the treetops, an immense flight of geese is moving southward, the din of collective honking carried before it. The angle of birds is perfectly formed, the point throwing a wake of two equal lines across the sky. Crouching down in the button brush, I wait to see if the geese will come within range. They are still impossibly high when the hunters across the pond open up. They must be firing automatics with the plugs removed. It sounds like a small war.

In the midst of this barrage, Richard stands up from his cover and yells over the water.

"What's that?" one of the gunners asks as the shooting tapers off.

"I said," Richard bellows into the sudden quiet, "that you're a pack of assholes!"

We sulk off through the woods and decide to split up. I make a long, careful stalk up a beaver canal that opens into a wide marsh but come up empty-handed. The morning is heating up and my woolens begin to chafe. I sit on the wreckage of an old beaver lodge and eat a mashed sandwich and don't see the pair of mallards dropping in until their wings whistle overhead. I swing on the drake, and the bird crumples into the marsh. Wading out, I pick up the drake and slip it warm and heavy beneath my arm like a loaf of bread. When I look back, the pond has already healed over, a few downy feathers floating on the still surface.

Much later, Richard shows up with a pair of greenheads hung from a sling around his neck. Uncertain the retrieving is over, the black Lab leaps up again and again to sniff the dead birds and snap her teeth. We reach the round pothole to find the hunting party already departed, their decoys left anchored in the water. Before we leave, Richard wades out and cuts all the cords.

At the riverbank, the channel looks lower to me, a translucent brown in the daylight, and I feel certain we can wade it. Richard is first. He cinches the belt tight around the top of his waders, slips into the river, shotgun held aloft, and begins working his way sideways to the current. Halfway across, Richard takes a long step and angles into the river, water pouring into his waders. His hat floats away as he kicks to shore.

Stripping off his wet clothes, Richard shouts encouragement from the other side as I slide down the grassy bank into the water. His dog, alone now, begins to whine and frantically pace the shore I have so recently abandoned. Finally the Lab lunges in and swims past me to the opposite bank. On tip-toe, I feel tentatively for the drop-off, losing heart because I know it's there. Stepping forward, I sink, weighted down with shells, into what seems like the Atlantic Trench. The river seals overhead in a wash of dim light until the bottom rises to meet me, and I push off, breaching the surface, and re-emerge on the far shore.

The next time I cross the channel, I'm swaddled in a life preserver worn beneath my canvas coat. But the river has fallen in the unexpected warmth of the late autumn and the crossing is easy. Richard's lab paddles ahead of us as usual, springing up the bank and shaking the river from her glossy black coat. Excited by the rich, humus smell of the river bottoms, she begins to circle, making false starts for the woods until we're clear of the channel. She doesn't appear to be dying.

We follow the distant trail of her barking through wild grape and prickly ash until we reach the round pothole we'd hunted earlier in the season. Richard takes the shovel I have carried and starts to dig through black muck and rootage. The shovel makes a sucking sound each time it lifts free of the wet earth. Richard is by now sweating, his movements jagged, and when he reaches solid clay he heaves the shovel into the tall grass. He calls the dog over, gently slips her collar off, and puts it in his coat pocket.

The dog is dying of a melanoma, a cancer that has bloomed and spread in her throat, slowly starving her to death. The veterinarian who examined the dog a week before suggested a lethal injection right there and then in his office. It seemed the thing to do. Most of us cannot bear putting an end to the things we care about and so willingly give up the task to strangers. But the dog had a quaking fear of the vet's office with its menagerie of fatal odors, so Richard declined, deciding to take the dog's life himself where it had seemed best defined, here in the river bottoms.

He breaks open a cellophaned dog snack and places it on the ground beside the hole he has dug. While the dog laps it up, he loads the .22 rifle and backs away to aim. But the dog has an unsettling way of looking up at him as she eats.

I am sitting on a tree stump, looking over the pond and wishing for invisibility.

"Call her," Richard says.

My mouth is too dry to whistle, so I face the dog and call out her name. She glances up from her meal before I can turn away and fixes me with a look free of implication.

The rifle shot claps over the pond. A pair of woodchucks whirr up from the windfall where they've been hiding, and I follow their flight as they clear the pond and disappear behind the dark smudge of bordering woods.

This is a weekend that I have my daughter. Halloween is a few days away and she's undecided about what to be. She watches unsqueamishly while I pluck the feathers from a plump mallard I'm sending home with her as a little peace offering. Then, declaring her boredom, she picks up an iridescent blue primary feather and puts it in her hair. The rest of the day, she wears it around the apartment, imagining she's an Indian.

Later, we drive to my ex-wife's house, but she's not there. I'm early or she's late. Whatever, I sit down on the back porch stoop and watch my daughter swing on a tire-swing hanging from a big walnut tree. All of this is just too familiar.

Her mother drives up with a carload of groceries. Of late, she's taken up racquetball and looks flushed and beautiful, a walking testimonial to self-assertion. I hand over the duck in a plastic bag, a husbandly gesture that seems, under the circumstances, absurd. But she is cordial, thanking me and sweeping up the gift with the grocery bags. For a moment, there is an awkward straining for talk so this won't seem like a hostage exchange. I try to think of something to say, but the words only come out faster and louder until I'm shouting. On that cue, she whisks daughter and groceries inside, the backdoor slams, and they're gone.

By November, migrations are no longer pouring down the northern flyway. The ducks you missed a month ago are lolling in a warm bayou while you cheerlessly watch football and contemplate another Midwestern winter. Still, there is always the question of one last trip to the river bottoms, knowing ahead of time it will be useless, and yet necessary to certify that it was.

A grey sky filled with shifting light hangs over the channel as I make the crossing. Pan ice has formed in scallops along the shore while the beaver ponds and canals have all frozen over. The ice shudders and cracks as I slowly cross a clear pane above black water. It's an edgy feeling, like walking on a skylight that might suddenly give way and drop you unannounced into a dimly lit room swirling with pike and old leaves.

Making the rounds of frozen potholes, I soon get the idea I'm alone in here. But there's a lead of open water running in one of the sloughs. The wind dies in the trees, and from around the bend I hear the quivering chatter of northern mallards. I bring the wooden duck call, strung from a lanyard around my neck, to my lips and give the Highball, a raucous call like the self-propelled laugh of a bore: Ha-Ha-Ha-Ha-Ha.

Like ourselves, ducks are gregarious and want to be let in on the joke, no matter how awful. This flock must be the exception or they've heard this one before because when I try to sneak them through the dry grass, they fly up like a window shade. As they head for the big water, I think: That's it.

Then from around a horseshoe bend a straggler calls, a hen mallard. Crouching in the grass, I answer with the Lonesome Hen Call, the torch song of waterfowlers. Each time I do, something like an echo answers from around the bend. Laments, real and contrived, pass from one end of the slough to the other until I feel a connection of some importance is at hand. I've almost lost interest in shooting the hen. But when she flies around the bend to see who's calling, that's exactly what I do.

The bird plummets, the sky no longer buoying her up, and drops like a stone into the open slough. I am already up and crashing through the reeds to reach the riverbank, but when I get there she's gone.

You always feel remorse crippling a bird, although the end is the same. Whether it ends up as a meal for you or a scavenging fox is a distinction the bird is unlikely to care about. Still, you want to redeem yourself.

I wade out into the icy slough, the bottom muck solid beneath me, hoping the duck will rise long enough for me to finish her off. Flurries are blowing across the water and my hands are going numb. I think how much easier this would be with a good birddog to sniff out the hen as she heads for cover in the reeds. I begin to wish that Richard's dog was not dead but revived beside me. And then I wish that I had never made the shot in the first place. And a whole flood of wishes follows.

Preoccupied, I nearly fail to see the crippled hen surface. The dusky brown head bobs just beyond the reeds, and very slowly I raise the shotgun barrel. But the mallard sees this movement, sees me, and for an instant fixes me in her stare before diving under.

Then the slough is utterly empty in the blowing snow. I wade ashore and wait on into the darkening afternoon, knowing I'm not going to see that hen again, knowing I've already consigned her to that long, long list of things done badly that no amount of wishing will undo.

Setting
the Lawn
on Fire

Mack Friedman

I t's the first day of school, third grade. Where are you? Are you
there? Do you remember the leaves starting to change, the
breeze cooling hips under shorts? Were you looking down at
your new shoes? I looked up on my way to the bus stop,
saw a boy.

And that's really my story. A nine-year-old stranger. Saucony
sneakers, gold-striped foam soles. Concrete squares, an arching blue
dawn, sunlit rooftops. The shadow I wound up in. Teeth as white as
sheets. A feeling, as he hugged me, of a dream. Not a dream I had
slept through, but a living reverie, a dream that followed me, the
way people are haunted by brilliance. Or a physical imprinting, like
the makers' marks impressed on the sidewalk before it turns hard
and impenetrable. Milw., WI. 1979.

Green *Journal* box, green light, WALK in pale letters. I ran to
him. He turned his head and grinned.

"Are you going to Golda Meir Elementary?" he asked.

"Yeah," I said, and was next to him, looking up at his face, where
the sky bored two holes to see through.

"So am I!" he said. "I'm in fourth grade." He threw himself at
me. We hugged so hard my backpack fell off my shoulders.

Cal was my guide. I barely noticed my new school. I couldn't
wait for recess, when I'd see him again. He was Cal with a capital C.
He lived around the corner. We were friends.

The boulevard where I grew up slid gently down the block, perfect for football. We played with his little brother Ron, who was in
second grade. I liked to outrun them. One summer morning I cut
across the grass and slammed forehead first into a concrete lamp-
post. It knocked me out just as I registered its flat enormity. Cal caressed me back into consciousness, as if willing the goose egg that
swelled on my forehead to hatch. He picked a dead dandelion and
blew off its head so the spores drifted under my nostrils. Ron ran for
my dad, who came out with ice. There remains of this scar tissue, a
mass of my cranium shaped like a tennis ball's extrusion into air
when it's floating on the surface of a pool.

In the summers we all took tennis and swim lessons. At first I was
jealous, but I learned to tolerate Ron's tagging along. Once we showered near a man who was shaving his crotch. We were entranced

enough to make fun of him walking home. I know I thought about pubic hair on me or on Cal, but the idea seemed so removed from what was there that I quickly got distracted.

I knew what was there by watching him change now and then. When he combed his straight blond hair, I'd survey his white Hanes for shit stains. One day Ron couldn't come, dentist or something. Cal and I walked back alone from the pool, four blocks up Locust from the riverside. It was in July, around our birthdays. He put his arm around me. His hair was slicked back, drying in the sun, like some Don Henley song. In the space of a pop tune, traffic receded into scenery, Cal's hand on my shoulder. He loved me right then.

I'd gone through the wardrobe and made it to Narnia.

That fall, the nightmares started. Alone in a forest, chased by bears, in a spiral of eight-fingered elm leaves and maple pod seeds. This dream recurred through the winter and most of the spring. Then, wandering naked, night after night, onto the stage in the school cafetorium. Standing, staring out. You have to confront your fears.

I got scared my first sleepover at his house and had to go home around 11. Our next try, Cal kissed me in his lower bunk while Ron slept above us. It worked. I stayed the night. When they got cable TV he'd call and we'd fall asleep to 3-D horror films on the pullout in the family room. We woke up to lawnmowers, Michael Jackson, blankets over bare chests, his red, mine blue; my arm around him, its sleepy tingle pinned under his weight. His upper lip was dewy and smelled like fresh-cut grass. If they say why, tell them that it's human nature.

Once, in a late-August lightning storm, while my parents tracked the crisscrossing electricity from the back porch, we snuck into their closet and pushed the bras, hanging like curtains, from our faces. We kissed once, fast, sweet, and the breeze from the bedroom window smacked the door shut like thunder.

Last kiss: in his bunkbed, in a blizzard. We'd walked in the street to the bus stop, digging our sticks deep into sidewalk snowbanks, carving three parallel tracks. Boys do things like that in fairy tales so they won't get lost, but it almost never works. We stood in the spindrift for forty-five minutes until we realized the bus wasn't coming. Cars fumed around us, graying the salty street. On the way back to their house, we saw that new snow had already covered our tracks. This being Wisconsin, all of our parents had made it to work. Naturally, Ron, Cal, and I were soon *au naturel* in their bedroom.

"One of us has to be the girl," Cal said. His lips drew back. He reclined on the lower bunk. I sat next to him, facing him, mouth tingling expectantly like when my mother sliced lemons to make lemonade. Ron stared, his back against the wall.

"What do you mean?" I asked. Edging so slightly away.

"One of us has to be the girl. Be Jenny. Otherwise, we're just two fags kissing." And then he laughed. It seemed so out of place. He wasn't sarcastic, characteristically. But he couldn't be serious.

"Okay," I agreed. "I'll be Jenny, but we have to switch later." I knew he wouldn't, but so what. When life gives you lemons . . .

Cal nodded, bent forward, nudged his face back into mine.

What he meant didn't sink in until much later, after we had played the bowling alley/restaurant game with plastic pins and a Nerf ball one last time. It didn't stick until long after we'd framed and clicked each other's dicks, hands shaped squarely into cameras.

What Cal said didn't hit until I was twelve, crammed into the way-back of my friend Favis's family wagon. We were driving to the birthday party of a kid named Dimitri.

One boy said, "Mike P. is gonna be there."

"Mike Pee," retorted another boy, pretending to urinate, "is a fag."

"You boys are too young to know that about yourselves," said Favis's mom.

I'm not, I wanted to speak, *too young,* and didn't. I stared through the parallel defroster wires at the hash marks sluicing endlessly away, turning from clear into blur.

That night Dimitri's dad gave me a facial massage that felt as good as Cal's hand over shoulder blades.

You don't have to stop, I thought of saying, *there,* and couldn't. Party boys danced in a circle as Dimitri's new Hall & Oates reached crescendo: *Because your kiss is what I miss when I turn out the light.*

I guess in time Cal felt embarrassed. He skimmed away like a water bug, swimming butterfly strokes that I couldn't catch up with. At practice I would glide in his contrail, stroke too close, choke in his wake. Water Safety seemed like a perfect excuse to perfect mouth-to-mouth. Instead, we tag-teamed an inflatable doll on the slippery pool deck. I nicknamed her Jenny; but when I kissed her, I pretended I was saving Cal's life.

Still, after swimming, he'd hang from my jungle gym, him and Ron peeing in bushes like bonobo monkeys. One blue summer day, when the breeze from the west was sweetly fervid, like cornfields and cowshit and brewery steam, I squatted in the wood chips and watched them climb our red-white-and-blue aluminum sticks. I threw bark shavings into the grass and imagined them splintered by my father's new gas mower. On the crooked plastic swing next to the clubhouse/outhouse, I felt more certain with every creaking return that when their mom realized I was a fag and a very bad influence she wouldn't let me play with them anymore.

My dad got me a magic trick box for my twelfth birthday, that July. It was a cheap kit, with weighted dice and invisible rope and cubist trinkets. Cal mastered this wizardry in two afternoons. The book that came with it, though, gave us some ideas. On its cover was a magician juggling flaming torches in the park. By August, we'd learned how to juggle Cal's plastic bowling pins, even passing one between us. We only dropped them once in awhile, or that's what we thought. We figured we were ready for more. I'm not sure whose idea it was. We just followed instructions. I collected three thick branches from the park the morning after a bad storm. Cal got some rags and wound them around the sticks, bundling them at the end with rubber bands. We dipped our kindling through the hole of the gasoline can in the garage, soaked the cloth through. Ron got some matches from my kitchen and a bucket of water. Then we set the lawn on fire. It all happened so fast. The flames were out of control, like my mom's hair. The neighbors called the fire department, but my dad unscrewed the sprinkler and managed to hose it all down.

In the fall when I went into eighth grade, I'd stand over my charred yard at the attic window, watch Cal and Ron play catch in their own fenced-off square, and try to make my phone ring. But what magic I'd learned from being Cal's assistant was useless in my hands. He ducked under the curtains in the middle of the show and left me sawed in two.

Our last date happened because my mom forced me to call him and drove us to *Footloose*. She was tired of my moping or sensed I was heartbroken. Suspecting it was a big conspiracy to show me a good time, I felt humiliated. I never called him again. I figured Cal's new trip was not a vacation. He'd never come back. Now I know I was right.

All over Wisconsin are kettles and moraines, molded by glaciers. Sometimes you can even find petrified stone.

Preserved in an icefall, life passed right by me. I fell in love with the autistic kid on *St. Elsewhere*. I thought I was enough for myself. I'd look in the glass day after day to make sure I was still there. My skin cracked from all the showers I took to get warmer. I just felt the same numbing cold all the time. In the resorts on the Upper Peninsula the snow is sometimes so frigid, alpinists get stuck on the summits because their skis can't create enough friction to glide them downhill.

There is something unbecoming to being stuck: You cannot become. I didn't know who I was becoming, or even if I was. I had a sense of it, looking at my friends, but my point of view was limited: skin-deep, and they always had clothes on. The only kid I'd strip for was the one the mirror showed. I wasn't sure which one was real. Myself, or my reflection? There was no way for me to see my face without distortion. The closest I came was closing one eye so I could see my nose, but that was blurry and too close, out of perspective. It reminded me of filmstrips. Somehow, I convinced myself the image was a counterpart: a flash of pink in my friends' retinas, a flash of pink in mine.

And so I made a friend.

I was thirteen then.

In colored pencil, I sketched friends in my grandfather's house, on the slim, madras couch in the den. Faces upon faces. My old friend was with someone else: The latest face was cool, she wore a jean jacket, no jelly bracelets. She looked like she had staying power.

When my parents were gone, my new friend came to visit. The oval, metal-frilled frame in the downstairs bathroom showed only the top of his head: wavy brown hair, narrow, lively brown eyes. The medicine-cabinet mirror in my bathroom was rectangular but curved on the top like the Liberty Bell. I saw every imperfection in the glass: the big nose with the sunburn line across it, chin pimple growing like a witch's wart, a kid's dumb veneer: uncertain, anxious grin.

In the laundry room mirror I focused on my body. I'd stand next to the washer and strip, fixating on my lack of pubic hair, as though that were all that separated me from the world. It was a metaphor for hopelessness, a locus I couldn't control anymore than my desire. I was repulsed and entranced to see myself such a child. In my parents' bathroom, between opposing green walls, I reflected a leaf from one mirror onto another and saw my pale ass, undistinguished. I flexed my butt muscles and all the laws changed, like levitation. I puckered up at the glass I had tilted, fogging over, and swabbed circles in vain. I fingered the words *I love you* over my lips in the glass, wiped them over with my hand.

At this mirror's lower counterpart, I learned I could push my penis back into my body with ease. When it was hot out, and humid, it would stay there, retracted. My veins were blue under translucent skin, like the invisible man in science class. When I looked over my shoulder, an ass gleamed like moonlight. Combining these two moves was sweetly negating, as ginger and soy sauce reduced over heat.

I watched my mom cook. I took long hot showers.

In seventh grade Spanish class I would imagine all my classmates, black white latino hmong japanese jewish, skinheaded and dyed, fat fit and skinny, big-tittied or flat, frozen at their desks, zippery parachute pants in sloppy piles for me to examine: leather cotton nylon poly fleshy bony skin like mine.

That spring, on the class trip to DC, my camera froze friends' asses under cherry blossoms. I liked it when schoolmates wore sweatpants. There was a swimming pool at the hotel. My friend Ryan, his bowl-cut and rat-tail a permanent beaver hat, got naked changing into his Speedo. I saw him through the mirror in his hotel room, the eyes in the back of my head. They flickered over Ryan's slight body, small penis curving over big balls like a banana split. His pubic hairs were chocolate sprinkles. I looked away, embarrassed for him in the Speedo: no one shows that much skin. Maybe I was the only one who noticed enough to care.

I knew from junior high that men could find me appealing. My gym teacher gave me special attention. He'd watch me bounce out of hot showers. It wasn't something that got to me, just subtle, unnamable, persistent, then awkward. I took in only its barest suggestions. I read Greek myths but the stories were censored. In this way, I could not identify as Narcissus, Peracles, or Geryon. I was Icarus, led by my father out of the maze, only to burn as the sun licked my wings.

That summer, I went to New York to visit my great-aunt Ana. She was eighty-three years old, quick and fierce as a goose, and she called me Benjie, my dad's boyhood nickname. Once when I was eight, and a flower-thrower at a family wedding, my dad gave me a plastic glass of champagne. I drank it all in one big swig in my grandfather's bathroom, like it was a cup of ginger ale or Tab. Then I put on some lipstick from a travel case that had to be Ana's: it was the brightest, pinkest color around. My mother asked, horrified, if I'd been putting on makeup. "Linda, darling, he's just been kissed by so many of us," Ana covered for me with a wink and a kiss.

Now I fought the desire to fly away naked down Columbus Avenue. Like exotic lovers, Trocadero and Charivari opened their rooms to prepubescent afternoons. And later that summer, new wisps consumed me. I spent the family trip to California in front of mirrors in hotel bathrooms, charting each strange brown hair extruding from white skin. My dad ran mousse through my waves, roughshod. My dad's friend fired buckshot with us in his sprawling SoCal backyard, piercing warm cans of Old Milwaukee. "It's the best use for your worst beer," Wayne told me, a beefy arm around my waist. "Here, hold it with both hands." He designed weapons for a living. I missed every time, but Wayne made them explode against a rock barrier. Foam dribbled like tears down the sandy cliff face and into his artificial creek.

My dad's friend's daughter, and her friend, took me to a dance club in Santa Barbara one summer night. It was muggy and smelled like plants drinking. They had to drag me away from the Frogger arcade when "People Are People" came on. I was in *depeche mode* but my body moved slowly. I got an erection in the Pacific Ocean in my Ocean Pacific swimsuit. No one noticed. Later, I showed the boy in the mirror. He kept it to himself.

One day I got lost at Magic Mountain. The last time I had been in California, I'd been eight years old. At that age I was in love with Cal. Now I wished I could touch my reflection, but I only re-absorbed it. Mirrors are imperfect conduits to other dimensions. Fenced inside the Lost Kids section (don't feed the animals), I hoped some nice man would kidnap me. Instead, my entourage found me and didn't. They didn't know how lost I was. I couldn't tell them. I did not know myself.

Thirteen years is time enough to see the world and circle back around.
   I follow his body, indistinct and stubborn, as it grows from one Sunday to the next.
   I see him in line for the diving board and follow him, because he looks cute. He's five-three, 100 or so pounds, wearing a navy Nike suit. He has medium brown hair, freckles on his shoulders, blue eyes, braces, the beginnings of a mustache. He walks the tacky aquamarine, slowly turns around, smiles down at me. He steps back toward me, my foot on the first rung of the one-meter. Then he turns again and runs off, his unrealized frame barely touching the board, an ugly duckling learning to fly by flailing. I wonder where his mother is. He tries a front flip and lands flat on his back. Behind me, a muscle-boy laughs. I do a simple backflip, sink down to the bottom, meet him back in line. He pirouettes and I eyeball his peach fuzz.
   "Are you going for a front flip?" I ask.
   The sweet sun blinks down on us from a cumulus cloud. The yeasty smell of harvest wafts in slow waves from the farms to the west.
   "Yeah," he says, with an embarrassed half-smile, as if torn from reverie.
   "You need to tuck more."
   "I keep telling him that!" says the bigger kid, dripping wet.
   "Practice. Are you guys brothers?"
   A six-year old girl ahead of us mounts the board, walks its length gingerly, and jumps feet-first into the blue Olympic pool.
   A whistle. "Has she passed her deep-water test?" screeches a lifeguard, to no one in particular, to the cornfields beyond this pool.
   "Yeah," says the older kid. "We're bros."
   The frail kid reddens his backside again. I do a standard pike, fuck

my neck up on entry. I walk into the locker room to massage it with a hot shower.

The skinny kid's there in less than a minute; I run into him on my way to piss. He wanders blindly around, holding a glasses case.

"Hey," I say. "Cool suit."

"Thanks. It's Nike."

"Yeah I saw." I move up to him. "Does it have a lining?" As the kid goes for broke, I think, considering the Doonesbury *book of the same name, where Andy comes out to Joanie Caucus. I read it the summer I turned fourteen.*

("I'm gay, Joanie," says Andy.

"How do they know?" asks Joanie.

"I know, Joanie. I know.")

I asked my mom what gay was then, in 1985. She told me, to her credit, though by then the point was moot.

I tug gently at his elastic band. He looks at me, bemused. I lift it, look down, but his genitals are all in shadow. I see a lining and nothing else. Blood rushes through me. The air near the showers is thick and sweet.

"Yeah, I guess it does," I sigh. "Cool."

We step outside under the concrete awning that connects the men's locker room to the pool. I lead, embarrassed at myself: What has gotten into me?

"Wait," he says.

It's almost a plea. I stop in my tracks, my toes already aglow in sun.

"It doesn't go down all the way."

I stare at him, confused.

"My lining," he repeats. "My lining doesn't go down all the way!"

My instincts take over.

"I don't understand what you mean. Show me." So I lead him back, to the back of the lockers, where no one can disturb us without fair warning.

He stands on one side of a wooden bench, me on the other, like we're astride a pew, without of course the Bible racks. The boy unties his suit. I wait, fascinated. He peels the elastic away from his belly, peeks down.

"See?"

"See what?" I peer over the pew and down his abs.

"See, that's my suit. That's my lining—it doesn't go down all the way. And that's my penis."

He giggles.

"Uh," I stall. "Yeah, I can see that."

His dick twists to the left, askew, half-hard and winking. His suit snaps back in place like a slap across the face.

"Is it the same way in back?"

"Same way in back." He turns profile so I can stretch his string backwards. I gaze at the start of his crack, let it go. "What about you?" he asks. "Does your suit have a lining?" His braces glint in artificial light.

"No—" I say, surprised to be the center of attention. "Look, it's like velcro." I unsnap the top two buttons and rip open the crotch. He ogles my dick, soft from shock.

"That's weird," he breathes, rapt.

"It's okay, but I should wear something under it—I feel sort of naked with just this. Feel how thin the material is." Cautiously, he feels the side of my nylon. We start to move out of our niche. "Plus," I say, "the velcro snags my pubic hair sometimes."

He has some, contained in area but unruly by nature, curling into Nike shadows. "What do you mean, snags?" he asks.

"You know, snags it—like, gets caught in it."

"I still don't understand what you mean." Oh. He wants me to show him.

His name is Eric. He doesn't like basketball but he plays it with me, moving in circles, asphalt burning his bare feet. He doesn't like football but his Dad makes him watch it. He says he likes IKEA and that male strippers were on Sally Jessy Raphaël once. Adolescence is a non sequitur.

He refuses to remove his suit in the showers. "I don't want someone thinking I'm gay," he explains. I peel my shorts away. Then he bones up and flashes me two dozen times, that being more acceptable. Eric takes the lead and vaguely segues into things, asking questions like he's God and it's Judgment Day. His more memorable queries, three Sundays in a row, are:

How much do you jerk off? Have you ever done it—had sex I mean? What kind of condoms do you use? Doesn't this shower make you hard? Are you circumcised? What is circumcision anyway? Are you Jewish?

Have you ever been to a church? (He says he's Catholic—my gramma knew Jesus, he cracks.) How do you jerk off? Is it like this I mean?—or do you do it like this? Are you jerking off now? Do you get a lot of stuff shooting out? Don't you think the water's cold today? What kind of car do you drive? Do you smoke? What kind of cigarettes do you smoke? How many girlfriends do you have?

On the third Sunday, as I'm drying off and ready to head home, he follows me to my locker with a hard-on wrapped under a towel—"I get hard just thinking of your girlfriends," as he puts it. There are a couple of women I'm seeing, but they, like my job and the rest of my life, seem immaterial at moments like this. As I'm wondering how to respond, Eric gets desperate and asks whether I ever wear Speedos.

"I don't," he says, "I'm afraid if I did, my dick would pop out, like this!" His penis jumps through the band and over his navel, disappears, and comes out through a leg hole. I'm down to my linings, blue Adidas short shorts. "You've got a hard-on!" he says. I'm kind of pissed. I should have better control.

"What should we do?" I ask.

"How big is yours?"

"I don't know. Let's match up."

He stands up from his bench, takes off his towel and pulls down his suit. I follow suit and stand beside him, eyes peeled for toddlers and daddies and grandfathers, nose sniffing for sunscreen or coconut oil or eucalyptus. My cock's over his, him taut and straight, me half hard and horizontal.

"They're about the same," I observe, thinking we need to make this quick.

"No, yours is bigger. You're so big and I'm so small!"

Eric bounces the bottom of my dick twice with the tip of his. He smiles, nice and easy. He sits back down and starts jerking immediately, like a gift he's unwrapping. I motion him to a safer spot, a foot away from me, straddling a bench. I sit across from him to scout for authority figures.

"Do you always cover your dick when you do that?" he asks.

My cock's still inside my trunks, and I'm going at it. I focus on my hearing, for soft footsteps on wet carpet, or the squeals of little children. There's nothing. For two minutes we're completely alone. That's plenty of time. It's just enough, I guess. I lob cum from my nipples to my navel and grab a towel right before he spunks out. Still I can't stroke him on the thigh as he comes. I can't touch him at all. It's like joining the Mafia: hard time and a lifetime registration, once you join the Sex Offenders you can't ever leave. "Look, look!" he shouts. He points to the salivary rubberbands that swing from his urethra to the floor.

"Jeez," I say, "Aren't you gonna clean off?"

"No." Eric grins at me and then looks thoughtful. It's too brilliant to witness so I look down for a sec. "I'm going to go swimming." He takes off his glasses and shivers, hugs himself with his towel, tiptoes off.

I see him in line for the diving board and watch him, because he looks cute. He walks the length of tacky aquamarine, slowly turns around and smiles at me across the Joshua "Jock" Glick Family Recreation Park pool. Then he turns again and runs off, bouncing full-force off the end and making very nearly a full flip. I stand still but not frozen. A little girl clambers up the metal ladder. I give Eric a thumbs-up as he emerges and leaves the deck. Outside, at the edge of the grove, I hear the name Eric quaver through the elms, and he runs off barefoot, shouting Coming! *To me,* Later!

A goosy horn, his name out loud, his vanishing replies; a slam of metal, low growl from the small, sharp stones leading him home. I get into my car and drive away. I'll never go back. I don't fucking know why.

One soggy August day just after I turned fourteen, my mom got back from the bookstore and tossed me a paperback called *What's Happening to Me?* It was, of course, about puberty. I kneeled in the hallway over a centerfold of a naked youth at successive stages of sexual maturity. I wasn't sure then if it was a photo or a sketch. My guess now is that it was a pointillist illustration based on photographs. When I saw the boy in the middle I fell in love. I took him upstairs to the laundry room mirror, to compare. We were the same, only my dick was rock hard. I thought, *What's happening to me?*

By the time I was sixteen, things were even more awry. When I cut class or procrastinated to avoid my biology assignments, I killed time flipping through the card catalogues at the University of Wisconsin–Milwaukee library. In short order, I discovered "puberty—boys—rites of passage," and "sexual abuse—males—case studies," and "homosexuality—Greece." After I had exhausted these resources, I tried the kiosk of computer screens near the reference desk, keying "art and boys and nudes," and "Klinefelter's syndrome," and "pederasty," and—when I got more advanced—"intergenerational male intimacy," which yielded detailed Dutch research that left me contending with certain inch-to-centimeter ratios.

One icy night, when I had six weeks' worth of homework due, I sprinted the short blocks from home to the library in my winter coat and soccer shorts, to wake myself up. There I tapped into a CD-ROM, the Medline, and came up with a reference to "priapism and adolescence" that promised black-and-white prints of synthetic growth hormone side effects. The journal in question was located in Compact Shelving, the electronically separable stacks deep in the basement. I found my call-number parameters and pressed the Operate button on the elevator box wired into the side of the metal bookshelf. A green light flashed. As long as I fingered the button, the stacks hummed to life, parting for me, acquiescent as passed-out friends. I headed down the newly created aisle, squinting for the 1987 *American Journal of Diseases in Children.*

Vaulted within five-hundred micro-thin pages was a doctor, frozen grasping teen male genitalia, like a spokesmodel displaying items up for bids on *The Price Is Right*—it's a priapic fifteen year old with delayed maturation! Start the bidding at $200! My heart sank to my guts, thumped into my prostate, and surged through my dick as I carried the book to the back of the basement, between the last closed stack and the blank stucco wall. I tugged my blue checkered soccer shorts under my balls, and jacked off over and alongside the fondled specimen.

A whim impelled me back over the tracks to examine the journal's annual indices. In the 1940s, Earle Reynolds and Janet Wines had taken thousands of pictures of fifty-nine boys from Yellow Springs, Ohio, some of which appeared in 1951, under "Physical Changes Associated with Adolescence in Boys." The seven sizes of the flaccid penis fascinated me. "We have also taken a few measurements of both stretched and erect penis," they wrote. "In four boys, there is a history of semi-erections at a number of visits. This is noted routinely on the physical examination record, and can also be seen readily in the photographs."

That night, I smeared semen on my tie-dyed boxers; over a library card slipped from its slot on the topside of the rack; across old folio maps crinkling on the black plastic shelf to my left. I'd never seen so much sperm. Hell, I'd never seen any; my girlfriend was always gobbling mine up. I was confused, this first night I successfully masturbated: what did I need Teri for now? My shorts slapped my abs as I slamdanced through the footnotes, hot on the trail. My eyes flashed on one title—*Somatic Development of Boys,* by Stolz & Stolz: MacMillan, 1951.

A whole book! I was sure that if I found the Stolzes, I'd never need anyone else. I thought *I must have this book!*

The Milwaukee libraries never had Stolz, but I memorized its Dewey decimal number, 612.661, and thus began my obsessive quest. From that night on, whirring stacks gave me erections. I learned to find joy in the permanent shelves, discovering *The Linked Ring: The Secession Movement in British Photography, 1892–1910,* which included some F. Holland Day expatriate scenes, listless surreal prints of unclad, wild youngsters emulating woodsy saints. I developed a fondness for case studies of abused kids, the only accounts I could find of boys having sex with other males. I shielded Theo Sandfort's *The Sexual Aspect of Pedophile Relations: The Experience of Twenty-five Boys,* held it close to John Money's *Love Maps* and *Paraphilia,* let *The Sexual Offender and His Offenses* kiss *The Boys of Boise.*

Sometimes I scaled locked doors and climbed into the study rooms on the library's second and third floors; there was a gap between the wooden doors and the acoustic ceiling that I could squeeze through, muscling up and then rappelling down onto the desk, where I'd pop open a Paul Kubitschek portfolio from the 1932 *Journal of Nervous and Mental Disease.* Entitled "The Secondary Sex Characteristics of Boys in Adolescence," the article was laden with soft, fuzzy photos of cherubic, denuded guys standing side by side under such captions as, "testicular size in this group varied from small almond to large walnut." Into the trash can I came.

My personal fave was Frank K. Shuttleworth's 1949 piece in the *Monographs for Social Research in Child Development,* "The Adolescent Period: A Graphic Atlas." As soon as I read the abstract—"consists entirely of half-tone reproductions of photographs of nude children, mostly serial photographs taken at different ages"—I clutched the burlap backing and bounded blindly for cover in a three-walled, cornered carrel. I thought of Andy, a freshman in my homeroom, as I obsessed over Shuttleworth's "late-maturer," a pasty kid whose face was obscured by a black box painted over it. Full-frontal and biannual from 11.5 to 17.1 years, he stood anal-receptive, juxtaposed to front the taller "early-maturer," a similarly defaced skinny kid. I copied their measurable attributes into my notebook, robotic. Then I took my blue Bic and wrote on the carrel's wooden wall:

"I'm 16, brown hair + eyes, 5′7″, 135 lbs, sparse copper pubic hair, none under my arms. If interested," and then my pen gave out.

I yearned for the opportunity to compare myself to a real, flesh-and-blood guy. In high school I got glances from one older kid in the weight room and wanted the kid to ask me out, or something. I trailed him one day past rotting piers and chalk-white boulders on Lake Michigan's shore, both of us alone, awash in the stench of poisoned alewives. But nothing came of it. Books were more dependable.

Invisibility makes you want to be seen. I stalked a footnote all the way to the West Side, past Milwaukee County Stadium to the Medical College of Wisconsin. There I found a one-of-a-kind folio supplement to an adolescence textbook: two European boys in oversize sepia stared back at me, frozen in time. In a trance I took the poster to the communal study table. Two white-haired doctors sat at each head, engrossed in thick journals. Next to me, a bald-spotted researcher jotted wet notes; across, a blonde female doc skimmed restlessly. I pried open the Dutch boys like a bucket of paint and moved my chair as far under the table as I could before my stomach hitting the edge. I unzipped one flange at a time, breathed in intermittent silent gasps. My cock hit the underside of the table and I dragged it against its own streaking effluvium and along the smooth grain. I left stalactites sweeter than bubble gum. How could no one have noticed?

Sometimes I found books I wanted, like *Control of the Onset of Puberty*, or J. M. Tanner's *Growth in Adolescence*, only to see that certain pictures had been removed with razor blades. The technique seemed so cold. I preferred to fold them over, crease them slowly, gently tear the boys away.

To exact revenge against the vandals, or maybe jealously wanting the boys all to myself, I started hiding my captives inside my official high school folder, the one they gave us in homeroom, with an etching of our prison silk-screened in blue on the cover. The ripped-out photos, musty with age, gave the folder the smell of bitter almonds. I liked to carry it down into my house's dank cellar and leaf through it, like the wind, during thunderstorm warnings.

On cold winter afternoons, in my junior year of high school, I'd be the first one home. My dad was a physicist. I imagined him solving equations written in Greek and methodically boinking his secretary. Whatever, he wasn't home until 5:30. My mom was an English professor whose meetings droned on until 4:30. That left me and the cat, and the cat went outside as soon as I got home, even though it was freezing. It was warm in the house.

The house was big and brick. In warm months it was covered with ivy. The third floor went completely unused. We used to rent it out to college students but my mom didn't like the creaks above her bedroom when she was trying to sleep. My dad's weight equipment was up there, and my grandfather's love seat. He died right after I got back from DC. The madras couch fronted three windows that looked over the boulevard. The afternoon sun lay shafts on the cushions, which were laced with gray cat fur. I imagined that the dust helices inside these sunshafts were evidence of the interplanetary beams that would atomize me, transport me to ecstasy, and return me unharmed and happy.

I brought my mom's long, freestanding mirror upstairs to witness this transformation, then sprawled on the couch to experiment. I wanted to see my down light up in the flares that made it through the window and the plastic storm in front of it. The small red patch of hair I'd grown was ablaze. Thoughts disappeared in the shaft of January sunlight. Me: skin and shadow, sperm, rising and falling, restrained only by breath, muscle, and gravity.

Every molecule in me strained to be seen. I wanted those two dimensions to replicate through some ancient, forgotten mitosis, so that the attic was an orgy of fun-house mirrors with naked teenaged boys inside. I wished someone would take nude pictures of me. I wondered what it would be like to strip on stage, and so pretended to be a stripper and came again five minutes later, in my skimpiest white briefs (Hanes size 12), or my mom's blue one-piece, straps slipped off the shoulders, vulva-liner scrunched into my ass. In the audience were men of all shapes, colors, ages. Their faces mattered much less than their presence.

That year my dad described a wormhole to me.

"There are enormous forces at work in space, son," he'd say. "Now, a wormhole is an almost infinitesimally small passageway that opens at one end in the space-time continuum, and comes out at another part of space-time."

"Like Pac-Man?" I asked him.

I pretended I could go into a wormhole and wind up somewhere else. That's where my body went, under the sun-shaft, and inside the mirror. The trick was where and when to come out, and I had no idea how to control that. When my dad was in the garage, tinkering with the cars (an old Toyota with a hole in the floor, and then a 70s model Ford Fairmont, a detective car), I would fantasize that he was building a time machine just for me.

I wanted to be eight again, but I didn't know why.

When I was eight, my dad was addicted to Pac-Man, and especially, Ms. Pac-Man. It got to the point where he wouldn't stop playing to order our Blizzards at Dairy Queen. Something about the arcade must have soothed this fiery man with the red beard: the way you could go in one side and out the other, or the way you could munch the ghosts. Ghosts scared me, their cold transparency, their demonic chattering. How could they endlessly regenerate? Why couldn't you get rid of them for good?

And what if you never came out the other side? What if you got stuck in that nowhere? Where would you be then?

Imagine you're fifteen years old. Your dick's eight inches and thick all the time. You like to show off. Last summer we showered once next to each other. We shared a dispenser: pink soap, my favorite. It smells like clean sheets and boy sweat. Water cascaded in sheets down your torso. Your stomach let the side of my hand rest against it. You moved into it, instead of away. Call it intuition.

I won't forget it. When I was fifteen, I strip-teased my local locker room as much as I could, balancing towels on my erection. You're the same way, but more blatant: you don't even work out first. You could be a von Gloeden model, swarthy and tawny. Your skin's olive and cherry, like a stiff drink. You keep score for the Hyman Piston thirty-plus basketball league, in which your dad plays. I watch a game. The hoops suck. You track stats. You stroke off afterwards in the urinals, smile at me on the way out, our only eye contact. Your eyes are pretty and green.

You're waiting for me by the vending machines forty-five minutes before game time, the next week. You're wearing a navy blue sweater over some jeans. You follow me into the locker room. I strip down, throw on shorts. You walk down a runway of scattered undress, to the bathroom in only a long charcoal shirt, like a teddy. You weigh yourself nude. You don't say a word. Your butt's a split coconut, ripe and sprouting brown hair. As I walk past, it seems to want to be touched. I'd flip it, but it's on a grill and I didn't bring tongs.

When I was your age, I wasn't attracted to men who would cruise me, aesthetic professors who'd ask me to model. Even turned down the beefcake straight from the weight room cuz he didn't seem right for me. You might do the same thing. I like, love you for it. I wonder if you like me.

You get dressed again and hit the first stall, leave the door open. I go to the bathroom, see you jerking off. You're way out in public, but that's how it goes. At least you're not laughing and making fag jokes. I move into your cube and ask coolly for two-ply. You turn yourself towards me, hand on the pump; it jumps upward. Don't know what to say, so I blow my big nose on Scott tissue, ask when basketball starts. You say, twenty minutes, and zip it.

You walk to the stairwell that goes to the gym. When you come on back down again, I'm on my way up. I say in passing, "There's another one on the second floor."

"Another what?" you ask.

"Another bathroom. It's empty."

You make an about-face and bolt up there past me. I run into a random 13-year old baller, who blocks me at the gym doors. He thinks I'm cool cuz I can dunk, so he half-hugs me, half-hits me, and says I look lost. I tell him I gotta make a phone call.

I trail you through the gallery of the community center, hung with nostalgia: streetside paintings of an America I romanticized growing up; diners and truckers and hungover June mornings, Roadway rigs in dappled light. I wonder if we'd have been truck-stop boys if we hadn't been Jewish.

You're where I knew you'd be, in the handicapped stall. You see my fresh Kobe hi-tops and swing free the door. I'm at the kiddie-height urinal right next to your toilet.

"Want some company?" I ask. God, I'm so lame.

You say, "I don't care."

"Your rules," I say, but that doesn't process, probably cuz they haven't been formalized.

I'm so into this I'm not even hard. I'm not sure who I am now at all. "I'm in shock," I giggle.

"Why's that?" You mutter, stretching your skin back and forth, real deliberate. There's a moment when I sense something has taken you over, a cosmic control over ebb and flow, this slow pulse of a boy in a coma.

"Cuz, like . . ." I stammer. I don't even know why now. I've never had bathroom sex, I feel like saying, though that's not true—at seventeen, my ass against palms creased and weathered in a park tearoom. "Cuz, you're cute," I say, joining you.

You sort of smile, content enough.

My knuckles flex for your left cheek, which blushes. You flinch and zip up. It happens so fast. Then you're half-gone, looking in sink mirrors and finding yourself. You wash your hands.

"We should meet up some time."

"I'm busy most days after school," you say.

"Maybe at . . . halftime?"

"Maybe," you shrug.

"I'm sorry."

"Don't worry about it."

"Shit. Is this too much of a trip-out for you?"

"Yeah." You're at the door now.

"I'm so sorry," I repeat, meaning, Next time I'll respect your silence.

"It's okay," you tell me, and I know you're saying it as politely as possible, if only to get the hell away from me, but you look into my frightened eyes with iridescent certainty, and somewhere inside, you're telling the truth.

I think, Sometime I'll make it all right. *But if it's not already, I won't.*

In the spring of my senior year in high school I partied until I got pneumonia. Delirious, I'd wait until school had let out and let my fingers do the walking. I called five guys from the junior varsity soccer team, two of Ron's cutest male friends, and a few youngsters from my little league days. I got some wrong numbers, but I knew Milwaukee neighborhoods well enough to make an educated guess. There were some things I needed to find out.

Shivering violently, cracking in and out of my deepest, most commanding voice, I would start by saying that I was a doctor who'd been given their number from their medical office. "Can I ask you a few questions about puberty?"

Almost always, the boys would hesitantly agree.

"How old are you, how tall are you? How much do you weigh? What color is your hair? What color are your eyes? What is your race?"

These questions usually came off without a hitch. The next set really separated the men from the boys.

"Do you have pubic hair? What color is your pubic hair? Do you masturbate? How much do you masturbate? When did you first cum? How long is your penis?" I crooked the phone into my shoulder and freed one arm from my poncho, shakily recording their responses.

Here's a sample of the results:

Name	Age	Ht.	Wt.	Hair/Pube/Pit	Ejac	mastur	pen length
Me	17	5'8"	140	br/red/light	yes/15	1–3x/day	6"
Derek	13	5'1"	135	blo/bla/none	n/c	heavy breathing click	
Renaud	15 (f/x)	*My doctor is in Antwerp, I do not see why I should be answering such questions.*					
Tyler	12	5'0"	95	blo/br/unsure	*huh?* click		
Bill	16	5'8"	135	br/br/br	yes	*Here, talk to my friend Steve*	

85

Steve   17   5′9″ 165   br/bla/bla   yes/12 *Whenever I can!*
    Laugh/click
Jeff   13   5′4″ 105   red/red/none   yes/12 *I'm doing it with my*
    brother right now!
Joshua 15   *Hey, Mackey is that you? What are you doing dude?*
    (Disconnected by caller.)

Three weeks after these phone calls, I molested another boy. We were in San Francisco for a Mock Trial conference, which was fitting, considering how many laws we broke there. Our high school contingent stayed at a hotel on Divisadero Ave., four to a room, two to a bed. My bedmate was Jim Lokker.

My friends and I were getting drunk in their suite; they'd stashed their parents' surplus whiskey in their duffels. Jim decided to join us—peer pressure. He never drank. He was sort of a dork, and looked like a hobbit. I liked him though. To prove his manhood, he took four plugs of Jack Daniels, spaced only by three deep breaths through his nose. Within minutes his eyelids were drooping. I was thawing, not toasted, and slowed down. Our friends had me haul him off to our bed. I carried him downstairs like a baby. Our roommates were gone. It was still early.

I propped Jim up and helped him into the bathroom, held him to the toilet. Jim tried to puke but couldn't. I poured glasses of water down his throat and he gagged.

"I need to go to . . . bed," he said slowly.

"Okay. I'll help you out of your clothes."

"It's . . . okay."

"You'll be more comfortable tomorrow morning. Where are those soccer shorts you wear?" He had folded them neatly and left them on the dresser. "Here they are. Here . . . help me take your pants off."

Jim closed his eyes, helped me pull down his underwear. I put his shorts around his ankles and pulled. He crashed onto the bed. I dozed off, beside him. When he started snoring, I woke with a start.

I circled around the bed in the thrilled languor of having what you want but not knowing how long it'll last or what you should do with it, admiring his big goofy ears and his wire-puff blond hair.

Then I took off the soccer shorts I'd just put on him, like committing insurance fraud. Someone knocked at the door. I left Jim half bare and let in my friend Mike. He was surprised but said nothing. Something stopped us from carting him, in all his glory, to the chaperones. Instead Mike walked back to his party and I returned to mine, turned Jim back over. I touched his penis, rolled my thumb and forefinger around the head. He was stone cold gone, and his dick was a rag doll. I gave up and tucked him back in. I didn't touch him again. It was so sexy and so sad to see his reaction in the morning, like he'd never, ever woken up naked before.

After my father had been dead for about nine months, he began to appear in the kitchen. I'm referring to the kitchen in England, where my parents had chosen to live in their retirement. They were musicians, and what they wanted to do with their retirement was listen to music, and England is a place for that. They bought a small red brick house in a village outside Reading, within commuting distance of London. After six months in quarantine, their dog was allowed to join them. They had been careful to buy a house with a fenced-in backyard, the fence hidden by a hedge ten feet tall. A munificent oak held court at the far end of the property, scattering a largess of acorns for those squirrels willing to brave the dog.

The day came, of course, when the dog could no longer chase the squirrels and my parents could no longer make the long trip to London. My parents now watched telly most of the day; at nine o'clock at night, they moved to the kitchen for ice cream. My father scooped up three dishes, setting one on the floor for the dog. The three of them were crowded into a kitchen barely big enough to hold the appliances. The furnace was in there too, inside a cabinet, warm as a hand, so that being in the kitchen felt like being held in somebody's palm. Whenever I visited them, I ate the mandatory bowl of ice cream and had that feeling of being held, being clasped and enclosed.

When the dog died, and my father no longer felt needed, sadness took over the house. Such sadness is not unlike what the English call "rising damp," a pervasive mold in rainy climates. My father declined rapidly. He was diagnosed as having Alzheimer's, and within a year, he was dead of a stroke. My mother weighed seventy-eight pounds, and had lost the use of one of her legs. She had end-stage emphysema. She could no longer manage the stairs. On my last visit there, which I had made wanting to see my father while he could still recognize me, I had gotten them a replacement for Blaze, the dog that had died. Oscar was a Shih Tzu who'd been born with a hernia that rendered him ineligible for breeding and who, at six months, was just a bit too old for consignment to a pet shop. Now he and my mother slept together on a single bed that had been set up downstairs in the dining room, next to the kitchen. When my mother wrote to me that she had seen my father sitting in his chair in the kitchen, I wondered if her mind was going too, and perhaps it wasn't even Alzheimer's—I knew from experience that losing someone you love can sensitize you to every memory of him, so that his memory is as present to you as he used to be. It would surely not be difficult to confuse the presence of the memory with the man himself. "Dear Nina," my mother wrote back, when I suggested this, "don't be a dope. I do not have a sentimental bone in my body, and if your father is not in the kitchen, who the hell is sitting in there scarfing ice cream every night?"

I was, myself, when I read this letter, ensconced in my Green Bay Packers chair—a club chair I'd bought years ago, that had a Green Bay Packers emblem on it; the department store was eager to unload it because even in Wisconsin nobody had been a Green Bay Packers fan since the days of Vince Lombardi—with my own little dog curled up beside me. My daughter was rocking in her rocking chair in front of the radio. Madison, which is so relentlessly populist that it feels that every musical faction, like every political faction, must be served even if it means that everybody winds up feeling shortchanged, refused to have an all-day classical station, and just then, the afternoon jazz program began. My little girl will tolerate nothing but classical. "N-O!" she shouted, stamping her foot on the floor. It was clear that if she had been old enough, she would have retired to England.

I got up and turned the radio off. She had never met her grandmother—who was also her great-grandmother, since her biological mother was my brother's daughter. I had adopted her.

"How would you like to fly in a big plane across the ocean?" I asked her.

"Can Teddy come?" He was sitting in her lap.

"Yes," I said, "Teddy can come, but this little piggy will have to stay home." I picked up my little dog, and he looked straight into my eyes as if saying, How can you do this to me after all we've meant to each other? "It's only temporary," I said to him. "I'll be back."

We Bryants clung to our animals as if they were our lovers, our lifelines. They helped us to have faith in ourselves. Maybe they *were* ourselves, or the most generous parts of ourselves. As the morning sun broke over the wing of our plane, light spilling ecstatically across the horizon, Tavy held Teddy up to the Pan Am window, pressing his button nose against the pane, showing him the sky, the clouds, the flashing blue-and-silver sea. "My nose is cold," she said in what appeared to me to be some kind of sympathetic confusion, falling back into her seat.

"You mean Teddy's nose, don't you?" I corrected her.

"Teddy's nose is a *button*," she said, amazed by my stupidity. She looked at me as if I was crazy. She didn't know I used to be. I smiled at her. "A nose by any other name would smell as sweet," I said, pretending to catch hers between my fingers, making the tip of a nose with my thumb.

My mother, who had been tall and beautiful, slender and strong, was now a wrinkled doll propped on pillows. She was an island in a sea of cigarette wrappers and ashtrays, Kleenex and toilet tissue, Rollo chocolates in gold tinfoil and half-full cups of cold cocoa, and the complete works of Dickens. Oscar, all gold fur, a live Rollo, sat at her side. I tried to straighten up the mess at the same time I embraced her and introduced Tavy.

I had been worried about this introduction.

As she gazed at her grandmother, Tavy's eyes grew rounder and rounder. They were green eyes—after the blue period of infancy, her eyes had turned green, though still a blue-green, elm-leaf eyes. My brother and my niece had both had true-green eyes, deep-green off-the-coast-of-Cozumel eyes; my mother's eyes, now weak and cloudy, had once been hazel-green, sometimes golden, sometimes gray. These subtleties of hue may mean nothing to anyone else but I had observed them with fascination. It was as if there were two branches to the family: the bold branch, with green eyes and outrageous energy; and the quiet brown-eyed branch, the observers.

"Why are you staring at me?" my mother asked Tavy. She'd had a minor stroke a few years earlier and the left side of her mouth seemed to resist any attempt at speech so that her words came out slightly scrunched, determined but fugitive, softly slurred.

Tavy said, "You're so old."

"Ha," my mother said. "You will be too, when you've lived as long as I have. And maybe by then you'll have something more interesting to say."

My mother had never liked children. Sometimes she would act as if she did, for the sake of her reputation among neighbors or co-workers, offering congratulatory comments over snapshots of new-borns or reports of grade-school genius, but she would tell her own children, speaking about children-in-general, "They're more trouble than they're worth. After all, what are they going to be when they grow up? People!" Her dislike of children was minor compared with her contempt for adults, to which it was teleologically related. She would have liked it better if human beings could have grown up to be dogs or dolphins.

This was one reason I'd been worried about this introduction.

I was used to my mother's ways but Tavy wasn't, and I didn't want her feelings to get hurt. "I'll take Tavy upstairs and get her settled in," I said, standing behind my adopted daughter. And with a pro-tective hand on each small shoulder, I tried to steer her away.

Tavy twisted free, turning back toward the bed. "Are you going to die?" she asked.

I watched my mother's parchmenty face crumple like a piece of paper history had wadded up and tossed into the trashcan of time. She had had such plans. Once upon a time, she had thought she would outlive my father by enough years to have a second, single life. She would travel to Scotland, take a boat trip through the Nor-wegian fjords; she would read every novel published before the twentieth century (twentieth-century novels being by and large not worth reading), have affairs for adventure's sake even if the sex was uninteresting, become a CEO, quite possibly an astronaut as well, and in short, live the life she had never had a chance to live. In-stead, she was an unhappy invalid, confined to her downstairs, and so far from being single that her late husband was still hanging around the house.

"Take Teddy upstairs," I said, pushing my daughter out of the room.

I sat on the bed and held my mother's hand. Oscar growled.

"I don't know what's wrong with me," she said. "All I do is cry. It's so stupid. I think maybe I've got Alzheimer's."

"It's not stupid," I argued. "On the contrary, it's completely logi-cal. When your husband dies, you're supposed to feel sad." I said this knowing that it was a statement that would not carry much force for her. She thought sadness was a waste of time—if not precisely a fungus.

"I'm worried about him," she said. "Why is he hanging around here unless it's because he's not happy *there*?"

"Maybe he misses you," I said, "the way you miss him."

She sank back onto the pillows. I pulled the afghan up and tucked it in around her arms and sides. "Yes," she said, frowning, "that would make sense. Your father was never any good at being on his own. I always had to take care of him. But sometimes I got sick of it," she added. "The responsibility." She had closed her eyes; now she opened them again. "It's lucky for him he was a good fiddle player." She meant she wouldn't have loved him so if he hadn't been.

In the life she had actually lived, she had played second fiddle to his first in a succession of string quartets.

"Take a nap," I urged. "I have to unpack and tend to Tavy. She's worn out from the trip."

"She's a cute kid," my mother said, but then she couldn't keep from adding, "as kids go." She closed her eyes again.

I stood there a moment, looking at her—my mother, a creature of such complexity that it had taken me years even to begin to figure out how to untangle my self from hers.

She had set standards of self-discipline, hard work, and sound reasoning that had for years seemed, no matter how I drove my-self, beyond my reach. Yet now, to my surprise, they didn't seem high *enough*—they were predicated on a need to disown everything human, and so were still dependent on everything human, whereas I had arrived at a point where my ambitions simply grew out of my work. I had an inkling of where it might go, my work, and the world's opinion of it or any art had become irrelevant.

I wished she would consent to understand this. I wanted her to believe, with me, that in adopting Tavy I had not been betraying her or her ideals, that I was merely being true to myself.

Oscar was a little larger than a caramel-covered apple, and about the same color. His coat was a heart-meltingly beautiful gold with light and dark streaks. His squashed-in face resembled that of an ancient Chinese emperor or sage. He glared at me.

By the next day, Tavy and I had recovered from our jetlag. I put Tavy out into the backyard, the same way my father had let Blaze out for his morning constitutional. Oscar went out with her but he was back in seconds, his fur fringed in dew; he refused to leave my mother any more than was absolutely necessary.

When I wasn't there, my mother managed with a patchwork system of part-time nurses, helpful neighbors, and a cleaning woman who came in mornings. In my honor, she had dismissed most of these. I spent the day plumping her pillows, fixing meals, helping her to the commode chair, emptying the commode chair, washing dishes, answering the telephone, handling business correspondence, bringing in the milk, doling out pills—and then there was Tavy. I hadn't a minute to myself, and before long, I was exhausted. So when I bumped into my father in the kitchen, I told myself I was seeing things. The power of suggestion coupled with repressed hysteria and total tiredness was causing me to hallucinate. My father just shook his head, slowly, sadly, the way he'd always done when he was feeling pessimistic.

"It's true," he said. "I'm really here." He sighed heavily, as if this was not only unlikely but lamentable.

"But why?" I asked.

"Search me," he said, shrugging his shoulders. "I don't have any idea what's going on. I've got a hunch it's like what Satchmo said about jazz: If you have to ask, you'll never know."

He was nicely dressed in a pale green long-sleeved shirt and gray slacks. He had always cared about clothes, although he'd rarely spent any money on them for himself.

He was thin, with dark, thinning, but attractively unruly, hair that had the right amount of gray in it. He looked stronger than he had in his last year of life, but he was still frail. When he took off his glasses to rub the bridge of his nose where they pinched, I could see, in his large brown eyes, the intelligence that had made him who he was, before Alzheimer's disease had come along like a thief, some sort of mental mugger, and snatched it away, leaving him someone he wasn't. In other words, I realized, this was indeed the ghost of my *father*— not the ghost of the pitiful physical envelope that had contained an Alzheimer's victim.

I wondered if something had happened to him that I was supposed to exact revenge for so his wandering spirit could find peace. I wondered if this kitchen were the modern equivalent of parapets and that was why he was here. Was he restless? Had he been wronged?

I sat down at the table. My mother had dozed off in the living room, in front of the telly, after the seven o'clock news. "I don't understand," I said, facing him. "I thought ghosts, if there were any, would be the residue of souls who died violently or at any rate before their time. You were seventy-eight. You had emphysema almost as bad as Mother's. You had arthritis. You had Alzheimer's. A stroke was probably the best thing that could have happened to you."

But even as I was saying this, I was remembering how alone he had been when he died.

He had been at the rest home for a week—not for his sake but to give my *mother* a rest. She could still walk unaided then, though barely, and she wore herself out day after day trying to take care of him. He thought that by going into the home for a short stint, giving her a respite, he could put off the day when she might feel compelled to send him there forever.

The day before he was to come home, she slipped in the bathroom and fell, hitting her head on the sink and also hurting her back. This was the bathroom she had tiled herself, a dark green paragraph of tiles punctuated here and there with the odd Dutch scene, Jack and Jill carrying pails, or a windmill in a tulip field. Confined to bed, she was unable to look after her husband, but his room in the rest home had been spoken for, so the doctor arranged to have him moved to a second rest home.

It wasn't far—a few blocks down the street from the little red brick house. His room was at the back and had a view onto a duck pond. It was Christmas Eve, and that afternoon the Salvation Army threw a party in the lounge for the "guests." Every so often, my father, the musician, would recognize one of the carols and shout out a word or two—a kind of rudimentary singing.

After the party, back in his room, he was sitting in the chair by the window, gazing at the ducks, perhaps trying to comprehend how it was that he'd once been a small, obedient boy in Rock Hill, South

Carolina, and then was a shy, intense young man in Chicago and Louisiana and New York, and then a middle-aged man in Virginia, and now had become a dotty old fool in a rest home in England, separated by illness and accident from the woman with whom he'd lived for over fifty years. Perhaps this would have been difficult to fathom even if he had not been senile. The ducks in the pond were so bright, as bright as paint. The sky was as gray as a goose, with pin-feather clouds.

Suddenly his heart seemed to double over, and his left arm, which had for most of his life been a kind of mast, holding his violin aloft in musical light, crashed against his chest with a killing weight.

He could still think, images were still vividly present to his consciousness even if the connections among them were sometimes scrambled, and what he thought about at this moment was his wife. "Is Mother all right?" he asked in the ambulance, on the way to the hospital. He pictured her at home, alone, ill and worrying about him.

But right after he asked about her, even before the ambulance had reached the hospital, the walls of his brain gave way, too—it was a general collapse, his entire body falling apart section by section, being demolished by the great wrecking ball of age. "The walls of his brain were incredibly thin," the doctor said. "There was massive bleeding."

His lungs and legs were still working. The doctor had said my father would die before daybreak, but Christmas afternoon, a nurse found him wandering the hallways. "A reflex action," they said; they said he could not have thoughts or feelings anymore. What did they know about his thoughts and feelings? He could still refer to himself as "I," as in "I'm thirsty." They decided not to give him water or food; he was starving to death. On the twenty-seventh, he died, unattended even by machines.

And so, he must have come back because he was lonely. I'd been right, I thought—he missed my mother. He nodded. "I never liked that little dog, though," he said. "I couldn't get used to his taking Blaze's place."

"Where is Blaze? Why isn't he here?"

"Imagine being able to do what you want to do and being able to do it forever," he said. "Blaze is in heaven, chasing squirrels."

So animals *did* have souls, I said to myself, satisfied to wipe out one very disagreeable strain in theological thought.

"And you play your violin," I said, sure that this was what he would want to do forever.

"No. After all these years, it just doesn't feel right without your mother next to me on second, smoking up a storm and criticizing my intonation. How is she?"

"She's okay," I said. "Demanding. You know how she is."

"She always kept us on our toes," he said.

"Yes."

"Don't let her make you feel too bad about the kid," he said. "She's a cute kid." (Like all parents, they sometimes quoted each other without knowing it. Or maybe he did know it—had been listening, invisible but not insensible, at the foot of my mother's bed when I displayed Tavy to her.)

All at once, I wanted to know what *he* thought about the fact that the mother of his children didn't like children, but I could hardly ask him this directly. It might disturb him, and I didn't want to make his restless spirit any more restless. "Do you really think Tavy's cute?" I said.

"Adopting her was the right thing to do. And I think you need her."

As he said this, his voice dropped to a spectral pitch, like an undertone, and I realized I could see the back of his chair through his body.

"You're fading!" I cried.

"I always did fade about this time of night. Good night, Nina," he said.

He was gone.

Oscar came tearing into the kitchen. He made a circle from the kitchen through the dining room and living room and foyer back into the kitchen—again and again.

"Oscar's gone crazy," I said to my mother, waking her up and helping her from the wing chair to the bed.

"Your father must have been here. He and Oscar never got along. They saw themselves as rivals for my time."

Oscar leapt onto the bed. He had a beard, a Confucian beard, and his eyes were clever. My little dog at home was not nearly so clever, but sweeter. And clever, just not so clever.

My mother wanted pills, a glass of water, a cup of cocoa, to make a list. Tavy was crying upstairs. "Mommy, Mommy, Mommy," she yelled. I ran upstairs, downstairs, upstairs. I felt as if I were running back and forth between my past and the future.

Tavy never saw my father. Apparently, since she had not known him in life, she was not supposed to know him in death. He took an interest in her, however.

"You'd better get her started on the violin right away," he said. "She's already almost too old."

He was resting his chin in his palms, elbows propped on the linoleum-top table.

"I don't know," I said. "I remember how painful it was when you gave me lessons. It felt like my arm was going to break off."

"That's ridiculous, Nina. Your arm couldn't have hurt. Nothing is more malleable than a young child's bones."

I remembered it hurting.

"She takes ballet lessons," I offered. In the Meadow Scene, she had been a bee, buzzing her way across the stage in a black leotard striped with yellow crepe paper.

When I said she took ballet, he started to fade. I knew he wouldn't consider ballet music real music, and I said, "You can't just fade whenever things don't go the way you want them to."

"I don't see why not," he said. "It's one of the advantages of being dead."

"Is that you, Arthur?" my mother called from the other room. "What are you two talking about?"

She pulled herself along in her walker, entering the kitchen by degrees. Finally she was in her chair across from him. They looked at each other over the table, a doll-size table for doll-size people in a doll-size house in a doll-size country.

"Well, Art," she said, "it's a hell of a note, isn't it. I'm just barely alive and you don't seem to be quite dead."

"Would anybody like some ice cream?" I asked.

They both nodded. I dished it up into three bowls; it was vanilla. They wanted chocolate syrup so I heated the open can in a pot of water on the stove. It was an aluminum pot and I wondered if it had been a contributing factor in my father's getting Alzheimer's. I drizzled the syrup over the ice cream. Tavy was asleep upstairs, snug in her dreams. Oscar sat on the floor at my mother's feet. Unlike Blaze, he liked peaches but not ice cream.

"What's it like over there?" I asked, perching on the tall stool at the sink counter. I felt like an overgrown child in a high chair. There wasn't room for a third chair at the table.

"I don't really know," he said. "I haven't had much of a chance to look around yet. The climate is better, I guess. Not so much rain. I suppose this is because heaven is not an island."

Was it a continent? Maybe heaven was the *ocean,* and our entire universe one small island in it. "Do you have to listen to a lot of harp music?" This had been nagging at me. The Mozart Flute and Harp Concerto was nice, but for an eternity?

"I don't think you understand. Being dead isn't at all like being alive. You don't *do* things over there, you just are them. I believe it's got something to do with everything's happening faster than the speed of light. Because everything happens faster than the speed of light, doing and being are the same thing. You don't listen to music, you *are* music," my father said.

"How lovely," said my mother, who had always had a running argument with the world as it was. She thought it would be desirable to shed both the body and the ego, emerging as a work of art rather than a worker of art. In this, she reminded me of Van Gogh. Or Buddha or Einstein, for that matter, since she was in no way parochial about the forms of beauty.

"A poem does not mean but be," I said, slightly disgusted.

"Close," my father said. "But still not exactly right. There's still meaning—nobody wants to eliminate that. It's just that it now resides in what *is,* not in what *isn't.* If you think about it, you'll see that on earth it is always absence that is meaningful. And that is the source of all unhappiness."

I found all this very disturbing. Although it sounded like a fine premise—heaven as eternal being—I was not at all sure I would in fact want to give up either creation or contemplation, which is what the premise seemed to entail. There had to be a separation between maker or thinker and the thing made or the thing thought about, or else there wouldn't be any making or thinking. If unity was all, there was no relatedness—and I liked the idea of relation. I liked being in relation to the thing I was trying to bring into being and liked losing myself in that effort. I liked the idea that the idea of union was predicated on the idea of divorce. It wasn't just the paradox that appealed to me; it was the idea of desire, of longing for achievement. Throwing that out would throw out a number of other things, too—the concept of development would go, for example, as in the sustained developmental passage of a Beethoven string quartet, and that was the linchpin of my philosophy of art. That was the baby I didn't want tossed out the window with the bathwater. (I had seen Tavy not so much as an opportunity to revise the story of my own life as the chance to write a sequel. She was the extension of me; she was my self projecting itself into otherness, my self losing itself, ultimately to become herself—the way a novel, muscling its way through time, emerges on the last page as something that can suddenly be seen to be both inherent in and utterly different from the opening sentence.)

In brief, if there was no gap, no shortfall between start and finish, there was no possibility of becoming.

That is to say—if my father was to be believed, and though reticent, he had always been a man of truth—the continuous tense had, in heaven, epiphanically revealed itself to be a predicate.

"Let me get this straight," my mother said. "Blaze is not simply chasing squirrels, he somehow *is* chasing squirrels. He is the very idea of a dog chasing squirrels. Similarly, if I wanted to fly, I would just *be* flying."

I saw her with her arms outstretched—or at least the good arm outstretched, the other, flattened by stroke, tucked against the side—homing in on Heathrow.

"And if," she said, taunting him (she was ever the tease), "I wanted to make love, though God knows I never would, I would just *be* love."

"Lovemaking, actually," my father said, a glint in his eye.

"I'd rather be the idea of flight."

"Not the idea. The thing itself."

"I like the ideas," I said, feeling threatened, as if somebody were about to deprive me of them—as my father must have felt, as he sensed his illness encroaching on the private property of his brain. "I don't want to give them up. They're what make the things themselves interesting. A thing without an idea would be like a plane without an engine. It *wouldn't* fly."

"I should never have told you two about this," my father said, fading. "I should have known that if anybody would have criticism to make about heaven, it would be the two of you."

"You come back here, Arthur!" my mother called. "It's not fair of you to keep slipping away like this!"

But he was gone. I washed the dishes.

The house was in a close, a dead-end drive like a sclerotic artery to the heart of the development. Dogs and cats and children played on the front lawns and welcomed the paperboy, the milkman, the greengrocer, the butcher, the cleaning man, the window washer, the refuse collector, the television serviceman (in England, only the rich own television sets; everyone else rents), and the teenage boy who came to mow my mother's lawn.

To my mother's house also came the doctor, the district nurse who bathed her, the physical therapist who exercised her muscles, the hairdresser who washed and set her sparse white hair, the elderly female postal clerk who came out of her way to bring the stamps she allowed my mother to order over the telephone, and the neighbors—even when the part-time housekeeper and the part-time private nurses and the handyman who did her grocery shopping and the woman who stopped in to get her breakfast for her were not, as they now were not, there.

Among the neighbors was a retired constable who now donated his time to the local volunteer squad, taking sick people to the hospital and collecting them when they were well, accompanying the elderly on their visits to the clinic at Mortimer, and serving as my mother's banker. The first of the World Wars had shattered his family's fortunes and diverted his own future from its expected course, through university, into the police academy, from which he had emerged as a staunchly conservative supporter of the class system. I never could fathom this peculiarly English tendency to applaud one's own oppression. He was like a tall, silver-haired, barrel-chested bird alighting from time to time in our living room, bearing not twigs in his beak for our nest but the cash my mother had asked him to withdraw from her account. He was both kindly and argumentative. Like many Englishmen, he could never really believe that any woman would seriously oppose any of his opinions, and of course my mother opposed them all. In her old age, my mother had become radicalized. She sat in front of the telly making wisecracks about Maggie Thatcher. She styled herself a Social Democrat, but recognizing that her party hadn't a prayer, was willing to throw her lot in with the labor unionists. Malcolm, the male bastion of suburban conservatism, thought these political sympathies adorably female and unbelievably ridiculous. My mother invariably responded by acting adorably female, right up to the point where *he'd* say something ridiculous, and then she'd spring the particular trap she had set on that occasion. They were devoted to each other and had great fun playing this cat-and-mouse game, each being convinced that the other was the mouse.

"The trouble with Reagan," my mother announced from the wing chair one day as Malcolm towered in front of her, his back against the bay window as if he were shielding us from the world, "is that he's so stupid it's impossible for anyone to communicate with him. Now you take Star Wars. Everyone's running around building satellites and laser guns because nobody has ever stopped to figure out that in Reagan's mind this was a reference to *Gunfight at the OK Corral.* We could all get killed because he thinks being president of the United States is no different from being president of the Screen Actors Guild."

My mother's eyes were guileless, even blank: In age, they had the peculiar quality a television screen has in the dark when it's turned off, that ability to glow without light. It was the expectant thrust of her jaw, the way her chin was tilted slightly up—as if she were some-how ready to take it on the chin—that gave her away. I wondered how long she had been waiting to say this to Malcolm.

Malcolm has a high color. His face turned as red as the light on the washing machine in my mother's kitchen; he looked like he'd en-tered a spin cycle. Tavy, who had materialized in the living room holding Teddy upside down by one leg, looked up at him. "Are you going to die too?" she asked.

"This child is a necrophiliac," my mother said.

"Now, now, Tavy," Malcolm said, bending down to confront her at eye level. When he said her name, it sounded like Tah-vy instead of Ta-vy. "You must not think that everybody's going to die just be-cause your grandfather did."

We had not informed the neighborhood of the intricacies of Tavy's appearance on earth, so he didn't know that Tavy's grand-father was also her great-grandfather.

"If you die," she said, looking him in the eye and gnawing on Teddy's leg, "you can have some ice cream."

I looked out the bay window, both fascinated and embarrassed while she went on to explain her statement.

"That's what Grandpa does," she said. "He has ice cream every night in the kitchen."

"And do you say hello to him?" Malcolm asked, humoring her.

There were bluetits and coaltits crowded together on the ever-green, and a small brown wren in the sumac bush. The Woodbines' Burmese cat was watching the wren closely.

"No," she said. "I can't see him. But Mommy and Grandma do. I hear them talking to him when I'm in bed."

Malcolm stood up, knees cracking. He brushed Oscar's dog hairs from his trousers. "She certainly has an active imagination. I guess it's an artistic family, isn't it, Eleanor."

"More's the pity," she admitted.

"I should think that artists are well-nigh obliged to be a bit il-logical," he continued smoothly. "They say there's only a fine line between genius and insanity." He glanced slyly at my mother, as if he'd scored a decisive point.

I excused myself and went out to the kitchen and sat down in my father's chair at the table and laid my cheek against the cool linoleum of the tabletop. Because my father had made this table, I felt like I was placing my cheek next to his.

Nobody in the other room, I was thinking, knew how close I had come to crossing that line, once upon a time.

I opened an eye and realized that Oscar had followed me and was looking up at me. It was the first time he had treated me like something other than a potential enemy. I picked him up and began to stroke him. My little dog at home had density, solidity, a firm, round stomach emphatically real, not to mention greedy. Oscar fell across my lap as lightly as silk; he seemed to be made of cloth, I was wearing a live, gold skirt.

From the other room, I heard sounds of laughter. Malcolm called out, "I'm leaving now!" and I heard the door shut behind him. I shook Oscar off and went back into the living room. Tavy looked worried. "Mommy, do I imagine things?"

"Of course you do," I said. "Everyone does."

"But do you talk with Grandpa, or not?"

"Why not?" I said. "Why shouldn't people talk to the dead? Where are you going to find a better bunch of listeners?"

"Take it from me," my mother added. "Your grandfather makes a whole lot more sense than Ronald Reagan. Even dead."

Despite these brief (but for me, how shining!) moments of communion among my mother, my daughter, and myself, there was more often a tug of war going on, with me as the rope.

I was nervously aware of my mother's deep skepticism abut me, her feeling that my having elected to live with and care for a child made it doubtful that I'd complete the work I had always insisted I would do. She looked at me with the corners of her mouth turned down in disgust and even fear, as if I'd betrayed her, as if my action had been a wanton assault on everything she'd tried to teach me. To myself, I thought, Beethoven had his nephew—why shouldn't I adopt my grandniece? But I had more sense than to say that out loud.

When Tavy was being cute, I felt vindicated—but also guilty, for proving my mother wrong. And when Tavy was cranky or mean, banging a spoon against the floor just because she enjoyed the distress it caused us, or screaming until she seemed to have turned into a tiny human horn, all noise and out of tune, I avoided my mother's eyes, guiltily fearing a told-you-so look. All this guilt was getting me down, and I would no doubt have felt sorry for myself if there'd ever been any time to, but my days were cataracts of busyness, chores cascading from dawn to dusk, one long waterfall of obligation.

I had tried to do right by them both, and they both seemed to think I had failed them, I had abandoned them, each for the sake of the other.

What I would have liked was a stiff drink. What I got was ice cream.

In the kitchen that night, my mother and father and I discussed my brother. "It was our fault," my mother, in a breast-beating mood, said, referring to his spectacular decline and fall, which had ended in his death from alcoholism. My mother got into these self-blaming moods but perhaps they were more an expression of her perfectionism than of pity. "We had no money and couldn't give him any of the things he wanted. When he was a freshman in college, he had only one pair of pants. One day your father discovered he had nothing to wear under them."

This fact dazzled me. I had never understood exactly why we had always been so broke. According to my parents, my brother and I had made excessive demands on their finances, yet my brother had no *underwear*. Birthday presents were a Hershey bar. We seldom got books and never lessons or anything like that. Maybe the violins, the bows had consumed all the money. Maybe we were just poorer than I ever really understood.

"Alcoholism is a sickness," I said, "a disease. People know that now."

"He could have quit," my mother said. "People do."

"There's a problem here," my father interjected. "At what point does addiction override free will? If you quit drinking, are you still addicted?"

"Members of AA refer to themselves as recovering alcoholics," I explained, "no matter how long they've been dry."

"But then Mother is right, drinking *isn't* purely a disease. It's a disease you can choose to have or not to have, and what other diseases do you know of like that? Believe me," he said, "I could have used a choice when it came to Alzheimer's."

We were all silent for a minute. To lose your mind, I was thinking, what a sorrow, what a shock.

In the hospital, I had thought I was losing mine: It used to disappear for hours on end, then slip back, like a teenager into the house, at the last minute.

I'd never told my parents about any of this because they had said that they did not want to hear any bad news; they had had crisis-ridden lives, burdened with debt, they said, and they wanted no more stories of trouble. We were a family with secrets—where the money went, who was crazy, who slept with whom, whose child was whose, how anyone felt.

"You'd better be careful that Tavy doesn't start drinking," my mother continued. "Your father had a sister who drank." My father clicked his tongue against the roof of his mouth at this mention of Aunt Millicent, a husky-voiced redhead who had died at age seventy surrounded by empty vodka bottles, but who, he thought, my mother should now be willing to let rest in peace. "And your brother—"

"Your son," I reminded her.

"And I suspect Babette drinks, wherever she is."

Babette was Tavy's biological mother, a teenage runaway last seen heading for California. No one knew what to think about her. Suppose she was a hooker. Suppose she had AIDS.

Suppose, I thought more happily, she was a starlet in scarlet, a bikini'd bathing beauty in oversized sunglasses, lounging on a rubber raft in a Beverly Hills pool, tiny American flags decaled on her insouciant toenails?

"You don't know that," I said. "Babette could be a teetotaler." Though this seemed unlikely, if she was hanging out around a pool in Beverly Hills. "And it's a little early to worry about Tavy's drinking habits."

My father said, "What a morbid conversation this is."

"You're dead, Arthur. What do you expect?"

A still moon shone in through the kitchen door, which had a key-lock, a latch, and top and bottom bolts because a couple of years ago my parents had gotten worried about the wave of granny-bashing that was rolling over England. I undid all the locks and let Oscar out. He trotted down the narrow walk that led from the patio, along the hedge, ten feet tall, on the right side of the lawn, to the second patio, under the oak tree, where rhododendrons and rose bushes bloomed.

In the moonlight, his gold coat gleamed like a pound coin. I wondered again why my family had always fretted so about money. (I knew that money was one of my major themes, waiting for a critic who could trace and analyze its appearance in my various works.)

Oscar sniffed at the bushes, then raised his head and looked at the hushed night sky, as if listening to some constellatory music only animals could hear. Out there, in that darkness, there might be answers to all our questions. Or there might be just more questions. I shivered, unsweatered in the cold, and called to Oscar to come in. He turned around to look at me, and though he was at the other end of the lawn, in the dark, I could have sworn he was right in front of me, bright as dawn, hypnotic as a gold watch. In the cool dampness of the English dark, he was like some strange changeling, a silky, sulky midsummer sprite.

I slept in my father's bed. Tavy was on the cot in the extremely small room that my mother had used as an office for keeping the household finances. No one used my mother's bedroom; the fiction was that when she was feeling better she would move back upstairs.

On the wall facing the headboard of my father's bed was a window, and next to it, a framed photograph of my father's violin. The violin had been auctioned at Sotheby's. The photograph was actually four small photographs: From a book featuring his violin, among others, he had cut out four plates and had taped them behind four "windows" razored into a piece of cardboard; then he labeled the mat in his flowing composer's hand, and put a frame around it. I now wondered why he'd never felt entitled to have a photograph professionally made and framed.

The window faced west, so night clung to it as long as it could. As light began to reach down from the upper story of the sky, doves cooed under the eaves as if to welcome it. Magpies and humming-birds sent out their own BBC signals—Better Bird Casting. Still half asleep, I listened to that dreamy music as if it were a score—*the* score, the one I had always been trying to find out.

I couldn't lie in bed for long because my mother wouldn't permit it. At five-thirty, there'd be a huge pounding noise coming from the ceiling below, and I'd wake in a rush of adrenaline, thinking alarm. She was beating on the ceiling with her broomstick.

"If I don't have to sleep," she said, "I don't see why anyone else should have to." She actually said that to me, as I stared at her, bleary-eyed, from the foot of her bed. I was wearing an old shirt over a cotton nightgown, and socks that had caused me to slip as I ran down the stairs, banging my hipbone bad enough so a stabbing pain would sometimes radiate up my back. I wanted to tell her that her "toughness" was no longer cute. That it may have been cute fifty years ago, but now it was indistinguishable from a lack of considera-tion for other people.

But I just stared at her, amazed she could say such a thing and too afraid of hurting her to confront her. I'd always been afraid of hurt-ing her. The thing was, the older I got, the more I began to be angry about this. "We don't want to know about any problems," she'd said, but I wanted her to *know* me. This anger . . . it was as if part of me was regressing. At this rate, when I reached her age, I'd be a withered-up three-year-old, wanting everyone to make up for my mother's selfishness. It was figuring this out—that generalized anger, anybody's generalized anger, stemmed from a belated desire to have someone make up for early neglect and was a kind of regression— that saved my temper: I realized I was dealing with a three-year-old. And I already knew how to deal with a three-year-old.

Tavy, Oscar, and Teddy were taking tea in the living room. With each day that passed, Oscar had become a little less grudging toward Tavy, and now he was lying on his stomach on the green carpet, a thimble-sized teacup of painted wood just beyond his punched-in muzzle. Teddy was sitting up, leaning against the wing chair. Tavy was pouring.

When I saw the miniature dishes, bright golden wood painted with a delicate row of blue and green flowers, I felt myself being carried back in time, tugged out to sea by the strong undertow of memory, that current of images and sensations that has so much to do with the direction we take in life but which we are usually unaware of.

I fixed breakfast for my mother, Tavy, and Oscar. "You forgot Teddy's breakfast," Tavy said, looking at me accusingly. I gave him a dog biscuit, but then Oscar wanted one too. I unlocked the kitchen door and shooed the trio into the backyard.

On the brick patio under the oak tree, they played in the summer light. They were like creatures from another world, a world of timelessness whose dimensions had spread out by mistake and gotten ensnared with ours; otherwise, these small aliens would not be known to us even to the temporary extent that they were. I leaned against the doorjamb, letting my spine sag. I wanted to weep, thinking that one day Tavy would be my age. I would be a demanding old woman. One day Oscar would make a last trip to the vet. One day even Teddy would go to the vast grave of teddy bears, the stuffing knocked out of him, ears and eyes and button nose beyond repair.

"Come here," my mother yelled, snapping me out of my sad reverie.

I had helped her into the wing chair in front of the telly, but the screen was dark. She was reading a biography of Dickens. She lit a cigarette. I had to keep an eye on her because whenever she opened a new pack of cigarettes, she performed a ritual coda by touching the lighter to the cellophane wrapping, starting small fires in the ashtray.

"Yes?" I asked.

My mother the pyromaniac watched as the cellophane flared and died, the bitter odor of burning plastic a sudden, sharp note on the air. "What's going to happen to your work now that you've got Tavy to take care of?"

I knew that she had been waiting to ask me this just as she had waited for the right moment to taunt Malcolm with her remark about Reagan.

"It's going to deepen," I said. "It's going to widen."

I understood that she would feel compelled to argue the opposite case, since she had always believed that having children had hampered *her*. "It's not that we didn't want you," she rushed to assure me. "But you don't know what you're getting into. All I did for years was worry abut you children."

This last statement was not true, but it must have seemed true to her. She wanted to believe it. It even occurred to me that maybe the reason it had not been true was that if she *had* paid any attention to us, it *would have been* true. Maybe she had turned away from us not out of indifference or selfishness but fear, feeling that, if she were to acknowledge our existence, the attendant responsibilities would suffocate her.

Thinking about her blighted life, she started to cry. More and more, she was doing this, swinging between moods. She'd be angry one minute, disconsolate the next. If you said something to cheer her up or comfort her, she'd look at you with those clouded eyes that didn't seem to see you and say, "Ha." Like that: "Ha."

I yanked a Kleenex from the box and handed it to her. She let it drop, slamming her fists into her chest as if some internal mechanism had suddenly gone haywire and pulled her arms up short. The same screwed-up guy wires had twisted her face into a look of agony. I thought, Oh God, oh God. I grabbed the buzzer for the Lifeline Unit. A voice came over the speaker: "Mrs. Bryant? Mrs. Bryant?"

"This is Nina Bryant," I shouted. "I think my mother is having a heart attack."

In no time, there was an ambulance in the driveway. Malcolm had come over and was standing in front of my mother, trying to persuade her to let them take her to the hospital, where they could run tests to see if she had indeed had a heart attack. The ambulance drivers waited at the door to the living room, caps in hand. Tavy and Oscar had come in from outside and wandered among the grownups as if among tall trees.

"I don't want to," my mother said. "The last time I was in the hospital, I had to stay awake all night because a lesbian kept trying to pinch me."

The three tall Englishmen stared down at the carpet. I knew my mother sounded crazy to them: Scrunched-up old ladies weren't even supposed to know words like "lesbian."

"It's true," I said, as if my mother were on trial and I was her defense lawyer. "I was there once when it happened. The woman was ninety-three but she was horny. The nurses just laughed at her and took her back to her own bed, but from my mother's point of view, it wasn't funny at all."

Imagine what it would be like to be unable to get away, unable even to get out of your own bed, lying there in the dark, feeling like prey.

"It's important to find out whether or not you've suffered a heart attack, Eleanor," Malcolm said again.

"Important to whom?" my mother said. "It's not important to me."

"It's important to me," I said, and she started to cry again.

She wanted to die, or at least she said she did. She made jokes about how, no matter how hard she tried, she couldn't seem to pull it off. She said if she could just die, she'd give God a piece of her mind. It was a hell of a way to run a universe, she'd tell Him: all this evil and illness, death and decay and bad art.

She said she wanted to die, but the truth was she was afraid to. She had so much invested in being herself. Dying meant giving all that up, and nothing scared her as much as giving up.

I attributed this fear of surrender to some early-developed sense of being easily overwhelmed, perhaps in response to having two sisters enough older than she was that it was like having three mothers. Or maybe the loss of an Edenic childhood, lived among cypresses and water moccasins and bright birds as flamboyant as flying graffiti, in a bayou in Louisiana, had translated itself into lifelong anxiety about further loss. Or maybe, as the youngest, the baby of the family, her father's favorite, she had felt forever cheated, after she discovered that no matter how good a daughter she was, she was not going to be allowed to remain his daughter forever.

I think she had been shocked to find herself an adult, and with more than her fair share of responsibility. She had done her best to recover, tossing out all childish things in a wholesale psychological housecleaning. In the battle to define herself against whatever it was she perceived as a threat, she had defeated the almost pathological shyness of her youth and gone on guard against all revelations of vulnerability. The result was—my mother, the seventy-eight pound warrior on twenty-four-hour-a-day alert. She had not surrendered to herself; she wasn't about to surrender to anyone else; she could not bear the thought of surrendering to death—she kept thinking there had to be a way she could do this on her own terms.

It was because she hated the thought of surrendering that she disdained politicians. It was why she disliked sex, though she *said* the reason she didn't like sex was that it was about as interesting as having someone stick a pencil in your ear.

And yet, what a passionate romance she'd had with my father for fifty tumultuous years.

Now, in her old age, she was as small and brown-spotted as a mushroom, growing in the forest of her bed. Her skin, creased as leather, was as soft as suede. Her breasts had vanished, receding when they became no longer relevant. And this was a woman who had been five-six-and-a-half, with outstanding legs.

I made more of her beauty than she did. She hardly ever wore makeup; for her, her beauty was just a fact, like her height.

For me, her beauty was a standard. And it was a clue, as if, by deciphering it, I could understand why her youth had been so different from mine. It was interesting to me to imagine her at twenty, say, with her hair cut in a "windblown" style, and wearing a white coat bought specifically for walking along the shore on those lovely gray days in Gulfport when the breezes were cool and there was spray from the surf and a hint of storm in the air. She would look out over the Gulf in the direction of Mexico and South America, constructing the future as an exotic landscape just over the horizon. She danced the nights away with her boyfriends, who were plentiful, at a waterfront pavilion in Biloxi. Her mother had made her a white organdy evening dress, trimmed in red, for the Valentine dance, and a black-and-white striped dimity with a black velvet sash for afternoon parties. Sometimes she and her friends went to drive-in movies, or they organized torchlit expeditions to spear flounder in the shallow water at the base of the seawall. In the afternoons they sailed, or played putt-putt on the miniature golf course by the municipal pier, or drove up and down the beach road, stopping occasionally for Cokes and hot dogs.

When I was the age she had been then, I attended a banquet with my parents. During dessert, the man sitting next to me turned to me and said, as if this were a fact I had to be forced to face, "You'll never be as beautiful as your mother." I didn't realize he was in love with her, besotted as a boy. As soon as the coffee cups were cleared away and the dancing had started, I got the car keys from my father, excused myself and went out to the car, let myself in and curled up in the back seat and cried, long into the sycamore-scented night. I cried on the drive home. I cried all weekend, shut up in my room. My mother's response to all this unexplained self-pity was, as usual, disgust, but I was afraid that if I told her what the matter was, she would feel guilty. I didn't want her to feel she'd let me down genetically. My father came into my room and tried to get me to talk, but I couldn't tell him, either, because he would get worried that there was something going on between my mother and the man who had spoken to me, because he was always worried that he loved her more than she loved him and she might fall in love with someone else and have an affair and leave him. (He *could* be restless; he *could* be imagining that he had been wronged; he *was* always that jealous.) To make himself more attractive to her, he had recently spent nine hundred dollars on Arthur Murray dance lessons, in secret, so he would be able to dance with her at the banquet. I didn't know how to dance either, but girls weren't supposed to need lessons.

"Do you remember when Daddy went to Arthur Murray?" I asked her. Art imitating Art, I was thinking.

"Ha," she said.

"Ha?"

"Nobody's dancing now."

She had such a sad look on her face—her mouth dragged down and trembling, her eyes like one-way windows that she could see out of but you couldn't see in. She was wearing her favorite outfit, a pink "sweat suit" with a pastel-blue bunny over the heart. She had high cheekbones and in profile still looked like the young Katharine Hepburn.

Though she read constantly, she also liked to be read to. I sat at the foot of the bed, squinting, under the pale light of the overhead fixture, at the microbe-sized print in her gilt-edged "fine" editions with ribbon bookmarks. Tavy would join us, her small face screwed up in tight concentration as if she were following every word of *Barchester Towers*. One afternoon my mother broke into my reading to ask, "How far back can you remember?" I started to answer her when she said, "Not you, I'm talking to Tavy. Do you remember lying in your crib?" my mother asked her. "Do you remember the curtains in your bedroom blowing over your crib? I do."

Tavy stuck her thumb in her mouth.

"I remember tying and untying a gauze bandage on my big toe," my mother went on. "I remember the lavender kimono I was wearing when my parents took me to the hospital to have my tonsils out—and that was before I was two. It seems like the closer you are to these events, like Tavy, the better you'd remember them, but it's just the opposite, isn't it? They come back to you as you get older. Isn't that ironic!"

"Probably the older you get, the farther back you can remember," I said. "Probably one day you have a blinding recollection of being born, and in the same instant you die."

We looked at each other and started to laugh, a few collusive giggles at first and then we laughed harder and harder. Tavy just looked at us and continued to suck her thumb. I was afraid she thought we were laughing at her, but I couldn't seem to stop long enough to explain. I didn't know how to explain. Later, I wondered what she would remember of this.

I knew I was not paying enough attention to Tavy. Not that she was alone—Malcolm frequently looked after her, and she had become a great favorite in the neighborhood. She was also gifted at the art of amusing oneself. Lately she had taken to giving song recitals to Oscar and Teddy, who sat on the floor facing her. She revised the texts of these songs with abandon. "Where, oh where has my little dog gone?" became "Puppy gone. Where, oh where be?" "Oh come, let us adore him" was transformed into "Oh come little outside door him." There was one song she liked to sing that may even have been an original: "Oh Jeesy, Jeesy, Jeesy, they all play with toys, and they don't take up the nickels."

But I knew she felt I had deserted her. When I put her to bed at night, and she stared up at me without saying anything, or rolled over onto her pillow without throwing her arms around me to say good night first, I wanted to apologize. *I* wanted to apologize when she was *good*, because she was an active, risk-taking, free-spirited kid who was *supposed* to be misbehaving, who was *supposed* to be apologizing to me, and if she was being good, it was because she thought I had lost interest in her and believed the only way for her to get my attention back or please me was by changing her ways.

I knew what it felt like to struggle to impress one's existence on a parent by impressing the parent.

But Tavy did have an existence, and my mother might not have hers for much longer, so it seemed to me my first duty was to her.

But I also acknowledged that I might have been seizing on that fact to excuse another, which was that I felt ashamed, in front of my mother, to have been found out as a human being, a female human being at that, one with a desire to be a mother herself that had been so uncontrollable that she had dared to adopt.

And I felt ashamed, before Tavy, to feel such shame.

It was a mess. I was trying to be—I *was*—both mother and *daughter*. And I didn't want to lose my mother.

Since we didn't know for sure whether or not she had had a heart attack, I thought I'd better go on the assumption that she had. From the local health service, I got pamphlets on how to do CPR. But I knew it would be an iffy matter, blowing air into lungs already rendered half-inoperative by emphysema.

She would not consider a nursing home; that would've meant giving up Oscar.

They were a pair. She and Oscar would sit up side by side in the single bed, the one smoking a cigarette and drinking cocoa, the other chewing on a rubber shoe.

Malcolm said that after she died, he would take Oscar.

Because my mother was always cold, the house was usually sealed tight, even though it was summer. I imagined we might live there forever. I imagined us whirling through space and time like Dr. Who in his telephone booth: There was no telling where we would end up, except that wherever it was, it would be in our little brick house.

And if we were in our little house, we were probably in the little kitchen, talking. Sometimes just talking, and sometimes talking things over.

My mother liked to talk about how she had met my father. He had been even shyer than she, so that she had had to propose to him. When he said yes and asked her to set the date, she said, "Two o'clock."

Their timing wasn't great. It was 1933. The Depression years burned away any vaguely romantic notions they may have had about life. And made them afraid—if they had not already been afraid. They lived in an unending expectation of catastrophe, to which my father's reaction, had he been free to have one on his own, would have been flight, and my mother's was fight.

It could sometimes be hard to get past her "tough talk." My father would simply let her go on. While she criticized whatever it was she was criticizing, he placed his fingers on the edge of the table, spreading them wide, the heels of his hands hanging over the edge, raising the knuckles so that the tips flattened out, then letting the heels of his hands fall again so that the fingers became as straight as clothespins. He had used to do this as if he were studying his hands, or even admiring them. They were strong hands, flexible until he developed arthritis, unexpectedly large. Suddenly I saw him as he had been in 1933, matinee-handsome, darkly intense, completely naïve, and decked out in the wardrobe he'd acquired with his first paycheck— a white linen suit and yellow-and-white polka-dot bow tie with matching handkerchief protruding from the breast pocket.

As I stared at him, the green shirt and gray slacks reappeared and then re-metamorphosed into the white linen of yesteryear. It was confusing: His younger and older selves seemed to take turns appearing and disappearing like the images on the playing cards Tavy had at home, which were one thing when you held them at an angle

117

and another when you held them straight up. I blinked my eyes to bring him into focus.

It occurred to me that this was more or less the way my father had always related to us: wavering in and out of focus.

I had a question I wanted to ask him. It seemed to me that it had to be a question that was on my parents' mind too—my mother's to ask, my father's to be asked—and yet no one had dared to bring it out into the open. I thought the time had come. "You know," I said, as a kind of prologue, "this was a family in which there were always a lot of secrets. Too many, if you ask me—"

"Ha," my mother said, interrupting triumphantly. "Nobody asked you."

"You've got ice cream on your top," my father said to her. He tore a paper towel off the roll and rubbed at the spot. (Paper towels had always been handy in this household, because my parents were always bringing up phlegm; stress and nicotine had undone their once-young bodies so!) "Pink becomes you, Ellie," he said.

"Ha."

She was going to start crying again, overcome by his compliment. I was determined not to be deflected. Into the space of that instant during which her mood was shifting, I rushed with my question. I asked my father if he had seen my brother "over there."

My father pushed his empty bowl away with a sudden show of revulsion, as if he wanted to disown the ice cream—or his love of it. He crossed his legs. He took off his glasses and squeezed and caressed his nose where they pinched and settled them back on his face. I remembered that on sunny days he used to wear tinted lenses that clicked onto these regular glasses, and when he didn't need them, he'd flick them up where they overhung his face like little dark-green awnings.

"No," he said.

We were silent, absorbing this news, which wasn't really news since we'd half-known that if my father had seen him, he would already have said so, but which nevertheless seemed to increase in ontological stature by being spoken out loud. Then my mother said, "I was hoping that even if God had made the mistake of allowing evil on earth, He might have seen the error of his ways. But no, He had to go and create hell. What kind of God loves evil so much He can't get enough of it?"

"You're jumping to conclusions, El," my father said. "First of all, the fact that I haven't seen him does not necessarily mean that he's not there. Second, even if he's not there, it doesn't necessarily follow that there has to be a hell."

"Where else could he be?" I asked, taken aback by the brusque note in my own voice. I seemed to be saying that was where he belonged. Nina, I reminded myself, if you can't excuse even your own brother from hell, who's going to excuse you?

But then I thought, That's what we need a God for: to grant forgiveness where the rest of us can't quite manage it.

My father was saying to my mother, "Let's not beat around the bush here. The truth is, I never saw all that much of him when we were alive. I had to earn a living. I had to support us all. The result was, I never had time for him when he was little, and after he got bigger, he didn't want to have anything to do with me. He refused to believe that I had *wanted* to have more time with him. Well, if we didn't see each other on earth, there's really no reason for us to see each other now."

What he had just said was only partly true. My brother had had seven years of basking in the parental sunshine before I came along. But my attention had been arrested by something else he said. "Do you mean," I asked, finally registering what he'd said earlier about jumping to conclusions, "that you don't *know* whether there's a hell or not?"

"Of course I don't know. How could I know? Hell is about not-being, and as I've already explained, the whole idea of heaven is that it's about *being*. It's not about not-being. Being can't know non-being because it would entail a self-contradiction."

"Then let me ask you this," I said. "If being can't know non-being, how can goodness know sin, which is also a kind of absence since it means 'missing the mark'? And unless goodness can know sin, how can God know time?"

I was thinking that questions like these might have been why theologians had come up with notions like limbo and purgatory. Probably you went into that line of work out of a hunger for absolutes, an addiction to drawing dichotomies, but by the time you reached middle age, you felt surfeited, you were tired of your life-long binge, and you began to develop a secret craving for what was relative, for the in-between, maybe even, at least on rare, indulgent occasions, for the indefensibly vague. Oh my God, maybe you became a closet Hegelian.

My father said, "You were always one for the questions, Nina."

"As long as we are on the subject of specific persons," my mother said, "I have a question." A kind of timidity invaded and softened her voice. "What about my mother?" she asked.

My father laughed. "How could Saint Peter turn away someone who was buried wearing her Presbyterian pin for perfect attendance?"

"Is she happy?" my mother asked—and I knew she was holding her breath for the answer, though she had very little breath in her lungs that she could hold.

"She's with your father," my father said. This time, when he reached for a paper towel, it was to dry the tears on my mother's wrinkled face.

These nightly conversations were telling on my mother. In the morning, she looked haggard, the skin on her face not just passively sagging with age but *tugging* at her, trying to pull her down into old age and death. There was a tug of war going on, between her fighting spirit, which could not bear the thought of surrender, and a deep desire for peace. She had so little use for the world, and yet here she was, syllogistically obligated by her own sense of herself as someone whose essential nature it was to oppose, to side with the world, opposing death. She was a lover of abstraction now having to align herself with the world of physicality *against* abstraction. This battle was being fought daily, even while she was talking with my father. He drew her to him by his physical magnetism, but he himself—being a ghost— was an abstraction. These contrary vectors were exhausting her; they seemed almost to generate a friction that was wearing her down. Day by day, she seemed less *there*. Her bones were shrinking away from her skin, as if she were getting ready to molt. As for flesh, there was hardly any left. Just the dress of skin over the sewing form of her skeleton.

From lavender kimono to pink sweat suit with a pale blue bunny: This was the haute couture of a life, the sartorial arc of her passage on earth.

It was high summer. The neighbors to our left had gone to Spain; the neighbors to our right, the Woodbines, were in Florida (which Mrs. Woodbine, who had traveled the world over, insisted was the place on earth she found most different from England, more "exotic," she said, than Turkey or Egypt, or even Sri Lanka.) Malcolm and his wife had sent us a postcard from Devon, where they were walking twenty miles a day. The neighborhood was like a ghost town, and would have been even without my father's nocturnal visitations. Even when the ice-cream man came in his truck, the bell as clear and cool as an ice cube in the sweet lemonade of daytime, only one or two children dashed out from their houses, ten pence in their palms.

Some mornings we sat out on the patio, my mother wrapped in blankets, her face turned toward the sun, Tavy digging in the stone-potted geraniums, Oscar snoozing, the extravagant curlicue of his tail a kind of cadenza to the theme of his body, bluebirds and swallows threading their song through the bright seam of day. Butterflies floated on currents of air so light they were imperceptible—a phenomenon we knew existed, from the evidence of the butterflies, but which was inaccessible to our senses. My mother slept. For a few minutes, I felt as if time had stopped. Then a shadow passed over the sundial of my mother's face as if to remind me what time it was— and what time was—but nothing else moved except the butterflies with their delicate, soundless bobbing, Tavy's busy little wrist and spoon, and Oscar's twitching tail. Far off, an airplane homed in on Heathrow, but from where I sat, it seemed more like a bee making for its hive. I had the sense that I was intimately familiar with this scene. Not that I had experienced it before in exactly this way, but that I had been somehow prepared for it, perhaps *had* experienced it before but from a slightly different perspective, perhaps my mother's or Tavy's or that of someone who wasn't with us now.

Maybe time, I thought, was like light and functioned sometimes as waves, sometimes as particles. Maybe some of the time it flowed from past to future (or, as Augustine thought, from future to past), but maybe at other times it bunched itself up into a lot of not-quite-infinitesimal quantum-like balls, bouncing around like crazy, some kind of pinball machine, the universe a penny arcade, somebody— who?—racking up one hell of a score.

It was so strange, living through those weeks during which my mother grew ever more contingent and delicate, almost, in a sense, younger, because her mind, while retaining its wizardly sharpness, was relinquishing its scope, narrowing the range of its interests to concentrate on the one central fact of existence, the self, while my daughter, my mother's great-granddaughter, blossomed like some sort of small, rustling bush, progressing from toddlerhood to little-girlhood.

Tavy was walking with assurance now. Instead of looking always as if she was just about to trip, or as if she thought the world was not merely round but about to spin out of control, she raced through the house as if she were training for the four-minute mile. "Who's got happy feet?" I'd say, and she'd break into a silly dance and collapse giggling. For a moment, I felt redeemed: I was a good mother and I had a happy child. So what if she sneaked into Malcolm's kitchen when his back was turned—he had been babysitting her for the day, giving my mother a breather from the commotion Tavy couldn't help creating—and grabbed his jar of pickled walnuts, expensively sold at Harrod's, and carried them outside to feed to the squirrels, turning them all into baffled gourmets?

But it was hard on my mother, all this energy, this top wound up at birth and set to whirligig her way through a long, probably headlong, life. I suggested to her that we should leave, but she wouldn't have it. She knew what was coming and didn't want to face it alone. She had panic attacks that she wanted me to be there to see her through. When people have panic attacks, they feel as though they can't breathe, but I think it was *because* my mother couldn't breathe that she had panic attacks. When you have emphysema, there are times when no matter how hard you try to breathe, no matter how much air you manage to suck in, it seems to do no good because there aren't enough air sacs left in your lungs to hold the air. You try to breathe, you make the motions of breathing, but you still don't have any breath. Some stony gargoyle is squatting on your lungs. Some mysterious statue has been planted right in the center of your chest, and the intricately branched bronchioles beneath won't grow, the bellows won't blow. It's like being suffocated from the inside.

I fixed her a supper of peaches and cream. It was one of the few things she'd eat, though even with this, the bowl would be on the floor for Oscar before she'd finished half of it. I sat beside her, a human vending machine for Kleenex, paper towels, cortisone pills, blood-thinner pills, laxatives, cigarettes, matches, chocolate. We were deep into summer, having left a trail of shiny litter, but it was a trail that would never lead us out again. The leaves on the old oak tree were a restful, sleepy green, as if they'd manufactured all the chlorophyll they needed and could now relax for a while.

Under the high hedge, a hedgehog rolled itself into a prickly ball at Oscar's approach.

My mother asked me to plump up the pillows behind her back. Her legs, under the blanket, were so pathetically thin that they seemed to me to be, as she never was, apologetic. They seemed to want to apologize for being helpless, and I would have patted them in the reassuring way that you pat children or pets, except that the cortisone my mother took made her skin so thin that it tore like tissue paper, you could punch holes in it with your fingers.

Sometimes, at night, or in the early morning when the tree and sky and the chimney across the way that topped the tall fence at the end of the lawn presented themselves in the frame of the window like a painting, lying in my father's bed, I cried, not knowing what else to do. I cried quietly so I wouldn't wake Tavy or get my mother's broom handle going. To cry in front of my mother would have been, somehow, to steal the limelight from her, since this was her tragedy, not mine; and I didn't want Tavy to see me cry, because it might make her feel insecure. So I kept my crying a secret from both of them, but I couldn't keep it secret from Oscar.

Oscar came into my room, curious and wanting breakfast, and jumped on the bed. He put his face next to mine as if to ascertain that what I was doing was, in fact, crying, and then he sat down next to my face and simply watched me until I stopped. I don't mean to hurt your feelings, I whispered to him, but you're my mother's dog, and Blaze is in heaven with my father, and I miss my dog, who is in America. I felt such a wave of longing for my own little dog, who had been through so much with me, and who would soon be the only creature left on earth who knew who *I* was, who had experienced what I had experienced in the past eventful decade. Not even Tavy knew me the way my dog did. I was so tired of trying to understand what everyone else needed—I wanted someone who understood me.

Oscar was unmoved. When I still didn't get out of bed, he sat on my chest, his plumy tail feather-dusting my teary face, blocking my view. I got up, crawling into a pair of jeans and one of my father's shirts. I had always thought it would be creepy to wear a dead person's clothes, but now I found it comforted me. It made me feel close to him.

On the way downstairs, I peeked into Tavy's room. She was still asleep on the cot in the room that was my mother's office. The sun had crossed the windowsill and highlighted the open book of her face. She had her thumb in her mouth. She liked to pick a piece of fuzz from the lightweight summer blanket, stick it on the knuckle of her index finger and then suck her thumb. It was a kind of padding, I guess, designed to prevent her knuckle from irritating the tip of her nose. I laughed at the thought of such a sensitive little nose.

Through depths of dreams, she felt my presence. She stirred, kicking at the sheets and blanket. She opened her eyes, in which I was afraid to read how much she knew: I did not want to know if she knew that to the extent to which I was my mother's daughter, I was not free to be my daughter's mother. The sunlight shining on her face seemed, rather, to be radiated by it, every strand of her hair gleaming, streaming into rays. She held open her arms and I reached toward her, leaned into her. I sat on the bed, squashing Teddy, and picked her up and held her, held her tight.

Oscar, his tail as erect and sweeping and haughty as the Arc de Triomphe, posed at the doorjamb, facing into the hallway, poised for the trip downstairs.

It began as an ordinary day, a day like any other: breakfast for all, the toothbrush tray and a sponge bath for my mother, the "News at One." In the afternoon, I read to my mother from *Wuthering Heights,* and Tavy listened while she colored in her coloring book. After supper, after the evening news, I took Tavy upstairs and put her to bed with Teddy, and my mother and I talked for a while in the living room. Then I put her to bed. She could no longer traverse the distance between the wing chair in the living room and the cot in the dining room even with the walker. I tucked her in, brought her a glass of water. "Is there anything else I can get you before I go up?" I asked.

"Do you think he'll come tonight?"

"If you want him to," I said.

"I don't want to die alone."

She had never come flat out and said that before. It gave me the willies. "Why are you talking about death?" I said. "Dinner wasn't that bad." I had fixed her a soft-boiled egg but burned the toast.

"Will you stay down here tonight?"

Oscar was curled up on the pillow, on top of her head like a golden crown. She looked so small, so vulnerable. Her cloudy eyes were like leaded windowpanes. She was a little house that everyone had moved away from. "I'll sleep on the couch in the living room," I offered.

"If you hear Daddy, please wake me up."

"I promise," I said.

In the living room, I lay down on the couch, still in my clothes. Then, like a victim of carbon monoxide poisoning, I fell into a colorless, odorless sleep.

When I heard him in the kitchen, I rolled off the couch and went in through the foyer, trying not to wake my mother.

He was so handsome—he looked the way he had looked in his youth, dark and quiet and earnest and dedicated, a man who, though he was much too Protestantly reserved ever to talk about his beliefs, thought that there had to be a God and that it was clearly a God who loved him, the proof being that He had let him be born after Beethoven, which meant he could spend his life playing Beethoven string quartets. This was the greatest miracle of my father's life and he never ceased to be wholly thankful for it.

I simply could not understand how he could now be content merely to *be* a string quartet or even string-quartet-playing. Why, he had never even wanted to *be* Beethoven—that was a hubristic ambition his daughter might plead guilty to, but all he had ever wanted was to *play* Beethoven. "You *must* miss playing the violin," I said, desperately wanting him to be what, who, he was: himself—not an idea or a predicate, even an eternal one. *Himself.*

"It's like I told you, Nina," he said, patient with my impatience. "My intonation has just gone all to hell without your mother around to criticize me."

Then it was clear to me, what he was saying. "No," I said.

"Yes," he said.

I felt cold. I felt as if I'd just been pulled, dazed and trembling, from an icy pond into which I had stupidly, *stupidly,* stumbled. I was shivering with realization. I wanted to un-realize what I had realized. Maybe if I didn't know what was going to happen, I thought, it wouldn't happen. It would be the reverse of predestination.

"There are solo sonatas," I said. "There are records with one part missing. When Mother was busy, you used to practice by yourself. I stayed in my room, listening. In the hallway, listening. For years. In the end, you said, every member of a sting quartet is responsible for himself. Or herself. Nobody can play your part for you."

"That's right," he said. "That's the first thing you learn when you shut the door to the practice room and start to play scales for the first time. It's like anything else that matters. Nobody else can do it for you."

"I don't know if I agree with that," I said. "When you played the violin, when Mother played, it was like my heart was playing its own chamber music. I mean, I have always applauded you both. I hope you know that."

"Thank you," he said. And I realized that I had stumbled into the same pond all over again and that, no matter how I tried to circumvent it, that pond would always be there, waiting for me to fall into it and surface shivering and forever changed. My father's formal thank-you had signaled the fact that we had come to the end of something, but I still didn't want it to be over. I was an audience clamoring for an encore, while the musicians backstage just wanted to put their instruments away and go home. "Will you wake her?" he asked.

I hesitated. "Do I have to?"

"I'm here because she didn't want to do this alone."

"But you said everything that matters has to be done alone!" I was still the star pupil, aggressively blasting holes in everyone else's arguments so no one could draw a bead on mine.

"Death *can't* matter," he rebutted me, "because it *isn't* matter. Life matters, but death doesn't. Please bring her in here."

He had become so commanding—a presence, in spite of his non-existence. He was more real to me, at that moment, than he had been since I was a child, an infant even.

I remembered that I had seen him naked once, not so many years ago. He had talced himself after a tub bath and was drying himself off with a large towel. He had looked so pale, from the talc, almost snow-white, and yet so—*embodied.* That was how he looked now: pale as a ghost embodied.

When I had seen him like that, naked, I'd ducked into the next room, not wanting him to know, not wanting to embarrass him. I ducked into the next room now.

"He's here?" She said the words as soon as I touched her shoulder. She raised herself off the pillows. Her hair, tousled from sleeping, was sticking out in wispy white corkscrews. It looked like smoke, as if her scalp were smoldering. Or like fog—the white, twisted columns of fog that drift silently through bayous.

"He wants to talk with you," I said.

"He's come for me."

"I don't know what you mean!" I cried.

"You know perfectly well what I mean, Nina. Don't be an ass about this."

"It's hard on her, Eleanor," my father said, as we pushed through the swinging Dutch gate into the kitchen.

"It's harder on me." She sank into her chair. "Nina, fix us some ice cream, if you don't mind."

I got the glass bowls from the cabinet and spoons and scooped up four dishes of ice cream, placing one on the floor for Oscar in case he decided he liked Rum Raisin, but he refused to come into the kitchen. He stayed by the gate, inscrutable as the Dalai Lama.

Because it was night, because my mother was old and cold, the furnace was on. We three were held in the kitchen as in an embrace.

I forced myself to eat the ice cream because my parents obviously wanted me to. They wanted to think I was happy, they wanted to be released from all guilt, freed of all anxiety. There was nothing new in that—but how could I be happy when they were leaving me? How was I supposed to feel good about what was happening? I didn't have my mother's ability to detach herself from sentiment. I didn't have my father's humility, which had allowed him to be grateful for even the smallest favor from God, such as being born after Beethoven.

Instead, I was angry. I felt they had played a dirty rotten trick on me. They had let me think that my father had come back because he was lonely and he missed my mother, but he had come back to take her away.

I felt a despair that was like amputation. I had thought I was helping her—talking with her, reading to her, looking after her wants and needs. But what she needed was to cut off life. She was gangrenous with the past—maybe that's how we all become. To get well, she needed to be freed from it. I was the amputated appendage.

Nothing I had done had been enough to keep her from being lonely and missing my father.

They handed me their empty bowls and I ran water over the dishes in the sink. When I turned around again, my father was helping my mother out of her chair.

"You're not going already!"

It came out like a scream, a sort of scream or controlled shriek. I was afraid I had waked up Tavy. We stopped and listened to the house, but she slept on.

"Remember," my father said. "Violin lessons as soon as you get back to Wisconsin."

I nodded. My eyes were filling.

"Don't cry," my mother said. "It disgusts me to see anyone cry. Besides, I'm happy to be with your father again."

And how happy she looked! She was as radiant as a bride, she was a bride. Before my eyes, she had become again the vibrant young beauty who had liked to stroll along the Gulf shore and dance late into the salt-scented, breeze-blown nights. She was again the clear-eyed, firm-profiled young woman who, to my father's amazement, shared his love of the Beethoven string quartets. Who would have thought that there could be a girl like this, or that she would be waiting for him? When he finally had accepted this as yet another miracle he had no choice but to believe in, he gathered up his courage and drove to Gulfport, in a Buick he'd bought for seventy-five bucks at a bankruptcy sale. It was, as I said, 1933.

But now my father had picked up my mother and carried her in his arms to the door to the backyard. "Open the door, Nina," he said.

I dried my hands on my shirt—his shirt—and went to the door. Outside, the leaves of the oak tree were like hands, all playing the sky as if the sky were a musical instrument, the wind an invisible bow. I unlatched the latch, unbolted the bolts, unlocked the keylock.

"Stand over there, Nina," my father ordered, jerking his head in the direction of the little table he had made, the two chairs and the high stool.

I moved over to the table.

"Goodbye," said my mother. "I know you're determined to be a better mother than I was, but that may not be as easy as you think. In any case, you must not let Tavy keep you from your work. Make sure you get a decent price on the house. Vote Labour."

"Goodbye," said my father. "I'm sorry if you think I didn't love you enough, but I always had my hands full with your mother. So you see," he added, grasping her tightly, "nothing is any different from the way it's always been. Do you understand?"

My mother had her arms wrapped around my father's neck, and they were smiling into each other's young face.

She laughed.

And then my father carried my mother over the threshold of this world into the next.

Mission Work

Anthony Bukoski

When our priest has a stroke, the nuns lament what God has done. *"Jezu, Maryo, Józefie!"* they say as they clasp their hands together and look to heaven for guidance. In the bakery and butcher shops, people order sausage, poppy-seed cake, and extra bread to help them through the period of great trial. At St. Adalbert's grade school, children cry over the news about Father.

When he is well enough to come home from the hospital, his housekeeper, Lu sits him in a lawn chair on the rectory's front porch. Father's thirty-eight-year-old niece, Lu, takes this worse than anyone. To keep off the chill, she has dressed him in a car coat and snap brim cap, then ducked into the rectory to pace back and forth. If you are brave enough to ride past on your bicycle, you see Father sitting helplessly, Lu staring through the picture window. Maybe he waves or says something you don't understand. Then he starts crying from the stroke.

"The Lake Superior wind makes our eyes water, not Father Nowak's condition," I say to Gerald Bluebird so we will not be embarrassed about the tears in our own eyes. We are on our way to serve Mass.

"If I'm crying, it's because I'm hungry," Gerald says. He has large, round eyes, dark skin.

"I'm hungry, too. When I left home, my parents were just finishing breakfast before Dad goes to work. We can't eat now because we're receiving Communion. On second thought, I'm not sure I'm going to Communion. Do you think if we do, it will take the edge off our hunger? Do you feel bad about Father?"

"I feel awful," he says in Polish. *"Straszny."*

Nobody notices when the lone Indian kid in the neighborhood uses Polish words. His family has lived here a long time. *"Dzien dobry,"* he says to old women passing us on the way to St. Adalbert's this cool Wednesday in early June.

Gerald and I don't hurry to church. It's no fun serving Mass for the different priests the bishop sends to replace Father Nowak, especially when we know that by the time Mass ends, Father will be bundled up on the porch again, and Gerald and I, trying to avoid him, will pretend not to see him on our way home. The best priest in the world, he has served St. Adalbert's for forty years. He's kept Masses short, gone easy on penance, come into our classrooms for spelling bees, pitched to us during recess, given us money, and given us half the day off on the Feast of St. Joseph. Seeing him cry, Gerald and I will have to turn away.

"We're not going home after Mass. We have to go to the mission," Gerald says when we enter St. Adalbert's. "Lu called to ask us to serve two Masses today. We're scheduled for a home-and-away double-header. My ma told me about it when I woke up. It's an hour out there, plus the time it takes for Mass at the mission. We won't eat for four hours."

Hearing the bad news, I say, "Shit."

"That's what I said," Gerald says. "Why does Lu call me? I'm Indian. There are others she could get to do this."

"Lu doesn't like me because the Parish Report shows we only give $109 a year—two dollars a week in the regular collection, five dollars for special collections. My dad's embarrassed, but if we don't have money, what can he do? My grandma calls shit 'gowna,'" I say as we make the Sign of the Cross.

Genuflecting before the altar, we head into the sacristy. Until we hear him snoring, we aren't sure what (human or non-human) is in the chair in back by the closet where Father Nowak's vestments hang. Hearing us, a large shape opens its eyes, says, "You're awright, Padre. Too much altar wine last night." Struggling to get up, he shakes his head to clear it. "Priesthood's a tough way to make a buck," he says, looks over, sees us.

When we help him dress for Mass, he barely fits into his alb; then Gerald and I have to pull hard to get the chasuble over him. We don't know who he is or who he's talking to because he doesn't tell us anything about himself until, on the altar, he begins, *"In Nomine Patris, et Fílii et Spíritus Sancti. Amen."* We smell Mogen David on him.

By the part of the service called "The Confiteor," when a person strikes his breast three times and confesses he's "sinned exceedingly in thought, word, and deed," I believe I will faint from hunger. Suffering from starvation and malnutrition, I can't think of my sins. I feel worse during "The Kyrie" and the "Glory Be." Realizing I have to eat, by "The Offertory" I decide to receive Holy Communion knowing, in terms of filling me up, the Blessed Sacrament won't equal half a piece of dry toast. When the priest gives Gerald and me Communion, saying *"Corpus Domini nostri Jesu Christi . . . ,"* my mouth waters. I am grateful Jesus died on the cross so I can have this Host to eat. When the priest, done distributing Communion, is about to place the ciborium in the tabernacle, I say, "May I please have another?" but he frowns, shakes his head.

After Mass, Lu gives us the lunch she's prepared for us to take to the Dedham Mission. We can tell she resents the new priest and didn't like making him something to eat. She doesn't want anyone taking over for Father Nowak. To keep her mind off of him, she probably had to make the lunch or go crazy, though. Our parish priest has never been helpless.

Thirty-five miles away on country roads, the mission is called that not because it has something to do with Indians, but because it is too small a building with too few parishioners for a priest to be stationed there. When Father would take us to Dedham before his stroke, on our way back to town he'd buy us lunch at Shores Café and let us play the jukebox.

The new priest is different from Father Nowak. For one, he had a hard time kneeling, rising, then holding the Host aloft in his shaking hands during Its consecration. He was probably thinking if this is what it took to get a chalice of wine now and a good feed later, so be it, though probably he'd have preferred being wheeled around the altar in Father's wheelchair to conserve energy for what really matters, his stomach. Because of his weight, he sounds like he snores when he breathes. Now he has to squeeze himself behind the wheel of the Ford Fairlane we'll take to Dedham.

We believe Lu is right when she says lunch will be worth the trip. The cooler with the food in it weighs five pounds. Heading into the country on mission work, I dream of Lu's cooking, of my mother's cooking, of Grandma's, of Gerald's mother's Indian fry bread. At the creosote plant, we see guys on mid-morning break. Lunch buckets open, they are drinking coffee, eating a cookie or sandwich. Outside the Four Corners' General Store, kids eat Banana Flips and Eddie's Snowballs. At a gas station, a man lifts a sandwich, waves. From here on, it is mostly fields and woods. When we finally get to the mission, all during Mass, attended by nine people in the four rough pews, I dream of what we will soon have: Polish sausage, ham sandwiches, Lu's good pastries.

At the part of the Mass called the "The Introit," I bow. Camouflaging a whisper behind the Sign of the Cross, I say to Gerald, "I bet there's a doughnut waiting for you in the cooler." When the priest reads today's Introit, "My heart is become like wax melting in the midst of my bowels," I cannot look at my friend, knowing he'll be doubled over laughing at the word "bowels." Given our youth, giggling at such things is nothing we can help, though I soon quit laughing, for the Latin words the priest says next remind me of food. I think the priest is saying *"Dominus* Nabisco" instead of *"Dominus vobiscum,"* which means "The Lord be with you;" "Oreos" instead of *"Oremus,"* which means "Let us pray."

"I hope there's *strucla* in the cooler," Gerald says after "The Nicene Creed." *Strucla* is a coffee cake that looks like it's been braided.

After we laugh at "Homo" in *"Et Homo Factus Est,"* the Mass really drags. I fade out of the action until right before Communion, when God blesses us by leading us down the home stretch. Only Communion, Postcommunion, and a few other things remain. The priest is saying, "Lord, I am not worthy that Thou shouldst come under my roof . . . ," everybody replying three times the same way, only I am saying, "I am not worthy. Please feed a poor sinner."

Judging from the looks on their faces, the people receiving Communion are very, very hungry in a different way than I am. Holding the paten, which is a thin gold plate, under their chins to catch any crumbs from the Host, I see close up how others await the Blessed Sacrament, how they long to be fed. That is always a mystery to me, what people get from the Body of Christ.

When we are supposed to be praying afterwards—though I realize it is a sin to wonder about it—I ask Gerald, "How much longer?" Getting the nourishment he can from the Host, Gerald, still busy letting It dissolve on his tongue, winks to let me know we're almost done.

With the second Mass over, everybody gone home, I think the priest will let us dig in. Still in his vestments, he hands us the cruet with a little water remaining in it that wasn't used during "The

Transubstantiation," when water is poured into the chalice to mix with wine poured from another cruet. Next he pushes us out of the way. Lifting the chasuble behind him as he runs, he cries, "Oh, Lord!" The church doesn't have indoor plumbing. The priest is heading into the aspen trees for privacy.

"I'm starved," I tell my partner once the concussion of what the priest has done dies away. "If he had to go, fine. That shouldn't keep us from this treasure chest."

When I try opening the food cooler, Gerald stops me. Though he's as hungry as I am, he says, "We're at a mission. Sometimes missionaries go hungry doing mission work. They even starve. Father Nowak wouldn't like us eating before the priest does. Nor would my parents like it. It ain't the Polish way."

"I've got to have a snack," I say. "At least a cracker crumb, a carrot. Why are you so holy all of a sudden?"

"I can't let you eat," Gerald says. "I just received Communion."

"Then the heck with being foreign missionaries out here. What kind of priest doesn't care about the suffering? The sins we study in catechism are on display today. I went to Communion, too."

"He's sure not Father Nowak," Gerald says. "I guess we don't owe him anything."

"Who'd you rather be, Father or this guy who's so big he blocked our view of the tabernacle? He could live off his fat until Jesus raises the dead. He don't need to eat. We do! If I don't, I'll die. I'll play you 'Rock, Paper, Scissors,' to see whether we should eat or starve."

We pound our fists into our palms, extend two fingers.

"Scissors cancels scissors," Gerald says.

We both show rock the next time.

The third time I win. "My scissors cut your paper. You can't stop me from a lunch I won fair and square. I'm eating."

But Gerald doesn't have to stop me, for the priest, returning from the woods, says his first words in English to us: "Help me free of my vestments."

Not wanting to touch them, we let the priest himself place them in the trunk of the Fairlane. He holds out his fat hands for Gerald to pour water from the cruet over them.

"Wash your hands, then eat. Cleanliness is next to godliness," says the priest. "Let's investigate lunch. You boys move the cooler here in front and you both jump in back."

Gunning the car out of the mission's driveway, he heads down the road looking as though he's angry we wouldn't touch the vestments.

Admiring the sandwich he's selected from the cooler, the reverend says, "Turkey. White meat. My favorite." Tearing off the crust, which he sets on the dashboard, he bites into the sandwich. Several bites later, he tosses the remaining bread out the window, grabs another sandwich. "Are there pickles in here?" he asks himself, question sounding like a snort. "Old Dutch potato chips to finish the job!"

When I look at my sidekick, he has sunk into the seat. Seeing the hunger in his eyes, I feel my stomach ache. I bet Gerald regrets keeping us from eating when the big priest was in the woods. I think of Father Nowak, frail on the porch, think of his suffering.

"I'm going to eat up *everything*!" says the priest.

Unable to stand him, I whisper to Gerald, "He's practicing one of the Seven Corporal Works of Mercy, to feed the hungry. Only in reverse. He's stuffing himself and the hungry stay hungry."

"Just kidding about eating it all. There'll be enough for you two. I promise," the priest says. Nibbling a few items I can't see—maybe radishes—he goes back to the sandwiches. He doesn't finish until he has eaten all six of them plus whatever else we figured was in there.

Only then does Gerald ask, "Can Antek and I have the crusts, Father?"

"They might be dusty from the dashboard, but sure. Here you are. Eat them all."

This is not funny. No doubt our parents would tell us it is best not to say anything to a man of God, even if he's getting revenge on you. "*Aż was, zjadaczw chleba—w aniołów przerobi.* You lowly eaters of bread will be made into angels," they would say. Lowly eaters of bread? We eat dirty bread crusts, Gerald saving one in his shirt pocket. The thought of this offers little consolation to two famished, suffering missionaries now really near passing out. How could Jesus go forty days and forty nights in the wilderness without food? How could Father Nowak go forty years at St. Adalbert's Church giving everything he had to others?

"Now lookee," says the priest as his stumpy fingers snare the desserts he's hidden from us. Wiping his chin when he's done with the brownies and cake, he says, "You share what is left. *Dominus vobiscum*. The Lord be with you." But, sitting forward to look in the cooler, we see nothing in there, just the flat, white bottom. Going through a day's worth of food in twenty minutes, the priest has eaten his way back to the East End of Superior, Wisconsin.

Looking at his watch, realizing he's late for lunch with the bishop, he drops us at the rectory, then peels out, startling Father Nowak on the front porch, where Lu has parked him in his wheelchair with an army blanket over his shoulders.

Not wanting our hearts to break more than they have today, Gerald and I yell to each other, "Go!" and make our getaway for home and our mother's good cooking, but stop after a few steps, for Father Nowak is crying and saying he is hungry.

"So are we," we tell him, Gerald pulling the bread crust from his pocket.

With us on the porch feeding him bit by bit of the crust, Father finally calms down. Because we've come over to him despite his sadness, maybe he senses that we will some day be good men who practice the Seven Corporal Works of Mercy. Lu can't believe the change in Father until Gerald and I point to the crumbs on Father's car coat and tell Lu through the window that, lowly eaters of bread, we are feeding the hungry.

This was in a faraway land. There were gyms but no irony or coffee shops. People took things literally, without drugs. Laird, who wanted to fix her up with this guy, warned her beforehand in exercise class. "Look, Odette, you're a poet. You've been in po biz for what—twenty years—"

"Only fifteen, I'm sure." She had just turned forty and scowled at him over her shoulder. She had a voice menopausal with whiskey, a voice left to lurch and ruin by cigarettes. It was without a middle range, low, with sudden cracks upward. "I hate that phrase *po biz*."

"Fifteen. All right. This guy's not at all literary. He's a farm lawyer. He gets the occasional flasher, or a Gypsy from the Serbo neighborhood in Chicago, but that's as artistic as he gets. He's dealing with farmers and farms. He wouldn't know T. S. Eliot from, say, *Pinky* Eliot. He's probably never even been to Minneapolis, let alone New York."

"Who's Pinky Eliot?" she asked. They were lying side by side, doing these things where you thrust your arms between your raised knees, to tighten the stomach muscles. There was loud music to distract you from worries that you might not know anyone in the room well enough to be doing this in front of them. "Who the heck is Pinky Eliot?"

"Someone I went to fourth grade with," said Laird, gasping. "It was said he weighed more than the teacher, and she was no zipper, let me tell you." Laird was balding, and in exercise class the blood rushed across his head, bits of hair curling above his ears like gift ribbon. He had lived in this town until he was ten, then his family had moved east to New Jersey, where she had first met him, years ago. Now he had come back, like a salmon, to raise his own kids. He and his wife had two. "Little and Moist," they called them. "Look, you're in the boonies here. You got your Pinky Eliot or you got your guy who's never heard of Pinky or any Eliot."

She had been in the boonies before. To afford her apartment in New York, she often took these sorts of library fellowships: six weeks and four thousand dollars to live in town, write unpublishable poems, and give a reading at the library. The problem with the boonies was that nobody ever kissed you there. They stared at you, up and down, but they never kissed.

Actually, once in a while you could get them to kiss.

But then you had to leave. And in your packing and going, in tearing the seams, the hems, the haws, you felt like some bad combination of Odysseus *and* Penelope. You felt funny in the heart.

"All right," she said. "What is his name?"

Laird sighed. "Pinky Eliot," he said, thrusting his arms between his knees. "Somehow in this mangled presentation, I fear I've confused you."

Pinky Eliot had lost weight, though for sure he still weighed more than the teacher. He was about forty-five, with all his hair still dark. He was not bad-looking, elf-nosed and cat-eyed, though a little soccer ball-ish through the chin and cheeks, which together formed a white sphere with a sudden scar curling grayly around. Also, he had the kind of mustache a college roommate of hers used to say looked like it had crawled up to find a warm spot to die.

They ate dinner at the only Italian restaurant in town. She drank two glasses of wine, the cool heat of it spreading through her like wintergreen. One of these days, she knew, she would have to give up dating. She had practiced declarations in the mirror. "I don't date. I'm sorry. I just don't date."

"I always kind of liked the food here," said Pinky.

She looked at his round face and felt a little bad for him and a little bad for herself while she was at it, because, truly, the food was not good: flavorless bladders of pasta passing as tortellini; the cutlets mealy and drenched in the kind of tomato sauce that was unwittingly, defeatedly orange. Poor Pinky didn't know a garlic from a Gumby.

"Yes," she said, trying to be charming. "But do you think it's really Italian? It feels as if it got as far as the Canary Islands, then fell into the water."

"An East Coast snob." He smiled. His voice was slow with prairie, thick with Great Lakes. "Dressed all in black and hating the Midwest. Are you Jewish?"

She bristled. A Nazi. A hillbilly Nazi gastronomical moron. "No, I'm not Jewish," she said archly, staring him down, to teach him this: "Are *you?*"

"Yes," he said. He studied her eyes.

"Oh," she said.

"Not many of us in this part of the world, so I thought I'd ask."

"Yes." She felt an embarrassed sense of loss, as if something that should have been hers but wasn't had been taken away, legally, by the police. Her gaze dropped to her hands, which had started to move around nervously, independently, like small rodents kept as pets. Wine settled hotly in her cheeks, and when she rushed more to her mouth, the edge of the glass clinked against the tooth in front that was longer than all the others.

Pinky reached across the table and touched her hair. She had had it permed into waves like ramen noodles the week before. "A little ethnic kink is always good to see," he said. "What are you, Methodist?"

On their second date they went to a movie. It was about creatures from outer space who burrow into earthlings and force them to charge up enormous sums on their credit cards. It was an elaborate urban allegory, full of disease and despair, and Odette wanted to talk about it. "Pretty entertaining movie," said Pinky slowly. He had fidgeted in his seat through the whole thing and had twice gotten up and gone to the water fountain. "Just going to the bubbler," he'd whispered.

Now he wanted to go dancing.

"Where is there to go dancing?" said Odette. She was still thinking about the part where the two main characters had traded boom boxes and it had caused them to fall in love. She wanted either Pinky or herself to say something incisive or provocative about directorial vision, or the narrative parameters of cinematic imagery. But it looked as if neither of them was going to.

"There's a place out past the county beltline about six miles." They walked out into the parking lot, and he leaned over and kissed her cheek—intimate, premature, a leftover gesture from a recent love affair, no doubt—and she blushed. She was bad at love. There were people in the world who were good at love and people who were bad at it. She was bad. She used to think she was good at love, that it was intimacy she was bad at. But you had to have both. Love without intimacy, she knew, was an unsung tune. It was all in your head. You said, "Listen to this!" but what you found yourself singing was a tangle, a nothing, a heap. It reminded her of a dinner party she had gone to once, where dessert was served on plates printed with French songs. After dinner everyone had had to sing their plate, but hers had still had whipped cream on it, and when it came her turn, she had garbled the notes and words, frantically pushing the whipped cream around with a fork so she could see the next measure. Oh, she was bad, bad like that, at love.

Pinky drove them six miles south of the county beltline to a place called Humphrey Bogart's. It was rough and wooden, high-beamed, a former hunting lodge. On a makeshift stage at the front, a country-western band was playing "Tequila Sunrise" fifteen years too late, or perhaps too soon. Who could predict? Pinky took her hand and improvised a slow jitterbug to the bass. "What do I do now?" Odette kept calling to Pinky over the music. "What do I do now?"

"This," said Pinky. He had the former fat person's careful grace, and his hand at the small of her back felt big and light. His scar seemed to disappear in the dancelight, and his smile drove his mustache up into flattering shadow. Odette had always been thin and tense.

"We don't dance much in New York," she said.

"No? What do you do?"

"We, uh, just wait in line at cash machines."

Pinky leaned into her, took her hand tightly to his shoulder, and rocked. He put his mouth to her ear. "You've got a great personality," he said.

On Sunday afternoon Pinky took her to the Cave of the Many Mounds. "You'll like this," he said.

"Wonderful," she said, getting into his car. There was a kind of local enthusiasm about things, which she was trying to get the hang of. It involved good posture and utterances made in a chirpy singsong. *Isn't the air just snappy?* She was wearing sunglasses and an oversize sweater. "I was thinking of asking you what a Cave of Many Mounds was, and then I said, 'Odette, do you *really* want to know?'" She fished through her pocketbook. "I mean, it sounds like a whorehouse. You don't happen to have any cigarettes, do you?"

Pinky tapped on her sunglasses. "You're not going to need these. It's dark in the cave." He started the car and pulled out.

"Well, let me know when we get there." She stared straight ahead. "I take it you don't have any cigarettes."

"No," said Pinky. "You smoke cigarettes?"

"Once in a while." They drove past two cars in a row with bleeding deer strapped on them like wreaths, like trophies, *like women,* she thought. "Damn hunters," she murmured.

"What kind of cigarettes do you smoke? Do you smoke Virginia Slims?" asked Pinky with a grin.

Odette turned and lowered her sunglasses, looked out over them at Pinky's sun-pale profile. "No, I don't smoke *Virginia Slims.*"

"I'll bet you do. I'll bet you smoke Virginia Slims."

"Yeah, I smoke Virginia Slims," said Odette, shaking her head. Who was this guy?

Ten miles south, there started to be signs for Cave of the Many Mounds. CAVE OF THE MANY MOUNDS 20 MILES. CAVE OF THE MANY MOUNDS 15 MILES. At five miles, Pinky pulled the car over onto the shoulder. There were only trees and in the far distance a barn and a lone cow.

"What are we doing?" asked Odette.

Pinky shifted the car into park but left the engine running. "I want to kiss you now, before we get in the cave and I lose complete control." He turned toward her, and suddenly his body, jacketed and huge, appeared suspended above her, hovering, as she sank back against the car door. He closed his eyes and kissed her, long and slow, and she left her sunglasses on so she could keep her eyes open and watch, see how his lashes closed on one another like petals, how his scar zoomed quiet and white about his cheek and chin, how his lips pushed sleepily against her own to find a nest in hers and to stay there, moving, as if in words, but then not in words at all, his hands going round her in a soft rustle, up the back of her sweater to her bare waist and spine, and spreading there, blooming large and holding her just briefly until he pulled away, gathered himself back to himself, and quietly shifted the car into drive.

Odette sat up and stared out the windshield into space. Pinky moved the car back out onto the highway and picked up speed.

"We don't do that in New York," rasped Odette. She cleared her throat.

"No?" Pinky smiled and put his hand on her thigh.

"No, it's, um, the cash machines. You just . . . you wait at them. Forever. Your whole life you're just always"—her hand sliced the air—"there."

"**P**lease do not touch the formations," the cave tour guide kept shouting over everyone's head. Along the damp path through the cave there were lights, which allowed you to see walls marbled a golden rose, like a port cheddar; nippled projections, blind galleries, arteries all through the place, chalky and damp; stalagmites and stalactites in walrusy verticals, bursting up from the floor in yearning or hanging wicklessly in drips from the ceiling, making their way, through time, to the floor. The whole cave was in a weep, everything wet and slippery; still ocher pools of water bordered the walk, which spiraled gradually down. "Nature's Guggenheim," said Odette, and because Pinky seemed not to know what she was talking about, she said, "That's an art museum in New York." She had her sunglasses perched high on her head. She looked at Pinky gleefully, and he smiled back at her as if he thought she was cute but from outer space, like something that would soon be made into a major motion picture and then later into a toy.

" . . . The way you can remember which are which," the guide was saying, "is to remember: When the mites go up, the tights come down . . ."

"Get that?" said Pinky too loudly, nudging her. "The tights come down?" People turned to look.

"What are you, hard of hearing?" asked Odette.

"A little," said Pinky. "In the right ear."

"Next we come to a stalagmite which is the only one in the cave that visitors are allowed to touch. As we pass, it will be on your right, and you may manhandle it to your heart's content."

"Hmmmph," said Pinky.

"Really," said Odette. She peered ahead at the front of the group, which had now gathered unexcitedly around the stalagmite, a short stumpy one with a head rubbed white with so much touching. It had all the appeal of a bar of soap in a gas station. "I think I want to go back and look at the cave coral again."

"Which was that?" said Pinky.

"All that stuff that looked like cement broccoli. Also the chapel room with the church organ. I mean, I thought that looked pretty much like an organ."

" . . . And now," the guide was saying, "we come to that part of our tour when we let you see what the cave looks like in its own natural lighting." She moved over and flicked a switch. "You should not be able to see your hand in front of your face."

Odette widened her eyes and then squinted and still could not see her hand in front of her face. The darkness was thick and certain, not a shaded, waltzing dark but a paralyzing coffin jet. There was something fierce and eternal about it, something secret and unrelieved, like a thing not told to children.

"I'm right here," Pinky said, stepping close, "in case you need me." He gave her far shoulder a squeeze, his arm around the back of her. She could smell the soupy breath of him, the spice of his neck near her face, and leaned, blind and hungry, into his arm. She reached past the scratch of her own sweater and felt for his hand.

"We can see now how the cave looked when it was first unearthed, and how it had existed eons before, in the pitch dark, gradually growing larger, opening up in darkness, the life and the sea of it trapped and never seeing light, a small moist cavern a millions years in the making, just slowly opening, opening, and opening inside. . . ."

When they slept together, she almost cried. He was a kisser, and he kissed and kissed. It seemed the kindest thing that had ever happened to her. He kissed and whispered and brought her a large glass of water when she asked for one.

"When ya going back to New York?" he asked, and because it was in less than four weeks, she said, "Oh, I forget."

Pinky got out of bed. He was naked and unselfconscious, beautiful, in a way, the long, rounded lines of him, the stark cliff of his back. He went over to the VCR, fumbled with some cassettes in the dark, holding each up to the window, where there was a rainy, moony light from the street, like a dream; he picked up cassette after cassette until he found the one he wanted.

It was a tape called *Holocaust Survivors,* and the tile flashed blood red on the television screen, as if in warning that it had no place there at all. "I watch this all the time," said Pinky, very quietly. He stared straight ahead in a trance of impassivity, but when he reached back to put an arm around Odette, he knew exactly where she was, slightly behind one of his shoulders, the sheet tight across her chest. "You shouldn't hide your breasts," he said, without looking. But she stayed like that, tucked close, all along the tracks to Treblinka, the gates to Auschwitz, the film lingering on weeds and wind, so unbelieving in this historical badlands, it seemed to want, in a wave of nausea and regret, to become perhaps a nature documentary. It seemed at moments confused abut what it was about, a confusion brought on by knowing exactly.

Someone was talking about the trucks. How they put people in trucks, with the exhaust pipes venting in, how they drove them around until they were blue, the people were blue, and could be shoveled out from a trapdoor. Past some barbed wire, asters were drying in a field.

When it was over, Pinky turned to her and sighed. "Heavy stuff," he said.

Heavy stuff? Her breathing stopped, then sped up, then stopped again. *Who on earth was entitled to such words?*

Who on earth? She felt, in every way it was possible to feel it, astonished that she had slept with him.

She went out with him again, but this time she greeted him at his own door, with a stiff smile and a handshake, like a woman willing to settle out of court. "So casual," he said, standing in the doorway. "I don't know. You East Coast city slickers."

"We got hard hearts," she said with an accent that wasn't really any particular accent at all. She wasn't good at accents.

When they slept together again, she tried not to make too much of it. Once more they watched *Holocaust Survivors,* a different tape, out of sequence, the camera still searching hard for something natural to gaze upon, embarrassed, like a bloodshot eye weary and afraid of people and what they do. *They set fire to the bodies and to the barracks,* said a voice. *The pyres burned for many days.*

Waves lapped. Rain beaded on a bulrush. In the bathroom she ran the tap water so he couldn't hear as she sat, ill, staring at her legs, her mother's legs. When had she gotten her mother's legs? When she crept back to his bed, he was sleeping like a boy, the way men did.

In the morning she got up early and went to the closest thing there was to a deli and returned triumphantly with bagels and lox. Outside, the town had been museum dead, but the sky was lemony with sun, and elongations of light, ovals of brightened blue, now dappled Pinky's covers. She laid the breakfast out in them, and he rolled over and kissed her, his face waxy with sleep. He pointed at the lox. "You like that sort of stuff?"

"Yup." Her mouth was already full with it, the cool, slimy pink. "Eat it all the time."

He sighed and sank back into his pillow. "After breakfast I'll teach you some Yiddish words."

"I already know some Yiddish words. I'm from New York. Here, eat some of this."

"I'll teach you *tush* and *shmuck.*" Pinky yawned, then grinned. "And *shiksa.*"

"All the things a nice Jewish boy practices on before he marries a nice Jewish girl. I know those."

"What's wrong with you?"

She refused to look at him. "I don't know."

"*I* know," said Pinky, and he stood up on the bed, like a child about to bounce, toweringly naked, priapic. She could barely look. Oh, for a beaded bulrush. A train disappearing into a tunnel. "You're falling in love with me!" he exclaimed, gazing merrily down. She still had her coat on, and had stopped chewing. She stared, disbelievingly, up at him. Sometimes she thought she was just trying to have fun in life, and other times she realized she must be terribly confused. She narrowed her eyes. Then she opened her mouth wide so that he could see the train wreck of chewed-up bagel and lox.

"I like that," said Pinky. "You're onto something there."

Her poems, as she stated in letters to friends in New York, were not going well; she had put them on the back burner, and they had fallen behind the stove. She had met this guy. Something had happened to the two of them in a cave, she wasn't sure what. She had to get out of here. She was giving her final reading to the library patrons and matrons in less than three weeks, and that would pretty much be it. *I hope you are not wearing those new, puffy evening dresses I see in magazines. They make everyone look like sticky buns. It is cold. Love, Odette.*

Laird was curious. He kept turning his head sideways during the sit-ups. "So you and Pinky hitting it off?"

"Who knows?" said Odette.

"Well, I mean, everyone's had their difficulties in life; his I'm only a little aware of. I thought you'd find him interesting."

"Sure, anthropologically."

"You think he's a dork."

"Laird, we're in our forties here. You can't use words like *dork* anymore." The sit-ups were getting harder. "He's not a dork. He's a doofus. Maybe. Maybe a *doink*."

"You're a hard woman," said Laird.

"Oh, I'm not," pleaded Odette, collapsing on the rubber mat. "Really I'm not."

At night he began to hold her in a way that stirred her deeply. He slept with one hand against the small of her back, the other capped against her head, as if to protect her from bad thoughts. Or, perhaps, thoughts at all. How quickly bodies came to love each other, promise themselves to each other always, without asking permission. From the mind! If only she could give up her mind, let her heart swell, inflamed, her brain stepping out for whole days, whole seasons, her work shrinking to limericks. She would open her mouth before the library fellowship people, and out would come: *There once was a woman from . . .* Someone would rush to a phone booth and call the police.

But perhaps you *could* live only from the neck down. Perhaps you *could* live with the clothes you were taking off all piled on top of your head, in front of your face, not just a sweater with a too-small neck but everything caught there—pants, shoes, and socks—a crazed tangle on your shoulders, in lieu of a head, while your body, stark naked, prepared to live the rest of its life in the sticks, the boonies, the fly-over, the rain. Perhaps you could. For when she slept against him like that, all the rest of the world collapsed into a suitcase under the bed. It was the end of desire, this having. Oh, here oh here she was. He would wrap himself around her, take her head like an infant's into his hand and breathe things to her, her throat, her chest, in his beginning to sleep. *Go to sleep, go to sleep with me.*

In the morning she warmed her arms over the blue zinnias of the gas jets and heated water for coffee and eggs. Over the newspaper, she pretended she and Pinky were Beatrice and Benedick, or Nick and Nora Charles, which is what she always pretended in a love affair, at least for a few days, until the actual evidence overwhelmed her.

"Why are you always talking with your hands?" asked Pinky. "You think you're Jewish?"

She glared at him. "You know, that's what I hate about this part of the country," she replied. "Everyone's so repressed. If you use your body in the least way while you're talking, people think you're trying out for a Broadway show."

"Kiss me," he said, and he closed his eyes.

On a weekday Pinky would be off to his office, to work on another farm bankruptcy or a case of animal abuse. "My clients," he said wearily. "You would never want to go out to eat with them. They come into my office reeking of cowshit, they lean back in the chair, set their belly out like that, then tell you about how some Humane Society bastard gave them a summons because their goat had worms." Across his face there breathed a sigh of tragedy. "It's a sad thing not to have clients you can go out to eat with." He shook his head. "It's a sad thing, a goat with worms."

There was something nice about Pinky, but that something was not Nick Charles. Pinky was more like a grave and serious brother of Nick's, named Chuck. Chuck Charles. When you had parents who would give you a name like that, there was nothing funny anymore.

"What do you write poems about?" he asked her once in the middle of the night.

"Whores," she said.

"Whores," he repeated, nodding in the dark.

She have him books of poetry: Wordsworth, Whitman, all the *W*'s. When she'd ask him how he liked them, he would say, "Fine. I'm on page . . ." and then he would tell her what page he was on and how many pages he'd accomplished that day. "The Wadsworth is a little too literaturey for me."

"Wordsworth," she corrected. They were in his kitchen, drinking juice.

"Wordsworth. Isn't there a poet named Wadsworth?"

"No. You're probably thinking of Longfellow. That was his middle name."

"Longfellow. Now who's he again?"

"How about *Leaves of Grass*? What did you think of the poems in there?"

"OK. I'm on page fifty," he said. Then he showed her his gun, which he kept in his kitchen in a leather case, like a trombone. He kept a rifle, he said, in the basement.

Odette frowned. "You hunt?"

"Sure. Jews aren't supposed to hunt, I know. But in his part of the country it's best to have a gun." He smiled "*Bavarians,* you know. Here, try it out. Let me see how you look with a gun."

"I'm afraid of guns."

"Nothing to be afraid of. Just heft it and look down the top of the barrel and line up the sights."

She sighed, lifted the gun, pressed the butt hard against her right shoulder, and aimed it at the kitchen counter. "Now, see the notch in the metal sticking up in the middle of your barrel?" Pinky was saying. "You have to get the bead in the middle of the notch."

She closed her left eye. "I can feel the urge coming on to blow away that cutting board," she said.

"Gun's not loaded. Probably not till spring. Turkey season. Though I've got tags for deer."

"You hunt turkeys?" She put the gun down. It was heavy.

"You eat turkey, don't you?"

"The turkeys I eat are raised on farms. They're different. They've signed on the dotted line." She paused and sighed again. "What do you do, go into a field and fire away?"

"Kind of. You try to catch them mid-flight. You know, I should take you deer hunting. It's the last two days, this weekend, and I've got tags. Have you ever been?"

"*Pulease,*" she said.

It was cold in the woods. She blew breath clouds, then rings of cigarette smoke, into the dead ferns. "It's nice out here. You don't suppose we could just watch nature instead of shoot it."

"Without hunting, the deer would starve," said Pinky.

"So maybe we could just cook for them." They had brought along a bottle of Jim Beam, and she twisted it open and took a swig. "Have you ever been married?"

"Once," said Pinky. "God, what, twenty years ago." He quickly shouldered his rifle, thinking he heard something, but no.

"Oh," she said. "I wasn't going to ask, but then you never said anything about it, so I thought I'd ask."

"How about you?"

"Not me," said Odette. She had a poem about marriage. It began, *Marriage is the death you want to die,* and in front of audiences she never read it with much conviction. Usually she swung her foot back and forth through the whole thing.

She looked down at her chest. "I don't think orange is anyone's most flattering color," she said. They were wearing blaze-orange hats and vests. "I think we look like things placed in the middle of the road to make the cars go around."

"Shhhh," said Pinky.

She took another swig of Jim Beam. She had worn the wrong kind of boots—gray, suede, over the knees, with three-inch heels—and now she studied them with interest. One of the heels was loose, and mud was drying on the toes. "Tell me again," she whispered to Pinky, "what makes us think a deer will cross our path?"

"There's a doe bed not far from here," whispered Pinky. "It attracts bucks."

"Bucks, doe—thank God everything boils down to money, I always say."

"During mating season the doe constructs a bed for herself, and then she urinates all around the outside of it. That's how she gets her mate."

"So *that's* it," murmured Odette. "I was always peeing *in* the bed."

Pinky's gun suddenly fired into the trees, and the noise filled the woods like a war, spilling to the ground the yellowing needles of a larch.

"Ahhhhhh!" Odette screamed. "What is going on?" Guns, she was reminded then, were not for girls. They were for boys. They were invented by boys. They were invented by boys who had never gotten over their disappointment that accompanying their own orgasm there wasn't a big *boom* sound. "What the hell are you doing?"

"Damn!" shouted Pinky. "I missed!" He stood up and went crashing through the underbrush.

"Oh, my God!" cried Odette, and she stumbled after him, snapping the same twigs underfoot, ducking the same barbed wire. "Where are we going?"

"I've only wounded the deer," Pinky called over his shoulder. "I've got to kill it."

"Do you have to?"

"Keep your voice down," said Pinky.

"Fuck you," said Odette. "I'll wait for you back where we were," but there was a sudden darting from a bush behind her, and the bleeding deer leaped out, in a mournful gallop, its hip a crimson gash. Pinky raised his gun and fired, catching the deer in the neck. The air shimmered in the echo, and the leaves fell from a horse chestnut. The deer's legs buckled, and when it tipped over, dead in some berry bushes, its eyes never blinked but stayed lidless and deep, black as outer space.

"I'll leave the entrails for the hawks," Pinky said to Odette, but she was not there.

* * *

Oh, the ladies come down from the Pepsi Hotel

153

> Their home has no other name
> than the sign that was placed
> like a big cola bell: Pepsi-Cola Have a Pepsi Hotel.

Only a few of Odette's poems about whores rhymed—the ones she'd written recently—but perhaps the library crowd would like those best, the anticipation of it, knowing what the next word would be *like* though not what I would *be;* stanza after stanza, it would be a combination of comfort and surprise an audience might appreciate.

The local library association had set up a lectern near the windows of the reference room and had arranged chairs in rows for about eighty people. The room was chilly and alarmingly full. When Odette read she tried to look out past the faces, toward the atlases and the biographical dictionaries. She tugged on the cowl of her sweater and pulled it up over her chin between poems. She tried to pretend people's heads were all little ears of corn, something a dance instructor had once told her ballet class to do when she was seven and they had had to dance before the parents.

> They come down to the truckers
> or the truckers go up
> to the rooms with the curtains pell-mell.
> They truck down for the fuckers
> or else they fuck up
> in the Pepsi Have a Pepsi Hotel.

There was silence. A door creaked open then shut. Odette looked up and saw Pinky in the back, tiptoeing over to a chair to sit. She had not seen or spoken to him in a week. Two elderly women in the front turned around to stare.

> Oh, honey, they sigh; oh, honey, they say,
> there are small things to give and to sell,
> and Heaven's among us
> so work can be play at the . . .

There were other stanzas, too many, and she sped through them. She took a sip of water and read a poem call "Sleeping Wrong." *She slept wrong on her back last night,* it began, *and so she holds her head this way, mad with loneliness, madder still with talk.* She then read another long one, titled "Girl Gets Diphtheria, Loses Looks." She looked up and out. The audience was squinting back at her, their blood sugar levels low from early suppers, their interest redirected now and then toward her shoes, which were pointy and beige. "I'll close," she said loudly into the mike, "with a poem called 'Le Cirque in the Rain.'"

> This is not about a French monkey circus
> discouraged by weather.
> This is about the restaurant
> you pull up to in a cab,
> your life stopping there and badly,
> like a dog's song,
> your heart put in funny.

It told the story of a Manhattan call girl worrying a crisis of faith. *What is a halo but a handsome accident / of light and orbiting dust. What is a heart / but a . . .* She looked out at the two elderly women sitting polite and half attentive, unfazed, in the front row. One of them had gotten out some knitting. Odette looked back at her page. *Chimp in the chest,* she had written in an earlier draft, and that was what she said now.

Afterward a small reception was held out by the card catalogs. There were little cubes of pepper cheese, like dice, placed upon a table. There was a checkerboard of crackers, dark and light, a roulette of cold cuts. "It's a goddamn casino." She turned around and spoke to Pinky, who had come up and put his arm around her.

"I've missed you," he said. "I've been eating venison and thinking of you."

"Yes, well, thank you for coming, anyway."

"I thought you read very well," he said. "Not all of it I understood, I have to admit. Some of your stuff is a little too literaturey for me."

"Really," said Odette.

People shook her hand. They looked at her quizzically, came at her with assumptions, presumptions, what they believed was intimate knowledge of her. She felt unarmed, by comparison; disadvantaged. She lit up a cigarette.

"Do you really feel that way about men?" asked a man with a skeptical mouth.

"Do you really feel that way about women?" asked someone else.

"Your voice," said a young student. "It's like—who's that actress?"

"Mercedes McCambridge," said her friend.

"No, not her. Oh, I forget."

Several elderly couples had put on their coats and hats, but they came up to Odette to shake her hand. "You were wonderful, dear," said one of the women, gazing into Odette's nose.

"Yes," said the other, studying her own botched knitting—a scarf with an undulating edge.

"We come to these every year," said a man standing next to her. He had been searching for something to say and had come up with this.

"Well, thank you for coming this year as well," said Odette, stupidly, and dragged on her cigarette.

Kay Stevens, the woman in charge of the fellowship readings, came up and kissed her on the cheek, the sweet vanilla wax of her lipstick sticking like candy. "A big success," she said quickly, and then frowned and hurried off.

"Can I buy you a drink somewhere?" asked Pinky. He was still standing beside her, and she turned to look at him gratefully.

"Oy," she said. "Please."

Pinky drove them out past the county line to Humphrey Bogart's. He toasted her, flicked a sparkly speck of something from her cheek, looked into her eyes, and said, "Congratulations." He grew drunk, pulled his chair close, and put his head on her shoulder. He listened to the music, chewed on his cocktail straw, tapped his feet.

"Any requests?" the bandleader rumbled into the mike.

"O, give us one of the songs of Zion," shouted Pinky.

"What was that?" The words popped and roared in the mike.

"Nothing," said Pinky.

"Maybe we should go," said Odette, reaching for Pinky's hand beneath the table.

"OK," he said. "All right."

He struck a match to a candle in the dark of his bedroom, and the fire of it lit the wall in a jittery paint. He came back to her and pressed close. "Why don't I go with you to New York?" he whispered. She was silent, and so he said, "No, I think you should stay here. I could take you cross-country skiing."

"I don't like cross-country skiing," she whispered back. "It reminds me of when you're little and you put on your father's slippers and shluff around the house like that."

"I could take you snowmobiling up by Sand Lake," There was another long silence. Pinky sighed. "No, you won't. I can see you phoning your friends back East to tell them you'd decided to stay and them shrieking, 'You did *what*?'"

"You know us East Coasters," she said desperately. "We just come into a place, rape and pillage."

"You know," said Pinky, "I think you are probably the smartest person I have ever known."

She stopped breathing. "You don't get out much, do you?"

He rolled back and stared at the shadowed ceiling, its dimples and blotches. "When I was in high school, I was a bad student. I had to take special classes in this house behind the school. It was called The House."

She rubbed his leg gently with her foot. "Are you trying to make me cry?"

He took her hand, brought it out from beneath the covers, up to his mouth, and kissed it. "Everything's a joke with you," he said.

"Nothing's a joke with me. It just all comes out like one."

They spent one last night together. At his house, late, with all the lights off, they watched another cassette of *Holocaust Survivors*. It was about a boy forced to sing for the Nazis, over and over. Because he could sing, he was the last to be shot in the head, and when they shot him they missed the center of his brain. He was found alive. "I must think of happy things," he said now, old and staring off. "It may not be what others do, but it is what I must do." *He had a beautiful voice,* said a woman, another survivor. *It was beautiful like a bird that was also a god with flutes.*

"Heavy," murmured Pinky, when it was over. He pressed the remote control and turned away in the darkness, toward the wall, in a curve of covers. Odette pulled herself close, placed her hands around to the front of him, palms over the slight mounds of his breasts, her fingers deep in the light tangle of hair.

"Are you OK?" she asked.

He twisted toward her and kissed her, and in the dark he seemed to her aged and sad. He placed one of her fingers to his face. "You never asked about this." He guided her finger along his chin and cheek, letting it dead-end, like the scar, in his mustache.

"I try not to ask too many things. Once I start I can't stop."

"You want to know?"

"All right."

"I was in high school. Some guy called me a Jew, and I went after him. But I was clumsy and fat. He broke a bottle and dragged it across my face. I went home and my grandmother nearly fainted. Funny thing was, I had no idea that I *was* Jewish. My grandmother waited until the next day to tell me."

"Really," said Odette.

"You have to understand Midwestern Jews: They're afraid of being found out. They're afraid of being discovered." He breathed steadily, in and out, and the window shade flapped a little from being over the radiator. "As you probably know already, my parents were killed in the camps."

Odette did not say anything, and then she said, "Yes. I know." And at the moment she said it, she realized she did know, somehow had known it all along, though the fact of it had stayed beneath the surface, gilled and swimming like a fish, and now had burst up, gasping, with its mouth wide.

"Are you really leaving on Friday?" he asked.

"What?"

"Friday. Are you?"

"I'm sorry. I just didn't hear what you said. There's wind outside or something."

"I asked you if you were really leaving on Friday."

"Oh," she said. She pressed her face hard into his neck. "Why don't you come with me?"

He laughed wearily. "Sure," he said. "All right," knowing better than she at that moment the strange winding line between charity and irony, between shoplifting and love.

During that last day she thought of nothing but him. She packed and cleaned out her little apartment, but she had done this so often now in her life, it didn't mean anything, not in the pit of her, not anything she might have wanted it to mean.

She should stay.

She should stay here with him, unorphan him with love's unorphaning, live wise and simple in a world monstrous enough for years of whores and death, and poems of whores and death, so monstrous how could one live in it at all? One had to build shelters. One had to make pockets and live inside them. She should live where there were trees. Should live where there were birds. No bird, no tree had ever made her unhappy.

But it would be like going to heaven and not finding any of your friends there. Her life would go all beatific and empty in the eyes. And if he came to New York, well, it would bewilder him. He had never been before, and no doubt he'd spend all his time staring up at the skyscrapers and exclaiming, "Gosh, look how tall those suckers are!" He would slosh through the vagrant urine, shoelaces untied. He would walk through the dog shit awaiting him like mines. He would read the menus in the windows of restaurants and whistle at the prices. He would stare at a sidewalk drunk, prone and spread-eagled and fumbling at the crotch, and he would say, not unkindly, "That guy's really got his act together." He would look at the women.

And her restlessness would ripple, double, a flavor of something cold. She would turn from him in bed, her hands under the pillow, the digital clock peeling back the old skins of numbers. She would sigh a little for the passage of time, the endless corridor of it, how its walls washed by you on either side—darkly, fast, and ever, ever.

"What do you do, you stay overnight on the road somewhere?" he said, standing next to her car in the cold. It was Friday morning and spitting snow. He had come over and helped her load up the car.

"I drive until dark, then I check into a motel room and read until I fall asleep. Then I get up at six and drive some more."

"So, like, what are you bringing with you to read?" he asked. He seemed unhappy.

She had a *Vogue* magazine and *The Portable Jung*. "Something by Jung," she said.

"Jung?" he asked. His face went blank.

"Yeah," she sighed, not wanting to explain. "A book he wrote called *The Portable Jung*." She added, "He's a psychologist."

Pinky looked her deeply in the eyes. "I know," he said.

"You do?" She was a little surprised.

"Yeah. You should read his autobiography. It has a very interesting title."

She smiled. "Who *are* you? His autobiography? Really?"

"Yeah," said Pinky slowly. "It's called *Jung at Heart*."

She laughed loud, to please him. Then she looked at his face, to fix him like this in her mind. He was wearing a black shirt, a black sweater, black pants. He was smiling. "You look like Zorro today," she said, strangely moved. The spidery veins at his temples seemed like things under water, tentacular and drowned. She kissed him, long and at the rim of his ear, feeling in the rolls and spaces of her brain a winding, winding line. She got into the car. Though she hadn't even started up the engine, her departure had already happened, without her, ahead of her, so that what she now felt was the taunt of being left behind, of having to repeat, to imitate, of having to do it again, and now, and again.

"All this wandering that you do," he said, leaning in the window, his face white as a cream cheese, his scar the carved zigzag of a snowmobile across a winter lake. Wind blew handsomely through his hair. "How will anyone ever get close to you?"

"I don't know," she said. She shook his hand through the window and then put on her gloves.

And she thought about this all across Indiana, beneath the Easter hat of sunset that lit the motel roof in Sandusky, through the dawn of Pennsylvania, into which she soared like a birth—like someone practicing to be born. There were things she'd forget: a nightgown stuck on a hook behind the bathroom door, earrings on the motel nightstand. And all love that had overtaken her would have to be a memory, a truck on the interstate roaring up from the left, a thing she must let pass.

She would park the car right off Delancey Street; there would be a spot across the street from the hotel with the Pepsi sign and HOTEL in lights beneath. All night, sirens would keen, and traffic would whoosh and grind its way down Houston, down Canal, toward the Holland Tunnel—a bent sign that aimed straight at her window. She would get up in the morning and go for sundries; at the corner bodega the clerk would mispress the numbers on the register, and the toothpaste would ring up at $2,000. "Two thousand dollars!" the clerk would howl, standing back and looking at Odette. "Get a *real* toothpaste!" From a long distance, and at night, a man would phone to say, doubtfully, "I should come visit on Valentine's," history of all kinds, incongruous and mangling itself, eating its own lips.

If she had spurned gifts from fate or God or some earnest substitute, she would never feel it in that way. She felt like someone of whom she was fond, an old and future friend of herself, still unspent and up ahead somewhere, like a light that moves.

It's Freezing
Here in
Milwaukee

J. S. Marcus

Sometimes I am in excruciating pain, so excruciating that I can barely walk across the room. I prop my feet up on pillows to keep the pain away. It's very simple, really: The arches—the metatarsal arches of both my feet—are falling, and when I try to walk in any direction, or stand up, the bones of my toes throb, and my eyes begin to water. It's unbearable. My surgeon, the man who is supposed to operate on my falling arches, is in Italy, and I am waiting at my parents' house for him to get back. Every day I read the weather report in the newspaper: "Rome—84 degrees F." or "Rome—91 degrees F." My surgeon is in Rome, and my parents live in Milwaukee.

I don't have to stay in bed all the time. I could go down to the family room and sit on the La-Z-Boy, or into the basement and sprawl out on our old sofa. Sometimes, in the afternoons, I go into my parents' bedroom and lie down on their king-size bed. The bedspread, which is frayed and colorless, smells like the kitchen. It's like lying down on a tablecloth.

The surgeon is supposed to be the best in the country for this kind of surgery, so I gave up my apartment, took a leave of absence from my job, and came home to see him at his suburban clinic. After my second visit, the nurse gave me some cork-and-leather inserts so I could get out of the house and do things.

The cork-and-leather inserts, which are too big and slip underneath the soles of my feet, remind me of portable oxygen tanks. When I was in high school, I had a summer job at a factory on the south side of Milwaukee. The factory made portable oxygen tanks for people with severe respiratory illnesses so they could leave their houses without passing out. The company liked using employees instead of models for their brochures, and I remember one of the vice-presidents coming around every July to choose people. He would take them to the parking lot, fit them each with an oxygen tank, then get the photographer to take pictures of them getting in and out of a company car. Somewhere, in some part of the house, there is a brochure with a picture of me and a caption reading, "It really helps!"

I have spent the last three years of my life working on the metropolitan staff of a newspaper in New York City. Outside, everything seemed to be falling apart, but inside, in the newsroom, everything was getting better and better; new carpeting, new display terminals, record-setting circulation. I was a copy aide for two years, which meant that I clipped other people's articles and answered the telephones. In September of last year, the deputy editor called me in and said, "Danny, we're going to make you election coverage coordinator," which meant that in early October I was supposed to call the telephone company and order the extra telephones.

This last winter, I was promoted to editorial aide and sent to the Westchester bureau. My job there was pretty similar: answering phones and clipping articles. But about twice a month they would let me write a brief for the "Westchester in Brief" column. Right before my arches collapsed, they sent me on my first story: a python had escaped from a veterinarian's office in Tarrytown and gotten itself caught in the engine of a nearby station wagon.

A few weeks after I was sent to Westchester, Sally-Ann arrived. She had been a reporter for a Dallas paper and had just been hired by the metro editor. Sally-Ann lied about everything: her age, her salary, where she went to college. And she used me as a personal slave. "Daniel!" she would scream. "I need that clip ASAP!" The bureau chief, who is twenty-five (a year younger than I am), had been working on an investigative story for ten months: something about cocaine smugglers and a Larchmont pizza parlor. When he discovered a link with a pizza parlor in Amarillo, Sally-Ann said, "Let me work on this story. Get the paper to send me to Texas. I know Amarillo. I covered the Panhandle."

Sally-Ann had to stay in Westchester and was only allowed to cover the municipal courts. One afternoon in the courthouse, she saw Tony Seligman. (Tony Seligman writes for the national desk and has a Pulitzer Prize.) Sally-Ann came back to the bureau and started asking questions. Why was Tony Seligman in Westchester? What had he been doing at the courthouse? Sally-Ann got frantic and called up the national desk. "Hello, Tony?" she said. "This is Sally-Ann Hughes. Remember me? I work up at Westchester bureau? I heard you were doing a story up here at the courthouse, and I thought that if you need any help perhaps we should meet and talk. I know the courthouse. It's a pretty closed place without contacts." Tony Seligman didn't want to have lunch with Sally-Ann, and he wasn't interested in meeting any of her contacts. He was getting married in three days and had gone to the courthouse to buy his marriage license.

On my last day of work, Sally-Ann came up to where I was sitting and handed me a list of forty names. She wanted me to find out the people's phone numbers, and then call and invite them to her birthday party. "Of course," she said, "I would have invited you, but you'll be back in Idaho by then, won't you?" Most of the people on the list had to be reminded of Sally-Ann's last name before they remembered who she was. Tony Seligman and his new wife were on the list, but I couldn't get up the nerve to call them.

When I went downtown to ask if I could have the year off, the metro editor said, "Of course. We can't afford to lose you. The year you were election coverage coordinator, everything went as smooth as silk." A few times since I've been home, my father has bought the national edition of the paper and left it on the dining room table as a surprise. I spend the afternoon going through it as if I had never been inside a newsroom, and never lived in New York.

When I first moved to New York, I tried to get all points of view. I tried and succeeded in befriending the couple who lived across the hall. She had a genetics degree from MIT, a law degree from Harvard, and a medical degree from Yale. Her husband used to joke that the only thing left was divinity school. The first time I saw her, she was pregnant and wearing high heels, and walking down the stairs as I was walking up. After the pains in my feet became worse and I could think of nothing but my own suffering, she gave me a list of five specialists: four in New York, and one in Milwaukee.

Their names were Carol and Ron Platt, and they often introduced me to their friends. One of the friends, a man from India with advanced degrees in mathematics and philosophy, would throw dinner parties in his small apartment and explain things using mathematical metaphors. He would begin: "There isn't a society, there isn't an individual consciousness, that doesn't start out believing it is getting closer to one, and farther from zero. We move, step by step, from the latter and towards the former. But with each step our courage diminishes, and our steps become smaller. You see, we eventually realize—we sane ones—the infinity of numbers between zero and one. We realize that we have never been at zero, and we will never reach one. Our past remains a fiction and our future an impossibility." Then someone would ask him if he had ever been compared to Bertrand Russell, and he would say, "Of course, dear girl."

The summer before I was sent to Westchester, I slept with a woman who lived in the mathematician-philosopher's building— one of those giant fortresses on Second Avenue. It was August, and I was supposed to be on vacation. I couldn't afford to leave New York, and I went to a party with a copy aide. I remember a man of about thirty, slightly overweight, refusing to take off his suit coat. He was surrounded by people who seemed to know him, and who seemed to be chanting, "Take it off! Take it off!" Someone had put bottles of wine underneath the air-conditioner to keep them cold. I took one of the bottles and sat on the floor next to the window. I could see the copy aide looking around the room for me, then I could see him go into the hallway. Standing above me, leaning on the air-conditioner, was a woman in a green T-shirt and a long skirt. She moved closer, and the air-conditioner blew the hem of her skirt against my face. She was looking down at me, keeping her hair up in a bun with one hand, and holding a bottle of beer with the other. She seemed to be swaying back and forth, and I thought she might be drunk. As she came toward me, she let her hair fall down around her shoulders. She put the beer on the floor and ran her fingers across my forehead. "Hot?" she said. She had my head between her hands. "We'll have to make it go faster," she said, and tilted her head toward the air-conditioner. "We'll have to make it go as fast as it can!"

During the cab ride to her apartment, the driver stopped to buy cigarettes. She rolled down the window and started screaming. Then she opened the door and grabbed my hand, pulling me into the street. She kept saying she was a stockbroker and that she had a really bad day in the market. "Really, really bad," she kept saying. "Really bad." As we walked the rest of the way, I decided to ask if she had lost her job, if she had been fired. "Really, really bad day," she said.

Her apartment was on the twenty-third floor, and it wasn't until I looked out the window that I realized the man from India lived a few floors below her. She turned on the air-conditioner and stood in front of it, holding her hair above her head again.

I decided she was either moving in or moving out. There were paintings stacked on the floor, a very large television set next to its box. She must have sensed my confusion because she walked away from the air-conditioner and kicked a pile of paintings. She kissed me on the mouth, and we stood in the hot darkness, taking each other's clothes off, waiting for the room to get cold.

In the middle of the night, I walked around the apartment. There was a basket of unopened mail addressed to Judith Simms—her last name, I assumed, was Simms. In the bathroom, there was a bottle of French shampoo made from walnut leaves, and an unused bar of soap. I was hungry, and went into the kitchen. She had two gallons of olive oil, an empty refrigerator, and empty cupboards.

The next morning, I woke up and she was sitting on the couch, wearing her green T-shirt. She was wearing underwear, but as I got out of bed, she put her hands in her lap. "I don't know what's the matter with me," she said. "I really feel sick. Do you?" I thought about staying and taking a shower with the walnut-leaves shampoo, but she seemed to want me to leave. "I have to get to work," I said, lying.

It was about seven-thirty. I stood in front of the elevator with two men and two women, all in suits. After five minutes, I decided to walk down. The stairs were wide and well lit. I remember speeding down the stairs, flight after flight, talking to myself. I was sure I was the only person not waiting for the elevator. But I had overestimated my endurance, underestimated how long twenty-three flights of stairs are. I got to the point where I was so dizzy and hot that I had to sit down. There was something awful about the situation—spending my vacation surrounded by stairs, running away from some girl who I never wanted to see again. I leaned back against the concrete to catch my breath.

When I first moved to New York, I couldn't wait for anything: I could feel myself crackling inside. But it all changed. It must have changed because I fled New York the first chance that came along.

Here in Milwaukee, everything is beginning to freeze. Yesterday, my father took our cars in to have snow tires put on; the neighbors' yards are starting to look like tundra. I stare outside, and I can't help thinking about my surgeon. In Italy, they are having the hottest November in history. It's over one hundred degrees. People are passing out in the streets. I try to imagine what my surgeon is doing: Has he abandoned Rome and gone to the beach? Has he sacrificed his vacation to treat the heat-stroke victims? Or perhaps, like the Romans I saw on the evening news, he has given up and lain down in a fountain.

While I wait for him, I often lie in bed with my feet on the headboard. I follow the ceiling as it slopes down to the windows, then I look out to the backyard. When I was a child, we had a pear tree and an apple tree growing next to each other. In late summer, the ground would be covered with pale, green things; you could never tell whether they were apples or pears. From far away—from my bedroom window, for instance—they all looked round and indisputably apples. From closer up—the back porch or the driveway—they would become yellow and irregular, like hourglasses. Not until you got on your hands and knees, or picked them up, not until after that—could you possibly know for sure.

My parents cut down the apple tree so they could install central air-conditioning, and the pear tree has stopped bearing fruit. Its leaves are all gray and brittle.

In a way, nothing turns out to be what you think it is. Sometimes the yard looks empty—it doesn't even look familiar. But if I rushed outside, I could feel those pear leaves, like wet sticks between my toes, and know exactly where I was. And I could look up to my bedroom window, just able to make out a corner of the room, the place I'm looking at right now.

Several years ago, on the night of the first snow, our neighbor was apprehended for indecent exposure—a young mother, with a baby just a few weeks old. Someone caught her in the park across the road nursing a homeless man with no teeth. The rumor that went around was that someone jogging in the park had come across them on one of the benches. It was dusk, the streetlamps had just come on, and in the glow of the new snow falling, there it was: a patch of skin or maybe her nipple, I'm not sure which.

My husband Al, out with the dog, came in and said, "You're not going to believe this." He hung his hat in the hall, untethered the dog, the smell of wet wool filling the room. "Dr. Crawford's wife," he said, breathlessly, easing his dark feet out of boots, "caught feeding a homeless man by the swing sets."

I was stumped for a second, my hips pressed to the stove where I was making soup stock. It was no secret that a few of us in the neighborhood made occasional food drops in the park—not to temporary vagrants, but to two old women who pushed grocery carts through the park in the summers, one of them in bedroom slippers. They camped on benches for a few days at a time, then disappeared, always together. Docile, child-like, made up like brides, their eyes rarely left the elms where birds built their spring nests.

"Breastfeeding," Al clarified when he saw I didn't comprehend. He rose up on the balls of his feet, wide-eyed, snowflakes suspended in the fine gray hairs around his ears. He was wiry and excitable. I could almost see the blood pulsing in his temples.

"Isn't her name Sharon?" I asked dryly, tying some parsley together with kitchen twine. "Or is it Shelly?"

Al gave a little snort and left the room. I heard him open the drawer where he keeps his pipe, then came the sound of the TV news. In the pot on the stove, I watched the chicken carcass from the night before bob below the surface, its limp bones flapping like a tired swimmer.

That same year my father began leaving his house in the middle of the night across town. Calls at 2 a.m. The police found my father in the middle of a field, barefoot, wearing nothing but tattered pajama bottoms, the bare skin of his chest smudged with dust. Another time, we found him walking down the middle of the highway with his Bible, dressed in a suit, wearing only one shoe.

Back in his kitchen, my father let me fix him toast fried in bacon grease. He nibbled the edges, holding onto it with both hands, looking from me to Al and from Al to me, eager as a squirrel. Then for days, he ate nothing.

I'd stop by daily with Styrofoam dinner trays full of his favorite things—catfish, slaw, pudding—and find the trays out on his stoop, full of teeth marks from raccoons.

Of course I knew her name was Sharon. For a year, I watched her. And even before that, I dreamed her face—her jaw, narrow as a bedroom sandal, and those great big unfocused eyes, like decade-old fruit in a murky jar.

She appeared one night, stepping out of Dr. Crawford's great black car, a blonde ghost carrying armloads of angel-thin belongings. As the lights went on in the upper rooms of Dr. Crawford's great Colonial house next door, I could see her moving behind the blinds, a shadow that paced long into the night. I knew why she was there.

Before her, Dr. Crawford had been married to our good friend Kay. Twenty-one years, two kids in college. Now Kay lived in a duplex with her mother in Rockford, where she called from time to time, a faint voice, to talk about the rain clouds, to ask finally, "What's she look like? What's she doing now?"

With Kay on the other end of the line, I'd draw back the curtains and watch the girl sunbathe. It was summer. In her bikini, she didn't look more than seventeen. No one but me could have guessed she was pregnant, except that she slept all day on the lawn and got up a few times to vomit in the bushes.

To Kay I'd say, "I don't see her. She's never around."

In the fall, sometimes I came home on my lunch break. From the kitchen window, I would watch her roam the living room, large as my own aching. Or sometimes floating all through the house, one hand trailing along the walls.

Sometimes, she would almost see me. She'd hang by the window, her eyes hungry, her head cocked. Inside that house, I knew what it smelled like—like smoke, like cat piss. I put on my coat but couldn't sort the injured from injury, not enough to cross the grass, not enough to offer a hand, a hello, a sandwich.

She licked paint chips from around the sill. She dipped spoons into dark jars going bad in the fridge. Once I saw a razor glint whisked from a sleeve. But she lived. At a distance, I followed her on foot when she walked downtown to mail letters, crossing Church Street, cutting through the cemetery. All the way, I tried to imagine what those letters might say. I knew what I'd say: *This town is all ghosts.*

My father liked to come over and work on our house when she was around—clean our gutters, check the flashing on the roof. Once, he gave her a ride to the post office. He said she didn't even know how to drive and that her voice, low and whispery, was like a gas leak.

From one day to the next, your life can disappear before you. I've seen it happen, the night Kay drove away to live with her mother, the day Velma came home and found her husband collapsed by the radiator, the morning Jack Trotter up the street found his son hanging from the beams in the shed. One minute, the world is a perfectly ordinary place, and the next minute, you're hanging from a spider web, clinging for dear life to your own spit.

The day my father had a stroke was like that. I went to the hospital and put my arms around a pale ghost. He blinked, lips trembling with the effort of speech. Hooked up to an I.V., he was already more plant than person. I said to the nurse, *I want to feed him. I want to feed him something myself.*

She looked at me and frowned. Outside, I smoked for the first time in a decade under the hospital eaves and dreamed of a life in my arms. It made me dizzy to open up that part of me, to allow hunger a shape of its own. I wanted to nestle down with it, to rest exhausted against its dark form. At that moment, I might have done anything—walked into the traffic, lit my hair on fire, wept—but Al appeared, the day still heavy on his clothes, his eyebrows furrowed and knowing.

All it takes is one person to save you from the hollows.

She was on bed-rest all that fall. Near dark, Dr. Crawford drove up on his Honda Goldwing, singing to himself. Before dawn, he left again, a quiet purr toward the highway. No one else ever entered to visit Dr. Crawford's new wife, no sister, no mother. No one but Dr. Crawford with an occasional bag of groceries.

Once, I saw her descend the front staircase, crack an egg into her mouth, and disappear upstairs again. Sometimes the windows were dark for days, a mysterious cat with white eyes lurking around the hedgery.

I said to Al once, *How do you think she stands it in there?*

He said, *She's waiting for the next intervention of fate.*

In my mind, I dared her to rise from that coffin and sing. I know what loneliness is. That's how this neighborhood is, each house a box of quiet roaring. People divorce and die, children grow up and leave home, but there's always that one person who gets left behind. It would be impossible to keep a secret here, and yet it's the easiest thing in the world to be alone and to go deeper into that loneliness, to die inside it while the body appears, day after day, to go on living.

The women with their shopping carts know this. Each spring, I hear the wheels clattering across the ravine, and their shapes form out of the trees, staggering like lost elk. They bend with plastic bags that sway from their elbows, and cross the brittle field on legs neatly taped with gauze to keep their ankles from swelling. Somewhere, someone has given them a bath. Somewhere they have a home, family. Still, they come and go like ice. No voice except for the rattle of wheels, the whispery sound of their slips rustling under housecoats.

On the day of the birth, the shopping cart women randomly reappeared, one of them with a gash across her cheek, the other limping slowly behind, wearing a little pink knit cap with earflaps. My neighbor Velma called at work to tell me. By the time I got home, all I could hear were the shopping carts rattling in the distance, and somewhere—in the cold air beyond the trees—a baby howling.

It was days before she came home from the hospital. During that time, my father was back on his feet. He called three times a day to describe the things he was eating, to assure me he had just stepped from the shower without falling, to admire the red cast of the sky before dusk.

We drove by and caught my father eating uncooked rice on the roof of his house one Sunday evening. I was bringing him some clean sheets, walking up the gravel drive in my clogs through the mud, when I saw him up above, from the back, his head bobbing strangely.

After Al helped him down, we found the front pockets of his overalls full of Uncle Ben's, the pockets of his windbreaker too. He was sick to his stomach for days and wouldn't do anything but cuss at the birds and maybe eat a few prunes. Al asked him if he was finally out of his mind. My father just shook his head and said he felt brand new, brand goddamn new.

For days though, he walked around dazed, looking for something to touch up, feeling along the walls for cracks. He'd come over to our house when Al was at work and ask for a spade, then work at turning over all the dirt in our garden though the earth was still frozen.

One day, I fed my father lunch, and he turned to me out of the blue and asked, "Why aren't you pregnant yet?" I stood dumbfounded at the stove while he ran a handkerchief over his mouth.

"Dad," I said, "I'm fifty-two." In the next house, I saw Sharon pass between the upstairs curtains in a dark bra. I hadn't even seen her come home. She looked like black branches.

After she left, I hungered for her. And whatever I ate made me hungrier. I haunted the grocery for peaches, plums, and brought home only waxy apples, oranges with dried out sections like dead sea-life. Still, I ate them, thinking of her on the park bench, thinking of her nipple in the mouth of the homeless man, the streetlamp a dim glow around them and the snowflakes melting against their warm skin.

Just thinking of it warmed me all that winter, like a hot stone at the base of my stomach. I nursed that story, letting it grow inside me until I could see between the hairs of the homeless man's beard where the lint of her sweater hid. I could feel the cold bench slats under her body and hear the sound of snow falling on snow, like the first welcome silence.

When I made soup from chicken stock, I imagined her milk. It was an earthy taste, like the forest floor itself, like places in the ravine where I had never set foot. I woke up, knowing just where to find mushrooms, just where a nest had fallen, and when I went out with my flashlight to put the nest back into the tree, there were long strands of blonde hair wound around the twigs.

If anyone in the neighborhood noticed I behaved strangely, no one said anything. We spoke with our eyes. For years, we had watched the same things. I saw Velma and her eyes told me she had seen it, too, the way Dr. Crawford had backed his car out of the drive, loaded with the girl and her things. We had all watched. We saw her cross the snow in her parka, the baby closed tightly against her stomach. We watched her climb into the backseat. We waved quietly from behind curtains, not knowing where she would go—back into the pocket where Dr. Crawford found her: behind a bar or at a restaurant or across the state line where he still sometimes made house calls.

Of course I dreamed of her still. For weeks, her face surfaced before me in the dark, her eyes floating just off shore, her arms aching, the baby nowhere to be seen. I'd wake up at the kitchen table in my nightgown, crumbs around me from things I ate in my sleep, strange things: tulip bulbs, tea leaves, fresh earth, raw hamburger.

Then I heard her coming—there I was at the shopping mall in Rockford, looking for a birthday dress—I heard her coming through the racks of empty dresses before I even saw her. She was alone, and just as thin or thinner than before. A great bracelet of wooden beads looped around her wrist rattled like teeth.

I let her show me to a dressing room. Her great floating eyes stared blankly at me, her thin face framed by that same ice-blonde hair I'd watched so many days from far away. She said nothing, her body like a cold shard—not warm, not warm the way I had wanted her to be.

When she pulled the curtain on my little room, I stood there, looking at the pink dress I had chosen. But I couldn't move. She had frozen me there. I heard her beads coming and felt her cold breeze pass. "Sharon," I said through the curtain.

It was the first time I had called her name. The curtain looked like it was made from a Mexican blanket, coarsely woven and frayed around the edges. I could feel her icy stance on the other side; I could feel the air in the dressing room harden.

I reached my hand through the curtain, so that I was almost touching her through it. The chill to the air was suddenly gone. There was no sound of her wooden beads rattling from beyond. She was simply gone, out of the store, out of the air it seemed, as if she had never been real to anyone but me.

Still, in that one instant, in that one touch, I felt I had told her my whole story, as if I had pinned a piece of string to her shoulder, so that when she flew off I kept unraveling. I drove home with the pink dress on the backseat, and felt my whole body loosen and stir, bits flapping like the straw under a scarecrow's shirt.

I drove across town to my father's house, where he was lying on his bed staring out the window, quizzically, as if he could see things moving across the empty fields. Maybe he could feel the unfurling. His head didn't move when I set my bags on his table.

I changed into the pink dress in his kitchen, almost naked, right there before his stove, something I never would have done, even with his back to me. And before I buttoned up the front, I said, *Dad, turn around and look at me.*

When he didn't move, I said, *I want to show you the scar.*

Slowly, he rolled over, with great difficulty. His eyes were clear and blue and distant. When he saw me, his jaw trembled.

I pointed to my stomach, the great red riverbed that runs across it. *This,* I said, *is where they took out my uterus.*

My father just looked at me, as if under a spell. I could tell it was one of his days when things didn't quite come together. I crossed the room and sat down by him and saw there was rice in the creases of his blankets.

Dad, I said, *You're going to puff up like a little bird. Why don't you eat when I try to feed you?*

He shivered though the room was not cold. I helped him get under his blankets and folded his sheet down over his chest the way he likes. I brushed his white hair away from his temples, and for a moment, it was all too clear, how within the year, I would look down on him like this again, his eyes closed, his body breathless.

I rested next to him, my dress still half open, and pressed my scar against his side. He stared wide-eyed at the ceiling, where a thin thread of spider web hung between the eaves, the world's thinnest streamer.

Slowly, the light fell across the blankets, leaving the sky, erasing the ceiling, until even my father's face had disappeared. For the first time my scar ached a little, like the pocket it was with its deep folds shifting.

When the trees started to rustle outside, my father began to grind his teeth. I wondered what he was dreaming, who he saw on the other side, if he ever went back to my mother, met her halfway, the way I believe some people do—living half in this world, half beyond the shadow. The question for me has always been, where? Where do those curtains part? If you feel along the walls long enough, can you find it?

My father trembled in his sleep; his face flinched. He let out a little squeal. Without thinking, I reached up and put two fingers to his lips to quiet him.

Later, when I left, I could feel something following me, not a person but a presence, something I couldn't name. Halfway to the car, I stopped in my father's drive, determined to turn around, to run back in and check on him. But I didn't. I could feel a cold wind, then a hot wind sweep past my ankles. It was enough to be let in, however much, however briefly, on the secret—a patch of snow, a patch of skin. In that moment, all of me melted from within.

After she left, Dr. Crawford took off on a long trip, or maybe took an apartment somewhere closer to the hospital. He came back to put in his storm windows and left on his Goldwing with just a few things stuffed in his saddle bags. His face in the headlights looked fat and froglike. I thought about Kay, whom I hadn't heard from in weeks, and wondered if she knew. Of course she knew, as people in all small towns do, that the doctor's second wife had been caught with her shirt open, letting a homeless man suckle.

I knew just how Kay would laugh, with her head back, the roots of her dark hair exposed, her fillings gleaming. *Doesn't that just beat all?* She'd say, *That's what I call natural justice.*

It was all I could do not to break into Dr. Crawford's house, to look into the fridge for those dark jars along the door, to check for twigs in the trash, to touch the pillow in the bed where she slept all those months. How quickly she was there, how quickly gone, like a fire. All around, I sensed the burn. I felt her unearthly grace. And like a forest that has been charred and then slowly takes seed, I saw how the neighbors came out of themselves that spring.

With Dr. Crawford gone, we crossed his lawn with pans of brownies, sang across the fence with a handful of not-too-wormy apples, pulled back our curtains to let the light in and the dust motes settle. I broke out my good tablecloth one night and had the widow Velma over for a glass of elderberry wine, and when Sue from across the street saw the candles glowing, she came over with a tin of shortbread, and we sat around in the kitchen with the dog sleeping at our feet until the sun climbed to the base of the trees. Then we all retreated, deeply satisfied, to our own beds and dreamt of the shopping cart women and of the rabbits layering their warrens with the fur of their stomachs.

Unknown
Donor

Judith Claire Mitchell

Here lies Lois Mello spread on an examining table, shivering in a backless johnny, wishing she'd kept her socks on. This wing of the clinic is cold; if the nurse was still here Lois would ask her to adjust the thermostat. Though no doubt the nurse would laugh at that request. No doubt the nurse would list all the bona fide medical reasons for keeping the heat so low. Maybe in warmer temperatures, the eggs go runny. Frozen sperm melts. An image comes to Lois. The dark bay near the shabby triple-decker in Fall River where she grew up. Spring thaw. Slush. Minnows.

If only Unknown Donor were here, she thinks. He would warm her feet in the palms of his large and generous hands.

"Hop up, lie back," the nurse had said. "Butt, slide on down." This had been nearly thirty minutes ago. Even then the doctor had been running late. The nurse glanced at the wall clock, shook her head. "So now all we need is that boss of mine to show up and do his stuff," she said. "Not that he's got that much stuff to do. I'm sure he's told you the whole shebang takes maybe a minute or two."

"Yes," said Lois.

"It's completely slam bam thank you Ma'am, just like in real life." The nurse looked again at the clock. "Let me go track him down."

"Thank you," said Lois.

She spent the next few minutes checking out her surroundings. Stirrups and speculums, gizmos and gadgets, silver and steel. After that her attention moved to the ceiling, and that's where it's largely remained. There's a poster up there. A border of primroses and robins, a numbered list in the middle. Ornate script. The Fifty Best Things About Life. *Number twenty-three: a playful puppy. Number one: love.* It's that sort of poster. *Number thirty-eight: chocolate ice cream. Number thirty-seven: chocolate ice cream with sprinkles and whipped cream.* If one of Lois's students ever handed in something so sappy, so sentimental, she would draw mean-spirited hearts and violins all along the margins.

And what, she would like to know, is someone in her situation supposed to make of number ten? Number ten, looking down at her, innocent as can be, sandwiched between *number eleven: moonlight* and *number nine: autumn leaves,* is the smell of new babies.

Insensitive, is what Lois makes of it. Insensitive at best, cruel at worst. And yet it's a risk, isn't it, for the clinic to display a poster that includes number ten? Number ten is the only item on the list likely to trigger true emotions in this place. Taking risks. Daring to evoke genuine feelings. Surely those things are worth something, Lois thinks. Surely those are worth a few extra points.

And surely the poster isn't meant to be cruel. Was the list-maker supposed to leave out number ten just to avoid making people feel bad? Either the smell of babies makes life's top ten or it doesn't— that's reality. Which, she notices, doesn't appear on the list at all. She agrees with the omission, most everyone would. But not absolutely everyone, she knows that for a fact. Because wouldn't reality be on Daniel's list? Wouldn't it be number one on her ex-husband's list, number one with a bullet?

Daniel is a corporate litigator, a partner at a law firm in downtown Providence, a logical and fastidious man nearing fifty; that is, a man nearly fifteen years her senior, who eats every meal with a silk tie slung back over one shoulder but who never forgets to right it as soon as he's finished his espresso. Manuel Daniel Santos, Esquire. Face the facts is one of his favorite sayings. He began shaving his head the morning he noticed his hairline receding.

Face the facts. Sometimes he came out with variations. Get real, Lois. Or, Wake up, Lois. Or this, which he claimed a Black Panther said in the sixties when Daniel had been in law school and she'd been five: *reality, baby—you takes it and you deals with it.*

"Even blocked fallopian tubes?" Lois had asked Daniel. They were still married then. "I have to even takes blocked fallopian tubes and deals with that?"

"Especially blocked fallopian tubes."

"But I don't get it. Why don't you think this is a viable way to deals with it? What's going on with you? You all of a sudden don't believe in medical science?"

"I believe in playing the hand you're dealt," he said. "I believe in facing the facts."

And so she knows the calligraphied slop above her head wasn't compiled by Daniel. Nor, truth be told, would any of her students have written such tripe; she doesn't seriously have to worry about that. *Number forty: fresh laundry. Number sixteen: shooting stars.* If she ever asked her kids to write about the best things life offers, not one of them would come up with shooting stars or laundry. *Reefer,* they'd write. *Blow jobs. New clothes.* Once she assigned them to write a composition called "My Ideal Day." They pretty much all wrote about getting laid or driving to the mall.

She can imagine who did write this list. A marketing firm. A marketing firm's computer. What's harder to imagine is the actual hanging of the poster, the event itself. Which clinic employee actually entered this chilly room holding a ladder, thumbtacks in her pocket, and mounted the thing to the ceiling? She can't imagine this sort of poster appealing to the staff here. That nurse before, her comment about slam bam thank you Ma'am. That was more in tune with the culture of the place.

It's a staid-looking medical building. Blond brick on the outside, nubby mauve upholstery within, and in the parking lot, near the entrance, a group of protesters parading like a tiny merry-go-round, prim fillies in bulky white cardigans and comfortable flats. Ex-nuns, she'd been told by the receptionist who added, "It's all I can do to stop myself from ramming them with my car every morning. Why can't they go harass a frigging abortion clinic like everyone else?"

And yet despite the architect's attempt at a veneer of respectability, despite the circling reminder of the serious procedures that take place here, the nurses are always cracking wise. The time there was that expose all over the news—a doctor in California implanting the eggs of one patient into the womb of another—a nurse here had referred to it as the case of the poached eggs. Lois had winced and the nurse had grinned, pleased with herself. "Just a little egg humor, dear," she had said. "We like to keep our sunny sides up around this joint."

And once, when Lois asked where the sperm donor unit was, the receptionist had nearly leered. "Why? You want to look at the dirty magazines?" she said.

"I'm serious," Lois said after a moment. "I would like to see it."

"Well, you can't," said the receptionist. "There's nothing to see anyway. It's closed now."

Maybe they didn't let the boys in on the same days the girls were there. Maybe they were worried about what all would go on. Men and women getting together, eliminating the middle man.

"Anyway," the receptionist added, "you read the contract. 'Recipient shall not seek any information pertaining to nor in any way attempt to identify any anonymous donor of semen.'"

"I don't want to ferret him out," Lois said. "I'm just trying to get the feel of the place."

And what if she did want to meet him, this stranger who for reasons Lois would never learn had decided to ride to her rescue? This masked man whose identity never would be revealed? Unknown Donor who fights the crimes of oblivious nature. Unknown Donor who, disguised as an accountant, a sales clerk, a mild-mannered medical student, maybe even a doctor or lawyer, masturbates, then moves on. Comes and then goes. Her hero, her secret lover. Her imaginary friend.

"All you'd see there is what you see here," the receptionist said. "A waiting room."

The receptionist is a busty woman with pink and blonde hair and fake brown fingernails. How has Dr. Finney come to hire someone so frowsy to greet his clients? He himself is such a sweet man, short and pudgy, appropriately ovoid. Something comforting in that, in how round-faced and utterly, but naturally, bald he is. No morning stubble on that egg head of his.

And gentle, so gentle. Whenever he's touched her, whether with one of his gadgets or one of his fingers, he's never hurt her. Her former physician used to roll his eyes if she dared cry out. "Oh, for pity's sake," he'd say. "That didn't hurt." But Dr. Finney is tender.

Charmingly disheveled, too, in his baggy khakis, scuffed loafers. Never a tie. Sometimes, an old tweed jacket. "Dress-up day," Lois says to him when he wears the tweed. Shortly after she began coming here she had a dream about that jacket. In her dream she was so small she fit in its breast pocket. She crawled in alongside a fountain pen, stood on her toes, peeked out at the world. It was nice in there though she had to cover her ears with her little hands; his heartbeat was deafening.

Lois teaches Pre-Remedial Freshman Comp at a community college just two exits south of the clinic. "Don't get excited," she told her aunts when she was first offered the job, when they did get excited and called her Professor. Her aunts were delighted that one of their own had not only graduated from a real college, but now taught at one, too. Like her parents, her aunts were immigrants from Cape Verde, that Portuguese colony off the African coast. They were women whose own mothers—grandmothers, too—had married Europeans, and their skin was the color of overdone pie crusts. Her own skin was even lighter than theirs. "It's not a real college," she had to tell them. "It's a junior college. It's a bad junior college. It's where kids too dumb to get into the worst of the four-years go."

"You mean a school for greenhorns," her Aunt Filomena said.

"Mostly," said Lois, "though there are plenty of descendants of moronic Pilgrims, too."

Some of her aunts had persisted in remaining excited on her behalf. "Does it have ivy all over it the way they do?" her Aunt Maria asked. Then Lois had to explain that not only was it a college for dumb kids, it was grim and depressing as well. The entire campus consisted of a single poured-concrete building surrounded on all sides by parking lots. The building was as huge as it was homely, everything and everyone stuffed into it, the empty swimming pool, the nearly empty library, the surly administrators and underpaid faculty walking the halls with their heads lowered, muttering about pearls and swine. And the cafeteria and the bookstore and student health services and several bowling alleys and a video arcade with surveillance cameras to discourage the students from breaking into the change machine.

And the students, of course, the swine themselves, so many of them her own students, her eighteen-year-olds with their piercings and tattoos and dreams of making fortunes writing about vampires and spies. The piercings didn't distress her. She liked a glint at the nostril, a flash on the tongue. But, oh, those dreams and tattoos. Hard to say which of those got to her more. The tattoos, she supposed, since they'd last forever. They were such awful tattoos, so unpleasant in both appearance and sentiment. Bargain-basement

186

tattoos if there were such things, always the same shade of blackening green, the color of long-rotted vegetables.

Early in the current semester one of her boys had come to class with the word assassin misspelled across his biceps. *Assasin,* his tattoo said. "Look at this," he said to her. She was glad someone else had already pointed out the error. She was forever correcting them, their essays and the handwritten notes they left in her mailbox, lined paper torn from spiral notebooks, her name nearly always spelled Mellow. Professor Mellow, I will not be in class due to the fact there's this fucking rad group I gotta go see play in Boston. Hope you understand. Professor Mellow, this is to inform you I am going off Ritalin and my doctor says it might make me disruptive in class. Hope you understand.

The boy flexed so she could better see his tainted muscle. "I trusted the asshole," he said. "He looked like he knew what he was doing and first it looked right but then this other guy there, he's all like, hey, man, that's like 'ass, a sin,' and I'm all like shit! And now I feel like I been fucking raped, you know what I'm saying? You think I can sue?"

"Probably," she said. She wanted to reach into her handbag, find a moist towelette, rub at his forearm. You weren't supposed to touch them, though. She said, "Now do you see why I take off for spelling?" He nodded miserably. "Here," she said, and then she did reach into her handbag, scrummed around till she found one of Daniel's cards. Why not? Daniel had paid her grad school tuition. He had continued to mail her checks even after the divorce; he sent them even now. Why not give him a referral, pay him back as best she could?

Daniel had been the first person she called when the junior college hired her. Daniel, first. Only then the aunts who had raised her.

"Ah," he had said. "So. Freshman comp."

"Well, not really." She'd been sitting on a yellow chair in the former supply closet that is still her office, her feet on her small metal desk. The desk was so empty and flimsy it hummed under the scant pressure of her shoes. "You know how there's freshman comp? And then there's the course for kids too dumb to handle that? Well, I'm teaching the course for kids too dumb for that one. English as a second language for native speakers."

"Oh," he said and she waited, certain he would tell her to get real, face the facts, she did not want to take such a menial position. "Well, still," he said finally. "Still, all in all, it's pretty good news. It's a good first step and there are health benefits and it will be something to put on a résumé. And God knows it's better than working in Bed and Bath."

"Hey!" she said. She didn't like him disparaging Bed and Bath. It was where they'd first met, the linen department of Filene's. He had come in a little before closing. She had noticed him immediately, the skin olive-brown just like hers, the expensive suit, and in his earlobe, the tiniest of gold studs. "M. Daniel Santos," he had said, extending his hand. He had charged a set of Ralph Lauren towels in hunter green, fringed fingercloths to bath sheets. Hundreds of dollars. She worked on commission.

Now the earring was gone. The hole in the lobe had repaired itself, sealed. He was remarried to a young associate in his law firm, named Ferguson Miller.

Lois had met Ferguson at a law firm barbecue shortly after she'd gone back to school for her masters. She'd watched Ferguson bring Daniel a drink, stirring it, as she walked to him, with her pinky. "Do people call you Fergie?" Lois had asked.

"Not twice," Ferguson replied. She didn't smile. Lois smiled broadly, feverishly. *Number twenty-three: a playful puppy.*

"And what did you do before you came here?" she asked.

Ferguson looked over Lois's shoulder. "I used to clerk for Justice Bouchard in the Second District."

"What a coincidence," Lois said. "I used to clerk for Filene's in the North Dartmouth Mall."

Ferguson didn't smile. Lois hurt from smiling. "I know," Ferguson said. "Danny's mentioned." She had long blonde hair, curls everywhere like those party favors, the ones that explode from cans. She wore very dark sunglasses and a Lily Pulitzer sundress, expensive if not quite appropriate to the occasion, tight, with a tropical fruit pattern. There was a sliced mango on her right breast. "Excuse me, Lois," she said, and went to join a group of lawyers.

On nights Daniel said he was working, Lois sat up and pictured him in bed with Ferguson. She imagined them in a suite at the Providence Biltmore, laughing at her. Foreplay, acrobatic screwing, all followed by postcoital laughing at Lois, a full and merry evening, and she hated the part where they laughed at her even more than she hated the part where they tenderly kissed.

And yet she does the same thing, doesn't she? She laughs at people. The young man with *ass, a sin* on his arm. She feels sorry for him, true, but equally true, she's repeated the story to everyone. Face the facts, she has lectured herself, it's not a kind thing to do. Although she forgives herself for it. She's only human, and they are so damned ignorant, the young men and women who sit in her classroom. Has Dickens written anything a little more up-to-date? they have asked her. Their favorite playwright? Tennessee Ernie Ford. Stunning, stunning, and she finds it unnerving that there is no statute precluding the entire student body of her little school from voting in national or statewide, even in local, elections. And so, doesn't she have the right, just like any other terrified human being, to belittle what scares her?

She has shown their essays to some of the men she's dated since her divorce. A quick way of sharing her life, herself. The how-to's are her favorites. Usually she just reads the titles—*How to Find A+ Reports on the Net, How to Steal Stuff from the University Bookstore, How to Make a Really Fine Bong*—but there was one man she'd gone out with six times, a post-Daniel record, and before she lost interest and lied, telling him she'd reconciled with her ex, she read him the entire first paragraph of *How to Make a Girl Come with Your Fingers*. He was a successful accountant, this man, and he drove a navy blue Jaguar with gold license plate frames and yet when you looked at him you could still tell what he'd looked like when he'd been a boy, and so she'd been hopeful and they'd begun sleeping together on the third date. "As is the law," she told Daniel over the phone.

"Stroke her," she read. "Remember the clit. Open her up. Don't forget your thumbs."

"That's sickening," the man said. "I can't believe kids actually have the balls to turn in that kind of puke. What do you do when you get a piece of smut like that?"

"I correct the spelling," she said.

Other than the spelling, the paper had been fine. She had asked the class to be as precise and specific as possible, and this boy had fulfilled that part of the assignment perfectly. She could have taken that essay to bed with her, followed the directions step by step, fallen asleep content and purring—and if she'd refrained from doing just that it was only because the paper conjured up the image of its author, a scrawny kid, a child really, with a face like a Boston terrier, big bulging eyeballs, an expression full of worry and urgent needs.

She had intended to read the entire essay to the man she was dating, but his reaction to the first paragraph had so discouraged her she'd put it away. And yet it was the second paragraph she really admired and would have liked to have shared with someone. "After she goes home be sure not to call her. Even if you want to. Make her worry and suffer and think about you. Tell your friends everything you got off her. This is because of the time you fell in love like the dumb shit-for-brains fuck-lug you are and what it felt like and now you are out for blood." She'd held her red pen over that paragraph for a long time. What to write? This is an inappropriate subject for a how-to? This is sad? Watch out for fragments/run-ons? See me?

There are always the same five ex-nuns protesting outside the clinic. Lois is a lapsed Catholic herself. They must have a lot in common, she and the nuns. The day one decides to walk away from that which one used to hold dear. The day of cold wind and black ice and you slip and fall on your ass and suddenly realize nobody cares. You takes it, you deals with it, you struggles to your feet. You brush yourself off, count your own fingers and toes, see that, except for your faith, you are whole.

The nuns tell Lois they do care about her. Each day when she shows up at the clinic they shriek their care in her face as they rush at her, encircle her, order her home.

"Why don't you adopt?" they say. Or, "New life is the exclusive purview of the Lord."

"Yes," Lois once summoned the nerve to respond, "which would make this place holy."

She was as shocked as the nuns at the sound of her voice. She felt she'd been rude and she lowered her head and scurried to the clinic's entrance where she threw herself into a wedge of revolving door that, sensing her presence, began to spin on its own much too fast until it threw her into the lobby flustered and graceless. Her legs shook and she had to sit for a while on the bench by the pay phone that she suddenly found herself longing to use.

Unknown Donor, oh, Unknown Donor. Come for me, comfort me. Tell me your name.

That was the first and only time she talked back to the nuns. Since then she's just navigated through them, barely listening, constantly nodding. "We're praying for you," they shout at her and sometimes they hold hands, forming a five-person chain, an embarrassingly silly effort to prevent her from going inside. "Thank you," she says then, and walks around them.

They are annoying and presumptuous, but at least they're reliable. And in some ways they're more equipped to deal with the world than Lois. They bring oranges with them, offer her sections which, though she's always hungry, she always turns down, fearing they're poisoned. And they always have those cardigans with them, even on the sunniest days. If only Lois had thought today to bring a sweater.

She has long ago kicked off her useless paper slippers. Now she is rubbing her feet together trying to make sparks. She tries to summon a hot flash. Suddenly, she realizes, she's longing for the bout of faux menopause brought on by the Lupron. She shakes her head. "I'm going crazy," she says to the ceiling. She has to be crazy to want to relive for even a moment that brief foray into sweats and soaked sheets, those thudding stomach aches, the nausea and pounding cramps the hormones had triggered.

This is how the procedure worked: Every day for three weeks she came to the clinic for her hormone shots. That is, every day for three weeks she left school, skipped lunch, and braved the nuns so a wisecracking nurse could lead her to a small examining room where Lois would lift her blouse, pull her slacks to her knees, bare her belly, bite her lip, and take it stoically in the stomach just as if she'd been bit by a mad, foaming dog and now needed rabies shots.

In the fourth week she received the injection of Pergonal and Metrodin. The cocktail, the nurses called it as if it were happy hour and they were barmaids. That shot went into the hip; she'd limped for days after. Then last ("but not least," said Dr. Finney with a bashful smile), there was the single shot of human chorionic gonadotropin. Thirty-six hours later they harvested her eggs.

She has called Daniel throughout the ordeal, has kept him apprised of her progress. He is, after all, paying. Her benefits at school turned out to be negligible and he seems to feel guilty about her situation, about her being alone, unprotected. The checks he sends aren't her only clue. At first she was the one calling him, Lois missing Daniel, her new apartment so quiet, the shadows at night so unsettling, but now he picks up the phone just as often, maybe more. "Did you want something special?" she'll ask after they've chatted a while. "Not really," he says. "Just checking in. Just making sure no one's libeled you recently or tripped on your welcome mat. I'm still your lawyer, you know."

Face the facts, she has ordered herself whenever she finds herself wondering if it could possibly be love or desire or searing regret making him dial her number. It's only guilt. Guilt compounded by his jaundiced view of the procedure. From the moment she told him she was going ahead with it, he hated the idea though he had to concede it was no longer any of his business. But he hated it anyway, was convinced something bad and actionable would occur. Dr. Finney would make a terrible mistake and someone else's eggs would be forced into her womb, outraged hatchlings beating on the inside of her rubbery belly, screaming to be let out, demanding their real mother. Or an ex-nun would plant a bomb in her car while she was off getting a shot in the belly. Lois comes out, jumps in the Toyota, fastens the seatbelt, turns the key and, boom, there lies Lois dead and scattered. And here comes Daniel, all motions and writs, suing the clinic on behalf of her estate. It would be a high profile case, good for his career. And hence, the increase in his phone calls.

"Human chorionic gonadotropin," he had repeated when she described that last shot to him. "I dare you to say it three times fast."

"Gonadotropin, gonadotropin, gonadotropin," she said, and that made her think of a recent essay in which a student proposed the school teams be renamed The Nads. "Then the cheerleader bitches would have to shout, Go Nads! in front of the whole fucking school!" the boy had typed in all caps.

"Brother," Daniel said. "I remember coming up with that same imbecilic pun when I was, I don't know, maybe ten. How old are these kids?"

Lois remembered her friends coming up with that same childish joke, too. Middle school in their case, all her friends greenhorns like herself, dark-eyed, light-skinned children of Cape Verdean and Portuguese immigrants. Their mothers were maids or factory workers or, like Lois's mother, worked in the school cafeteria. Hair nets, plastic gloves. Her mother ladled sloppy-joe mix onto a Wonder bun, squirted whipped cream on Jell-O. It hadn't seemed like the most strenuous job in the world to twelve-year-old Lois, but her mother came home weary, too exhausted to talk. "So tired," she'd say and head directly to bed. "Bone tired," she'd say, and then one day she went to sleep and died, and though Lois was not the only girl in her crowd whose mother had died, of all the dead mothers, Lois's had died the most efficiently, with the least drama or mess, the fewest farewells. As for their fathers, they were without exception fishermen, rarely at home or even on land. When she thought of fathers, she thought of calloused hands, gold teeth and tattoos, but bright tattoos, reds and blues, ocean greens, tattoos of anchors, of mermaids, sea horses, the names of their wives.

"Go Nads!" Lois and her friends whispered to each other as they watched the cheerleaders practice. They giggled and agreed how funny it would be because those girls were too dumb to understand what would be coming out of their own mouths. They wouldn't get it, not those big yellow-headed girls, each as overwhelming as a sunflower in a city garden. This must be why her students' tasteless essays don't offend her the way they offend others, the accountant for instance. They are her childhood friends, these pierced, dreaming kids. They are Rosa Tavares, Ruy Silva, Nanda Medeiros.

"What frightens me," Daniel said, "is how someday we're going to be old and feeble and completely dependent on these imbecile kids of yours to keep the economy going. Not even someday. Any day now. Tomorrow, sometimes it feels like." He sounded sad and worn and then he grew quiet. "So," he said after a bit. "I've been wondering. Why don't you learn how to give yourself the shots?"

She was caught off guard. "Stick a needle into my stomach?" she said.

"I know, but how much is it, a clinic visit every day? It must cost a fortune. And it must be incredibly inconvenient, running over there all the time."

"I just don't see myself sticking needles into my stomach. How would you like to do it?" She meant how would he like to stick a needle into his stomach, but he misunderstood, thought she meant how would he like to stick one into hers.

"I guess I could," he said, "if someone showed me how."

She imagined him coming by her office every day. He would test the needle, squirt water into the air to get rid of dangerous bubbles, then pierce the skin of her tummy. He would press his handkerchief against the pinprick of blood.

"I could, I suppose," he said again.

For a moment there *was* longing, his, hers, she couldn't deny it. She had a quick and vivid fantasy of him kissing the spot of blood, then continuing to kiss her, his mouth moving lower, one hand opening her legs, the other covering her mouth so students in the hall wouldn't hear her moaning his name. He would climb onto her and the metal desk would shimmer beneath them and Ferguson would be back at the law firm, slaving away.

But her hormones were hectic that day making her overly, artificially emotional, given to daydreams she knew not to trust. And she was not allowed to have sex during the procedure under any circumstances; Dr. Finney had made that clear.

"They don't charge extra to jab me," she told Daniel. "I'm not squandering your hard-earned money."

"I wasn't implying you were," he said. "That's not at all what I meant."

In some ways she has enjoyed visiting the clinic so frequently. She likes the meetings with Dr. Finney. She even likes the encounters with the staff, the awful jokes about boiled eggs and scrambled eggs and eggs over-easy. Sometimes the nurses sneak the dirty magazines down from the sperm donor unit—they really do have dirty magazines there, it turns out—but though Lois laughs at their bad girl routine, she doesn't read them. She prefers the dog-eared issues of *People.* Actresses, princesses, some jilted, some dead. They go on just the same, glamorous and loved. *People Magazine.* Talk about smut. But she likes it. Bad coffee and junk magazines and smart-ass girlfriends. Even the ex-nuns, so much like the cheerleaders. This must be what it's like to live in a sorority house or spend time in a beauty parlor. In the movies the beauty parlors are always like this. A row of ladies chatting under big metal hoods. She fits in here. College she squeezed around her job at Bed and Bath, and it took forever to finish, the oldest student in her class by the time she got her degree. And grad school, all those dreary classes in rhetoric and pedagogical theory. She commuted to Boston from home, made hardly a friend, somehow lost her husband along the way.

And what about those ghastly law firm parties? She never fit in at those, not for a second. She always felt like the least consequential wife in a room full of inconsequential wives. The prettiest, Daniel used to say back in the days they'd just begun, the sexiest he whispered into her straight dark hair, but also the only greenhorn, that was for sure. He, at least, was third generation. The wives, Junior Leaguers in floral skirts, forgave him his roots. But "Where are your people from?" they always asked Lois, and Daniel would take over, answer for her. "Massachusetts," he'd say. "Just like yours, Alice."

How different it is at the clinic. Here she feels welcome and wanted, one of the girls. A sister to Dr. Finney's fountain pen. Even the protesters—what would they do without her?

And yet today they've all abandoned her. It's been nearly an hour now that she's been here alone, freezing and shivering, flat on her back, thinking about Daniel, and reading the ceiling. She slides her hands under her bare bottom, uses the remaining heat of her body to warm her fingers. She wishes she could summon the nurse. "Not to be a bother, but could you please bring me my socks from the changing room, please?" She could get up, she knows, fetch the damned socks herself, but as soon as she did, as soon as she rounded the corner, that would be exactly when Dr. Finney arrived. She won't risk missing him. And she's not convinced, really, she could find her way back to the changing room, not without someone to guide her. The winding halls in this unfamiliar wing of the clinic made her dizzy before. Even the nurse had commented on them.

"Rats in a maze," the nurse said as she held Lois's johnny closed in the back and steered from behind. A few yards ahead of them, another nurse was leading a couple down the same hallway. The man walked close behind the woman, using his body to shield her rear end. "Rats in a maze," the other nurse sang back, "with their tails hanging out."

For a brief, alarming moment Lois thought the couple might be Daniel and Ferguson. Something about the man's gait, his suit, the way his ears were attached to his head. But the woman was too tentative, sloshing along in her paper slippers, too vulnerable, much too exposed. And the whole idea of it was crazy. Daniel would never come to this place. Nor would he ever need to. It would be too much of a coincidence for the second wife to require the clinic's services, too. When Daniel and Ferguson have a child, they will have it the regular way. That will be their reality, Lois knows, and she knows, too, it's likely to be something they do soon. Tempus is fugiting, passion must be dulling if only a little, and surely Ferguson must be aware of the increased volume of calls to Lois. Maybe she stands outside Daniel's office and listens, wondering what she should do to reclaim his full attention. A baby is what she will do. A baby is what women do.

Several months ago, Lois began checking the birth announcements in the paper. Born to Louis and Camille Izzo, a girl Kimberly Morgan. Born to Hartoon and Seta Kazarian, a boy Michael Kyle. She is looking, of course, for Daniel's name. So far it hasn't appeared. And, yes, it is spying, but what choice does she have? He never talks to her about his wife. Sometimes, needing to be reminded that the girl is still in the picture, Lois will say, "And how's Ferguson?" as if she's referring to someone they're mutually fond of, a goddaughter, a niece, and he'll say, "Fine, thanks," and then change the subject.

And how are her fallopian tubes? That's what Lois really wants to ask. Have you had them checked out? Are they all aglow, as translucent as alabaster? Her own tubes are so blocked her former physician called in several interns to look at the ultrasound image and marvel. It crushed her with shame, made her think about bathroom pipes clogged with hair.

Daniel had put his arm around her shoulder. "Come on, now, don't take it like that," he said. "What do we care? So while everyone else is spending a fortune on tuition and braces, we'll be on a beach in Belize."

Only weeks after they'd met at Filene's, she moved into his duplex. They had sex constantly—one afternoon he rolled off her, caught his breath, and said, "Not that I'm complaining but I don't think we've spoken more than two words to each other this whole weekend," and she said, "No, I'm sure I've said at least these three: *Dios, Caro*—again?"

He laughed at her jokes and bought her presents that became more expensive as he moved up at the firm. Short leather skirts, silk scarves, Italian shoes, suede and strappy, showing some toe cleavage. He liked to take care of her. "Why keep such a menial job?" he said and she cut back her hours at Bed and Bath, then quit all together. She liked to take care of him, too. She spent most of her time cleaning the house. It sounded all wrong, degrading, she knew, yet she didn't mind, *she didn't,* she liked housework. Arranging pillows on the bed. Shining the brass rods that kept the oriental runner smooth on the staircase. She liked the whine of the floor buffer when she polished the parquet. She liked the magic of taking something worthless and turning it into a thing of use. Old rags became hooked rugs. Dried beans became stew.

But still—an old story—he had worked so hard, too many hours. She'd been lonely, as simple as that. Maybe he'd been lonely, as well. If there were a poster listing the fifty worst things life had to offer, loneliness would be number one. Would be the other forty-nine, too. "I'm not interested in laying around a beach somewhere," she said when he brought up Belize. "You forget I grew up on the beach. I'm sick of the beach."

"Lying," he said.

"No, I mean it."

"Not laying. Lying."

"Don't correct my English. I went to college."

"Speak like it, then. And you didn't grow up on the beach, for Chrissake. You grew up on an old polluted seaport."

Her tears always surprised them both. "It *was* the beach. There was sand. There was saltwater. There were fucking sea gulls."

She used to go to the shore to look for her father's boat. At dusk she followed the footprints the gulls left in the dunes. Their paths lurched and veered as if the birds were barflies staggering home after last call. Sometimes, before she erased her own footprints from the parquet in Daniel's home, she would make herself a tall Coke and Jack in a pretty frosted glass and totter through the house in the same crazy way.

She had gone to the clinic on her own and brought home the first contract. It was a simpler affair than the one she eventually signed, though that first one had been complex enough. She had showed it to Daniel after dinner. He took the document, weighed it in his hands, shook his head. "One of the many members of my profession who thinks he gets paid by the word," he said. Then he read the title out loud, projecting as if he were giving a speech: *Informed Consent and Contract for* In Vitro *Fertilization with Spousal Semen.*

While she cleared the table he turned pages, scowling. Finally he looked up. "You didn't read this, did you?" he said.

"Of course I did." She had skimmed it. It was dense, single-spaced.

"You're such a liar. No one who read this thing would go ahead with this procedure."

She went to the kitchen. He followed and while she washed dishes, he read parts of the contract out loud. "Article Roman Two," he said. "Recipient—that would be you—hereby acknowledges the *in vitro* fertilization failure rate to be more than eighty percent."

She drenched forks and knives under a rush of hot water.

"Article Roman Three. Recipient—"

"That would be me."

"—hereby acknowledges that the practice of medicine is not an exact science and therefore, that reputable practitioners cannot guarantee results and that no guarantee, warranty or other assurance has herein been made."

"I told you I read it."

"Get real, Lois," he said, and so she had applied to grad school.

Now here she is, doing it on her own. She decided to on one of those days she was scanning birth announcements. She came across another D-name who was married to another F-name, and that was close enough for her, she felt her heart screech like a skidding car. She went out, took a walk. She came home, overate. She slept one more time with the man with the Jaguar. The next day she called Daniel. "Are you happy?" she asked him. "What's happy?" he said.

The hell with all this, she thought, and she made an appointment, drove to the clinic and signed the contract, this one even thicker than the first, this one called *Informed Consent and Contract for* In Vitro *Fertilization with Unknown Donor Semen* and containing even more warnings. Article Roman Four: Recipient hereby acknowledges that in the event a child shall be born as a result of aforesaid procedure, such child may be mentally or physically abnormal or may have undesirable hereditary tendencies or conditions, or such child may be stillborn or may have congenital defects or sexually transmitted diseases or may otherwise suffer from the complications of childbirth.

The complications of childbirth. The phrase should have scared her. It only touched her. She initialed the bottom of every page, checked the box marked nonapplicable where it asked for her spouse's name. She invented a signature so ferocious it sliced through the notary clause.

She is remembering that signature, the fierce dot over the small *i* in Lois, her surprise as she wrote her own name, Mello, that funny Portuguese name, but hers or at least as close to hers as she was ever going to get, when Dr. Finney opens the door. He is over an hour late but here at last, and the slam bam nurse at his side. The nurse is smiling and holding a tray and on that tray is a catheter and in that catheter is Unknown Donor's sperm and Lois's eggs. "So finally," says the nurse. "It's egg plant time."

"Oh, Lord, Lois," Dr. Finney says. "It's freezing in here. Jeanine, can you turn up the heat?"

"You should feel my feet," Lois says.

He grasps a foot, that's how agreeable he is, so ready to tend to her needs. "Lord," he says. "Lois, I'm sorry to have to tell you this, but in my professional opinion I think you're dead." But he's already rubbing the foot back to life, rapid movements, efficient as a scout with two sticks. "I'm sorry," he says, rubbing, rubbing, "but it's been one hell of a day. We had a bit of a crisis with the folks before you. Lost the eggs and the couple, well, you can imagine—just bereft. And furious. I mean, you can only imagine. And of course, the clinic feels terrible, but the thing is, it happens."

"It's right in the contract," the nurse Jeanine says. She has opened a closet, adjusted the dial of a thermostat hidden inside.

Dr. Finney returns Lois's right foot to the right stirrup, now takes the left in his hands. If Jeanine wasn't here, Lois thinks she might cry out from this touching, might beg him never to stop. She might press her bare foot against the front of his trousers, press and rub against him. That's why a nurse always accompanies him. Not to protect her, but to protect him from her affection, her gratitude.

He touches the inside of her calf and she opens her legs for him. Then there is no more touching. With gestures, he gets her to spread her legs wider, with gestures he gets her to wriggle closer to him.

"It's all in the contract but no one pays any attention," Jeanine is saying. "And then something goes wrong like you warned them it could, you tell them you lost their eggs, and they get all bent out of shape. Like they think you misplaced them. Like you ought to be running around looking for them. Like they rolled behind the file cabinet or something."

"People think," Dr. Finney says as he puts two gloved fingers inside her, "that when we say eggs are lost we mean lost as in I lost my keys when what we really mean is lost as in we lost grandma to influenza."

"Even if they had rolled behind the file cabinet, we couldn't just look and see them."

"The human egg is microscopic," Dr. Finney explains as he wriggles his fingers, feels something that makes him smile and nod, murmur good.

"Smaller than a bubble of spit," says Jeanine. "But people always picture Easter eggs."

"Life is sad," says Dr. Finney. He has withdrawn his fingers. "Some days all I see here is sad followed by sadder." Now he's reaching toward her again. "Here comes cold and gloppy." He is smearing a thick gel on her, inside her. "But you, I'm happy to say, have no reason to feel sad today. Can you relax for me? Can you open up just a little bit more?"

Not long after she first began with the Lupron, Lois read about yet another corrupt clinic in California. The doctor there was fertilizing his patients' eggs with his own sperm. Everyone had been outraged; people pressed charges. Lois understands, of course, but she also knows she would never sue Dr. Finney if it turns out he's introduced his sperm to her eggs. They charged the California doctor with an act of fraud, but Lois thinks it may just as well have been an act of love. Isn't that what love is? A pleasant kind of fraud? Your imagination running away with itself but in a nice way, the way the dish ran away with the spoon. A happy if mismatched couple in the moonlight, and isn't that another lovely fraud, *number eleven: moonlight?* There's no such thing, the moon is not a source of light at all, and yet at times Lois has read by it.

The day she signed the contract they led her to a room done up like a den. Brown leather sofas, shelves full of books about pregnancy and motherhood. Displayed on the coffee table like bright modern sculpture, a plastic model of the female reproduction system. There were also a half dozen notebooks containing hundreds of Unknown Semen Donor Profiles.

She picked one of the notebooks, opened it at random. She accepted that the profile she turned to was the one meant for her, that her hand had been guided to it the way a magician guides you to the queen of hearts though you never understand how, though everyone, including yourself, feels they've witnessed an act of free will.

"Are you sure?" she was asked. "Don't you want to spend a little more time?"

She shook her head. She was given a photocopy of the profile. "Keep it somewhere safe," she was told, and Lois put it in her new apartment's linen closet, beneath the clean sheets and extra washcloths.

Dr. Finney has withdrawn the catheter. "All done," he says. She surprises herself by starting to cry, hot fat tears that roll sideways. "Oh," Dr. Finney says. He puts his hand on her forehead as if he

were her mother and she a sick child. "There now. You're all right."
She closes her eyes and imagines what's happening inside her. Her
own, fertilized eggs—or maybe they are really the eggs of some other
woman; it doesn't matter, really, it doesn't—these eggs that have by-
passed her vaginal canal, these eggs that her doctor has ferried past
her cervical lock, these eggs are now affixing themselves to her uter-
ine wall like barnacles on a hull. "All right now," Dr. Finney says.

"You take good care," he says before he leaves. "We'll be thinking
about you."

When she gets home, she goes to the linen closet and takes out
the Anonymous Donor Semen Profile. Then she goes to the bathroom, runs a hot bath. As the tub fills she sits on its side and reads
the profile. On one side are his vital statistics—height, weight, hair
color. Also a list of his talents. Circle all that apply, the form says.
Unknown Donor has circled musical, athletic, math.

On the reverse side is the release he signed, his name blotted out.
She's read the release so often she knows it by heart, can recite it like
a poem:

> Unknown Donor hereby
> agrees to make no attempt whatsoever
> to locate Recipient
> and/or aforesaid child.

She steps into the tub, one foot, the other. She sinks down. The
water burns but bearably, and she closes her eyes. When, at last, she
is thoroughly warm, she sighs and she opens her eyes and she reaches
for the profile again. She folds it and folds it again, until it is very
small, an origami swan. She floats it in her bath.

> Unknown Donor hereby
> irrevocably releases and gives up forever
> all rights to his donated semen
> and to any child that results from its use.

Forever. It touches her. She reaches for a towel, stands.

And now she gets out of the bath. Slowly and gingerly she walks
to her bed. She will treat herself well, take care of herself. Then, if
she makes no mistakes, she will get to have this baby. She will get to

suffer and worry and think about it forever. And if she makes no mistakes, if she is good, if she is lucky, then one day she will be doing something very ordinary, maybe riding a bus, and a man will bend down to retrieve the rattle dropped by the infant in her lap and his hand will brush hers and he'll look at the baby and then into her eyes, and he'll begin to say, to ask. . . .

At the same time she knows that one clumsy misstep and nature, like a stranger lurking on a playground, will lure those eggs from her. Then what will she do? She'll pick up the phone and when Daniel answers, she'll tell him what happened. I'll be right there, he'll say. Don't be silly, she'll tell him. You can't come here now. Don't you have clients who need you? I'll be there in thirty minutes, he'll say. Twenty if the lights go my way. He'll burst into her office, find her there, folding essays into swans, into paper planes, and he'll duck when she lets one soar past his big moon head.

Clarissa's first labor was a quick, businesslike affair, lasting only three hours. She endured it with as much good humor as possible, the way her mother had taught her to endure all life's difficulties, refusing to cry out for painkillers. Jason, her husband at the time and father of the child, rushed into the delivery room in his muddy hiking boots only a half-hour before their daughter arrived. After the birth, Clarissa got up and walked back down the hall to her private room, carrying the swaddled newborn with her. She refused to have her photograph taken with the baby until she had put on lipstick and a decent bra. When she phoned her mother with the news, she airily dismissed her husband's late arrival. "You know Jason—just back from one of his expeditions. I won't let him touch the baby until he's checked for ticks."

The hospital's La Leche League volunteer showed up in her long braid to help with the first nursing session, but she could only sit there uselessly as Clarissa affixed the baby to her breast as if she'd been doing so her whole life. Back at home, she put the infant in a shoulder sling and hung the newly washed baby clothes (picked up at garage sales for a song) on a sunny clothesline. For dinner, she baked one of the many casseroles she had prepared the month before and stored in the freezer. In a few days, the baby was sleeping in five-hour stretches. By the end of a week, she was sleeping through the night. At the child's first checkup, the pediatrician (a mother of three herself, with that tired look around the eyes) announced that she had never seen anyone take to motherhood as naturally as Clarissa. She lost the baby weight almost immediately and her complexion, which had gone ruddy during the last month of pregnancy, turned pale and smooth again. A quick stop at the hairdressers for a henna rinse and trim restored the silky elegance of her auburn hair. Her alert green eyes showed no sign of worry or strain.

The only problem was picking a name. Left to her own devices, Clarissa would have settled the matter long before the birth. Jason, however, refused to be pinned down. He favored Irene, and then, for no apparent reason, threw his lot in with Suzanne. Now that the child was born, he insisted on pseudo-hippie possibilities (Prairie, Larkspur) that Clarissa found laughable. She repeated her mother's dictate that a proper name should lend itself to a diminutive (for instance, Kittie from Katherine) yet, in its full form, be suitable for publication, when the time came, in the obituary column. Above all, Clarissa explained, a name should have a certain pedigree. "My family is Irish. We know where we came from. But your family—your names have no history. They don't mean anything."

As they discussed the issue for the fifth or sixth time in two weeks, the scent of mildew rose from the basement stairs. They lived at the edge of a Midwestern university town, in an aging development built on top of what used to be a meandering streambed. The olive green ranch house they rented was slowly sinking into the swampy ground, and every spring (they'd been there for four while they both attended graduate school) Jason had been forced to bail out the basement. He was a man who understood the danger of chronic dampness and had repeatedly urged Clarissa to put her grandmother's Persian rugs into storage until they could afford to move somewhere nicer. He stared at the fading mandala pattern on the living room rug while Clarissa suggested the names of several Irish saints. He nodded his head to everything she said but silently refused to yield. When she was finished, he went down to the basement to inspect the widening pool.

Clarissa stood at the top of the stairs and waited for Jason to sigh, roll his shoulders back, and get to work mopping up the mess. This time, he didn't. He yanked the string hanging from the bare bulb to turn off the light.

This abdication of duty was alarming. Clarissa stared into the dark cellar a moment, and then retreated to the living room couch to nurse the baby. She had fallen for Jason when they were both counselors at summer camp and he had performed an act of extreme devotion to duty, if not actual heroism. A red-haired boy had slipped off the branch of a sycamore tree and dislocated his shoulder. While another counselor ran to get the camp nurse, Jason turned the howling boy on his side, jammed his booted foot into an armpit, and pulled the boy's arm so hard the bone slipped up over the socket and back into place. In the weird silence afterwards, when the boy was too shocked to make a sound, Clarissa's eyes met Jason's. He was tall and strong—ready for anything. She chose him then and there.

Now, as she nursed his nameless child, she wondered if a twenty-year-old camp counselor had any business performing a stunt like that—especially with an actual nurse on the way. Jason had always gone in for showy acts of manliness. There was nothing about him anymore that Clarissa would call heroic, especially after having just been through childbirth herself. She had, with barely a cry or moan, expelled a seven-pound baby from her body. He, on the other hand, was most proud of his ability to start a fire with two dry sticks and a pile of moss. Typically, he'd been off roaming the woods along Lake Superior through most of Clarissa's pregnancy, gathering data for his doctoral thesis on woodland carnivores. He disappeared for weeks with hardly an apology. Of course it was only a matter of time before he'd disappear again. At this point in her life, Clarissa was more interested in the boy whose shoulder Jason had so violently forced back into position. At last she understood his mute astonishment at the end of his ordeal. How long had he stayed there on the ground, gazing up at the branches of the sycamore tree, readjusting to life after that wrenching transformation?

The next day, Jason surprised her by capitulating, sort of. Fed up with the chatter about names, he got out a map of Ireland and threw a dart, which landed on a little town called Adare (luckily for the baby—it was just a hairsbreadth away from Caherconlish). So Adare it was, Addie for short.

Once the name was settled, Jason engineered his own triumph: he moved out. In the midst of a drizzly fog, he left their ranch house in favor of a dirty apartment shared with three undergraduate wrestlers. After persuading Addie to accept a plastic bottle in place of Clarissa's breast, he insisted on having the baby three and a half days a week. Since space was tight, he put her crib in the closet and her few clothes in a suitcase. He continued working on his doctorate and took Addie with him wherever he went, to his lab, to the library, even on hunting expeditions in the frozen woods outside town. He slipped into his new life as a father instinctively, the way dogs gone feral adapt to life on the margin.

From Wednesday mornings through Saturday afternoon, Clarissa faced an empty house. The first time Jason drove away with

Addie for his half-week, she looked at the rattles, stuffed bears and boxes of baby wipes that littered the living room rug and felt helpless to clean up the mess. The clutter remained, scattered about like shrapnel, until Addie returned. One night Clarissa stood in the basement flood until the dark water soaked into her pink slippers. She wanted to reach up and pull the cord, to turn on the light, but she was afraid of getting a shock. She stood there for the longest time, with her feet getting colder and colder.

The next day, Clarissa started therapy. She didn't tell anyone, particularly her mother. Her therapist, an imposing woman in a black linen suit and expensive pumps, invited Clarissa into her office. Clarissa sat on a wing chair, picking at a hole in her jeans, and said: "I feel like I'm losing all definition, like a cloud that's fading away." The therapist strode around her office saying things like, "You just got tired of being his mother," as if Clarissa were the one who'd walked out of the marriage.

It wasn't exactly true, but it sounded good. After all, this sort of thing wasn't supposed to happen to women in her family. They did not allow themselves to be abandoned. So, taking courage from her therapist, such a loud and well-defined woman, Clarissa e-mailed her mother a lie: "It's over. I threw him out." She knew her mother would be concerned about her and the baby, but at the same time wickedly pleased.

Mamie herself had left her own husband, Clarissa's father, years ago, and since then had floated from one love affair to the next, sometimes conducting several at once. She bought herself a small house at the edge of a semi-tropical city, grew cucumber vines up her front porch, and refused to share her home with anyone. Mamie admired high spirits, hated complainers, and had done her best to cultivate a sort of genteel wildness in her daughters. Only one of the girls, Kathleen—who had gone through three charming husbands by the time she was thirty—had ever really lived up to their mother's ideal. More than anything, Mamie admired people with a fully developed point of view. You could do anything in her book—walk out on a marriage after a spat about the laundry (as Kathleen had done once), buy a one-way ticket to Pakistan and then disappear without a trace for a full month (as Jason had done once in their early days). For Mamie, all choices were good choices, as long as you made them swiftly and with determination, as if you had no other options.

Clarissa's problem, she now realized, was that, for the first time in her life, she could see other options. And they were all in the past. The world was suddenly a maze of might-have-beens, one path leading to a bookish home in the Cotswolds with a husband and three Irish wolfhounds; another leading to a convent in Michigan with a group of radicalized nuns studying liberation theology; another leading to the kitchen of an organic restaurant in Berkeley. At various moments in her life, Clarissa had rejected each of these options. Instead, she had charged (for no good reason she could think of anymore) down another path, a path leading past Jason to her present life as a divorced, half-time mother of one and graduate student in the women's studies department of a large university.

In her daily life, she masked her aimlessness with a bravura that was pure Mamie. She swooped through the department hallways shouting greetings to friends. She wrote a furiously argued dissertation about rural quilting bees in the nineteenth century. Yet the woman she used to be had somehow come undone. In her dreams, she literally broke into pieces, dropping an arm in the grocery store, a foot in her office.

Each Wednesday, Clarissa packed up Addie and her few belongings to hand over to Jason. She tucked Addie's pink lamb, rag doll and teething ring into the car seat with her the way the ancients loaded their dead with familiar trinkets to comfort them among the shades. When they were apart, Clarissa was alarmed by how little the child came into her thoughts. During her half week away, it really did seem as if Addie had slipped into another world, far beyond her mother's keeping.

Without quite knowing how, in the year following the divorce, Clarissa finished her doctorate in women's studies and started a teaching job at a local college. She found a nice apartment with enough bookcases to accommodate her collection of Victorian novels. She checked the basement to make sure that, this time, she wouldn't have to think about dampness damaging her grandmother's rugs. By the time Addie was four Clarissa had created a life for herself, more or less. She had a few flings at out-of-town academic meetings and then, one day in September, met a kindly botanist named Rob.

They had been set up by mutual friends, and when he arrived at her house for their first date he brought a bouquet of prairie grasses. She could hear the stems rustling before she opened the door.

His overcoat was neatly tailored. He laid his soft leather gloves on the dining room table while he waited for Clarissa to get a vase for the bouquet.

"You don't need any water," he advised. "The grasses get prettier as they dry."

Clarissa liked the fact that Rob was on the short side. In fact, he was exactly her height, so that she could look straight into his gray eyes. Rob was unusually nice, too. Over dinner, he listened to Clarissa in a way that made her self-conscious. As she described the course she taught on romance heroines, she became aware of a persistent pulse at the corner of her mouth.

During their married life, Jason would come home with scratches and bites from the animals he kept caged in his lab. He saw the natural world primarily in terms of the food chain. The question he perpetually asked was: Who eats whom and why? Rob, on the other hand, perceived the world as a web of mutual dependencies between pollens and pollinators. The wetland grasses he studied depended on the gentlest freshwater currents for their survival.

They spent pleasant Saturday afternoons together, shopping for groceries and then cooking complicated vegetarian meals. The first time they went to the store together, Rob threw a can of chicken soup into the cart along with the lentils and baby artichokes. Clarissa didn't notice it until they got to the checkout line.

"What did you get this for?" She asked. "You don't eat meat."

"I thought you'd like it," he said, as he paged through a magazine.

That small act of thoughtfulness stunned her. If she hadn't been stuck on the other side of the cart, she would have flung her arms around his neck and kissed him wildly right there. Rob continued to scan the magazine, unaware he'd done anything out of the ordinary.

It wasn't easy to explain Rob to Mamie. She'd always loved the bad boy in Jason and was biased against Rob from the beginning. She didn't meet him, though, until Clarissa brought him along to the family's vacation cottage the next summer. It was a short flight away, followed by an hour-long drive in a rental car.

The cottage was a crumbling old farmhouse that had been moved, years ago, to the edge of a small northern lake. According to family legend, Mamie's grandfather had won it in a poker game shortly before he turned religious and took up life as a Catholic deacon. Mamie had spent every summer of her childhood playing on the edge of that cold deep lake, and so had Clarissa and her sisters. Addie, who was four and half by now, already considered the place her second home.

First-time visitors to the cottage were always surprised by the sight of a four-square farmhouse perched on the rocky shore. Instead of barns and silos, it was surrounded by scrubby pines and a couple of old rowboats. The ground it stood on was treacherous—rocky and laced with twisting tree roots. After Clarissa parked the car, Addie ran to the cottage, as sure-footed as a goat in the familiar terrain. Rob twisted his ankle slightly on the way to the front steps.

Mamie waited for them on the porch swing with her gin and tonic. Everything about her was sleek and neat. Her silky white hair was trimmed chin-length and curled under to frame her face. She wore typical north woods attire (khaki pants, a denim shirt) and yet the clothes fit her so perfectly, the pants narrowing elegantly at the waist, that she gave the impression of having dressed for a special event.

She hugged Addie with one arm, without setting down her drink or standing up. She accepted Clarissa's kiss and shook Rob's hand.

"Did you hurt yourself?" she asked, gesturing to his ankle.

"A little," he said. "I'm not sure how bad." He swayed, slightly off balance from having shifted all his weight to one foot.

"That's a shame," she said. "And we were going to hike over to the sandbar tomorrow for a picnic." She smiled and sipped her drink. She did not slide over to make room for him on the swing.

"Why don't you carry your suitcases upstairs. Take the room on the right, the one with the red bedspread."

They had been assigned to the guest room, not to Clarissa's old white room with the macramé bedspread, the one she and Jason used in the past. The house smelled of conifers and lake water. To Clarissa this had always been the scent of summer freedom. Now it suggested years of neglect. She remembered how the pine sap used to drip onto her arms and hair as she passed through the woods, leaving black sticky stains that only turpentine could remove. Addie would be a mess by the end of the week.

Rob got up early the first morning and tried to make popovers. He poured the batter into a muffin tin but couldn't get the electric oven to start. Mamie found him in the kitchen with tools scattered on the floor, preparing to unplug the stove and take apart the outlet.

"You don't have to do that," she said. "Just hit it, like this."

She whacked the wall just above the outlet with a wooden spoon. The interior light came on and the oven began to warm up.

She looked down at the tools. "Next time something doesn't work, just ask me. Please." She pulled a towel off a hook by the door, tightened her white robe around her waist, and went down to the lake for a swim.

Apparently, the best Clarissa could hope for was a lack of open hostility. She retreated to the couch and read one mass-market historical romance novel after another—ostensibly as research for an academic paper on love stories but really because she couldn't get enough of the formulaic tales. She felt physically lightened every time one of the long-suffering heroines fell in love. Just the term "falling in love" pleased her. It described a collapse, a giving in, a complete submission to the forces of gravity. The rakes in the stories didn't deserve the love and devotion the heroines showered upon them. It was all senseless and impetuous, and by comparison her relationship with Rob seemed like a charitable argument. He was good to her. He was simply the right choice.

At the dinner table that week Clarissa paid more attention to Addie than to Rob. She was pleased to show off the child's table manners to her mother. Later, after Clarissa got over the initial shock, she was even more pleased by the way Addie ran down the path toward the lake and dove wildly off the dock into the deep water. The child thrashed around a bit but eventually made it back up to the surface so Mamie could fish her out.

That night, as Addie's clothes hung dripping from the clothesline and Addie herself was tucked warmly into her sleeping bag upstairs, Clarissa picked her way down the rocky path to the beach. In the fading light, she could just make out Flat Rock, a piece of granite about 100 yards from shore. As its name implied, the top of the rock was level, creating a kind of stage out on the water. When Clarissa and her sisters were younger, Mamie organized swim races out to the rock. Clarissa nearly always won the longer races, to the opposite shore, but Kathleen was the sprinting champion. She would haul her long, lean body out of the water and do a kind of hula dance before Clarissa, breathless and blotchy in the face, managed to touch the rock.

One summer morning, when Clarissa was twelve, her mother got up early and paddled out to the rock in a metal rowboat. She stayed there for the rest of the day, refusing to come in out of the sun and throwing fistfuls of lake weed at anyone who dared approach her stronghold. Clarissa's father, a professor of Old English who devoted his summers to compiling lists of Anglo-Saxon verb structures, was annoyed by this disruption in the rhythms of the cottage. After Clarissa, and then Kathleen, had come knocking on his study door to tell him that their mother was on the rock and wouldn't come in, he sighed and waded out knee-deep into the lake. He shouted, "You can barely swim! You shouldn't be out there without a life vest. Come in at once. The children are hungry!"

What he really meant was that *he* was hungry—and confused by this sudden willfulness. Clarissa and her sisters watched the proceedings from under a willow tree. The clumps of lakeweed Mamie lobbed his way fell far short. Her inability to strike her target seemed to enrage her more, driving her finally into absolute withdrawal. She turned her back on him, on the girls crouching under the willow, on the cottage with its unmade beds.

Late in the afternoon, when Mamie seemed to be napping, Clarissa swam out quietly, holding a cheese sandwich and a bottle of strawberry soda above her head. She left her offering on the edge of the rock. Looking out later from shore, Clarissa saw that the bottle had been drained and the sandwich consumed. Mamie, however, never mentioned the meal to her—not that night, when she rowed back in the dark, pulled the boat up onto the gravelly shore, and went to bed; not the next morning, when she got up and made cinnamon buns as if nothing had happened; not the next day, when she loaded Clarissa and her sisters into the station wagon and drove them cross country to Berkeley; not the rest of the summer, when, as Clarissa set up housekeeping for all of them in an upstairs apartment, she started college and filed for divorce.

A few times since then, Clarissa had almost mentioned the sandwich and her mother's long day on the rock, but the moment never seemed right. How could she even describe her mother's behavior? Was it really just a temper tantrum? Clarissa preferred to dwell on Mamie's decisive departure, the way she flipped up the rear-view mirror as she drove away from the cottage to blot out everything she left behind.

In the end, Mamie didn't really leave the cottage behind. It had belonged to her father and so was hers by right. Clarissa and her sisters continued to spend their summers there, and nothing pleased Clarissa more than to see Addie climbing over the same rocks she had played on as a child.

For indoor play, Addie came up with a new game called Suppose That. Addie loved to play Suppose That with any adult, but preferably with her mother. It only required that Clarissa keep doing whatever she was doing—setting the table, making a salad, folding towels. Addie followed her mother around and said, "Suppose that we're at the cottage on vacation, and that you're setting the table. Suppose that . . ." Addie paused while Clarissa paused to remember what she needed from the closet. As Clarissa reached for the tablecloth on the shelf, Addie continued: "And suppose that you get out the tablecloth and we spread it on the . . ." Here another pause as Clarissa hesitated between the kitchen table and the front porch. As Clarissa moved toward the front door, Addie continued, ". . . and spread it on the picnic table on the porch."

The only difference between Suppose That and the real world was that, in Suppose That, Addie called herself "Blink" and her mother "Baker Girl." (Where the names came from no one knew.) At first the constant narration got on Clarissa's nerves. Then she got used to it. In a way, it was soothing to have her life narrated like this. Baker Girl was a busy person. She got things done and moved on to the next thing. She swept the porch, she emptied the mouse traps without flinching, she spoke sharply to the neighbors who left a campfire unattended.

But with Rob, Clarissa was on her own. She didn't always know what her next move should be. Her attempts to dominate him with a brisk display of purpose often backfired. "Time to get up," she announced one morning, sweeping into their dark upstairs bedroom. As Rob struggled out of a deep sleep, she snapped up the shades and pushed open the casement windows. "I'm afraid I need you to do a few chores. The gutters are filled with pine needles and the propane tank is almost empty."

In the old days, Jason would have grumpily crawled out of bed and gotten right to work, only to disappear into town halfway through his list of chores without a word. Once Rob got over his surprise at her bossiness, he was amused. He smiled at her from his nest in the warm sheets. He pulled back the covers and patted the space next to him. Clarissa hesitated at the window. She wanted to crawl back into bed with him, but she was already dressed, fed and ready for the day. There were things to do. So instead she picked up a damp towel from the floor, threw it on him, and left the room.

Rob shouted after her, "Hey! That's cold! Why'd you do that?"

Clarissa hurried down the stairs and wondered: Why *did* she do that? He was only trying to make things nice.

Such awkward moments continued throughout the fall. Clarissa didn't know how to conduct a relationship with a man who truly had her best interests at heart. The two of them didn't struggle for supremacy, as she and Jason had. Instead, Rob seemed content simply to be with her. This created a kind of hole that she didn't know how to fill.

Despite Clarissa's uncertainty, Rob persisted. He filtered through all her objections like a stream through a stand of cattails. He carried her along with him until she found herself out on open water, disentangled, with the sky wide open above her. What a relief to learn at last what she really wanted. A good, reliable man. Someone she could count on. They married in December and bought a house in January. In the coldest week of the winter, Clarissa conceived for the second time.

This pregnancy was much harder than the first. Clarissa knew it was partly due to her age. She was in her late thirties now. Her body was less desperate to reproduce itself, less willing to accommodate another life. Partly, too, she blamed Rob. He wanted so much to be helpful that it pleased him when she complained, so he could rub her back or fix dinner. She disapproved of whining, but Rob made it so easy. He encouraged her. Ultimately, she felt, he weakened her. She cried when her back ached after a long day of teaching. She took naps in the middle of the afternoon and allowed him to bring her crackers in bed. She gave in, and he loved her more for it.

All this Clarissa was willing to forgive because of one thing: she believed that Rob would never, under any circumstances, leave her after the baby's birth. After all, he was the one who had wanted a child in the first place. He had actually begged. She felt certain she could depend on him. She knew he would be a good father. And though she occasionally mocked his ministrations, she found herself bound closer to him by ties of affection and need. Every day she grew bigger; she expanded enormously. If he'd wanted, he could have turned her on her back and left her stranded like an overturned beetle.

Her labor finally began with one painful contraction in the middle of the night. Rob called Jason, who appeared a half-hour later to watch over the sleeping Addie. Rob bundled Clarissa into the car and sped off down the empty streets to the hospital, running three red lights on the way—not because it was strictly necessary but mostly, Clarissa thought, for effect. At the hospital they were ushered into a plush birthing suite, complete with a hot tub and pull-out bed for Rob. After awhile she barely noticed her surroundings. In an hour she angrily demanded a shot of painkiller. Later, still in agony, she looked Rob square in the eye and hissed, "Stop strok-ing my fucking hand and do something!" Rob obediently called the nurse, who found an anesthesiologist. After her spine was numb, she labored on for 18 hours more. When the baby, a girl, was finally born, Clarissa took a look at the howling, bloody thing and fell asleep.

This time around, Clarissa thought, there would be no uncertainty about the name. She would be called Madeline, after Clarissa's mother. But the first time Clarissa used the time-honored family diminutive, "Mamie," Rob objected. "You know," he said, "I think I like Lina better. Or how about Maddie?" Clarissa was too tired to argue. Rob reached over to stroke the baby's forehead. "Honey," he said, "don't you have to support her head better than that? Look, it's just hanging there like a potato."

While Clarissa rested, Rob gave the baby her first bath, cradling her head and back in his hand and pouring warm soapy water over her belly. "That's okay little Lina," he whispered as he massaged her bent, froggy legs. At home he did all he could for the child short of nursing her. During her colicky phase he strolled around the house with her all night, apparently unaffected by the lack of sleep. He spent an hour each day showing her special black and white cards designed to stimulate neural growth in newborns. Each morning and night he swabbed the remains of her umbilical cord with a cot-ton ball and alcohol, and when the dead stump finally dropped off he buried it out back in the rhubarb patch.

In the past such an earnest ceremony would have made Clarissa snort with laughter. As she peered at him through the lace curtains now, she felt she was missing out on something. The attention Rob had once lavished on her was falling on Lina like warm spring rain. He might as well have been having an affair.

Then the first time Rob went back to his office, Clarissa dropped the baby.

To be more precise, she accidentally allowed the infant, wrapped in a blanket, to slip off the edge of the couch into a basket of laun-dry. Lina wasn't hurt. In fact, she barely whimpered. When Rob found out, he was horrified.

"You dropped her?" He left his briefcase on the living room rug and ran over to scoop Lina out of her portable crib. As he clutched her to his chest, his forehead turned red, as it always did when he got emotional.

"Oh Lina," he moaned into the baby's ear, "poor little Lina."

Clarissa tried to maintain control over the situation. "Get a grip on yourself. She's perfectly fine. I was just reaching for the phone—I thought it was you calling—and the couch cushion is so slippery. She's fine. I shouldn't even have told you about it. These accidents happen to kids all the time."

Rob didn't see things Clarissa's way. The incident left him suspicious of her abilities as a parent. Whenever Clarissa put Lina in Addie's old sling, Rob followed her around the house. "Look out!" he exclaimed as she stir-fried carrots in the wok with one hand and cradled Lina in the sling with her other. "What if the oil flares up?"

He constantly looked up "developmental issues" in his stack of reference material and reported back to her, book in hand. They had been doing something wrong—say, using the wrong kind of soap. He would tap his finger on a page, confident that he had discovered the proper course of action.

At three months, Clarissa wanted to give up breastfeeding in favor of formula. She had never particularly liked nursing. She hated the way her breasts dripped milk onto her shoes whenever she heard Lina crying in the other room. After conducting an Internet search on the topic, Rob begged her to go on nursing for at least another year. At first Clarissa laughed off his concerns. She was an experienced mother. But in time, his constant worries undermined her confidence. Truth be told, she was surprised by the amount of basic information about infants that she had simply forgotten. When was the first smile to be expected—at six weeks or twelve? At what age should a baby be able to roll from back to front?

She watched Addie, when she came to spend her usual half-week with them, and wondered if her assurance as a mother was in any way justified. She had always assumed Addie was perfectly comfortable living part-time with Jason because she had done it since birth. Perhaps, though, the damage would only be noticeable later. In fact, since Lina was born Addie had begun throwing temper tantrums.

She slammed doors when told to turn off the television and, in the mornings, clung to the stairway railing, refusing to leave the house for kindergarten. Was this to be expected with a new sibling in the house or was something darker at work? Was Addie displaying the effects of neglect and upheaval experienced in her infant years? Perhaps if Clarissa had spent fifteen minutes each day stimulating Addie with neural growth cards she would be happier now, less inclined to fling herself on the carpet and scream when refused a third helping of ice cream.

Addie sensed the uncertainty in her mother and became even more demanding. One night before bed, she locked herself in the attic rather than brush her long tangly hair. "Addie come out here right now," Clarissa shouted, then pleaded. In the end Clarissa gave in, and Addie went around for days with unbrushed hair that grew ever more snarled and wild.

As her relationship with Addie deteriorated, Rob insisted on having Lina in their bed at night, claiming such an arrangement produced a stronger parent-child bond. He plopped her down in the middle of the mattress, pulled a pillow over his head, and fell fast asleep. Clarissa, however, had never quite recovered from his accusations of carelessness after dropping the baby. On her side of the bed, she was too worried to sleep—worried that she would roll over and suffocate Lina. Just about the time she allowed herself to drift off Lina would wake up to nurse, and the whole cycle began again. The lack of sleep fogged her brain. Sometimes she could get through a day only by playing Addie's old game. "Suppose that I'm a mother," she said to herself, "and suppose that I have to make breakfast for my oldest daughter and then change the baby's diaper. Suppose that the baby has been screaming since five. Suppose that she cannot, will not take a nap."

That spring, with the baby in the bed and Clarissa so exhausted, they made love only three times. She felt thick and unkempt. She remembered the days when Rob would pounce on her the minute she walked in the door from work; sometimes they would give up whole weekends to creative sex. These days lovemaking was more like itch-scratching. They went at it quietly on the couch, trying not to wake the children. For Clarissa, the primary pleasure was the weight of

Rob on top of her. Afterwards, in the brief moments before they got up off the couch and went to bed, she liked to curl up around his back, reminding herself how they used to sleep before her pregnant belly and then the baby made such coziness impossible.

When their annual trip to the cottage rolled around, Clarissa ceded all the preparations to Rob. She sat on the couch nursing Lina through a concealed opening on the front of her boxy cotton dress. Rob ran back and forth to the car with suitcases, toys and the portable crib. In the plane heading north, Clarissa had to resist the urge to unbuckle her seatbelt at the moment of takeoff. She wanted her whole body to ride the upward momentum and float free over the narrow second-class seats. It felt that good to be leaving her everyday life behind.

Mamie was all smiles when they arrived. She had that brightly mischievous look Clarissa remembered from her childhood, when she would serve cold coffee or unsweetened lemonade to her husband as a joke. Clarissa wondered if Mamie had planned something along those lines for Rob, as punishment for being too much of a father and not enough of a husband.

Whatever Mamie's motives, she couldn't keep her secret for long. "I hope you don't mind, but I've planned a little dinner party."

When Rob went to get the luggage out of the rental car, she told Clarissa confidentially, "I think you'll be especially interested in Kenny, an artist friend of mine from California. He's leasing a cottage nearby for the summer. He specializes in painting portraits of people in one long, curvy line. I don't know how he does it."

Clarissa didn't like the idea of a dinner party, but there was no stopping Mamie once she got an idea in her head. Besides, Mamie was locally famous for her talents as a hostess. This was something Clarissa would have to endure. "You need a long nap," her mother said. "And then we're going to have fun."

After lunch, Clarissa rested on her old bed, what she liked to call her vacation bed, and fingered the macramé coverlet. Imagine—she was being lured into infidelity by her own mother. A crude trap had been laid in the form of a guy named Kenny. It was like an old black-and-white safari movie, where the natives dig a big hole, spread a few palm branches over it and hide in the bushes until the hero comes along and falls right in. And maybe she would fall in. Maybe she'd even jump. Why not? It would be so easy, a relief really. She might choose to keep on doing this kind of thing secretly, whatever it was she was about to do. She couldn't bring herself to name it because the words—one-night stand, liaison, affair—seemed too overwrought for her mundane life.

Rob took the kids down to the shore so she could get ready for dinner. She borrowed a gauzy wrap-around dress from her mother's closet, smeared on apricot lipstick, and anointed her pulse points with a fruity perfume she found in the back of the bathroom cupboard. She even went so far as to put a silk flower in her hair. By the time she was all dressed, she felt embarrassed by her complicity in Mamie's plot. When she walked into the dining room, her mother barely looked up. She polished the candlesticks and asked Clarissa to check the goblets for spots. This made her feel even sillier. Had she made this all up? Was it really *just* a dinner party? Clarissa ran back into the bedroom to pull off the flower and wipe off the lipstick.

Finally the guests began to arrive. For a moment, she felt the old sense of anticipation that always kicked in before one of Mamie's parties. No one quite understood how Mamie could pull off such elegance so far from civilization, in a place where the grocery stores stocked more fresh bait than fresh produce. Somehow, she'd done it again. She had laced fragrant hemlock boughs in among the dishes on the white linen tablecloth. Small candles floated in a silver bowls filled with water.

Barbara and Steven Bronson, neighbors from down the road, arrived first. Barbara was a large woman who never tried to hide her size. Tonight she was draped in a flowing red silk blouse and matching pants that rippled when she talked like a tent in a breeze. The effect was something like a harem girl's outfit, except for the tennis shoes Barbara always wore because she hated getting tripped up on the rocks. Steven was more fastidious, dressed in a creamy white linen shirt that had been perfectly pressed. Clarissa had known them all her life and greeted them at the door with a kiss. Like a lot of the summer people, they had a winter life about which Clarissa knew very little. She could say only that Steven taught German at a southern college, that Barbara had once published a poem in a prestigious literary magazine, and that they had three grown children.

Clarissa knew much more about their summer life, how thin, ruddy Steven liked to float in an inner tube for hours at a time smoking cigarettes and reading cookbooks, how Barbara arranged herself on a ledge on the shore to dry her long white hair in the sun. Mamie felt this hair was an old hippie affectation and often urged Barbara to have it cut and styled. Once Barbara explained to Clarissa why she wore it so long. "When Steven and I first married, I told him he could have hair or hairdo. He chose hair."

Barbara hugged Clarissa and pulled back to have a look at her. "Honey, you need some sleep! I can see it in your eyes." She caught sight of Addie, in her tie-died sundress, hiding behind her mother. "Well look at you! Come here, Addie. I have something for you in my purse."

Barbara took Addie by the hand and walked off with her into the house.

Clarissa made a gin and tonic for Steven and one for herself. Having a drink would mean she'd need to give Lina a bottle of formula at bedtime rather than nursing her. She hoped Rob wouldn't make a big deal about it. She could see him on the dock, holding Lina up and pointing to a pair of loons out on the water. He must have come in earlier to change for the party. He had on his sky blue shirt and the khaki pants that fit him so nicely around the hips. She stood for a moment, spying on their privacy. The sun hung low across the lake, lighting them from behind and etching their bodies in gold. The baby's head glowed, and Rob's long arm, stretched out over the water, shone. As she gazed down on them, she felt grateful for his ability to care for Lina. He was a good father. How many women could say that about their husbands? Here she was, cocktail in hand, free to enjoy the party, while he happily looked after the baby.

From the porch, Clarissa could also see Flat Rock. As two loons sailed serenely past the rock, one dove under the water, looking for food. Startled, Lina wailed. Clarissa heard Rob trying to comfort her, using baby-talk rhythms ("Birdie went bye-bye . . .") that she found annoying. She tried to keep the irritation out of her voice as she called, "Rob, come on in. Everyone wants to see the baby."

Actually, that wasn't true. No one had even mentioned the baby. It was typical of Mamie and her friends to express no interest in such a new, unformed creature. Mamie cared too much for adult pleasures—books, conversation, love affairs—to be swept up by adoration for any child. In the case of her own daughters, she had always provided the necessities and then stayed out of their way, looking forward to the day when they grew into people capable of real conversation.

As she waited for Rob to make his way up from the lake's edge, Clarissa watched a silver Cadillac pull into the drive. Mamie hurried down the steps to open the car door. Out came an elderly man with a dark tan and impeccably trimmed white hair. He wore a navy blue golf shirt with white slacks. He looked down at the rocky path and reached back into the car for a metal cane with a tripod on the end. Clarissa was surprised to see the solicitude with which Mamie helped him across the path.

"Harvey," Mamie said, as they came up the steps, "this is my oldest daughter, Clarissa. Harvey is a good friend." She gave Clarissa a look of triumph mixed with apology, as if to say: "I'm sorry I haven't mentioned him to you before. Isn't that just like me?"

Clarissa was accustomed to meeting her mother's male friends with very little warning. Mamie didn't talk much about her romantic life, preferring to spring her love interests on Clarissa before she could form an opinion. In any case, Mamie's involvements were always temporary, lasting only six months or so. The most recent had been with an academic who'd published an important book a long time ago. Before that, Clarissa had heard mention of a socialist, retired from his political pursuits, who was hoping to have a little fun in his later years. Clarissa sensed something different with Harvey. Perhaps it was the way he leaned on Mamie's slender arm, as if he had already grown accustomed to her support.

Harvey shook Clarissa's hand. "Nice to meet you," he said. He nodded toward his cane. "I had hip surgery recently and I'm still getting my bearings. Your mother was kind enough to help me after I came home from the hospital." He licked the inside of his bottom lip. It was a habit Clarissa associated with old people. What interest could Mamie have in someone who carried a cane? Had she turned old when Clarissa wasn't paying attention? She scrutinized her mother's face, which was wrinkled but still somehow ageless.

Just then, an enormous SUV roared in behind Harvey's car. "Oh," cried Mamie. "It's Kenny!"

She nodded toward Clarissa. There was that look again. Now Clarissa felt thoroughly confused. Was she or was she not being set up? Mamie introduced Clarissa to Kenny and disappeared to mix up the sangria. Clarissa looked him over—not so young, brown hair pulled back into one of those ridiculous middle-aged ponytails. Still, he had nice brown eyes and impressive shoulders. It might work, for one night anyway.

Then again—a guy named Kenny? His fingernails were long and too beautifully manicured. His embroidered vest fit him too perfectly, like a banker's suit. Once the party had moved inside, he sat her down on the couch to demonstrate his famous one-line portrait technique on a cocktail napkin.

Barbara came into the living room carrying a tray of bacon-wrapped scallops and paused to look over Kenny's shoulder. "I think you've caught Clarissa's expression. Don't you, Steven?"

Clarissa couldn't see any expression at all in the drawing. To her, it looked like a scribble. That's not me, she thought. She said out loud, "I don't see myself there at all." She knew—Rob had told her often—that she had a nicely shaped face, with good cheekbones. To look at his drawing, she was nothing but a tangled extension cord.

Rob walked past the couch with the baby. She looked to him, hoping he would jump in to agree with her. But he was too absorbed in showing off Lina to notice the drawing. She cringed as he handed the baby to Steven, who she knew had no interest in getting spit-up on his nice linen shirt.

Kenny laughed at her confusion, the way a Zen master might laugh at an apprentice. "That's you, my friend," he said, smiling. "You just don't know it yet." Such presumption from a stranger was hard to take. Yet something about Kenny—his ponytail, his embroidered vest—gave him the faux exoticism of a fortune teller. It was as if she had just paid five dollars and gone into a tent with him to have her lifeline read. She didn't believe a word he said, and yet it startled her to think that this stranger might have intuited something about her—that he, at any rate, believed he had.

Addie appeared with her hair elaborately braided and fastened with a sequined barrette. "You look nice," Clarissa said, pulling her close. "Was that barrette a surprise from Barbara?"

Addie nodded and squirmed out of her mother's arms. She squeezed between Rob and Steven and ran out the door. Clarissa turned to Barbara. "How did you get her to sit still?"

Barbara shrugged and reached for an appetizer. "You know little girls. They'll do anything to please an adult." Earlier Clarissa had thought she might entertain the group at dinner with the story about Addie locking herself in the attic. Now she changed her mind.

Mamie waltzed into the living room, calling everyone into dinner. She wore a vinyl apron with a cartoon drawing of a cranky golfer and the words "I'm Teed Off" emblazoned across her middle. She did a quick curtsy, to show off the apron as a kind of joke. To Harvey, who was sitting in an old wing chair by the window, she said, "See, it's perfect!" He waved vaguely and smiled. It wasn't clear if he'd heard her or not.

As everyone got up to go into the dining room, Mamie turned to Clarissa. "Isn't this a silly thing? Harvey won it as a door prize at his golf club. I've been thinking of taking up golfing myself."

Golfing? Mamie? Clarissa nearly laughed out loud at the thought of her mother in a gingham golfing skirt and a plastic visor, tooling around in a rented cart. She caught Rob's arm and pulled him into a corner of the living room to tell him about it. "Can you imagine?" she laughed, wanting him to join in. Rob looked nervously past her toward the kitchen and shifted the sleeping Lina from his right arm to his left.

"Shouldn't you lower your voice? Your mother's right there."

Clarissa hissed: "She won't hear me, for God's sake." This was the first real conversation they'd had all day and already it was going bad. She changed the subject. "I feel like I haven't seen you since we got here. Just talk to me for one minute. Can't you put Lina upstairs in her crib and come sit by me at dinner?"

"No. She doesn't know this place. What if she wakes up and finds herself alone?" He spoke with such compassion that Clarissa felt guilty. She glanced at Addie, who was parked in front of the television with a cheese sandwich and a bag of potato chips. Clarissa had picked out a long video to ensure some quiet time during dinner.

"Okay, we'll put her on the floor in the living room. You'll be able to see her from the table."

He shook his head. "I'll just hold her. Besides, I don't really feel like talking to a lot of people I don't know."

Rob looked down at Lina and smoothed her thin dark hair. From the forehead up, she looked like an old man.

"Go enjoy yourself," he said. "Mamie threw this party because she wants you to have some fun."

"But it's a dinner party for grown-ups. I want to enjoy it with my husband." Clarissa was practically whining now, like Addie begging to stay up late. All she wanted was to have Rob sit by her at the dinner table. Was that too much to ask? She leaned toward him, trying to arrange the two of them, plus the baby, into some kind of embrace.

The front of his shirt was stained with spit-up. She pulled back. It had been months since she'd even noticed the sour smell of the baby's vomit, but suddenly, coming off Rob, it was overpowering.

"Stop picking a fight," said Rob. He clenched his jaw as if he were in pain. So far no one had noticed their conversation in the corner. "Can't this wait until later, when everyone's gone?"

"Later!" she almost wailed, her eyes filling with tears. "I'll be too tired to talk later. And you'll be asleep anyway. And tomorrow I will have started to think it was at least partly my fault and then we'll never have this conversation."

She expected Rob to soften in response to her distress, but instead his eyes narrowed in a new, fierce way. "What do you want?" he hissed. "An argument in the middle of a party? I'm going upstairs. You need to sit down and join your mother's friends."

In the dining room, Barbara laughed about Steven's attempts to teach her German. "In the end I only learned to ask for whipped cream. Schlag—right dear?"

Clarissa glanced at the carefully arranged place cards (who but Mamie would use place cards at a vacation cottage?) and realized she was supposed to take her place next to Kenny. When he noticed her in the room, he picked up the card and waved it at her from across the table.

"Hey," he said. "We're partners. I guess it's our destiny." He said "destiny" ironically, which surprised her.

Clarissa wondered whether she should sit down. Maybe he was right, in a way. Maybe all of Mamie's obscure schemes amounted to a kind of destiny. Her eyes burned from crying. She hoped they hadn't turned red and puffy. Kenny smiled up at her. She thought about it. At least he was someone to talk to. She might have joined him and enjoyed the dinner if she hadn't heard her mother calling.

"Clarissa, don't sit down yet. I need your help."

In the kitchen, Clarissa ladled curry into white china bowls, sprinkled chopped cilantro on top, and arranged the steaming dishes on an ornate stainless steel tray that, in the right light, Mamie claimed, was often mistaken for silver. As she worked, she asked Mamie about Harvey.

"I met him at the grocery store, of all places," Mamie explained. "He runs a construction business. And I know what you're thinking. He's not my type." Mamie paused at the kitchen door. She caught Harvey's eye, waved her hot pad, then turned back to the stove.

"Well, he's a good man," she continued. "He reminds me of Gregory Peck. Don't you see it around his mouth?"

Clarissa paused to glance at Harvey. "No, I don't," she said. He was chewing on a roll, not bothering to wait until the hostess was seated. In the kitchen, Mamie sprinkled more cilantro on the bowls Clarissa had already garnished. Her elbows protruded hard and bony.

"I think we have enough bowls," Clarissa said. "Rob took Lina upstairs so she could sleep in her crib. He won't be eating with us."

Mamie raised her eyebrows. "Had a fight about it?"

"Not exactly a fight. She could have slept on the living room floor."

"I saw you two in the corner. I could read it all from the way you held your shoulders."

Mamie arranged chive blossoms among the bowls for decoration. She picked up the tray and paused, with her eyes closed, to breathe in the fragrant curry. "You know," she said, "in a way raising kids is like living in a state of war. The life you used to know, the life before parenthood, is blasted away. The people you thought you knew, your husband for instance, act like strangers. You walk around in shock for years, and then you raise your head and realize that it's over, that they're grown, or almost. You find a kind of peace, and it seems like you have your whole life before you."

Clarissa waited for Mamie to add something to this speech. Something like, "Of course, I loved being a mother." But Mamie just turned and walked into the dining room. She set the beautifully arranged tray on the table and bowed as the guests admired her creation, as if she'd done it all herself. Clarissa watched from the kitchen and then slipped out the back door into the twilight.

She walked around the back of the cottage, below the bedroom where Rob had retreated with Lina. The baby was crying, probably because she wanted to nurse. Clarissa felt a tingling in her breasts. She could feel her milk leaking out, soaking her bra, and spreading out into the dress she'd taken from Mamie's closet.

She hurried under the overhanging trees, down the path to the shore. The night was calm and cool. In the twilight, every dark thing had lost its texture. The tree trunks, normally bumpy and gnarled, were now only black. Each looked like a slash of open space—a narrow doorway into some other place. Flat Rock had turned even darker against the rippling water, as if it had absorbed all color into itself.

Clarissa imagined rowing out to the rock just as her mother had done all those years ago. How peaceful to spend the night out there, to leave everyone behind. Was that why her mother had done it? Just to get away? Clarissa had always assumed she'd meant it as some sort of punishment aimed at Clarissa's father. Maybe she'd meant to punish Clarissa and her sisters too. Had she seen them hiding under the willow branches on the shore and, for a moment, hated them for it? Rob's words to her in the living room came back to her now: "What do you want?"

A small splash disturbed the quiet like a glass breaking. It might

At the end of the summer Walter spent several days at Lake Margaret trying to envision his future. It was an embarrassment, to be in his late thirties and straining, still, to see what came next. He hoped that no one was spying on him as he sat on the pier watching for a light to shine from somewhere out in the dark years before him. He had struggled to find his way as a teenager and as a college student. It was humbling to be in the future, in the time that should have been filled with satisfying labors and triumphs. How was it that he was sitting in the same chair, trying again to divine the path ahead? Most of the people he knew seemed to have had little difficulty long ago choosing a profession and stepping into the role, using the jargon naturally, looking the part. His cousin's husband, Roger Miller, had decided in the third grade to be an optometrist; Susan had always been on the ballerina track; Daniel had wanted to become a marine biologist.

Through his twenties and thirties, Walter had worked at a dollhouse shop on the Upper East Side in New York City, selling furniture and house kits, and teaching his customers how to install the dinkiest marble tile, hardwood for floors, period molding and slate shingles. He understood the allure of the miniature because he had grown up helping Joyce put together and decorate her three-story town house with a dormer. They'd wired the downstairs with electricity, so that at Christmas the impossibly small candles clipped on the three-inch tree in the parlor filled the room with what his father called a homier-than-thou yellow glow. Walter knew that for his adult customers the simple delight of reducing real life in all of its detail to fit on the coffee table was worth eyestrain and aching fingers. There was also the more complicated charm of creating a kingdom so small that a person could perfect it. What woman wouldn't find it gratifying to make something incorruptible by human beings? No slob was ever going to track mud through the $4,000 Georgian brick town house with twenty-six hundred hand-laid mini bricks, or the English baby house with dentil molding, or the southern colonial, fourteen rooms, full attic, with clapboard siding and a cedar shake roof.

Walter had been sympathetic to some of his clients at the shop, ladies who, like himself, loved the spirit of a house as much as the particulars of design and structure. To his way of thinking there was nothing hokey or Oriental in the idea that a house had a life and sensibility of its own. He would never have said that a building had an aura, but the long and the short of it was that some places felt right and others did not. He indulged himself in the pleasure of communion with his customers as together they bent over veranda spindles and newel posts and finely turned balusters. For a while he thought he might fill his studio apartment at Ninety-sixth and Amsterdam with a replica of his old neighborhood in Oak Ridge. His boss would have given him the materials at cost, the construction would occupy him for years, and when he finished, decades later, the *Smithsonian* magazine could do a feature on him—he, an old man with a hobby. He supposed at the root of the project was the normal longing to fashion his own history and commemorate what was past. A friend had dragged him to the Y, to a seminar on taking charge and living in the moment, but the theories and techniques were suspect, Walter thought. The moment, after all, was a flash in the pan. Life, he knew, had meaning and was fully possessed only as it was remembered and reshaped.

It had taken Walter several years to admit to himself that he couldn't go on indefinitely selling Lilliputian Coke bottles and microscopic toilet-roll dowels. What, then? How was he to spend his days and how was he to earn his bread and butter? Maybe through his childhood he hadn't focused, hadn't crossed his legs at night on his bed, eyes closed, concentrating on Walter in a pinstriped suit, Walter shaking hands with the boss, Walter on the front page of the *New York Times* sealing a $70 million deal with a great American company.

He had not visualized prosperity and fulfillment, and so he was thirty-eight years old, sitting at the end of the pier at Lake Margaret wondering where to live in the years before retirement. The wind blew across the lake, driving off the sailboats and turning the water a darker green. Already some of the leaves had yellowed, drifted to the ground and stuck in the bushes. The neighbors were burning brush and to Walter the air smelled of autumn. He watched the chipmunks darting to the holes in the cracked seawall with wads in their mouths, and he thought that if he were a small animal in Wisconsin he would know by the smell to expect great change. Smoke filled the air, spiraling into the pale blue sky. He used to think there was nothing as sad as Lake Margaret in the fall, and it seemed so again. Summer was over, school would begin, winter was upon them. All green things, the moss, the vines, the children at their desks, would soon experience a prolonged state of near death.

In the daylight Walter sat far into the old white Adirondack chair, drinking coffee, and in the night he sat there also, under the heavens, wrapped in a quilt. He had never been out of doors by himself for that long, and it seemed to him enough of an occupation, watching the water change color, watching the fishermen holding their rods hour after hour in their metal boats. A morning went by, and he had only looked, and remembered, and looked, in the honest labor of smelling the change of season and waiting for absolutely nothing. He looked across the lake to the cow pasture and he looked at the water, where he sometimes saw his ghostly boyish form swim up to the surface. His was an ordinary tragedy, he knew. He had been happy as a child and had not realized it. But happiness was spent so quickly, he thought, and identifying it, feeling it, trying to hang on to it, made him nervous. Maybe it was better to be ignorant of bliss, unselfconscious, and later have the sense to recognize its traces.

In May, Walter had applied for a job teaching English at Otten High, in Otten, Wisconsin. He had been back to school part-time in the last four years for his certification. It had been a marvel in the spring during his inquiries to hear the secretary at the school say "Otten," and then "Wisconsin," as if her vowels, the broad Wisconsin *o,* were on display for a freak show. Walter could have supplied good reason for wanting the job, but he had applied primarily on a whim. It was the secretary, Mrs. Oldenberg, and her bewitching voice, and it was also the fact that Otten was an hour from Lake Margaret. The town of three thousand people had been named for a temperance leader, Samuel Otten, an easterner who had hoped to build a temperance utopia out in the wild Wisconsin territory. Well over one hundred years later there were taverns dotting the village map. Walter didn't know if such an inception, followed by the abandonment of the ideal, was a good sign. He and Samuel Otten were perhaps cut from the same cloth, two men from the East with ridiculous expectations. Maybe it was absurd to imagine he could teach farm boys Shelley's "Hymn to Intellectual Beauty," but from a distance it didn't seem impossible. They might not heckle him; it might be worth a try.

He had learned, a week before, that from the fifteen applications he'd submitted had come only two offers. It was a choice between a school in Queens and Otten High. He had grown accustomed to life in New York, and he wasn't sure he could make the adjustment to a town with a one-screen movie theater, no bookstore, no cafe, no opera company, not one ballet troupe and no chain clothing stores. It was unlikely, too, that there would be very many of his own kind in Otten. Either pick involved the risk of death, he considered, one literal, the other spiritual. The Queens high school had metal detectors at the door, equipment that weeded out assault weapons and handguns. Box cutters, apparently, were not detectable by the scanner. A math teacher had bled to death after his throat was slit in May.

Walter sat with his feet in the water pitting one place against the other, thinking of irrelevant specifics, weighing the appeal of the mangy city rodents, slinking along the subway tracks, against the type of rat sure to be found in Otten, the sleek, well-fed beast that made its living in the grain elevators on the edge of town. He listed the famous people who had grown up on Wisconsin soil: Spencer Tracy, Georgia O'Keeffe, Thornton Wilder, Harry Houdini and, of course, Liberace. Wladziu Liberace, born in the working-class town of West Allis; Wladziu, Polish for Walter, had been called Wallie when he was a boy. Surely the Liberace connection was as good as a marker, showing him the right direction.

Mr. McCloud, from Otten, Wisconsin, Walter said to himself. He rolled up his pants and slowly let his legs slip into the lake. If it warmed up he might swim out to the raft. There were very few boats around on the weekdays, and if he got a cramp and started to drown no one would see him flailing. In the years that he had been gone from the Midwest, his father and Uncle Ted had planted cedar and maple trees along the fence line to keep the neighbors from the family's intimate moments. Francie and Roger Miller had gotten married at the water's edge with a string quartet in the grass on one side of them and a brass ensemble on the other. There had been two memorial services, three weddings and numerous office parties. Walter had missed a good many of the celebrations. He couldn't help reminding himself that Daniel would not have strayed so far from home, would not have fled the way Walter had after high school. Daniel had not ever really left the 600 block of Maplewood Avenue in Oak Ridge. He was forever eighteen, forever the child who would not willingly leave his parents for adult life. It was so easy to imagine that Daniel would have become successful in a conventional way, someone who moved confidently through the halls of a venerable financial institution in the heart of the city. Daniel might well have bought a house down the street from the McClouds, calling on Joyce and Robert in the evenings, to ask their advice, to dispense his own wisdom.

It was a trap, rusty, clanking, stinking, Walter knew, to glorify the lost brother, the kind of son who would have driven up to Lake Margaret every weekend to spare his father the trip, who would have mowed the lawn, checked the locks, weather-stripped the windows, cleaned the gutters. Walter tried to imagine himself on the tractor mower, wearing a chambray work shirt, a baseball cap, canvas pants with compartmentalized pockets down the thigh that snapped shut. It didn't require more than five or six minutes to get the picture in focus, to see all of the accoutrements dearly: Walter, revving the engine, wearing a dark blue cap, Ray-Bans, and his new mail-order fanny pack, complete with water bottle, securely fastened at his waist. After struggling for nearly seventy-two hours to imagine a future, and coming at last to the vision—Walter McCloud dressed for lawn care—he said to himself, Maybe. Maybe I could live in Otten.

He had read in the paper that there was a trend, a tide that could be charted, people of his generation who had moved away from their birthplaces and were coming back home in middle age. Walter could be part of a legitimate trend, a pattern that as far as he could see was not harmful to his or anyone else's health. "A trend," he said out loud, as if the word might charm him into casting the deciding vote: Otten or Queens. Aside from the comfort of being at last a part of a movement, he thought that it was probably time to return to a place where he had imagined himself, even if the image was farfetched. He leaned back against the Adirondack chair and pictured himself mowing the slope down to the lake, the sunset in the distance, through the trees, the bats hanging by their little feet in the barn, staying put, and all the summer insects, everyone of them, fluttering around the yellow porch light.

On Walter's fourth day at Lake Margaret his old friend Susan drove up from her parents' house in Oak Ridge with her two children. She lived near Miami now, in Coral Gables. There had been very few students at the Kenton School of Ballet who were star quality, and from her beginning there she was best girl. She'd left Illinois for Manhattan when she was seventeen, and at eighteen she became a member of the New York City Ballet. She was one of the last dancers to be handpicked by Mr. Balanchine for the roster, before his illness. At his Russian Orthodox funeral all of the ballerinas stood in the darkness of the vaulted cathedral holding lit candles. Susan, tears streaming down her face, was in the center of the photo that ended up in *Time* magazine. A year later she shocked her friends and relations by quitting the company. She hadn't the heart for it, she said. Didn't like the new management. She failed to mention that she'd met a man named Gary Morgan at a party, that she'd fallen in love with a normal, nonartistic person, the owner of a bookstore in Coral Gables. She moved to Florida, decorated Gary Morgan's house, signed on with Edward Villella to dance with the Miami Ballet and got married. "There's more Balanchine in Miami," she always insisted, "than there is in New York." When Walter visited her he was always freshly horrified by the tiny lizards that skittered like mice across the sidewalks.

In the afternoon Susan and Walter stood up to their ankles in Lake Margaret while the two boys swam. She had not aged much in the twenty years since her high school graduation. Her hair rippled from her forehead and went all the way down her back just as it had when she was seventeen. "I don't know anyone else whose hair cascades," Walter said. "It wimples. And rumples. I don't think there's any amount of money the average woman could pay to get the effect, right from the roots, of undulation."

"You're getting corny, Walter," she said, pulling the mass over her shoulder and inspecting it for split ends. "Is that what happens when a person is nearly forty?"

Her nose was a little bit stubby, her one flaw, but otherwise Walter thought that, counting the hair, she was close to the ideal. She had large blue eyes, thick blond lashes, the right amount of mouth, curving lips that had a certain elasticity, and she wasn't too thin. He had seen plenty of dancers who had starved themselves and looked like plucked chickens.

"Speaking of old age," she said, "I've been meaning to tell you. I met someone recently who reminded me so much of Daniel."

"That happens to me, sometimes," he said, splashing water up along his arms.

"No, but this man was so much like him. And it occurred to me, afterwards, that you and I, as close as we are, have never really talked about that year Daniel was sick. We avoid it. There, I've said it. Well, anyway, it was startling to be with this person who had some of Daniel's mannerisms and what seemed like the same sort of organizing principle in his brain, if that makes sense. In many ways they are nothing alike, but there was something uncannily similar about, I don't know, maybe their chakras."

"You're getting wonky in your old age, darling. Are your earrings—they're crystals, right? Are they functional? Do they tell you where to go, what to buy, who to trust?"

"It's just fashion, Walter, and we haven't even hit forty, so let's stop this talk, please. I admit to thirty-three in the company, even though everyone probably knows it's a lie. But I've wondered through the years who Daniel would have become—and this man seemed like a good approximation. His face could have been a computer simulation of Daniel's, those renderings of how a person, at seventeen, will look when he's forty-five. Or maybe I'm making it up, and it's only that we're still somehow looking for him, missing him. Is that ridiculous after all these years?"

Walter squinted across the lake, at the pasture that had grazed cows since his grandfather's era. "In books, death is what often propels the plot," he said, "either ignites the action or finishes it. Death or marriage, one or the other. For me, death has always been right under my skin, not doing much to move me in any real direction, no plot device. It's just there, lurking, a spot, the Daniel stain, in every cell. I can't say that such a presence is useful, or has taught me some great lesson the way it would in a novel. The law of thermodynamics, you know, the idea that nothing is lost, that a loss in one area equals a gain in another, was actually not invented by scientists but by the people who write redemptive fiction. Stories that are praised for being a testament to the human spirit. Actually, in real life, we lose things all the time and they're gone. Lost, period."

That was as much as Walter had said about Daniel in years. Susan reached under the water, picked up several snail shells and turned each one, snail by snail, over in her hand. After she had examined all of them she said, "I used to think that Daniel, when he died, had really gone to India or Burma, and that I could go there and find him walking down the street—"

Just then her nine-year-old boy, Tim, stepped on a sharp stone and yelped. She sprang up on the pier and ran down the rickety wooden slats to hoist her son to safety and examine his big toe. Walter climbed the rock steps to shore and went for the Band-Aid box in the boathouse. He was grateful to the child for putting an end to the conversation. He didn't want to speak about Daniel, or Susan's role that year, the year they glossed over when they reviewed their history. The cut toe was bloody. The Band-Aid swam in the wound, wouldn't stick, and in the end they bound it in a rag Walter found in the tackle box.

They hobbled up the gravel path to the house to get warm and find something to eat. The boys huddled in their bathrobes on the lawn, in the sunshine, eating Oreos. "What's this town like, Walter, where you've decided to teach?" Susan said, licking the filling out of a cookie and crushing the rest into the grass. He noted, as he always did in her company, that she used his name when she spoke to him, as if she liked to say it, liked the feel of her tongue to the back of her teeth, making the l, anticipating the explosion of the t. In college, when he had had no idea what to study in order to have a profession, he looked up "Walter" in the *Oxford English Dictionary*. There was no hope, no consolation in the definition, a rendering that was so at odds with the tidy and productive Virgo Mrs. Gamble had once promised him. "Walter" meant: to roll, to be tossed on the wave;

to wallow, or revel in; to move or go unsteadily, totter or stumble; to surge or roll high. He was therefore living up to his name when he was drunk or stoned, a condition he found himself in regularly during his college years, rolling high and tottering at the same time, behaving, without question, like an ass.

"Walter," Susan said again, "what's this town like, this Otten?"

"I don't know much about it, but it strikes me as a barren, inhospitable place, about as cozy as Siberia, although not as far from train service. I suppose in the drabness there are probably fabulous wildflowers and stunning native grasses. It's a sleepy, ugly little town in the middle of nowhere, and as far as Otten High goes, although the management doesn't come out and say, it's basically a technical school. Twenty percent are college-bound."

"Oh no! You'll be casting your pearls before swine!"

"My pearls? Yes, well, there's certainly no harder task than that, is there, but maybe there's no better one either. Imagine those poor pigs having nothing but slop all their lives. The school retains a Latin teacher—how's that for an idiosyncrasy? She's about a hundred and sixty-five years old and of course cuckoo, as all Latin teachers are. Either they haven't the heart to let her go, or some codger on the school board can recite Catullus and values the subject. And, I hate to have to break this to you, sweetie, but you cast your pearls before swine at every performance. There are people out in the audience who are falling asleep, having spent their money on a ticket so they can dress up and be seen doing something high-minded. And there are probably plenty of situations where we're the swine and we don't even know it."

"Oh, all right. You win. But still, why choose Otten? Isn't there a middle ground, a place like Oak Ridge, a suburban school with adequate funding and serious students?"

"Why choose it?" he repeated. "I could go into a hypnotic state with the aid of your earrings and tell you that it chose me. The truth is, I don't really have a choice, not now, not this late in the season. I'm behind everyone else, having been in the miniature business half my life and looking for work in midsummer. Fire or ice, those were the options.

"Queens or Otten," Susan murmured.

"It's been easier to justify Otten than you might think. I'd love to get to know my niece, Linda, for starters. For once I'll be close enough to act like an uncle. And I'd like to spend time with Sue Rawson. It's unlikely that she is ever going to die, but in the event that she does pass on, I will be glad to have been in her company. Plus, I'm an hour from Lake Margaret and can help Mom and Dad look after this place. I went up and visited Otten the other night and I got a little bit of an *Our Town* kind of glow. There was a man on the school baseball diamond running his toddler daughter around the bases. That seemed promising. There was a great big retarded girl riding bikes with her younger sister, and that also seemed sort of hopeful in its own way. A real estate agent named Penny took me around and showed me the rental properties, all four of them. I could have a house for six hundred dollars a month, a whole house, with shrubs and tulips in the yard, an island in the kitchen, a living room with windows that look out to woods, to nature. There are deer antlers hanging on the garage and people will think I'm a sportsman. They'll call me Mr. McCloud. I'll buy a compact car and a speed bike and a Weber grill. I don't know, for some reason it doesn't sound that terrible."

The younger boy, Toby, shouted to the older one, "That shovel is mine, I hate you! I had it first."

"And there won't be racial conflict in Otten. I'll have garden variety discontent to cope with, such as we see here, but not gang warfare." Walter left the children to their mother. He went to the woodshed to find the old puppet theater and the accompanying trunk. He didn't remember ever fighting with Daniel, although they must have occasionally had words and come to blows. They had grown up like ghosts to each other, a shadow in the hallway, a clink at the breakfast table, a breeze coming across the porch. Sue Rawson had constructed the red and green plywood box and sewn a crimson velvet curtain for the front and the back of the puppet theater. She had at one time done elaborate productions, in the days when she had only a handful of nieces and nephews, before she realized that they were fundamentally uncivilized. Walter dressed the French hand-carved wolf in Red Riding Hood's cloak and an old pair of Barbie's stiletto heels.

Over the years a few stray items had made their way into the trunk, corrupting the contents.

On the lawn Walter lay behind the theater, making the wolf heroically sing, in his heels and cloak, and with a strained falsetto, "O mio babbino caro." The performance did not mesmerize Susan's boys, and before the aria ended Tim whacked Toby on the nose, yet another bloody scene. Susan, with no pity in her gesture or her voice, handed Toby a mass of tissues from her purse and ordered both of them into the station wagon.

"Sometimes," she hissed at Walter, "I despise them." She began picking up her things, talking more to herself than to him. "I love them best when they're asleep or when I'm gone—there, that's the horrible truth. When I dance I use that love to set me spinning. But the reality of them, God! I'm not sure I'm cut out for this, Walter."

He watched her gather their towels, plastic shovels, buckets, trucks and wet suits, compressing what was strewn over the lawn into one beach bag. Mothers, he thought, had the ability to rake up possessions and compact them, make the whole impossible load portable. Their proficiency was probably encoded in their genes, the packing skill having been selected for first in nomadic days, carried forward into the covered-wagon era and on into the age of mass-produced toys. Despite her agitation and her comment about mothering he could tell she was a good parent. Her boys were high-spirited, but they weren't cocky, they weren't cruel. She'd wanted a normal life with children and that had been one of the reasons she'd left the City Ballet, given it up. He stood aside, watching, telling her about how the ten Klopers on Maplewood Avenue used to go on vacation, and because seat belts had not yet been invented, Mother Kloper used to cram five into the middle seat, four in the back, the baby up front. They each had a paper lunch bag with the one plaything they were allowed to take along.

"One toy"—Susan snorted. "Ah, those halcyon days."

"They were halcyon all right," Walter said. She was getting into the car, leaning over the front seat to give Toby the evil eye. "Do you remember Aunt Jeannie's anniversary party?" he asked. "Do you remember how my mother made the wall of pictures topple over, and the frames shattered?"

"No!" Susan held her seat belt halfway across her chest. "Not your mother! She didn't make that happen."

"I wouldn't be so sure. I sometimes think she might have given it a nudge. She was the only one who wasn't shocked by the noise or the mess. Sometimes I think of it, and I wonder." Walter bent down and kissed his friend through the open window. She hardly noticed, immobilized by the idea of Joyce McCloud willfully committing a destructive act.

"I don't believe it," she said, shaking her head. "Why? Why would she have done such a thing?" She let the belt go and pulled it again, this time all the way across herself. "We never gave your mother a literary personality, did we? It's so interesting, to think about who she was in those days. We are her age now, Walter, do you realize that?"

He put his hands to his forehead to make a visor. He studied the sky, trying to look as if he was making an effort to remember. Joyce was outside literature, he thought, not someone they could easily peg. Through high school he and Susan, and Mitch too, had had the habit of assigning one another parts from their current favorite novel. The practice gave ordinary life the weight it would never have, and also lent substance to their own personalities. It was only lately that Walter had seen the obvious: Mitch as Charlotte Stant, and himself as Maggie Verver. But in the old days Susan was always the moral or immoral beautiful and intelligent heroine: Elizabeth Bennet, Margaret Schlegel, Anna Karenina, Dorothea Brooke. Mitch in that era was naturally the romantic lead and Walter the character part. Susan was the only dancer Walter had ever known or heard of who read serious novels.

"It was ingenious of you, to marry a bookseller," he said.

"All the uncorrected proofs I can read," she said, smirking at him. "A brilliant career move. Oh, Walter, you've got me thinking about that anniversary party. Daniel was supposed to come, wasn't he? He had been going to bring the girl on the tennis team—Eleanor O'Reilly was her name. But he got sick that morning. The very day. And the old bag, the neighbor lady of yours, Mrs. Gamble, was so angry at your parents when you got home. She took your mother by the shoulders, said she had no business leaving a kid with a tumor on his neck at home by himself."

"There hadn't been a diagnosis yet," he said, "but she seemed to know already that it would kill him."

"God, she scared me. I thought she was going to attack your mother. Or maybe it was those dogs of hers. They were all going crazy behind her fence." She chewed on her lip and Walter noticed that she had fine lines—wrinkles—on her brow. "Anyway, now you're leaving your old life and moving back here. I hope your students can read other things besides the gearshift panel of their John Deere tractors." She stroked her forehead as if she knew he had seen the creases, as if she was trying to smooth them away. "I'm a lot dumber than I ever thought I'd be. I planned to be a famous ballerina, an artist, and deep down I'm just a suburban mom with a paneled station wagon, domestic problems, two bratty kids who sleep on cotton sheets patterned with trucks. But you, you are going to teach your swine to walk and talk!" She reached both hands out of the window, pulled Walter's head in, and solemnly kissed him on the mouth.

"Ask your mother if she made the pictures smash and why," she called as she started down the drive. "I'll bet you a million dollars she didn't."

"She'll never tell," Walter shouted after her. "That's what I bet. She will never tell."

Before school began in Otten, Walter drove to Schaumburg, Illinois, to visit his baby sister, Lucy. She had been born in 1974, when a good portion of the family's life, in Walter's view, was over. She had missed growing up with his brotherly instruction and he couldn't keep himself from thinking that such an absence might explain why she was living in a place like Schaumburg. He was arrogant, he knew, but he couldn't help it, couldn't help wanting to improve her, to make her see what was hollow about her choices. He was, after all, thirty-eight years old, and she only twenty-one.

There was nothing good about Schaumburg, in his opinion, not the mall around which the town had recently been built, not the corporate headquarters, not the concrete sprawl of it, not even the sweet backward intentions of the planners who wanted to build a Main Street with a mock downtown. He did not like the wide new streets in Lucy's subdivision, with culs-de-sac that were supposed to prevent undesirable people from speeding and pillaging. All of the homes in the neighborhood—a term he used loosely for Lucy's environs—had two-story foyer windows and skylights in the master bedrooms, but they were alike in a way the Oak Ridge houses had never been. Maplewood Avenue, he knew, had once been a tract and many of the Queen Anne–style houses had identical floor plans, but all the same those structures had grace and beauty, and also character. In fact, there were certain houses that seemed to attract handicapped or troubled people and others that assured a type of normalcy. It was as if the buildings themselves determined the owners. In Schaumburg there was probably an ordinance that broadly defined and prohibited weirdos. Nothing, Walter believed, neither a range of owners nor the ravages of time, would add texture or variety or interest to the houses. And where was the alley? In Oak Ridge, Mr. and Mrs. Kloper and the ten girls had lived to the south of the McClouds, and their cousins, the other Klopers, were in the yellow house straight across the alley, all twelve of them, all boys. For years there had been jokes about the water, the air, the soil on one side of the alley versus the other, and the effects those elements had on determining gender. The alley itself was the great divide, the place where the children spent the daylight hours, but after, in the dusk of summer, they split away, each to his own turf, and went to war.

Walter couldn't imagine that there was one personality in Schaumburg as peculiar as Mrs. Gamble, not one woman who would storm out of her house with a bullwhip when the little children begged from the milkman. He was stubborn and not altogether reasonable about his dislike of his sister's town. It was middle-aged of him, he realized, to feel irritated by a place, to be bothered by the fact that there were driveways instead of alleys, that there were no stay-at-home mothers, no tired housewives in curlers, no women who started drinking whiskey sours at three in the afternoon on their porches. Where was that leisured class, the Mrs. Gambles, who took it upon themselves to police the families, the dogs, the village employees? Mrs. Gamble could detect the tantrum of a spoiled child in a faraway house. The squall of a husband and wife. The low rumble of the garbage men, always late, coming from the west side of Oak Ridge. There was no point and certainly nothing attractive in

middle-aged despair, and yet, Walter thought, someone had to have
angst. It should not have been surprising that the old neighborhood
would slowly vanish as the children grew up and their parents
moved away and the world changed, but he was on hand to say, I am
surprised! I am dismayed. I don't like it!

There was a quietness about Lucy's street, as if each house were
stranded on its own lawn. It was hard to believe that men and
women were really behind their closed paneled doors, couples thinking, cooking, making love, banging on a piece of wood with a ham-
mer down in the basement, something, anything, for home improve-
ment. The shades were drawn all down the street as if a president had
been assassinated, as if one a day got a bullet through his head.

Walter arrived in Schaumburg on Saturday morning, just as his
three-year-old niece was getting ready to go to her ballet class at the
park district. Lucy had invited Walter especially for the class, because of his interest in the dance. He was standing on the blue mat
that said Welcome! in red cursive, talking to Lucy before she appeared. "Linda's too young," he was saying as the door swung open.
"Do the park district officials look at the feet? Would they know
what they were seeing if they did? Who does she take after, you or
Marc?" He waved his hands in front of his face. "It doesn't matter—
the fact is she's too young."

"Walt," Lucy said, smiling at him. "I'm fine too." She was the
only person who had ever called him Walt. He had also once looked
up "Walt" in the Oxford English Dictionary. It meant to revolve in
the mind, to consider. It meant to fall into anger or madness. His
name, in any form, did not portend an easy life.

Lucy took him by the arm and led him into the entry that was
as large as the New York studio apartment he had left behind. His
sister's house always had the gift-shop aroma of dried flowers and
scented candles. Walter took a whiff and coughed. He wondered
how a suburban girl had taken to the country craft movement, if
it was pure chance, a mutation that had made his mother's home-
decorating gene run amok in Lucy. There were plaid bows around
the stems of the brass candlesticks on the mantel, checked gingham
curtains with tiebacks, and at every turn a fabric goose, a wooden
goose, a porcelain goose, a stenciled gaggle of geese. There were pigs

too, pink pigs, white pigs, stuffed pigs, china pigs. The house had come with the opulent foyer chandelier, a dazzler, all right, with several hundred prisms hanging from ever smaller steel circles that went up to the ceiling. The fixture clashed with the barnyard motif, but unfortunately it seemed to be attached to the main beam without hardware, a natural and permanent outgrowth from the ceiling. Walter's niece was sitting on the carpet through the way into the living room, picking out bits of pink lint in the white tulle skirt in her lap. "Hello, Miss Queen Dido," he called to her.

Linda looked up, slowly, blinking, as if she'd been asleep. She hadn't rushed to the door, calling his name, spinning around, wriggling with excitement. "Hi, Uncle Walter," she said dutifully.

He thought her terrifyingly well mannered, as quiet and closed as the houses in the neighborhood. To Lucy he said, "Her feet are not ready for ballet. Her bones are too malleable. I looked at them last weekend, at the lake. They're baby feet, soft, like pudding. In Russia they don't start children until they're nine or ten, and only after each one has had a complete physical, only if the child is suited for the rigorous training. I'm serious, Lucy. She's too young."

"You? Serious?" She reached around him with slack arms, and laid her head on his shoulder.

"Take her to *The Nutcracker* when she's eight," he commanded, absently patting her back. He called out to Linda, "Cover your ears." She obediently clapped her pudgy hands to either side of her head. "She'll want to be Clara more than anything in the world," he said into Lucy's silky sweet-smelling hair. "Blue satin dress, golden curls, white pantaloons, pink shoes. After the performance, tell her you can't afford the lessons. Apologize. Keep telling her about your impoverished state, even when she weeps, begs, beseeches. Pretty soon she really will want lessons more than a puppy, more than Barbie's dream house, more than getting her navel pierced. She'll take up religion. She'll pray. When her demands reach a feverish pitch you say, 'Maybe. Maybe, Linda.' Right before she goes over the edge you acquiesce, although grudgingly. It will be perfect timing, you see, because at that point she will be ready to submit to the torture, and find the path to the divine." He took a deep breath. "This park district thing is all wrong."

Lucy had moved away from Walter halfway through his prescription for her daughter's dancing career. She'd enrolled Linda in the ballet class thinking it would please him. She laughed a little as he spoke, as she wrangled the child into her yellow and white tutu. "There's no telling what goofy old Uncle Walter will say or do," she whispered. Linda was already wearing white tights and yellow ballet slippers. The yellow headband, with pink and green flowers sticking straight up on a thick wire, wound in a white ribbon, gave her the antennaed look of an ant.

"She loves her class, don't you, Lind," Lucy said, jostling the whole girl to free the skirt of lint. It was not a question and Lucy didn't wait for Linda to answer. She took Walter by the arm again and pressed gently. "Marc thinks she's so cute in her dancing outfit. Relax, Walt, and look at how cuddly she is."

"How what?" he called to her.

Linda followed her mother out the door, her unfortunate knock-kneed walk making the stiff tulle of the skirt bounce up and down. She buckled herself into her own car seat in the back of the New Dodge Caravan Limited Edition, which was a glittery sand color called Desert Romance. Walter wished Linda would cry and buck, get down on the floor and be a head banger. She fastened her seat belt and adjusted her antennas. When Lucy turned on the ignition, Kenny Loggins came on with the air-conditioning.

"You were born too late to enjoy this kind of thing," Walter said. "This guy's voice is clotted with—with goodness and self-satisfaction. Why aren't you listening to something you can argue with, Mahler, or Bjork, or Liz Phair?"

Lucy tilted her head toward Walter and smiled without opening her mouth. He was different, that's how she thought of him, when she described him to her friends. A different drummer who wouldn't hurt a flea.

"Walt," she said pleasantly, "would you please just give up on me?"

She had a knack, Lucy did, of occasionally saying something that betrayed a certain acumen. Walter had actually come to Schaumburg determined not only to nag at her but also to talk. From what he'd gathered, neither one of his parents had wanted to make a set of stories about the past. They had discouraged her questions, nipped

248

her native curiosity in the bud. Joyce and Robert had apparently believed that Lucy could make a clean start if she wasn't burdened by
the family's previous history, if she was not encouraged to read difficult books or take up an art form beyond making cakes from boxed
mixes. Walter had occasionally wondered if Joyce hadn't had the
heart to raise another child, if she had gone through the motions
hoping for a healing effect, hoping for something that never came to
her. He wondered if his mother had not had the strength to rescue
Lucy from her mild temperament and her ordinary aspirations.
Joyce had allowed her only daughter to go to junior college and
marry at nineteen.

Who could tell what had shaped Lucy or who had given her her
best self? By the time she was kindergarten age the neighborhood
was already lost. The swarm of children had grown too old to play
war in the summer nights and so she had missed shinnying in the
Kloper trench after the phantom bounty. There were moments
when Walter had truly believed that if the big boys caught him they
would slit his throat with their pocket knives and bleed him like a
lamb at slaughter. Fear, he'd believed early on, had a metallic taste,
and also smelled of dirt. Across the alley, on the safe side, Mrs. Gamble leaned against her fence, her burning cigarette providing the bea-
con and the scent of the home country.

Walter had asked himself a number of times why Lucy should
care about the history of Maplewood Avenue. Why should she be
interested in the texture of his boyhood? There was no clear reason,
and still he wished that retarded Billy Wexler had not been killed
by a car, gone before Lucy had had a chance to see him stealing
the trash-can lids. Year after year Billy seemed never to grow older,
always a four-year-old in the same adult body. His tantrums, his
shrieking, had had the same grounding effect as church bells, a noise
that is both heard and unnoticed, day after day. By the time Lucy
was in third grade the genius twins were doing liver transplants at
competing university hospitals. She'd missed the boisterous secrets
the porch mothers told about their husbands, and she'd missed the
pack roaming the block barefoot from Memorial Day to Labor Day,
as if they were all living on a farm. But it wasn't exactly an elegy that
Walter wanted to deliver.

He wanted to talk to Lucy not because he wished to cast a golden light on his past but because finally, in his premature middle age, he was afraid. Afraid, he guessed, of life itself. He was afraid of the boys who sat in their bedrooms in the glow of their computer screens, communing in sentence fragments with people they would never meet. When he thought of all those little zombies his stomach hurt. So many people seduced by a technology that bred impatience and greed. What was good, what had stood the test of time and had value, was being thrown out and replaced with a perpetual present that was slick and speedy and shallow. His stomach juices churned, the muscle clenched. He was well aware of the fact that others before him had been frightened by the next generation's ignorance and bad manners in just the same way. It was certainly not abnormal to believe that the new crop was deficient, but perspective did not make the distress less keen. In his blackest moods Walter feared that the books, music, art—everything he loved—were going to be overlooked by this coming spiritless and nescient generation.

Walter would make a point of listening to Lucy as much as speaking himself. He would listen. He wanted to find out from her that he was mistaken about the next century, no cause for sleepless nights. He would admit that he had become like the old lady shaking her black umbrella at the unruly boys loitering at the bus stop; he had become dowdy and out of touch, as Wordsworth had, mumbling on his walks over the wold, depressed about the general evil of the civilization.

He hoped to find, too, that he and Lucy, even without the old neighborhood, had something in common. He was willing to probe, to take a risk, to see if there was anything, besides duty and the assumption of love, that linked them. If there was not, then he would rest. He would let duty and familial love be enough. But how exhilarating it would be if they had reason for a bond, if there was something that in all of their years Walter had overlooked.

Even when he tried to dismiss his gloominess as something characteristically middle-aged, he could not move beyond his impression that Lucy and her husband, Marc, were lacking in substance, and that living itself would not provide them with insight. They were poorly equipped. They seemed to have missed their chance to build an inner life. They didn't read, they didn't discuss ideas, religion or politics, as far as he could tell. Lucy, he feared, had an interior dialogue that was as still, as silent, as a deaf girl's.

On the way to the park district building Lucy pointed out Marc's favorite features in the new van, which he had managed to acquire below cost from the dealership. There was a white quilted piggy with a red satin bow around its neck hanging from the rearview mirror. At a stoplight she took a deep breath and she said, "I'm so happy you're living close to us. We'll be able to have all the holidays together, not just Christmas. Mom said that even Mrs. Gamble is thrilled to have you back in the Midwest."

"Thrilled?" Walter said. "I didn't know that Mrs. Gamble was capable of registering delight. Indignation, yes. Rage, of course. Is there an emotion that invariably goes along with the act of snooping? What does one feel when one skulks? Titillation, perhaps." He took a tissue from a red and white container that had been embroidered in counted cross-stitch, and wiped his nose. "Do you notice that we always speak of her? When we meet, one of us always brings up Mrs. Gamble. Is she like that problematic third party, the Holy Ghost? I never understood what the Holy Ghost was, but maybe Mrs. Gamble is as good a definition as any. Otten is three hours from Oak Ridge and that's surely close enough to be in her force field again. That's the alarming part about moving to Wisconsin."

"She's an old dear," Lucy said.

Walter turned slowly to look at his sister. He was unable to move his mouth, to ask her to repeat herself. He felt as if he'd snorted the words, as if they'd gone up his nostrils and were doing their bad magic.

"But think," she persisted, unaware of his shock, "think. You'll be able to have Thanksgiving with us, with the whole family, at Lake Margaret. And Easter, too. I don't think I ever remember you at any of the Lake Margaret holidays."

He had been absent for most of her childhood, it was true. He had gone far away to college because at eighteen he knew he was in danger of never leaving home, of making his baby sister the center of his existence. It had been a wrenching departure, and even now he couldn't recall the leave-taking without feeling sorry. He regretted the distance and the fact that they had very few overlapping stories. It was funny, though, the way she seemed to think that he'd never had a Thanksgiving at Lake Margaret, that his life before her birth was unlived. After college at Columbia he'd stayed in New York. He hadn't the vacation or the money to come home, he told his mother. He hadn't the inclination, he told his friends. With a few years between them there was something about his parents and little Lucy that made him uneasy. It was as if his family had died and an all-new McCloud unit had moved into 646 Maplewood Avenue. He didn't know them anymore. He'd had trouble thinking and talking in what felt like the sedated calm of that household.

Without them he managed to have some glorious times in his twenties, in the city. He had partaken of the pleasures consigned to youth, to excessive sex and drink and drugs. He didn't get drunk much anymore and he rarely smoked dope or did cocaine, and as for sex he occasionally went looking for that someone, that high-wide-and-handsome moment. But Lucy, he was sure, had not ever given herself up to either sin or joy, had never conceived of real experience. It was a waste for a person as beautiful and capable as she was, never to have run like a gazelle across the sand on a beach and talked at high speeds about the intricacies of nothing at all, and woken later in the arms of some improbable boy.

Walter and his group had grown up, gotten tenure, or at least regular jobs, developed paunches. A few had bought homes and toupees and plastic Christmas trees. Some were dead. Some had come through, made it so far, nursing sick friends and lovers. The playwrights of his generation insisted that they were hanging on with emboldened hearts. Walter doubted that his heart was emboldened by either the deaths of his friends or their political struggles to fight the disease. Still, his young wild life, his secret, lived on in him. For all the ridiculous and petty intrigues of that spent time, he thought of the secret as a force of its own, a current, strong and clear, that ran through him, informing his older, wiser, stodgy self.

Lucy had no such thing, and now and then Walter wanted to wake her, a simple slap, one, two, three, back and forth, hello, wake up, here you are, twenty-one years of age, on this remarkable and sensitive planet, a place where single cells suffer shock if the pressure changes. Suffer shock, he wanted to demand. An old dear, indeed! He remembered that neither his parents nor Daniel had ever suggested that Walter be other than he was, and yet he wanted to grip Lucy's shoulder and insist that she be different. He noticed, as he reached for another Kleenex, that the car tissue box said, in red cross-stitch, "Happy is the house that shelters a friend."

Emerson, on Lucy's tissue box.

"Who wrote this saying?" Walter asked, testing her.

"Marc's mom gave that to me," she said. "I don't think anyone wrote it. Those phrases, ones that are true, get passed on and on." She nodded, as if to agree with herself. Looking over her shoulder, she parallel-parked the van in one dream-come-true Driver's Education continuous maneuver.

On the blue linoleum strip in the basement of the Schaumburg park district building, Linda and twenty little girls in spandex and tulle finery made a line. They scratched their legs and talked to one another, some of them making the age-old feminine gesture, slapping their hands to their mouths as they giggled over their three-year-old fancies. Melissa, their teacher, born and bred in Schaumburg, was sixteen. A schaumie, Walter thought. He wasn't sure if her hair was supposed to look teased and in place, a great puff of it in a second tier of bangs, or if she'd had a nightmare just before she'd rolled out of bed. There was no telling. She was wearing a black leotard that didn't quite cover the last tuck of her bottom, but the shortage kept her busy, yanking at the material every few minutes. Once her charges were in line she stood in front of them demonstrating the steps. She did not turn around to see if they were bending their legs correctly, or safely, if they were keeping their backs straight, their feet pointed. There was no barre for them to hold. She motioned to her boyfriend in the corner, her extended index finger jabbing the air, the sign that he should hit the button on the tape deck. There were several girls who didn't have any interest in following Melissa, and they wrung their friends' hands and spun until they fell down.

Walter sat on the folding chair on the side, next to Lucy. He tried not to look as if he were watching his homeland go up in flames. In spite of his need to educate, he would keep his outrage at bay and refrain from pontification. He would not keel over into his own lap. He'd sit erect and behave himself. This type of suppression was like holding his breath for a long period, and he intended to see the effort as an exercise, something that would at least firm his stomach muscles and possibly develop his character. When the girls on the dance floor started to turn around and around to the song "I Can Show You the World," tottering on half-pointe, their arms overhead in the shape of diamonds, rather than the elongated classical ovals, Walter clenched his teeth and gripped the chair. It was going to take all of his strength to prevent himself from scooping up Linda, chasing away, kidnapping her from her life of plenty and horror.

"Lucy," he nonetheless found himself saying out of his closed mouth. "Lucy." Classical ballet was the last fruit of Renaissance art. It began in the fourteenth century and came through Russian imperialism into the twentieth century. Imagine if the masters, if Petipa or Fokine had been able to anticipate Linda and all her cohorts and Melissa crucifying the form. "If I had seen this in the future, when I was thirteen," he muttered, "I would have slit my wrists."

She had no idea that he was really overwrought. "Sourpuss," she murmured lovingly.

Walter again turned to gaze at her. She had their mother's slender nose and hazel eyes. Her light brown hair was pulled back in a ponytail, her application of pink lipstick still holding. She was lovely, small-boned, a lightweight girl Marc picked up and spun around. She was happy with her job in customer service at the bank, happy watching her daughter doing what was expected of her, along with her Schaumburg neighbors. Linda, too, might grow up to have run-of-the-mill desires, reasonable expectations. He had watched her only a week before at Lake Margaret, asleep in a bed that used to be his. He had admired the sweaty sheen of her sleeping face. He'd kneeled at her side to look at the line of her eye, the white mother-of-pearl, showing under her slightly open lid. For an instant he believed he might, through that small thin line of white, see into her dreams. It was possible that like her mother she would aspire to a job, central air, a deck out back. There were moments when Walter felt wonder at the feat of his own sister's normalcy. It was so far beyond his notion of average. She and her husband were average to a marvelous exponential power. Lucy and Marc were like a skating pair, all made up, with matching satin outfits, sequined bodices, hair sprayed, in place, always in place, zigging and zagging over the ice, doing their synchronized moves, glowing, smiling, arms up, waving.

Lucy leaned over and patted him on the shoulder. "Maybe it's just not all that it's cracked up to be, Walt, to feel tortured so much of the time."

He had taken her to see Swan Lake, starring Natalia Makarova and Mikhail Baryshnikov at the Civic Opera House in Chicago, when she was eight years old. He would have liked to shout at her, to remind her of it, over the noise of "I Can Show You the World." "I don't feel tortured all the time," he said. "I'm one of the happier people I know, except for, maybe, Kathie Lee. I'm not as happy as Kathie Lee, but almost, Lucy, almost."

She laughed and slapped her hip. "Wait! Just wait until I tell Marc that one."

Walter began to say that it wouldn't hurt her to experience a bad day, that a brief depression would do her good. He bit his tongue. At thirty-five she would probably succumb, and he feared that she would have nothing, no good words, no music except Kenny Loggins's lullaby CD, for guidance. He looked out to the dance floor, to Linda, already cursed by her dull name. She was standing, frowning, while all the other girls tried to follow Melissa's combination. She looked small and bewildered. He wanted to go to her and whisper into her ear, offer her a pink-and-white swirling sucker, a new bike, a dollhouse, anything, so that she'd know it was all right, that life wasn't always like this moment, standing in the middle of the dance floor, standing, while everyone else breezed past. But it happens sometimes, he'd say, and believe it or not a person learns to make use of the loneliness.

Walter turned to his sister and whispered, "Linda is very, very cute. She'll be a great little dancer."

When they got back to the house Lucy's husband, Marc, was on the deck, firing up the gas grill. "Hello there," he shouted into the kitchen to Walter. "How's it going?"

Walter came through the sliding doors, grinning at Marc, grinning as hard as he could. "Good, good," he said. "Yourself?"

"Great, just great." He pointed past Walter, back into the house. "How's Miss Dance on Her Tippy Toes?"

"She did everything right," Lucy said from the dark kitchen. "Walt even said so."

At first, during Lucy's courtship, Walter hadn't wanted to like Marc. But as her high school career wore on he found that it took too much energy to repress what he supposed could be called fondness. He admired Marc, especially at a distance, when he was out in the yard mowing the grass or washing his newest car in the driveway. Marc worked eighty hours a week at the Chrysler dealership. He was skilled, giving his customers high fives, remembering their first names, and their children's names, but Walter sensed that his brother-in-law was embarrassed by his calling, that even at nineteen, when he'd started in the business, he'd felt apologetic. He worked out and he had his blond hair styled and he let Lucy dress him in pink short-sleeved polo shirts. His were the honest good looks you'd think you could trust, a man who would not lose his boyish appeal into his forties, who would grow up to be the salesman of the year, time and time again, until at last he owned the dealership.

It was the pleasantness in Marc, always moderated to the same pitch, that rendered Walter speechless. He wondered if Marc was capable of fighting for a school-bond issue, or seriously thinking about a presidential candidate, or feeling a wave of sadness at the sight of poor lost Linda on the dance floor. Walter once dreamed that Marc was dressed in gold lamé, flying on his own power in a powdery sky. When Walter concentrated on liking Marc, on getting to know him, he was bored to tears, and if he focused on the elements of his dream, what might have been an indicator, a peek into Marc's soul, what was lurking and probably forever stunted, Walter fell silent.

"She buys this meat from the Jewel," Marc was saying, "that doesn't have any fat in it. Zip-o fat."

"Wow," Walter said, marveling not at the meat but at a twenty four-year-old who had already reduced his wife to a pronoun.

Lucy opened the sliding door and stuck her head into the

September heat. "Walt, Linda wants to show you what she made at her art class."

Walter excused himself and followed Linda into the living room. Lucy had just bought a white velvet sofa and loveseat, new end tables, and two ceramic lamps with frilly shades. The living room was not large, but there was a vaulted ceiling with rough-hewn beams that was supposed to make the place feel spacious. Next to the rocking chair, the one relic from Maplewood Avenue, there was an antique wooden wagon with blocks arranged inside to spell Linda, Lucy and Marc. Linda stood at the shelf where Lucy stored the Childcraft set of reference books, and the Parents magazines in binders. Perhaps she had so many classes she couldn't decide what handicraft to show him, or maybe, Walter thought, she too was struck by the decor of the room.

"Sit down, why don't you, Linda," Walter said, taking the child by the hand and helping her onto the sofa. "While you're thinking about where you put that art project, I want to show you something. That's right, you get settled, and here, give me that headband, if you don't mind."

Linda watched without a word while Walter first stretched the band and then fit it on his head. "Your great-aunt, Sue Rawson— you remember, the tall old lady who looks like an endangered bird— she used to take me to the ballet when I was little and it pretty much changed my life. She was always changing my life, if you want to know the truth." He adjusted the band again, so it wouldn't pinch behind his ears. "Now," he said, "picture that I'm a swan, a cygnet. Little swans in ballet are called cygnets, which is something you will have to know about if you're going to be a ballerina. A cygnet is the greatest thing you can be when you're a dancer."

He was wearing khaki shorts, his blue paisley boxers sticking out above his belt in the back, black leather tennis shoes, green socks and a matching green T-shirt. "I'm at a disadvantage, Linda, because I'm minus the three other swans in this dance of the four cygnets from *Swan Lake,* and also I don't have a tutu like yours. Don't close your eyes, don't do that, but use your imagination anyway." He hummed a few bars of the music, broke to explain how the four dancers were linked up, arms hooked together in a basket weave, and then he did the entrechats, jumping in place, and retire, bent leg, foot pointed at the knee, and head to the right, down, and to the left. "In *Swan Lake*," he said, already panting as he did the jumps, "these swans are girlfriends. They're happy in this dance—but whatever they feel during the ballet, they are together—together in their happiness, and their misfortune, and their beauty. A lot of people like me, not just dancers, but fellows like me, happen to know and love this ballet and especially this variation. I got into big trouble once doing a scene from the third act—but that's another story.

"Anyway," he puffed, "there's a prince, Prince Siegfried, and it's his birthday, and his mom is going to make him choose a wife. She's going to throw a party for him and invite all of the prettiest girls and he's going to have to marry one of them. So he's in a really bad mood. He goes out to the lake—which is what I always do when I'm depressed—you can do it too, when you're older and sad—and in this peaceful glade he sees the most spectacular creature. Her face is half covered in swan feathers, and her white dress is made of this soft-downy swanny stuff."

He was going to have to start an exercise regime once he got settled in Otten. He was breathing heavily, but Linda was smart, of course she was, and she was getting the idea. "And, naturally," he went on, "the prince falls in love with this bird-girl. She sees him and she's scared out of her ever-loving mind—she thinks he's going to shoot her and have her for Thanksgiving—"

"Walt," Lucy said, appearing in the arch between the living room and the entry, "what are you doing?"

He continued to move, hopping on one foot, his leg stretched behind him, head down, one arm to the side, the other in front of him. "I took your mother—to see—*Swan Lake*—when she was eight, Linda," he sputtered. "She doesn't remember. Sometimes—that's all I want to ask of her—that she remember." He continued hopping, head to the left, down and to the right. "Am I being overly dramatic?" He gasped. "It was with Makarova—one of the greatest ballerinas—Russia—and the world—for that matter—has ever produced. Do you notice the plié—that bend Melissa was teaching you—it's about the most basic movement there is. In this four-minute dance—there are about fifty thousand pliés. Eddie Villella—my friend Susan's ballet master—believes that the battement tendu—the pointing of the foot—the stretching outward of the leg—is the way to Nirvana—but I differ with him—I prefer the plié as my personal route to the—."

"I do remember," Lucy said. "You wouldn't buy me Jujyfruits at intermission. You gave me a long speech about how movies could be about food and the movie, all at the same time, but that the ballet was separate from the body, that going to the ballet was—spiritual, I think you said, and did not mix with Jujyfruits. Sue Rawson probably never let you have candy when she took you to the ballet and so for you it was like a rule or something, a commandment."

His left leg, at that moment, extended in a knobby arabesque, came slowly to meet his supporting leg. He stood breathing out of his mouth, his headband antenna quivering. She had twisted her hair into a French knot, so that she looked grown-up, womanly. "A commandment?" he said. There was sweat running down his forehead, dripping off his brows. He balled his fists and rubbed his eyes.

"You don't have to start crying," she said, holding out a frosted glass of lemonade to him. "I got over it. All those people onstage running around made me hungry, that's all. Take this and drink. And yes, I do remember *Swan Lake*. The—couple, or whatever they are, die in the end, but you're supposed to be happy for them. I've got some lemonade for you too, honey," she said to Linda. "Just think, Walt, if your students could see you now, they'd transfer right out of freshman English into shop. If they could see you, what would they think?"

Walter looked up to the ceiling, wished for a double Manhattan and then took a long cool drink of his sister's brew, made from a powder of sugar and lemon flavor. He had temporarily forgotten that he was going to be a high school English teacher. "Oh well," he said lightly, "Freshman English is a requirement. You can't transfer out of it." His sister meant no harm, he knew. She had propriety to think of, her daughter's moral upbringing as well as her husband to protect. He was getting uppity on her own turf, and she couldn't condone it. Her reaction was understandable. But if he was ever the

Once upon a time—September of 1974, to be exact—I went to New York. I was twenty-three. I'd been out of college for a year. I could read, I could conjugate Latin verbs, I could discuss the contributions of the Venerable Bede to Western civilization, and I could handle a mop and a bucket. The last skill I'd picked up the previous winter in Nashville, where I'd cleaned the offices and bathrooms of people in the music business. This was a night job. During the day, I'd lain on my friend Mac's sofa and read novels and waited for the moment when I'd be ready to go to New York.

As I drove east, I sometimes checked myself in the rearview mirror. I had longish hair and full cheeks from which the baby fat had never quite disappeared. My small, turned-down mouth showed the effect of wanting to be taken seriously. In my eyes I thought I saw something flashing, a twitchy eagerness I'd failed to suppress in my desire to be a person whom life wouldn't burn. When I stopped at the George Washington Bridge tollbooth and looked at myself a final time before entering Manhattan, I saw someone who had drunk seven or eight cups of coffee and smoked a pack of cigarettes between the Ohio River and the Hudson. The thrumming I felt at my temples was almost visible.

I'd made arrangements to stay at my Aunt Vi's apartment on the upper West Side. Aunt Vi was my mother's older sister, a painter, twice-divorced. She had a house out in Westchester, her primary residence, which she shared with two Airedales. I was supposed to get the keys to her apartment from a man named Elvin.

It was after eleven when I found my aunt's building, a brownstone between Central Park West and Columbus Avenue. A man was sitting on the stoop, taking the mild September air. He wore a suit that was a lizardy green. The trousers were flared and the jacket lapels were as big as wings. The suit brought words to mind—*predatory, naive, hopeful*—but none of them seemed quite right. The suit glowed in the sulphurous glow of the streetlights, but it would have glowed in pitch dark, too.

The man, who wore a white T-shirt beneath the jacket, didn't look at me as I came up the stoop with my luggage. He was smoking a cigarette. He had thick, dark, wetted-back hair, like an otter, and a pale, bony face that was not unhandsome despite the crooked nose. Under his right eye was a purplish smudge—the remnant of a shiner, perhaps. I thought he might have been in his late twenties, older than me by several years, anyway.

Across the street, two men were shouting at each other in Spanish. Their curses flew back and forth, blurring the air.

"I'm looking for somebody named Elvin," I said to the man on the stoop. I remembered that my aunt had mentioned that Elvin was from down South—Mississippi, maybe. "He's a hick just like you, honey," she'd said, "except he's got a lot of mustard on him."

The man picked a piece of tobacco off the tip of his tongue and flicked it away. "You're looking at him, bro," he said.

"You're the building superintendent, right?"

"I guess I am," Elvin said. "I'd rather be the Sultan of Swing, but you got to deal with the cards that get dealt to you, don't you?" He was watching the two Hispanic men; one stalked away from the other and then turned back quickly to deliver an elaborate, gaudy curse. New York was like opera, I'd read somewhere—people in costumes discussing things at the top of their lungs.

Elvin said, "So you must be Violet's nephew. Come to get down in the big city." He smiled and brushed something visible only to himself off the sleeve of his jacket. Where, I wondered, did Elvin go in his suit and his ankle-high black boots that zipped up the side?

"Peter Sackrider," I said, holding out my hand.

"Pleased to meet you." He clasped my hand soul-brother style. "What you got in that box there?" He pointed to the case that held my new Olivetti, a graduation gift.

"A typewriter," I said.

"Ah," he said. "Tap, tap, tap into the night, right?" He dragged on his cigarette and then launched it toward the sidewalk. "I used to know this writer who lived in New Orleans. He OD'd or something." Elvin rose from the stoop and looked skyward. He'd been sitting on a magazine to keep his trousers clean. "Looks like we got a big, old, hairy moon on our hands."

I'd seen the moon earlier, driving across New Jersey. It was a harvest moon, the dying grass moon. Seeing it had made me shiver a little. Then it had slid behind clouds. Now, when I saw it again, hanging above apartment buildings topped with water tanks, it seemed no more than an ordinary celestial body on its appointed rounds, a cratered thing shedding some extra light on overlit New York.

"My old man used to say 'Katy, bar the door' when the moon got full," Elvin said. "I used not to believe any of that ass-trology stuff, but I might have to change my mind. I'm feeling sorta werewolfish tonight." He undid the middle button of his jacket.

"You're going out now?" I asked. "It's kind of late, isn't it?"

"Never too late for love, bro," Elvin said. "Never too late for some of that."

A few days later, I took a typing test at a temporary employment agency. Even though I made a number of errors while typing at close to a crawl, it was decided that I was a "pretty good" typist, and the agency sent me off to midtown companies in need of secretarial help. I worked for a direct-marketing firm, a bank, a company that sold gag items such as hand buzzers, an oil company, a cosmetics firm. I wore my tweed coat with the elbow patches and read Faulkner on my lunch breaks. I doused my typing mistakes with correction fluid, hoping I wouldn't be exposed as a charlatan. Late that winter, the agency sent me to a publishing house on Fifth Avenue. I was put in the office of a vacationing editor and given a piece of a manuscript to re-type. "Be careful you don't spill anything on the original," an editor, a woman in a black pants suit, said, tapping the top of a Thermos of coffee I'd brought with me. The manuscript pages were faded yellow second sheets; they looked as delicate as dried flower petals. After the editor went back to her desk, I held a page to my nose and sniffed it.

The section of the manuscript I typed was about an American couple traveling in the south of France. She had cut her hair short to make herself look like a boy. He wrote stories in cheap notebooks with sharp pencils. They swam naked in the cold blue sea and drank absinthe in cafés and made love. I had read most of the prescribed Hemingway in school, and I thought that what I was typing now, on an old manual Olympia, must be more of him or at least a very good imitation. I was excited. I was enthroned in an office a half dozen flights above Fifth Avenue, black New York coffee was running through my veins, and sunlight was flowing in the windows—late-winter sunlight that seemed to illuminate the pleasure I felt in being where I was (however fleeting my tenancy was likely to be) and to promise more: spring, love, a life in literature. Now and then, the editor put her head in the door to check on me. Once, when she came all the way into the room, I felt an urge to tell her how much I liked her black pants suit, which was Asian in style and made a little swishing sound when she moved. But I lost my nerve.

A few weeks later, I got a permanent job at a publishing house called Church & Purviance, a sleepy, old-line company. I worked for an elderly editor named Mr. Stawicki, who had a corner of the C & P building all to himself. He was responsible for the house's military history books. He had white hair that streamed away from his mottled forehead—one could imagine him on the deck of a frigate, spyglass in hand, studying the horizon for enemy cutters—and in close quarters he gave off a scent that was a mix of talcum powder, butterscotch candy, and decrepitude. Mr. Stawicki had trouble getting my name right, for some reason that seemed only partly related to his age. He called me Son or Champ or, once, William, which was the name of a nephew of his who sold bonds on Wall Street. "Well, William," he said, "I think it's time for Mr. Powell's morning constitutional." Mr. Powell was Mr. Stawicki's thirteen-year-old Sealyham, whom I was required to walk two or three times a day.

One reason that Mr. Stawicki may have been unable to utter my name was that my predecessor's name, Petra, was close to my own. Mr. Stawicki carried a torch for Petra, who had left him to work for a C & P editor named Marshall Hogue. On the one occasion when Mr. Stawicki and I went to lunch together, at a dark Lexington Avenue bar where both he and his dog were known, he said, following his second Rob Roy, "You know, son, you're a nice boy, but I can't forgive that man Hogue for stealing Petra from me." He pronounced her name with a soft *e* and a trilled *r*. And then he predicted that he would soon be lying in the "dust bed" of history, "along with Max Perkins and that gang." Drinking seemed to make him gloomy.

I got my job at C & P through Mr. Hogue, whom I'd met at a party at my aunt's house in Westchester. He grew up in Louisville with Aunt Vi and my mother, who sat next to him in fifth grade. He went away to boarding school, and then to college and into the service, and he returned to Louisville only for the occasional holiday. The time spent elsewhere made him more interesting to the young women of my mother's set. My mother considered it a coup when he asked her to a Derby ball. But he wasn't planning on sticking around. Like Vi, who'd gone to New York to study painting, he was bound for other places.

At my aunt's party, Mr. Hogue and I drank wassail and ate salty country ham on beaten biscuits and talked about the town where we no longer lived. His voice had been swept clean of all but a trace of an accent. He had a tidy grayish beard and close-cropped hair and he wore wire-rimmed glasses. He was tall and thin, like a swizzle stick. He told me that I looked like my mother. I swallowed some wassail, the scent of cinnamon riding up my nose, and said I'd take that as a compliment. Then Mr. Hogue told me that I should come see him whenever I decided to give up the temporary employment racket. Spaces opened up at C & P now and then, he said. Of course, the pay was dreadful and much of the work was humdrum, but literature must be served, mustn't it? He laughed a small, refined laugh.

In the evening, after I had finished my work for Mr. Stawicki, I went home to my aunt's apartment. The building was near the Columbus Avenue end of the block, the less genteel end, across the street from an empty, paved-over lot where kids played stickball and a man once stood in the rain and shouted out passages from the Book of Isaiah. Aunt Vi had moved into the building in 1959, after bouncing around the Village for more than a decade. For a number of years, she used a second apartment in the brownstone as a studio. Then, around 1970, she decided to move her easels to the countryside. The apartment I sublet didn't receive much light, but the ceilings were high and the claw-footed bathtub was large and the bedroom looked down upon a kind of courtyard that the two Irish sisters who lived below me had planted with vinca and lamium. Sometimes I would see Grace and Betty down there on warm evenings, sitting in matching aluminum-tube lawn chairs, sipping Dubonnet.

Aunt Vi's apartment was sparsely furnished. There was a card table, folding chairs, a metal cot, a worn red velvet sofa that might have passed for cathouse furniture, kitchenware (including several Kentucky Derby souvenir glasses), a small pine desk, and a couple of Aunt Vi's paintings. One was a *nature morte*—a sea bass on a platter, its mouth agape and eye bulging. In the other, Aunt Vi stared at the viewer through large, black-framed glasses. She had a cigarette in the corner of her mouth. Her chin was uptilted, as if she were waiting for an answer to a question. Her skin she'd painted a hazy rose color, the color of smoke mixed with the tomatoey hue that years of drinking produces in some people. The painting was hung above the desk where I sat most evenings, trying to write a story called "The Green Suit." After several months of looking at my aunt looking at me and failing to make much progress with "The Green Suit" or its spinoffs, I decided to cover the painting with a dish towel whenever I sat down at the desk. Covering the portrait seemed less radical than taking it down or moving the desk to the opposite wall, where the dead fish was hung. I imagined that if I removed the picture of my aunt scrutinizing me, I'd be upsetting a certain balance of forces in the apartment.

One reason I had trouble writing was that I had my own crush on Mr. Stawicki's former assistant, Petra Saunders. I sometimes found myself thinking about Petra in the midst of trying to imagine what Elvin did when he stepped out in his green suit. (I'd learned that he sometimes went to New Jersey—"the land of opportunity," he called it—and so I thought of his suit as his going-over-to-Jersey outfit.) Or I would find myself thinking about Petra while trying to light upon the word to describe the complexions of Grace and Betty, who were both tellers at a bank in Chelsea, who both wore white gloves to work. Grace and Betty were going to be in "The Green Suit," a story in which the narrator, a boy from the provinces not unlike myself, is drawn into the peculiar New York life of a man not unlike Elvin. I foresaw the story turning violent at some point—Grace and Betty mugged? Elvin wild with anger? But I was a long way from reaching that point. The distance between where I was and where I wanted to be seemed immense, and I often found it easier to retire to Aunt Vi's dilapidated sofa, where I could give myself up to thoughts of Petra.

Not too long after I'd been hired at Church & Purviance, Mr.

Hogue took me out to lunch. Petra came along. "You don't mind, do you?" he asked. We went to an expensive Chinese restaurant. I drank two gin-and-tonics and struggled with my chopsticks and confessed to liking Faulkner and Hemingway. "Faulkner more," I added.

"The big boys," Mr. Hogue said, pinching a snow pea with his chopsticks.

Petra didn't comment on my literary tastes, though I guessed, from the way she sipped her ice water and averted her eyes, that she didn't approve. She was quiet—even, I thought at first, evasive. Some part of her face always seemed to be in shadow, eclipsed by her long, dark, wayward hair or by a hand pushing the hair back. When I asked her where she'd grown up, she said, "Oh, you know, all around. My father was in the Foreign Service." She said this as if it were common for American children to grow up in Rome, Addis Ababa, and Bethesda. When I went back to the office that afternoon, my head full of gin and tea and fish sauce, I got my diary out of my desk and wrote, *Is she stuck-up, or am I blind? She doesn't drink—at least not at lunch. She's reading an obscure Japanese novelist—obscure to me, anyway— which Marshall, as she calls Mr. Hogue, recommended. She looks at Mr. Hogue fondly. When she says the words* Addis Ababa, *I think of all those soft a's tumbling around in her mouth. She has a large mole between her collarbone and left breast. She wore a scoop-necked summer dress—blue, beltless.*

One afternoon a couple weeks later, after I'd walked Mr. Powell and returned him to his cedar-scented bed in Mr. Stawicki's office, I went downstairs to the C & P library. Mr. Stawicki had asked me to look up something about a diplomat who had attended a naval conference in London in 1930. By the time I reached the library, I'd forgotten the diplomat's name. The library, which was small and windowless, smelled of orange. Petra was sitting at the table, a handsome old oak piece on which the first Mr. Purviance (so the story went) had once been pinned by an author armed with a penknife. Petra didn't look up when I entered the library. She was reading, one hand lost in her dark hair. Then I saw that hand reach for a slice of orange—it was laid out in sections on a napkin—and convey it to her mouth. The name of the naval conference participant suddenly came to me, or almost came to me, but when Petra looked up, her mouth full of orange, the name squirted away, leaving a bubbly trail in my brain.

"I'm doing research for the Admiral," I said, referring to Mr. Sta-wicki by his nickname. "For his encyclopedia of warships. The two-volume thing. I can't remember what I was supposed to look up."

"That's a problem," Petra said. She was wearing a plain white blouse and a dark skirt. The mole below her collarbone wasn't visible. With her book and her lunchbox, she looked like a proper schoolgirl. Except that her lunchbox had a picture of Mickey and Minnie on it. I took this to mean that she might have a sense of humor.

"Are you still reading that Japanese guy?" I asked. I waited for his name to surface. "Tanizaki?"

"I finished him," she said. She put another section of orange in her mouth. "Marshall asked me to read this Yugoslav writer to see if we should commission a translation." She held the book out toward me. I came closer. Her fingers and wrists were bare, no jewelry. On the cover of the book, crows or bats were swirling around a man wearing a derby and a clownish cravat. "It's sort of a surrealist satire of life under Tito. This is the Italian translation."

"Does Mr. Hogue—Marshall—send you home with work at night?" My hands were deep in the pockets of my khakis. Though swimming with desire to know what she did when she wasn't at the office, I hurried on to the next question. "Is Mr. Hogue fun to work for?"

"He does interesting books." She put the orange peels and napkin in her lunchbox, which, I saw, also contained a Milky Way candy bar. I found it comforting that she had a vice.

"And you don't have to walk a dog," I said.

"No," she said, latching her lunchbox and getting up from the table. "But I didn't mind walking Mr. Powell. I went all over town with him. I could be gone for two hours and Mr. Stawicki wouldn't say anything."

"He's sweet on you," I said.

"He's kind of lonely, don't you think?" Petra said. "Well, good luck with your research."

After work that day, I walked over to Korvettes to buy a window fan. The weather had turned hot, summer having laid its heavy hand on the city even before May was out. The day's heat was in the sidewalks, in the buildings I walked past, in the sweaty, pockmarked face of the blind man who stood with his tin cup and his guide dog at the corner of Fifth and Forty-eighth, rocking back and forth, like a man taken over by spirits.

When I came out of Korvettes with my fan and began to walk up Fifth Avenue, I saw, a half-block ahead, Mr. Hogue and Petra. They seemed not to be walking so much as gliding—as far as that was possible on a crowded sidewalk. At several points, Mr. Hogue, who was wearing an olive-green suit (cuffed trousers, narrow lapels), touched Petra on the arm and guided her around a clot of slow-moving tourists or out of the way of some speeding local. I remembered that my mother had said of Mr. Hogue in a recent phone conversation, "He was quite a dancer in his heyday. All the girls wanted to be led by him. Little did they know!"

"Little did they know what?" I'd asked.

"That he preferred men to women," she'd said. "Haven't you figured that out yet, honey?"

Instead of turning left, toward Sixth Avenue, where I could catch an uptown train, I followed Petra and Mr. Hogue up Fifth Avenue. Where were they going—Petra with her lunchbox and musette bag, Mr. Hogue with his Moroccan leather satchel? Neither lived in the direction they were walking. (Petra lived way over in the East Eighties; once, after going to a movie in her neighborhood, I'd walked by her building.) Perhaps they were going to meet an agent or an author for a drink. Perhaps they were going to an early movie and then to supper at some Turkish or Balinese place Mr. Hogue would know about and then—my mother's assertion about Mr. Hogue's sexual preferences notwithstanding—to a mutual bed. Wasn't it possible that they were lovers, even if Mr. Hogue was old enough to be Petra's father? There was that moment, for instance, outside the tobacconist's at Fifty-fifth, where Mr. Hogue held Petra's lunchbox while she fished around in her musette bag for money to give to a legless man who rolled himself along the sidewalk on a little furniture dolly. And then, after Mr. Hogue returned the lunchbox to Petra, there was the way, too delicate to be fatherly, he touched the small of her back, nudging her toward wherever they were going.

I followed a half-block behind, humping my three-speed fan and my briefcase, sweating through my seersucker jacket. At Grand Army Plaza, where I stopped to light a cigarette, I got caught in an auto-pedestrian crosswalk snarl and fell a block behind. I lost sight of my quarry for a minute, and then I spotted them disappearing under the canopy at the Hotel Pierre.

I walked across the Park, toward the West Side, secure in the knowledge that the life I wanted to possess was going to elude me. I saw a man drinking a carton of orange juice while riding a unicycle. I saw some Hare Krishnas crossing the Sheep Meadow in their saffron robes. Then, on a path near the Lake, a man wearing a floppy red-velvet beret-like hat on top of his Afro stopped me and asked for my wallet. He showed me an X-Acto knife, no more than an inch of blade sticking out of its gray metal housing. I gave him my wallet and stared at the carotid artery in his neck, which seemed to be throbbing. He went through my wallet without saying a word. I felt I should say something, and so I asked him if he wanted my fan, too.

"No, I don't want your dumb-ass fan, you dumb-ass bitch," he said. He dropped the wallet on the ground and walked off. He'd taken the cash and a ticket I'd bought for *La Bohème.*

I walked out of the Park and up Central Park West. By the time I'd reached the Museum of Natural History, I'd stopped shaking. By the time I reached my street, I felt oddly at ease, as if I could float the final half-block, past the spindly young trees whose trunks were wrapped with tape, right on up the stoop, on which Grace and Betty had set a pot of geraniums. I picked a cigarette butt out of the pot, flicked it away, and went up to my apartment. The door was ajar. I heard Aunt Vi's voice, and then I saw Elvin slumped on the couch, smoking.

"Hey, bro," Elvin said. "You're just in time for cocktails." Elvin was wearing a black sleeveless T-shirt and blue jeans. No shoes. The shirt was made of a shimmery material, like his green suit. He was all muscle and bone, and he gave you the impression that he'd done nothing to achieve it, except, perhaps, smoke to curb his appetite. At one time, he'd told me, he'd worked as a mud logger on an oil rig in the Gulf of Mexico and commuted with wads of cash between New Orleans and New York. Before that, he'd been in the Army, but had somehow avoided a tour in Vietnam. More recently, he'd worked as a car jockey in a parking garage in Midtown. Now, he did odd jobs for the landlord to pay off his rent. And occasionally earned beer money by modeling for Aunt Vi.

Aunt Vi came out of the kitchen with a drink in each hand. "I let myself in, Petey," she said. "I hope you don't mind." She gave Elvin his drink and surveyed me through her black glasses. The glasses made her seem both distant and overbearing, like a bird of prey.

"No, I don't mind," I said, setting down the fan but leaving my jacket on for the moment. I didn't consider the apartment to be mine, any more than I considered myself to be a resident of New York.

"I had to come into town to see Dr. Bickel, so he can pay for the addition on his summer house in Quogue," Aunt Vi said, laughing her heavy, nicotine-stained laugh. "The old buzzard would cap every one of my teeth if he could."

I looked around the room, as if some clue to my existence were to be found there. On the mantel above the nonworking fireplace, I saw the wine bottle that I'd not quite emptied the night before while sitting at my desk, waiting for inspiration to blow through me and prickle the hairs on the back of my hand. Beside the sofa, not far from Elvin's bare feet, the bony dogs that had carried him far from Mississippi, were one blue sock and a packet of newspaper clippings my mother had sent me from Kentucky. On the wall was Aunt Vi's painting of her ripe, florid self. It was a stroke of luck that I'd taken down the dish towel last night; I'd used it to mop up a puddle of wine.

"You look like you could use a drink," Aunt Vi said.

"You've been working too hard, bro," Elvin said, hoisting his glass. "Take a load off."

"I wouldn't mind having a drink," I said to Aunt Vi. I thought I probably wouldn't tell her and Elvin about my run-in in the Park.

My aunt went back into the kitchen. Elvin said, "I'm thinking of going over to Jersey on Saturday. You want to come?"

"What do you do there?" I asked.

"Study the landscape, do a little recon," Elvin said, blowing a stream of unfiltered smoke toward the ceiling. "Go bowling. See this girl I know."

I wondered if Elvin went bowling in his green suit, or if he took a change of clothes.

"Sounds interesting," I said, not wishing to offend Elvin, who was, after all, the building's super and could requisition me an extra door lock, if I should ever need one.

Aunt Vi returned with my drink, a gin-and-tonic, heavy on the gin, in a Derby glass. The gin went straight to that part of me that wished to lie down, and so I excused myself, saying I was going to change out of my work clothes.

"Sound your funky horn, man," Elvin said, snorting.

"What's that supposed to mean?" Aunt Vi asked.

"It's just a song I used to sort of like," he said, dreamily.

I went into the bedroom, undressed, polished off the gin, and lay down on the cot. I looked at the Monet poster I'd stuck on the wall—a sun-drenched beach scene, flags rippling in the breeze.

"The boy needs to get laid," I heard Elvin say. He made two syllables out of "laid."

"I'm sure he'd be touched by your concern," Aunt Vi said. "When are you going to sit for me again?" Elvin was one of my aunt's favorite subjects. She'd painted him clothed and unclothed—once in repose on a couch, in the manner of Manet's "Olympia," with a Mets cap covering his genitals. His eyes were near to being closed. "Drowsy Elvin," my aunt called the painting.

Three weeks later, a warm mid-June evening, I lay on the same bed, absorbing the breeze generated by my fan. I was wearing basketball shorts and a Shakespeare in the Park T-shirt. Now and then, I heard firecrackers explode. The Fourth was approaching, and every kid in the neighborhood was armed to the teeth. Below my window, in the dim courtyard, Grace and Betty sipped cocktails and discussed the events of the day: the rudeness of a young officer at the bank, the elderly Negro man whom they no longer saw on the No. 11 downtown bus, Elvin's failure to fix a dripping faucet.

I'd been home since about three in the afternoon, having fled the office in the wake of Mr. Powell's death. I'd taken Mr. Powell for a lunchtime walk over in Turtle Bay, where trees provided shade and there was the occasional poodle or Boston terrier for my charge to sniff. On Second Avenue, I slipped Mr. Powell's leash around the top of a fire hydrant and went into a deli to buy a sandwich. Mr. Powell, being old, wasn't frisky, and I expected him to do no more than wait patiently on the curb while I got my turkey on rye. But he stretched his leash and wandered off the curb into the gutter, where there was garbage to be inspected. I didn't witness the accident, but I was told by a pedestrian, a well-dressed man walking a chow, that a cab turning left and cutting the corner close had struck Mr. Powell, that the driver had hit his brakes but then had gone on, perhaps at the urging of his fare.

Mr. Powell had been killed instantly, but as I carried him back to the office, in a black garbage bag that the deli manager had given me, I kept thinking, absurdly, Maybe he's just sleeping. When I'd picked him up out of the gutter, there hadn't been any blood on his thick white coat or his curious, moist nose. However, he didn't stir as I bore him toward his master, and toward, I felt increasingly sure, my own termination. Mr. Powell grew heavier as I rode in the elevator to my floor, accompanied by silent Jimmy, the uniformed elevator operator, who was the most phlegmatic man in New York.

When Mr. Stawicki saw me with the garbage bag, he said, "Please don't tell me that's my dog." I said it was and that I was sorry and that it had happened suddenly and that Mr. Powell hadn't seemed to suffer much, if at all. Mr. Stawicki looked stricken. He waved me out of his office.

I sat down at my desk and wrote him a note of apology, restating (possibly overstating) my remorse at his loss, saying that I planned to look for work elsewhere but would stay on until he found a replacement. I put the note in the In box outside his door. Then I went downstairs, to the main editorial floor, to see Mr. Hogue and tell him about Mr. Powell and my decision to leave Church & Purviance.

But Mr. Hogue wasn't in his office. Nor was Petra in her adjoining nook, though the coffee in her mug was warm. So I went back upstairs, got my briefcase, and walked home, via the Park, where I encountered no muggers, only a violinist dressed up in a bear suit. At the apartment, I put Mississippi John Hurt on the stereo and lay down on the bed. I fell asleep and dreamed about Grace and Betty.

Later, awake, listening to the drone of the fan and the voices of Grace and Betty, I considered the idea of returning home to Louisville and hooking on with my grandfather's brokerage firm and eating high-cholesterol lunches with my father at the downtown club where he played penny-a-point bridge and marrying any one of several young women I knew whose interest in literature was about the same as their interest in ethnography or limnology. This notion occupied me for several minutes—deeply enough that the sound of my door buzzer didn't immediately rouse me. When I did finally go downstairs, I at first saw only Elvin, shirtless, standing in the vestibule, where the mailboxes were. Then, beyond the outer door, on the stoop, I saw Petra, her musette bag over her shoulder. She was leaving. I opened the door and called her name.

Elvin, scratching his flat, bare belly, said, sotto voce, "Hey, man, if she's the reason you bugged out on me, I forgive you."

I hadn't gone bowling with Elvin in New Jersey. I'd pleaded a tight schedule.

"Thanks," I said. I was happy to be on Elvin's good side. I stepped out the door onto the stoop. Elvin remained in the vestibule.

"I was sorry to hear about Mr. Powell," Petra said. She was wearing a white, open-necked blouse and a blue jean skirt.

"Thanks," I said. The stoop felt warm on my bare feet.

"I'm coming from my dentist," she said, "down on Eighty-first. Dr. Fingerhut. This sweet little Austrian. He plays Schubert or Mozart while he's cleaning your teeth. 'Ah, my dear, you haf vut looks like a very sweet tooth. Ve must repair before it becomes a very dead tooth.' Marshall told me about him." She paused, as if to consider her presence on my stoop.

I didn't know what was more improbable: a suddenly chatty Petra or the fact that she was standing near me on a warm summer evening. The air—the grimy, hazy, fume-laden air of Manhattan—seemed almost fresh. There was nearly enough oxygen in it to make your head spin.

"Dr. Fingerhut told me about this Cuban-Chinese restaurant on Amsterdam somewhere," Petra said. "I thought you might be able to help me find it."

"I'll get my shoes."

We found the Cuban-Chinese place, up Amsterdam, in the shadow of a new housing project, but it didn't serve liquor, which, it turned out, Petra avoided only during work hours. We walked back over to Columbus, to a bar called the Yukon, down the block from the Laundromat that I and Elvin and Grace and Betty frequented. I'd watched some baseball in the Yukon, and had even, once, tried writing there. Except for the refrigerated air, there wasn't anything in the Yukon that suggested the remote Canadian Northwest. No pictures of Jack London or sled dogs, anyway.

We sat toward the back, in a booth that had a view of the dartboard. A fat, bearded man and his petite female companion were playing.

"Tell me again how Mr. Powell got killed," Petra said. She'd been in a meeting for much of the afternoon, and had heard about the incident third-hand.

I told Petra the story, and then I said that I was going to look for work elsewhere and was even thinking of moving back to Kentucky, where I could whittle sticks with my friends. I was hoping, of course, that she would try to dissuade me from the latter idea and give me room to imagine that I could displace Mr. Hogue as her lover. The notion that she was Mr. Hogue's lover continued to flourish in the little hothouse of my mind.

"I've never been to Kentucky," Petra said, turning the frosted glass that contained her vodka-and-tonic. "Marshall talks about spring down there, how pretty it is."

"Yes." I let pass the chance to ask about her relationship with Mr. Hogue. A couple more beers and I might have managed it. "What was spring in Addis Ababa like?"

"It was nice, mild. Addis Ababa is eight thousand feet above sea level, you know." She was looking past me. She laid her hand on my free hand, the one that wasn't gripping the bottle of Rheingold, and nodded in the direction of the dart players.

"Look," she whispered. "On the floor. The bag."

I turned and leaned out of the booth and saw a gym bag under the table that held the dart players' drinks. Then I saw the man, who was wearing a billowy Hawaiian shirt, flick a dart toward the target. The motion his hand made was dainty and precise; it was if he were dotting an *i*.

"What?" I asked Petra. She'd removed her hand from mine almost as quickly as she'd put it there. If she touched me again, I thought, that would mean something. I was a boy who required reassurance, an appalling trait to have in a place like New York.

"The bag," Petra said. "It's moving. There's something in it."

I turned again, and saw that there was indeed something moving inside the bag, flexing it this way and that.

"Maybe it's a ferret." I looked at the mole below her collarbone; I wanted to put my thumb on it.

"No," Petra said, firmly. "It's a snake. Those people are snake owners."

I turned around once more. The woman was studying us. She did somewhat resemble a person you might see at a roadside reptile farm—the proprietor's thin-lipped wife, who keeps the books and dreams about running off with the guy who stocks the farm's Coke machine. She had a hard face that was once pretty.

"You don't like snakes?" I asked Petra.

"I don't expect to see one in a bar," she said. "It kind of takes the wind out of your sails."

"I know what you mean." As she finished her drink, I thought I could see her considering whether to take a cross-town bus home or to spring for a cab. If she was going home, that is. In any event, it seemed clear that she didn't wish to spend any more time in the Yukon.

I paid for the drinks and waited by the jukebox while Petra used the ladies' room. When she came out, she stopped to talk with the dart players. Then she came on toward me, the news that she'd been right about the contents of the bag written on her face. She was a person who took some satisfaction in being right.

"It's a python," she said. "A baby python. They have a bunch."

We walked out into the warm, jarring air. The sky was still an hour short of turning the smudgy color that was the local version of nighttime. Yellow cabs were streaking down Columbus. A man wearing beltless, crimson slacks and a shirt of several hideous colors came up the avenue, cutting a wide swath, singing, muttering, nodding violently to himself.

"I guess I'll go now," Petra said. She stepped off the curb and waved for a cab.

"OK," I said.

A cab cut across two lanes and came to a halt a yard or so from Petra's sandaled foot. She didn't flinch. "Don't feel too bad about Mr. Powell," she said. "And don't go home to Kentucky with your tail between your legs." She gave me a quick kiss on the cheek. Its delicate placement reminded me of the way the fat man had thrown the dart.

"What are you reading nowadays?" I asked, as she got into the cab, a part of her leg that I'd not seen before becoming briefly visible.

The thought that I was homosexual had, of course, occurred to me—for instance, on those occasions when I'd lain on my narrow, squeaky cot, solemnly holding myself. But if this were true, why did the sight of Petra's thigh, not to mention the touch of her mouth, move me so?

"Proust," she said, pulling the door to. "He's great. You should try him. He'll make you . . ." The cab shot away, like a cork flying out of a bottle, leaving me to imagine what she thought Proust would make me want to do. Proust, I knew, had been homosexual. That was about all I knew about him. He hadn't been on the syllabus at my college in Tennessee.

I headed back up Columbus. Standing in the doorway of the Laundromat, smoking, watching the world rush by, was Elvin. He signaled to me. Over his jeans he was wearing what looked like a pajama shirt, v-necked, with red piping. His muscle shirts must have been in the wash.

"Hey, bro," he said, "maybe we can double sometime."

"Double?" I asked, thinking this was street slang I'd failed to absorb.

"Double date," he said. "You and your chick, me and mine."

"Yeah," I said. "Maybe we could do something like that."

Elvin drove up the Henry Hudson Parkway, slaloming in and out of the Saturday afternoon traffic like a stunt driver—a style that made it difficult for me to concentrate on the long sentences describing the amatory practices of M. Swann. So I put the book down. But watching Elvin drive while he sucked on a joint was too frightening. And looking out the window at the river, sparkling though it was in the July sun, was insufficiently distracting. So I fixed upon the dark, shag-cut head of Connie, who was Elvin's girlfriend and who was not much older than sixteen. She seemed to have a driver's license, anyway; she'd driven over from Jersey before giving the wheel to Elvin. But she was nervous, too—something I thought was in her favor. When Elvin had laid down rubber at the last stop we'd see until we hit the Spuyten Duyvil bridge, she'd said, "My father's going to kill me if you wreck it." To which Elvin had said, "Be cool."

We were going to my aunt's house in the green hills of northern Westchester. It was her fifty-fifth birthday, and she was giving herself a party. She'd invited a great flock of people—painter friends, Village friends, Grace and Betty, my parents, Mr. Hogue, other Kentuckians, her dentist. Grace and Betty declined (they were going to Mystic with a church group), and so did my parents. But Mr. Hogue was coming, and so was the dentist. Petra was supposed to be there, too. I'd asked her, and she'd said yes, though the yes was provisional, dependent on whether she could resolve something in her schedule.

I'd invited Petra to Aunt Vi's party about a week before I was to leave Church & Purviance. One effect of being nearly unemployed was that I didn't feel my usual diffident self around Petra. Anyhow, the sight of her standing next to the copy machine, a cranky, unreliable thing that wheezed and heaved before disgorging paper, had emboldened me. She'd gotten her hair cut quite short; her exposed neck was as pale as a photographic negative. And so I'd asked her for a date, and after she'd startled me with her yes (provisional though it was), I'd also asked if she were no longer seeing Mr. Hogue.

She'd looked at me with her bright, critical eyes for as long as it took the copy machine to cough up two pages of somebody's five-hundred-page bildungsroman.

"I like Marshall and he likes me, but we don't 'see' each other." Her smile revealed her teeth, which were imperfect. She had a snaggly upper right canine. "He has other interests."

"Ah," I said, which was the sound of my mind opening slightly to receive important information. Air entering the hothouse.

Two weeks later, rocketing up the Saw Mill with stoned Elvin and his barely legal girlfriend, and without Petra, who would get to

Aunt Vi's on her own, if a lunch date she had with Ethiopian friends
of her father didn't take forever, I heard myself make a sound like
"ah" again. It was the sound of fear escaping from between my teeth.
I thought there was a good chance that Elvin would fail to negotiate
one of the many curves on the narrow Saw Mill, or, if we got that far,
one of the many curves on the even narrower Taconic. I thought,
too, that there was a good chance that I wouldn't see Petra, even if
Elvin didn't wipe us out. She'd made no promises.

Connie passed me a bottle of beer and smiled. She was wearing
a retainer, which made her look even younger than she was. She had
a pretty mouth with a fleshy underlip, and brown eyes clouded by
worry. How had Elvin acquired her, I wondered. Had he been wearing his green suit when they met? I drank my beer rapidly and asked
Connie, who was keeping pace, for another. We made more eye contact. Elvin, singing along with a disco number called "Rock Your
Baby," miraculously steered us off the Taconic and down a snaky,
wooded road to my aunt's house.

It felt wonderful to have my feet on the ground, and after I'd
kissed my aunt (who was wearing a huge, brocaded sombrero), and
after I'd gotten a plate of food and another bottle of beer, I sat down
on the grass, under a large sugar maple, next to Beau Jack, one of
Aunt Vi's two Airedales. Elvin took Connie to see Aunt Vi's studio,
an old implements shed that she'd fixed up. Beau Jack panted and
watched me eat barbecued chicken. It was a hot, breezeless afternoon. The whirligig on top of the studio didn't twitch. Insects crack-
led. A group of guests sat on the screened-in front porch, under a
ceiling fan. I gave Beau Jack a chunk of chicken, and then I saw Mr.
Hogue walking across the lawn toward me. He wore long, white
pants (cuffed) and a blue polo shirt. The heavy July air seemed to
part for him. Sweat didn't sit upon his forehead and it didn't mark
his shirt. His wire-rimmed glasses caught the light and scattered it.

He settled himself in the grass with his drink, something with
a wedge of lime floating in it. "How do you like being retired?" he
asked. There was amusement in his eyes. He had offered to help me
find a job at another publishing house, but I'd declined, saying I
hadn't decided what I was going to do next.

I took a gulp of beer. "Retirement is O.K. so far. I sleep in and read Proust. Slowly. All those long sentences, you know, that drag themselves across the page like serpents after a meal." I was high and was hoping to get higher. I hoped to see Petra soon, before I peaked.

"Petra is reading Proust, too, I think."

An old wood-paneled Country Squire station wagon rolled up the driveway, crunching gravel. Four men in white shirts got out. Musicians.

"I'm in love with Petra," I said, in a voice that one might use when taking an oath of office.

"I gather you're trying to say you're not queer," Mr. Hogue said evenly.

"No," I said. "I mean, yes, I'm not." I drained my beer and looked toward my aunt's studio. Elvin stood outside the shed, pouring beer down his throat. In the flat mid-afternoon light, he seemed somehow two-dimensional, tinny: Man with a Big Thirst. I didn't see Connie.

"How would you know that you aren't queer?" Mr. Hogue gazed at me in a kindly, schoolmasterly sort of way.

Was there a correct answer? "I can just feel it," I said.

Mr. Hogue rose from the grass and laid his hand on the ridged trunk of the sugar maple. There were tap holes at the tree's waist. "A young friend of mine told me about a drug he once took—MDA, I think he called it—that made him want to fuck trees. Even skinny saplings excited him. He was out in the woods, you see, trying to get in touch with his soul. And he spent hours, under the influence of this drug, dry-humping anything with a trunk. And he was perfectly happy. Don't you think it's odd that a little chemical adjustment, a jot of this or that, is enough to make you surrender to a tree?"

"You have to watch what you put in your mouth," I said smartly.

"But then a tree is always there for you, isn't it?" Mr. Hogue said. "Well, let me know if you change your mind and want to get back into the publishing business. I won't tell anybody that you killed Stawicki's dog." He smiled pleasantly and walked away.

I drank more beer and kept an eye out for Petra while playing croquet with Elvin, my aunt, and Dr. Bickel. With a cigarette clamped between her lips and her sombrero set securely on her head, Aunt Vi drove the dentist's ball thirty yards off the course, into the weeds beyond the edge of the lawn. "Oh, doctor," she shouted joyfully, "when you fetch that ball, beware the stinging nettle and the wily copperhead!"

The band, which was set up on the other side of the house, played "Blueberry Hill." Elvin sang along and drove my ball into the nettles and fleabane. "Take a hike, bro," Elvin said, and then cruised around the course in a single turn. "It's scary how good I am," he said. "And I'm stoned out of my mind."

The band played a slow blues and I went for a hike. I walked by Aunt Vi's studio, where, through a window, I saw a large canvas of Elvin sitting in a high-backed rattan chair in his green suit; he looked like a small-time criminal dressed for dinner. Then I walked through a field toward a spring-fed pond that was at the back of the property. I'd had five beers, but I could still walk a fairly straight line and identify some of the plants that grew in the field: goldenrod, wild carrot, fleabane. Down in a swale, fifty yards from the pond, was a clump of purple loosestrife. The sun shone brightly and the high grass brushed against my shins, making them itch. I felt a throbbing in the neighborhood of my left eye: pain gathering for a frontal assault. I'd just about given up on Petra's coming. I was looking forward to sticking my head in the water.

There was a swimmer in the pond—three, actually, if you counted Beau Jack and his mother, Cornelia, who were wading in the reedy shallows. The human swimmer was Connie. She was naked as a baby, her white bottom pointed at the pale blue sky. Her head was turned away from me. Then she dove under and when she re-surfaced, her black hair sleek and shiny, she saw me. I was standing on the grassy bank, unbuttoning my shirt. She seemed unalarmed by my presence. She'd given me that lingering look in the car, after all, which I'd interpreted to mean: I wouldn't mind it if you saved me from Elvin. Though this reading of things was perhaps nothing more than vanity on my part. I had a habit of seeing sparks where there were none.

"How's the water?" I asked. I put my shirt on the ground, next to Connie's pile of clothes. The dogs came over to sniff me.

"OK," she said. "Cool."

She looked away as I got out of my underwear. Had she seen me trembling, my heart whanging away under my bare chest? Proust: "We do not tremble except for ourselves, or for those whom we love." I didn't love Connie, needless to say.

I waded into the pond, soft, oozy mud sucking at my feet, and then I dove out toward the middle, beneath the sunstruck surface. The cool water gripped me, held me under. I could see nothing. If I kept swimming, I thought, I'd end up on the other side of the world, far from harm.

I came up behind Connie, my mouth inches from shoulder blade and knobby vertebrae. She turned and pushed away from me a bit. Her arms were folded across her breasts. She was wearing a cross around her neck.

"Where'd you meet Elvin?" I asked.

"The Moon Bowl," she said. "In Moonachie. Where I go bowling."

"Do you like him?" I heard the band—the boom-da-boom of the bass, an undulant melody from the saxophone. Cornelia caught the scent of something and ran into the field. Beau Jack continued to work the pond shallows.

"Yeah, sure," Connie said. "Except he's kind of crazy, you know." She smiled and I saw the retainer wire across her teeth. "He has this, like, Saturday Night Special that he bought from this guy at the bowling alley. He got it so he could protect himself from nuts."

"Would he shoot me," I asked, "if he saw us getting it on?" I moved toward Connie. The pain above my eye had increased.

"Don't," she said, backing toward the shore, her hands still covering her chest. I saw the fear on her face, the way her wet, dark hair framed her tightening features. But I said nothing. I half-closed my eyes and lunged at her. Bone knocked against bone as she fell back. Her head went under for a second. I pulled her up toward me. She'd swallowed water and was coughing. I pressed my mouth against hers and tried to insert my tongue between her teeth. She shook her head free.

"I'm sorry," I said.

"Go die," she said. She coughed and wiped her mouth against

her forearm. She was sitting where the water was perhaps a foot deep. Her breasts were small and waifish.

I turned away and drifted toward the middle of the pond, where the water came up to my chest. I squatted there, in the brilliant sunshine. I heard Connie get out of the water, but I didn't move. I heard Beau Jack's collar tags jangling. I stayed in the water for a long time, watching the skin on my fingers pucker, waiting to hear Elvin's voice. Would he ask me to turn around before he shot me with his Saturday Night Special? If, for some reason, he didn't shoot me, I thought I might try to resuscitate the story I'd been writing about him.

The sun slipped down the sky and swallows made passes over the pond. I wanted a cigarette and got out of the water. My clothes weren't where I thought I'd left them, however, nor were they anywhere nearby. Connie had removed them, apparently. I walked out into the loosestrife and found one of my sneakers. With the sneaker in hand, I walked back and forth across the field, stepping lightly among the milkweed and fleabane and hairy-stemmed ragweed, looking for the rest of my clothes. After a while, I sat down, using my shoe as a cushion. I was a hundred yards from my aunt's house. I could see people playing croquet, my aunt among them, with her absurd flying saucer of a hat. I could walk naked to my aunt's house now or later. Or I could simply sit here and wait for the turkey vulture, making black circles in the sky to the south, to descend upon me.

Then I saw two figures crossing the field. One was Elvin, his shimmery blue muscle shirt hanging out of his jeans. The other was a young woman wearing a dark skirt and white shirt. Petra. She trotted to keep up with Elvin, who was making tracks, despite being unable to walk straight. They were talking. I heard Elvin say, "I don't know what exactly he did. All I know is what my girl told me."

Petra stopped and held her hand up against the declining sun. Elvin came on. I rose to my feet. I held the sneaker in front of my crotch.

"You look like fucking Mr. Pitiful, bro," Elvin said, squinting, angling his head so that the sun wouldn't strike it so directly. I did not think it was to my advantage that he was wobbly drunk. "But I'm going to hit you anyway. You know why."

I didn't say anything smart or brave. I didn't say anything at all. I just stood there, hiding my privates behind my shoe, looking past Elvin at Petra, wondering where she and her Ethiopian friends had gone for lunch. Wasn't there an Ethiopian dish called *wat?* A hot, peppery dish that made your lips burn? Perhaps she'd had some of that for lunch, perhaps the taste of it was still there on her tongue.

Happy

Dean Bakopoulos

When he was twenty-nine years old, Charlie Pappas left Vermont and moved back to Detroit after suffering from what—in a more innocent, big-band-playing, hat-wearing era—would have been called a crack-up.

The many factors leading to the crack-up included Charlie's disillusionment with teaching in private schools, a tendency to self-medicate with six-packs of Blatz, and his fiancée Jana's affair with a prominent sculptor named Harris Mills. One day, a little drunk on after-school martinis, Charlie was searching for the checkbook in Jana's backpack. There, he discovered a note that said: *Jana, I know we were meant to be together, because after we make love, I dream of God and his angels, and they are dancing and they are made out of the most beautiful clay.*

He waited for her all night. She often worked late in the studio and sometimes came home after Charlie had fallen asleep. That night, however, Jana did not come home at all. It was if she sensed that Charlie had discovered the note.

Charlie finished a case of Blatz; he stayed awake, watching the darkness slip out of the sky.

In the morning, Charlie crumpled to the floor in the middle of teaching a lesson on the Transcendentalists. He began to whimper, then turned on his stomach, slowly and softly pounding his head against the tile floor, murmuring, *There is no Oversoul, there is no Oversoul, there is no Oversoul.*

The children in his class, sensitive, wholly tolerant, and intellectually gifted offspring of wealthy ex-hippies, ex-activists, and ex-organic farmers, sat in silence for a moment, and then, led by Skye Nelson and Prairie Masterson, they joined Charlie in his mantra. Some students even tapped their foreheads on their desk, so that, minutes later, when the headmaster arrived in the doorway, he found the tenth grade American literature class tapping their heads on desks and denying the Oversoul in unison.

And there was Charlie, twitching on the floor.

Charlie arrived in Detroit during a May that was still damp with the last chill of winter, carrying all his belongings in a duffel bag. His father, Jimmy Pappas (The Restaurant Supply King), to whom he had not spoken in three or four months, picked him up at the airport. Charlie had spent very little time with Jimmy since the age of twelve, but his father had money and a house, and Charlie did not. On the way home from the airport, Jimmy Pappas's driver, a college student named Ray, talked more than Charlie did. There was not much to catch up on between father and son; they barely knew each other anymore.

Charlie moved into his father's five-bedroom, three-bathroom home in Elk Ridge, a ridge-less, elk-less subdivision in Livonia. Now that Charlie felt himself without options, he figured it was time to accept his father's invitation to visit. Jimmy had been sober almost two years. Ever since Jimmy had gotten out of his six weeks in rehab, he'd been asking Charlie, his only child, to come home for a visit.

The first night of the visit, just before bed, Charlie looked at his father's bare white skin and noticed the small black band around his ankle. His father was still under house arrest for four drunk-driving convictions. He had to wear an electronic tether to prove to the police that he was home by dinnertime each evening. There was a whole year left on his sentence, but he'd avoided prison and was allowed to keep working. Jimmy had a lot of friends.

Charlie looked at the red light of the tether as he followed Jimmy up the stairs and down the hallway. Jimmy flipped on the light to the room at the far end of the house.

"See, you've got your own can," Jimmy said, showing Charlie to a white-carpeted guest room. "You can't beat that."

There was something poetic in convalescing in his estranged father's guest room, spending the summer largely in the climate-controlled indoors, reading novels from the public library, and watching documentaries on PBS. He felt a bit like an eccentric, weak poet in an E. M. Forster novel, and for weeks, he shuffled around as if he were a bastard cousin in a Merchant & Ivory film, grimacing and trembling, exaggerating his mood swings for dramatic effect. He had lost weight, had gone from slim to skinny. His father allowed him his space, cooked egg-white omelets for him on weekend mornings, and brought bland meals heavy with starches to his room.

Sometimes Jimmy would ask questions: "Do you think you might want to call your mother?" or "Do you want to tell me what happened with Jana?"

Charlie would always shake his head. "I'm not ready," he'd say. "Not yet."

Some afternoons while his father was at work, Charlie walked to the corner Rite-Aid and bought Canadian Club whiskey and magazines. Charlie hid the whiskey in his sock drawer. He was happy for his sober father, and did not want to tempt him. He'd skip home from the store, holding a brown bag. He'd read Blake before bed, sipping from the whiskey, and all night he dreamt of angels and tigers and flames, and, of course, sometimes, Jana.

Jana would call every week, and Charlie kept refusing her calls. Charlie did not know how she had found him there, since his family should rationally have been the last place he turned to in times of emotional crisis. Charlie suspected that Jimmy had called Jana, just to let her know Charlie was okay.

"She really wants to talk to you," his father would say. "She wants to hear that you're okay."

"Tell her I'm dead," Charlie said. He raised his voice and made himself sound woeful and breathless, hoping Jana would hear him on the other end. "I've withered away and disappeared. Tell her I no longer exist!"

"I'll tell her," his father would say.

Charlie would bury his face in his pillow. From down the hall, he could hear his father's voice: "He's in the can, honey. Can he call you back?"

Charlie had been in his father's house that whole summer, but he'd spent it largely locked in his room, and it wasn't until August that certain things about his father really began to sink in: Jimmy Pappas was not just thinner than Charlie remembered, he was trim. The decades of drinking had melted off his body like wax. Jimmy was only five-seven, three-inches shorter than Charlie, but had always been bigger, sturdier. Jimmy was once a man with big shoulders, a barrel chest, and a gut like a beer keg. Charlie figured that his father's waist was now maybe six inches slimmer, and his chest and shoulders less like massive slabs of meat than they once were. He also had stopped dying his thick and wavy black hair, which had now gone completely gray. And Jimmy wasn't smoking, he was barely even swearing. Charlie, at first, imagined this was just a sign of old age. His father was sixty now, and had begun living with a little less day-to-day intensity, letting the vices of youth and middle-age fade into the acceptable, lovable eccentricities of an old man. But one morning in late August, Charlie awoke and heard his father singing "Old Rugged Cross" in the shower across the hall. Charlie got up, showered and dressed, and came downstairs just after dawn (his earliest rising yet) and found his father eating a bowl of Fiber Madness cereal and reading the Bible.

"Pop?" Charlie said, walking into the kitchen. "Is that what I think it is?"

"Yeah, bran flakes," he said. "Have to keep an eye on the old ticker."

"I mean the book," Charlie said. "Is that . . ."

"The unadulterated Word of God?" Jimmy said. "That it is."

Jimmy pulled up the leg of his khakis to reveal the black, plastic band with a small box the size of a pager on his inner ankle. He tapped the device.

"This is what saved my life," Jimmy said. "Getting this sumbitch on my ankle."

Jimmy had, thankfully, lost his driver's license after the arrest, and for the last year had to hire Ray, the college student, to drive him on his sales calls. He now attended AA meetings at least five days a week. But Charlie already knew all of this. What Charlie was just learning was that Jimmy had also left the Greek Orthodox church, more a social club than a place of worship, and now attended New Promise Evangelical Free, a giant suburban church where Jimmy became involved in a group known as the Covenant Men.

"That fourth accident," Jimmy said. "You know, I ended up on the lawn of Stevenson High School, your alma mater, crashed into the statue of the giant Spartan, and right then and there, I said, 'Pappas, you've fought your last battle.'

"I had a bottle of vodka left," Jimmy said. "And I sat there sucking it down, knowing it was the last drink I'd ever take. I waited for the cops to come, and when the first officer responded to the scene, he poked his head in the window, saw me, drunk, with a bloody nose, and he said, 'Sir, do you know Jesus Christ as a personal Lord and Savior?'"

"You were converted by a cop?" Charlie said. "Can they do that?"

"The Spirit just moved him," Jimmy said.

"How could you keep this from me? You never told me you'd been born again."

Really, though, it all made sense. His father was more sensitive, more earnest than ever before. Charlie felt like he was living with some rich, gay uncle.

"I had a vision," he said. "I wanted you to work on your problems before you had to listen to mine."

"Jesus Christ," Charlie said.

"Amen," Jimmy said.

Jimmy shoveled a spoonful of bran flakes into his mouth.

"Son," he said, milk dribbling down his chin. "I want you to come and work for me. I know you've had a rough go of it lately, but you need to get back in the game, get back on the horse. Let go and let God."

Charlie was twenty-nine, homeless, broke, and out of options. So he said yes. "One day at a time, son," Jimmy said. "Easy does it."

Jimmy went to give his son a long hug. Charlie kept his arms at his sides.

"You start tomorrow," Jimmy said. "Shave. Wear a clean shirt."

The next morning, Charlie woke up, shaved, put on a blue oxford, and began working as his father's driver. Ray was demoted back to warehouse picker, and from that moment on he would look at Charlie with sharp glares of resentment and scorn. "Ignore him," Jimmy said. "He was a lousy driver and talked too much. I was about to can him anyway."

Jimmy called Charlie a "sales assistant," but Charlie's duties were obviously those of a chauffeur. He would shuttle his father from one appointment to the next. He would make eleven dollars an hour, two dollars more than Ray had been paid.

His father, always the salesman, put a lovely spin on things: "Jimmy Pappas, the Restaurant Supply King," he said, "has found an heir to the kingdom."

"Let's not get ahead of ourselves," Charlie said. "I am, technically, a professional educator."

"I know," Jimmy said. "One day at a time."

After a few weeks of work, Charlie was feeling better. By Labor Day, he was able to dress, comb his hair, and speak in complete sentences about his ex-fiancée without crying. He'd cut back on his drinking, no longer hiding Canadian Club in his sock drawer. In fact, while sitting with Jimmy in those court-ordered nightly AA meetings, Charlie slowly began to have the realization that he was not really an alcoholic at all. Charlie only made himself drink out of sadness and boredom; he'd almost quit drinking entirely, without any withdrawal or effort. It almost depressed him—all of that drinking, and still, he'd failed to become an alcoholic. He was a fraud; he'd been faking alcoholism. He quit going into the meetings with his father, and instead, waited in the car, listening to *All Things Considered* like any normal, sober citizen.

Jana continued to call. She'd been working as a development officer at an arts colony when she'd met Harris Mills. Charlie liked to believe that she had had enough of passion; she was calling because she craved the comfort of Charlie. He imagined going back to her, maybe after a brief fling with a Hooter's waitress, and for the rest of his life having a moral upper hand in their relationship. But no, he knew, they would not get back together: soon, he would have to return one of her calls and discuss the details of their break-up—who got their jointly owned assets, what to do with the engagement ring, the Volvo, the tandem bicycle. They had lived together for almost seven years and this break-up would not be easy. It would have logistics.

But before he dealt with Jana, Charlie wanted to visit his mother. He had not called her all summer, because he was not sure he was in any condition for such a meeting, but now he was ready to see her. One day at a time, he thought. He wondered if she knew he was in town.

One morning, after dropping off his father at the Restaurant Supply King warehouse in Wyandotte, Charlie drove down Jefferson Avenue, past abandoned homes with plywooded windows, abandoned cars without wheels or windshields, abandoned factories, warehouses, storefronts. It was easy to imagine that somewhere, amid the wreckage of abandoned industry, there were hundreds of aimless, abandoned children, mouths ajar, clamoring for attention.

His mother, like his father, was a drunk—but she was a drunk without money, and thus her life was more reckless and riskier than any life Jimmy Pappas had ever lived. Jimmy always had money; Mary did not.

Jimmy and Mary divorced when Charlie was ten, right after Jimmy's first arrest, a DUI that discovered him driving naked with a real estate agent named Tina.

His father moved to an apartment downriver, near the Restaurant Supply King warehouse. Charlie lived with his mother, who was furiously upbeat and struggled to be sober. She was a painter, and after the divorce she shifted to painting landscapes and bland nature scenes because she could sell them for inflated prices at craft shows. She remained that way—a hard working, housekeeping, rock-solid Mom—until Charlie went to high school. After that she entered a string of gradually worsening relationships—an alcoholic professor, a violent truck driver, a homicidal chef—and began painting in the abstract. She accelerated her social drinking and lost her job at Wayne State University, where she had been teaching studio art as an adjunct. By the time Charlie started his first year of college in Ann Arbor, his mother had lost the house and had moved back to Detroit, where she lived in the small ranch that had once been her childhood home.

While he was in college, Charlie fell into the pattern of bringing his mother nutritious groceries and maintaining the modest house. When he moved to Vermont, he began to give up on her, slowly. He wrote letters, called every other Sunday, and visited when he was in town, which was (deliberately) rare. His mother had been living with a security guard named Frank Geary, but just before his crack-up, Charlie had learned that Frank Geary had moved to Alaska with most of the contents of his mother's modest savings account. He knew his worrying about his mother was another factor in his crack-up episode.

He pounded on the door. "Mom," he said. "It's me, Charlie."

He waited for a moment.

From the small house next door, a dark, bearded man dressed in white pants and a black shirt emerged. "What do you want?" he said, his voice thick with a Middle Eastern accent. "What are you looking for?"

"My mother lives here," Charlie said.

"Oh, of course," the man said. "I recognize you from the pictures now, from up close."

"I'm Charlie," he said.

"Sam Alireza," the man said. "I am the neighbor of your mother."

Standing in the front yard, Charlie learned that Sam was from Yemen, and lived next door with his two brothers. Sam was trying to earn enough money to bring the rest of his family to the U.S. He owned a dollar store on Warren Avenue called Dolla-Palooza.

"My brothers and I help your mother out sometime," Sam said. "She, you know, she sometimes drinks too much wine."

"I know," Charlie said.

"I help her sometime. I check on her some days, take her for groceries. She is a nice woman. Very pretty, used to be, right?" Sam said. "She talks very nice about you."

"She does? That's nice," Charlie said. "I just moved back to the area. I've been trying to call her."

"Yes," Sam said. "You've been in Vermont."

Charlie took out one of the new business cards his father had printed for him the week before. On it was his new cell phone number. Seeing his name embossed on cardstock, a slew of printed digits beneath it, suddenly made Charlie feel powerful.

"Well, Sam, if my mother ever needs anything, my phone number is on this card," Charlie said. Sam studied the card and slipped it into his pocket. Charlie was feeling territorial. It's my wreck of a drunk of a mother, he thought. I'll take care of her, pal. You get your ass back to Dolla-Palooza.

"Do you want a house key?" Sam said. "I can let you in."

"I appreciate you taking care of my mother so well," Charlie said.

"It's what neighbors are for," Sam said. "Besides, your mother she's been very good to us. She gave us a car. She couldn't drive it anymore."

Sam waved to the Ford Tempo in his driveway.

"She gives my little brother, Ali, a little money when he cuts her grass and shovels her snow," Sam said.

Sam went inside his own house for the key to Charlie's mother's front door. Charlie did not know how he felt about this, a neighbor he had never met, with keys to his mother's home.

They found her on the floor in nothing but a slip. Sam apologized and back-pedaled his way out of the house, whispering, "I think she is drunk."

Charlie considered fleeing with Sam, but then Charlie saw his mother stir. She pushed her face off of the carpet, and looked at him.

"Charlie?" she said.

"Mom?" he said.

"Oh my God," she said. She managed to stand and hug him, and then backed away, put her hands on her sides and smoothed down her slip, realizing she was barely dressed.

"My God, you look terrible," she said. "What's wrong?"

"You look great," he said.

"Oh, God, I know, sorry. I was up all night, and just couldn't sleep. Back problems. I finally just stretched out on the floor, hoping to get rid of the pain. I took some Tylenol P.M. and it worked. I was out like a light."

She excused herself and went into the bedroom. "Help yourself to a Coke or something," she said. "I think there's some in the fridge."

The fridge was empty except for beer, a box of wine, and condiments. He opened the freezer, and found nothing but a tub of ice and two gallon bottles of vodka.

His mother came back to the room in a gray T-shirt and jeans.

"I called you a few times this summer," his mother said. "I never got an answer."

"I've been traveling," he said.

His mother had once been radiant, full of intellect and verve, and, even when he was a small boy at social events, he could tell that the men in the room wanted to be near his mother. They gathered around her, laughed at her jokes with great enthusiasm, helped her with her coat, admired her dresses, called Jimmy Pappas a lucky son of a bitch.

Jana reminded him of that, in some ways. Jana had always been the most beloved of the women in the room, and Charlie also felt as if people were muttering behind his back, Why is she with him?

Jana had fine, black hair, which she wore long, a small face with delicate cheekbones and a delicate chin, aqua blue eyes. Jimmy, when he met her for the first time, said, "Christ, Chuckie, she looks just like your mother."

When Charlie met Jana, it was in his last semester of college. An English major, he enrolled in Drawing 101 because he imagined it to be easy, or at least, to be free of required reading. His teacher was a graduate student named Teddy who wore oversized tweed coats and had a painfully wispy red beard. Charlie was one of the only men in the class, and Teddy didn't seem to like him.

After only a week of class, Teddy said to Charlie, "You have a tendency to depress people, Mr. Pappas. People have been complaining. Your sullen mood makes it hard for them to work."

On the day they were to try their hands at figure drawing, Jana entered the art room, shed her robe, and stood, completely naked, in front of Charlie. His instant erection proved to him that he didn't have the mind of an artist at all, but rather the temperament of a Greek from Detroit.

His hands were paralyzed. He couldn't draw the woman in the room. At the end of class, Teddy stood behind Charlie and said, "Pappas spent the whole hour staring at the model, but there's not one mark on the paper."

The class laughed as they gathered their supplies, Teddy smirked in Charlie's face, and Jana, on the platform in the middle of the room, put on her robe, and frowned. Barefoot, she walked right up to Teddy and said, "Last time I work in your class, fuckstick. That was completely inappropriate."

Charlie found himself at the bus stop with her a few minutes later, and stammered an apology. "I'm not a very good artist," he said. "My mother is one, though."

Jana smiled and nodded.

"It wasn't like I was just staring at you," he said. "Not like Teddy implied. I'm not some kind of sicko."

"Teddy's a fuckstick," she said. "But you were. Staring, I mean. That's not cool in an art studio, ogling the model."

A bus was coming and Charlie decided he was in love. He went for broke. "Every time I went to put a mark on the page," he said. "I couldn't. It was too overwhelming, the idea of catching any sliver of your beauty. I couldn't do you justice."

"Please," she said. The bus came by and she got on. It was not his bus, but he followed her. Maybe he was a sicko.

"Could we have coffee?" he asked her.

"I don't know," she said.

Three weeks later, he found her again at a small graduation dinner party hosted by a mutual friend. The mutual friend reassured Jana that Charlie wasn't a freak. (Later, Jana had said, she liked Charlie's looks so much—the olive skin and black hair of a Greek, with the blue eyes and slender frame from his mother's Ukrainian side—that she'd have dated him even if he had turned out to be a freak.)

At the end of the evening, Jana came up to Charlie and said, "I'll give you another chance."

"At what?" he said.

"At dealing with my beauty," she said.

It was already October. Charlie had settled into a comfortable routine. In the morning, he would drive his father from client to client, and then after lunch, he'd drop him at the office in Wyandotte and head over to visit his mother. He began buying his mother art supplies, helping her clean and organize the chaos of her basement studio, intent on helping her paint again. He'd been a bad son. He'd neglected her. She needed his help.

Though most business could be conducted via phone, fax, or e-mail—who really needs a salesman to sell plastic soup spoons and mint toothpicks?—Jimmy Pappas preferred to call on most of his clients in person.

"A firm handshake, a warm smile, a look square in the eye," Jimmy said that morning, "is the difference between a carton of toothpicks and a whole crate of them."

Jimmy had felt a burning need to go to an AA meeting that morning, so Charlie had to take him. Now they were behind schedule. Jimmy sat in the passenger seat, depressed and grim, looking over his order sheets, occasionally scratching the area of his ankle that was covered by the tether. Charlie's new cell phone rang, which it almost never did, and, because Jefferson Avenue was, as always, completely free of traffic, it was easy for Charlie to answer the call.

"Charlie," a thick-accented voice said. "This is Sam Alireza."

"Who's that?" Charlie said.

"Sam. Your mother's neighbor."

"Hey, Sam. What's wrong?" Charlie asked, though he already guessed at it.

"Your mother fell."

"She fell?"

"She's fine. She's okay, really."

"Can I talk to her?" Charlie said.

Charlie gripped the wheel tighter, glared in his rearview at an old LTD that had come out of nowhere and was tailgating him. What if he was in Vermont, he wondered? What would she do then? Who would Sam call?

"No, no, she not know I call you. She went inside. I found her. She was bleeding. I tried to call the ambulance, but she says she's fine."

"Thanks, Sam. I'll be right over."

"Okay," he said. "Don't tell her I called, okay?"

"No, Sam, I won't."

Charlie hung up the phone and Jimmy turned the radio back on, and looked down at his orders.

"We need to make a detour, Dad."

"A detour? I'm on a schedule today, Bub."

"Tough shit, Dad," Charlie said. "I have a driver's license, and you don't."

When Charlie pulled into his mother's driveway, Jimmy looked at the small red brick ranch, the same house where he picked her up for a first date thirty years ago.

"I can't believe she's back in this old place," he said.

"Well, she is," Charlie said.

"Is the neighborhood safe? It's full of Arabs."

"You coming in?" Charlie said.

"What do you think?" Jimmy said.

"Fine. Stay out here."

It took his mother a few minutes to come to the door. Charlie could hear her coughing and sneezing, which for some reason she did anytime she was drunk, and when she opened the door she looked dazed, a trickle of blood running down her forehead.

"What?" she said.

"Open the door," Charlie said. "Now."

In the light of the kitchen, Charlie cleaned his mother's head wound with damp paper towels and a little hydrogen peroxide before realizing that the gash was worse than he thought. She'd definitely need stitches.

"How much did you have to drink?" Charlie said.

"One beer," she said. "The steps were slick. I just fell."

"The day is dry as bone."

"Then I tripped on something. A stick."

"You need to come with me to the hospital," Charlie said. "You need stitches."

"I do not," she said, but her face was worried and her defiance half-hearted. She knew she had messed up, and could not get out of this mess alone.

On the counter, six empty beer cans were stacked on the cutting board. Charlie went and touched them, one by one. "Where's your coat?" he said.

"Wherever I left it," she said.

Charlie helped her with her coat, helped her with the buttons, and then led her to the car. Midway down the driveway, she stopped. "Who the hell is in the car?" she said.

"Nobody," Charlie said, and tugged on her arm. "Don't piss me off, Mom. I'm all you have left."

"Not true," she said. "You just like thinking that."

They got in the car, closed doors, buckled seat belts. Jimmy had turned off the radio.

"Dad? Mom?" Charlie said. "Jimmy Pappas? Mary Olszewski Pappas? I believe you two know each other, right?"

"I can't believe this," Mary said.

"We've met," Jimmy said, winking. "Hello, Mary."

Jimmy said you couldn't trust the hospitals in Detroit, because the emergency rooms would be full of real traumas—shootings, stabbings, overdoses. He had Charlie drive out to St. Mary's in Livonia. On the way, Jimmy busied himself by taking out his cell phone and rescheduling the day's appointments. "Family emergency," he told client after client.

In the backseat, Mary huffed and sighed.

"I don't need any goddamn stitches," she said, as more blood worked its way down her forehead. Jimmy handed her a clean handkerchief and said nothing.

At the hospital, Jimmy did all the talking. He talked to the nurse on duty, explaining the situation, helping his ex-wife fill out forms. He flagged down a doctor after they'd been waiting nearly an hour. The doctor, about the same age as Charlie, seemed to know Jimmy. The two men shook hands, and Jimmy mumbled something in the doctor's ear.

The doctor gave Mary three stitches and then presented a short lecture on drinking too much. He handed Charlie some pamphlets, *The Alcoholic in Your Life* and *When Someone You Love Can't Stop Drinking*. Charlie pictured a frantic family gathered around a man who was chained to a sink, his mouth fixed on the faucet. He smirked at his own joke. The doctor scribbled some notes in a file folder and frowned.

"You might want to consider getting your mother into a treatment program," he said to Charlie.

"That's a good idea," Jimmy said. "We hadn't thought of that, Doc. Thanks."

The doctor shrugged and left the room.

"Fuck you very much, Dr. Asshole," Jimmy said. The born again Jimmy would resort to swearing, Charlie guessed, if it would make his ex-wife laugh.

It worked. For the first time all day, Mary laughed, holding a hand up to her newly stitched forehead.

"Thanks, Jimmy," she said.

Charlie and Jimmy walked Mary to the door. Jimmy turned on the TV for her, and Charlie fluffed a pillow.

"You'll be okay?" Charlie asked.

"I know how to flip channels," Mary said.

"Are you dizzy at all? The doctor says you may be dizzy," Jimmy said.

"I've been dizzy for the last five years," she said. She was still a pretty woman, Charlie thought, her hair still black with a few strands of silver, her blue eyes, despite their weariness, a dazzling blue. Her skin, olive-toned, but perhaps, Charlie thought, it was now simply jaundiced. I've pickled myself, she said to him once, and now I don't age. She was thin, because she never ate more than a few meals a week. The slurring, wrecked voice, the snorting chuckles, seemed out of place with her graceful features, and the cut on her forehead stood out like a signal that the worst was yet to come. She slumped on the couch, took off her sneakers and socks, undid the button on her black jeans.

Charlie could see Jimmy scanning Mary's current life, the stray cups and plates on the end tables, tubes of paint and brushes everywhere, cobwebs in the corners, walls with crooked pictures.

"Take care, now," Jimmy said and turned to go.

Charlie went out the door a few minutes later, his mother, sober now, calling after him: "Don't be mad," she said. "Thank you, Charlie."

In the car, Jimmy said nothing until they were a few miles down the road.

"I had no idea," he said. "That it was this bad."

Before they turn for home, Jimmy said, "Maybe we can make the five o'clock meeting, son? I think it's a two-meeting day."

That night, exhausted and weary, Charlie fell into bed before dinner. Around eight, he heard the phone ring, heard his father answer it.

"Hi, Jana," he said. "I'm fine, thanks. Well, he's here," his father said. "But he's had a rough day. I don't think it's a good day to be talking to him."

"No," he said. "I think he just needs to sleep."

Charlie drifted back into sleep, and in and out of dreams for the next hour, he heard his father talking in a low voice. Could he still be talking to Jana? What could he possibly be saying to her? They'd only met a few times, brief occasions, and if Charlie had remembered correctly, Jimmy had been drunk every time.

Later, around ten, Charlie woke up to find his father standing in the doorway to the bedroom.

"Chuckie," Jimmy said, leaning against the doorjamb. His tether stuck out from his pajama bottoms like some mechanical tumor. "Chuckie, did I do that to your mother?"

Charlie realized something: It's the question he'd been waiting years for his father to ask. His mind raced to fights in the kitchen, to Jimmy's tendency to disappear for long weekends, Jimmy's failure to make school plays and soccer games, Jimmy, and his booze and his business and his women.

"Yeah, Dad. That was you," he said, though he didn't believe it. "That was all you."

Jimmy nodded and looked at the ground. "Okay, son," he said. "That's fair. I accept that."

That autumn was heavy with early frosts and clear nights, nights too cold for clouds. The skies speckled with stars. In the evenings, Charlie would read the stories of Cheever and drink tea by the gas fireplace. Charlie had fallen in love with Cheever, all that gin and sadness, gin and sadness. It stirred him; he longed to meet a woman who was also stirred by Cheever. It was the first he'd thought of the possibility of another woman since he'd left Jana.

One night, Jimmy, unable to exit the front door for fear of setting off his tether, hung his head out the living room window.

"Would you look up at all these goddamn stars," he said. "Points as sharp as daggers, I bet."

"Actually, they're giant balls of gas," Charlie said. "They don't have points."

"What's your point?" Jimmy said.

"My point is that the common representation of a star with five points is not the same thing as one of the celestial beings you so admire."

The window was still open, and the air was filling with a crisp chill. Charlie buttoned another button on his thick flannel.

"You know what, Chuckie?" Jimmy said. His face reddened, and tiny blue veins seemed to pulse on his cheeks and nose. "You know what? Sometimes I'm so fucking glad I'm not you."

"How's that?" Charlie said.

"You don't know how to have any joy in your life, do you?"

"I do, Dad. I'm just in a really weird place right now." Charlie didn't want to hear this, his chronic fuck-up of a father offering his hard-earned wisdom. Charlie looked to the floor.

"What the hell are you talking about?" Jimmy said. "You're in Livonia, in your old man's living room."

"I mean it, Dad. You don't get where I'm at."

"I get that you have a beautiful woman who is dying to talk to you, who wants you to come home, and you can't even answer her phone calls."

"What do you know?" Charlie said. "She cheated on me."

"People fuck other people, Chuckie. Then people say they're sorry. They make up; they're still in love. Or they split up for good, and they spend the rest of their lives a little heartbroken, but still breathing. And they start fucking someone new. That's life, Chuckie. You can't sit around in limbo all day. You know, if you want, pick up the phone and tell Jana to go jump in a lake, tell her you never want to see her again."

"My father the philosopher," Charlie said.

"I've taken my hits. I've licked my wounds. I know some things."

Jimmy shut the window and left the room.

Charlie closed the Cheever, folded his arms on the couch, thought of Jana. He could call her now, announce that he was coming home, and be done with all of this. Maybe they could reconcile, and he'd build the kind of life he once imagined he would build for himself in Vermont—quiet and peaceful, full of beauty, full of art and philosophy and every fine thing a fine home should have. He could quit chauffeuring the Restaurant Supply King to and fro; he could quit having to see his mother in the sad chapters of what had become a quiet, desperate life. Vermont would be covered in snow within weeks, and he could hide there in the mountains and go after his old life with passion and vengeance.

The weeks ahead were somber ones. Charlie still drove his father in the mornings, and visited his mother whenever he had free afternoons. His father seemed quieter, less enthusiastic than he had once been about their partnership. His visits with his mother were brief, he would go somewhere with her, to the bank or the grocery store or to the mall, and then he'd be gone.

By the first of November, the gold and red leaves had been erased from the trees. The air turned relentless with its wind and its gray dampness, and suddenly, one morning, the trees had bare black branches slick with frost and mist and looked like the skeletons of obsolete machines.

One morning, a Wednesday, Charlie agreed to go with Jimmy to a Covenant Men prayer breakfast at church, where he sat with his father and listened to ex–football coaches, broke businessmen, and former city council members recount how Jesus had freed them from shackles of adultery, alcohol, and pornography. Charlie was not buying into it, but it fascinated him. It amused him. He found something endearing in everyone in the room. He longed for a conversion, but knew conversions never came when one is dying to change course. They come only when you think you're happy, and Charlie was not yet delusional.

Afterwards, Jimmy suggested that instead of the usual morning rounds, they'd go and visit Mary. He was holding a box of leftover doughnuts.

"Why?" Charlie said. "She's probably still passed out from a night of drinking."

"Don't talk about your mother like that," Jimmy said. "Besides, I want to bring her these doughnuts. They're very good."

Charlie humored him. Jimmy also stopped at the Beirut Bakery and bought her a couple of loaves of dark rye. "Her favorite," he said.

They had to knock for five minutes before Mary answered the door in her robe. "What the hell?" she said.

"Red Cross," Jimmy said. "Care package."

Mary opened the door. Jimmy handed her his gifts.

"Uh, we can't stay," he said. "Uh, Charlie wanted to bring you this stuff for breakfast. And, uh, I wanted to invite you to Thanksgiving next week."

Charlie looked at his mother and nodded. What else could he do?

"That's sweet of you boys. I'll check my calendar. I'll let you know."

There was silence. Mary set the box of doughnuts and the bread on the coffee table. She held the top of her robe closed.

"I've got to get this house clean today," she said. "I've been so busy. It's a wreck."

"We wouldn't notice a dirty house," Jimmy said. "A couple of bachelors like us? Well, okay, Mary, sweetheart, we got to run. Keep the family business going."

Charlie nodded again. When he got in the car, he was about to say something, but he wasn't sure what to say. Before Charlie could speak, Jimmy put up his hand.

"It's my house," Jimmy said. "I don't need to explain a freakin' thing to you."

The day before Thanksgiving, winter gave way to a warm, yellow morning with wind barely strong enough to push a few dried leaves along the pavement. Charlie woke up a little after eight in the morning to the sound of his father vacuuming. Charlie got out of bed and went down the stairs. Jimmy was in boxer shorts, an undershirt, and black socks. His legs were thin and white and nearly hairless, and his arms no longer pulsed with definition. He was struggling with the vacuum on the steps, without his clothes, his thinning hair flopped over his forehead beaded with sweat.

My God, Charlie thought, he's just an old man.

"Morning, Dad," Charlie hollered over the vacuum cleaner.

His father hit the power switch and the machine coughed itself quiet. "Hey," he said. "Sorry I had to wake you. I've been up for two hours, and couldn't wait anymore."

"No, that's fine," Charlie said. He smiled. He wanted suddenly to be cheerful and full of youth and energy. "I'll get dressed and give you a hand."

"There's coffee," Jimmy said.

In the shower, Charlie began to believe that his father was trying for something specific here, with this Thanksgiving. What if his mother would be so moved by the invitation, what if she would be so impressed by the new Jimmy Pappas and his giant, clean new house that she would decide to go on the wagon herself? Charlie pictured his mother and father saying their morning affirmations together, exercising at some sterile suburban health club in matching His & Hers sweat suits, then, after breakfast at Big Boy, walking arm and arm into an AA meeting.

Is it true, Charlie wondered, that children of divorce could never quite come to terms with the end of their parents' marriage? Did they always, in their heart of hearts, believe that reconciliation and reunion are possible?

Down in the kitchen, Charlie whistled as he poured his coffee.

"You're in a better mood," his father said.

"I am," Charlie said.

"You're glad that your mother is coming over?"

"I am," he said. "Yes."

They spent the morning with the *Today* show on the television, dusting the furniture, washing the floors, cleaning sinks and toilets.

"I hope she notices all our hard work," Charlie said. Now, not only was he feeling like some naive, hopeful kid, he was sounding like one.

They ate an early lunch of tuna salad on wheat garnished with fat-free corn chips and then they went shopping. His father insisted on a twenty-pound turkey at the grocery store; he bought a cartload of food, enough for a family of twelve or more.

Late that night, after they'd cleaned every room in the house, prepped much of the food for the next day's meal, and called Mary to confirm the invitation (Jimmy was sending a cab), they sat in the family room, watching television. A van pulled into the driveway.

Charlie stood up and went to the door. The sign on the side door of the van read, A-1 Airport Transport.

"Don't say anything," Jimmy said. "Like I said, it's my freaking house."

Jana was wearing a long charcoal coat, black leather boots, black gloves. She pulled a small suitcase behind her. In her absence, Charlie had detested her, loathed her, wished danger and despair on her person. Seeing her coming toward the door in a dim flood of porch light, he loved her again.

"Hey," Jana said.

"Jana," Charlie said. "Jana."

"Charlie," she said. "I'm sorry."

"About what?" he said.

She looked at him crooked.

"Oh, oh that?" Charlie said. "I'd almost forgotten."

"Happy Thanksgiving," she said.

"Right," he said.

Jimmy shook Jana's hand, invited her inside. It was not how Charlie had pictured such a reunion at all. He'd rehearsed cold lines and steel-eyed stares. But he had not had any time to prepare, and he moved along with his whims. He hugged her.

"Is this you, Dad? Did you do this?" Charlie said, when he finally was able to let go.

Jimmy said, "Big freaking day tomorrow. I'm turning in."

Then they were alone in the kitchen; Charlie came up behind her and kissed her neck.

"There's a double bed in my room," Charlie said.

"And you'd have your own can," Jimmy called from the top of the stairs. "It's nice."

They'd been in love a long time, Charlie thought. They could talk in the morning. He didn't know what Jana was thinking. She had grown quiet. Maybe he didn't want to know what she was thinking.

He led her up the stairs. "We should talk," Jana said. "Don't you think this is a little odd? I should sleep in another room."

"Jana," Charlie said. "I loved you for seven years. So we've been apart for a few months, so what?"

"A lot has happened," Jana said. She was whispering.

"I haven't had sex in a long time," Charlie whispered back.

Jana did not smile, not at first, but then she laughed. "I can't believe you," she said. "But you look good. And it's been a long time for me too."

"It has?" Charlie said. He couldn't help beaming.

She nodded and kissed his lips.

"We can talk tomorrow," he said and took her hand.

Right now, he just wanted to lie in bed and be glad that she was there. He had no rage in him, he felt like a child who had thrown a tantrum and had finally come out of his room for dinner. He felt embarrassed by everything, the affair, his breakdown, how he would not come to the phone.

"I thought you hated me," she said.

"I did," he said. "Until I saw you again. I had planned to be mad."

"Did you know your father invited me?" she said. "He sent me the money for a ticket."

"No idea," he said.

"Does this mean you want to get back together?" she said. "Because, I don't know. This is still very odd, too fast."

"Jana, I want to be with you here, just for now. That's all I want. We might die tomorrow. Let's just be together tonight."

They went into the bedroom and closed the door. She touched his face and whispered to him. "Fine," she said. "I'd like that."

"Are you okay?" he asked.

"I'm fine," she said, taking off her skirt and folding it on a chair. "I've just been traveling all day. You're right. We can talk tomorrow."

"I missed you so much," he said.

The next morning, snow flurries. Charlie awoke to a window filled with gray light and downy white fuzz floating in the sky. It felt divine. Suddenly, Charlie understood his father's cheerfulness, understood what it felt like to have another chance. *One day at a time. Easy does it. Let go and let God.* His father's petty maxims somehow seemed wise and full of truth. He nudged Jana.

She seemed to take a few minutes to figure out where she was, and then she sat up in bed, pulling the sheet over her breasts.

"Look," Charlie said. "Snow."

"Oh boy," Jana said. And then she buried her face in her pillow.

They showered together in silence, as familiar as if there had been no five-month hiatus in their morning rituals. She sat on the toilet and peed as he brushed his teeth. They picked up their intimacy with ease.

Dressed and with wet hair, they went downstairs. Jimmy Pappas was brushing melted butter on the spanokopita, about to put it in the oven.

"Good morning, you two," he called, and Charlie couldn't help blushing. Jana looked annoyed and exhausted.

"Everything okay, Jimmy?" Jana said.

"Great, great. I've got a taxi picking up your mother around one, we should eat by three, and you don't have to lift a finger."

Jana looked at Charlie and mouthed the words, *Your mother?* Charlie had, of course, told her everything about his parents.

Charlie picked at some carrots that Jimmy was chopping.

"I did forget one thing," Jimmy said. "Cranberries."

"We'll go get some," Charlie said.

"If you don't mind," Jimmy said.

"That's fine," Jana said.

They kissed in the car, a long, slow kiss that Charlie wanted to last longer. Jana pulled away. "Cranberries," she said.

In the store, Charlie wanted to buy canned cranberries, but Jana insisted on fresh.

"Fresh is too much trouble," Charlie said. "I want canned ones. Open and eat."

"Buy fresh," she said. "I can prep them myself. I'll need some sugar and some oranges too."

The express checkout was crowded with men standing in line, all holding single items—butter, canned pumpkin, or breadcrumbs. Charlie flipped through a men's magazine. He found an article that said, "How do you know when she's cheating?"

He laughed, and showed the article to Jana. "Wish I had seen that article a long time ago," he said.

Jana walked out of the store, leaving Charlie standing in line.

He paid for the groceries and found her in the parking lot, standing next to the car.

"What was that?" Jana said.

"A joke," Charlie said.

"Not funny," Jana said.

"A little levity, that's all," he said.

"You know, I didn't come here to fuck you. I came here to settle things once and for all, to see what remained."

"I know," Charlie said. "I was wrong. It's weird. I'm adjusting. You had time to adjust. You prepared yourself for this. I was taken by surprise."

She wouldn't look at him. He set the groceries in the back seat.

"That's fair," she said. "Okay."

And then, when they were back in the car, the heater on, she told Charlie something she'd been waiting to tell him.

"Last night," she said. "It's just that I may have given you the wrong idea. I'm not saying it was bad, but I'm also not sure we should get back together."

"Why are you here then?"

"Your father, he begged me. He said that you needed closure. He said you were suicidal, he worried for your life. I didn't want you to die. I think he was exaggerating though. You seem fine."

Charlie felt his insides crumple, his organs deflating.

"Are you still with the sculptor?"

"No."

"Really?"

"He left," she said.

"So what was last night?" he asked. "I don't get it."

"It was closure, Charlie. I guess that's what it was. It was nice."

"It felt nice? Or it was a nice thing to do?"

"Both," she said. She touched his arm. "Oh, Charlie."

They drove back from the store in silence: Charlie with windshield wipers on although there was no rain, Jana looking at the package of cranberries in her hands.

"Hey, can we do one thing?" Charlie said, as they pulled into his father's driveway. "Can we deal with this later? Can we wait until tomorrow to tell my father? Could we just make sure he has a nice Thanksgiving? I mean, he's been very nice to me and . . ."

"Of course," Jana said. "Of course. I'm a human being, Charlie. I'm not some kind of monster."

"Whatever," Charlie said.

They turned on the Lions' game at noon, which helped to keep the conversation to a minimum. Jana seemed overly interested in the game, Charlie pretended to be concerned about the Lions losing, and Jimmy chattered incessantly while he cooked, about Greek men and their ability to cook without recipes.

"We make love without manuals too," he said.

Around one-thirty, Mary arrived at the door, shaky and pale, but with clean hair and perfume and a long-sleeved black dress Charlie recognized from years before. She had dyed her hair, Charlie noticed. There was no gray. She smiled when she saw Jana, and said, "This is so nice," she said. "To see the two of you together."

"Mary, how are you?" Jana said.

Jana embraced Mary. Mary appeared startled. Charlie's stomach turned under the weight of the fraudulent pleasantness in the air. He felt hot.

"Mary, you look radiant," Jimmy said, his voice booming. "A sight for sore eyes, welcome, welcome!"

He wiped his hands on his apron, gave his ex-wife a half-hug and kissed her on the cheek. Mary's hands remained at her sides. Jimmy almost knocked her over. She did look good, Charlie thought. She was trying. Jimmy was always barreling into people, hugging them without warning.

Jana seemed too practiced at insincere conversation, Charlie thought. He had always thought so, and now he was convinced. Jana engaged everyone in conversation, talking to Mary about painting, talking to Jimmy about the art of salesmanship, even getting Charlie to talk about his love of teaching, which was nonexistent. Jana punctuated the talking with spurts of high, delirious laughter. Her cheeks seemed flushed red with the effort. Jimmy left the room to check on the turkey.

"So, Mary," Jana said, "What do you do with yourself during the day? Are you teaching? Or do you just paint, paint, paint all day?"

"Jesus Christ," Charlie said. Jana knew Mary was a drunk who could barely hold a brush most days.

"Well, I'm between things," Mary said. And then her voice went up a few decibels, just loud enough so Jimmy could hear her in the kitchen, where he was basting the turkey. "My boyfriend, Frank, he's up in Alaska right now, looking for a place for us to live. He'll send for me soon, I'll sell the house, and then I'll go up there with him and paint some landscapes I've never seen before. Frank is very supportive of my work."

In the kitchen, there was the shattering of glass.

"Are you okay?" Mary called. "Jimmy?"

"Everything is fine," Jimmy said, walking into the room wiping his hands on a towel.

"Good," Mary said.

"You know, this is so nice," Jimmy said. "Maybe we should all move in here and it could be like this all the time. One big, happy family."

Everyone burst out in delirious laughter, even though everyone, Charlie thought, knew that Jimmy Pappas was dead serious.

The Lions lost, the turkey was done, and a little after three they sat down for dinner. Mary had a flask in her purse, and had gone off to the bathroom every twenty minutes or so for a hit. She was not drunk, but there was some color in her face and her hands had stopped shaking.

Jimmy said grace, a long rambling prayer that thanked the giver of all good gifts, especially the Lamb of God, Jesus Christ.

"Cheers," Charlie said. "Here, here." He lifted his water glass for a toast.

"Um, is there any wine?" Mary said.

"That'd be nice," Jana said. Charlie knew her stamina was leaving her. She would need alcohol to get through the rest of the afternoon.

"My father is a recovered alcoholic," Charlie said. "Goddamn, people."

"So," Mary said. "We're not."

Charlie wanted a drink as bad as anybody. In fact, the whole table seemed terrified of getting through dinner without anything to drink.

"I could run out and get some wine," Jana said. "I mean, that would be easy to do."

"Yes, great," Mary said.

"I'd rather we didn't," Jimmy said. "You know, I'm still in the early steps of the program. Lead us not into temptation, you know."

"People, I think we can have dinner without wine," Charlie said.

"Oh, I almost forgot. I got Vernor's," Jimmy said. "I'll get out the Vernor's. It's just ginger ale, Jana, but it'll knock your socks off. It's a Detroit delicacy."

"I've had it," Jana said. "In college."

"I'd prefer wine. Or beer? If you have beer," Mary said, "that would be fine."

"Yeah, beer sounds good," Jana said.

Charlie glared at his mother, who shrugged, and then at Jana, who glared back.

Jimmy came back to the table with four frosted mugs of Vernor's. He remained standing, and raised his glass.

"We should all say what we're thankful for," Jimmy said.

Nobody agreed aloud, but Jimmy was determined. "Jana, you go first."

"My art," she said, keeping things generic. "For good friends."

"For my boyfriend Frank and our new life in Alaska," Mary said. "I'm so thankful for Frank."

Charlie watched Jimmy's smile waver. "Besides Frank," Jimmy said. "What else besides Frank?"

"This is sad," Mary said.

"For Jana," Charlie said, going next, keeping the thankful train on the tracks. "Yes, for Jana. Jana, Jana, Jana! And for my family."

"That's so sweet," Mary said.

"Isn't it?" Jana said. "Except we're not getting back together."

"What?" Jimmy said.

"We're not getting back together," she said.

"Fine," Jimmy said. He took a note card from his shirt pocket.

He cleared his throat. "I am thankful for second chances. There is a woman I met over thirty years ago, who I never treated the way she deserved, but by the power of Jesus, I want to ask her forgiveness."

"Pathetic," Mary said.

Jana slumped down in her chair.

"Let him finish," Charlie said.

"He's a fool," Jana whispered. "Mary doesn't love him."

"I love Frank," Mary said.

"Frank left you," Charlie said. "Face it. He's gone."

"And your wife left you," Mary said. "How much did he pay you, Jana? Isn't that just like Jimmy? He paid you, didn't he? Paid you to fake happiness for awhile?"

Jana put her hand over her eyes.

"What, I'd say it's worth at least a grand or two?" Mary said.

"Did he pay you for the ticket?" Charlie asked. "Or did you make money on this? Is this a job? How much?"

"Charlie, what do you think I am, some kind of whore?"

Mary snorted. Charlie pounded a fist on the table.

"I need to call a cab," Jana said.

And as the shouting grew louder, Jimmy Pappas ran from the table, down the basement steps, and there was the sound of wood being split into pieces. They sat at the table; nobody said anything. Charlie started serving food.

"He'll be okay in a minute," he said. "He just needs to cool down."

After Charlie had heaped everybody's plate with food, Jimmy called to him from the basement. "Chuckie, come down here."

Charlie stood up from the table. He picked up a piece of white meat, and chewed it.

"Nobody leaves," Charlie said.

"Be careful," Jana said. "He might have a gun."

"He won't hurt anybody," Mary said. "Not Jimmy."

"Charlie," Jana said.

"You guys keep eating," he said. "I'll be right back."

"Chuckie, please," Jimmy called from the basement.

Charlie was picturing his father holding a pistol to his head, but found his father standing in the space beneath the stairs, looking at a large wooden crate that was nailed shut. He'd already pried one of the front panels off of the crate, but there was another panel underneath it.

"Son, the day I quit drinking," Jimmy said, "I came home and I spilled every drop of liquor I had down the sink. I was shaking the whole time. I felt like I was going deaf and blind. I was sick. No fooling, I even licked the sink out of regret after I'd gotten rid of all the booze."

Charlie nodded. He heard Mary and Jana coming down the stairs, and he felt them stop and stand behind him, but he didn't turn towards them at all. Jimmy kept on talking.

"But in this crate," Jimmy said, "in here, there are forty-eight bottles of wine. The last batch my father—your *Papou*—ever made. He wanted me to save them until your wedding day. It was his dying wish. He loved making this wine, and he thought it might help him be present in some way at your wedding."

"I see," Charlie said.

"You were the only one to carry on the family name," he said. "The only male grandson he had."

"I know it," Charlie said.

"This crate is nailed shut, and with God's help, I never tore it open, even at my lowest point."

"Well, Dad. It doesn't look like I'll be getting married anytime soon. Let's go upstairs."

"That's okay, son. Maybe you and Jana will get back together and marry. Maybe you won't. I just want you to know there is some happiness in life, and it's always there, lurking in the darkest corners, waiting to be set free."

Charlie nodded. He didn't know what else to do.

"Come on, Dad."

"That's all I want for you, son," Jimmy said. "Happiness. A nice, peaceful life."

Charlie turned back to see his mother rolling her eyes. Jana started to go back up the steps. Then Charlie followed her. "Mom and Dad, enough is enough. We might as well eat. There's all that food that Dad made."

Jana and Charlie sat back down at the table, waiting for Mary and Jimmy. "He won't do it, he won't open the wine, he's bluffing," Charlie said.

And then, suddenly, there was a sound that sounded like a hole being punched into a wall, and Charlie turned around. Then he heard Mary yell, "Atta boy!" and Jimmy could be heard huffing and stomping his way up the stairs. He reappeared, suddenly drenched in sweat; in each hand he held two bottles of his father's homemade wine.

"You're right, everyone, we need to drink!"

Mary was behind him, an open bottle already tilted toward the ceiling.

Charlie almost stood and wrestled his father to the ground. But he could not move, he had no idea what to do next. Jana clucked with concern, and looked at him, raising her eyebrows.

"That's the holiday spirit!" his mother said, and Jimmy and Jana laughed. Charlie just watched his father take the corkscrew to those long-saved bottles of wine, and did not move. His mother rummaged through the cabinets for wine glasses, which were hidden on a top shelf behind the flour and sugar. She took the glasses from the cabinet and brought them to the table.

"There's more where this came from," Jimmy said, as he handed each person a bottle of wine. "The best wine in all of Greece!"

Then he drank half of his down in one wild, frantic gulp. Charlie and Jana looked at one another, shrugged and then filled their glasses.

By the time dinner was over, the house had the warm, affectionate glow that can only envelop a house full of drunks. Everyone was touchy and feely, stumbling about the house. Twelve bottles of wine had been opened. Charlie and Jana had already snuck off to the bedroom once, taking pumpkin pie upstairs with them, but instead of sharing the dessert, they found themselves falling into bed, and making drunk, quiet love. Jana fell asleep in bed, her skirt still pushed up around her waist, her blouse unbuttoned, her bra open. She was snoring. Charlie helped her out of her clothes, knowing nothing was different, knowing the intimacy was as empty as any other intimacy. Tomorrow, she would leave him. He would not see her again. He felt sick. He wondered if he could get his father to an AA meeting that night. He knew they stayed open all the time on holidays. Maybe all four of them could go to the meeting. They could throw open the door and bellow, "Happy Drunks-giving!" as they took their seats.

Charlie went down to the kitchen. His mouth was dry. His body ached. He heard his parents' voices, and he walked slowly and softly, trying to hear what they were saying. What could they possibly have to say? He stood in the doorway to the kitchen, and saw his mother and father sitting at the table covered in half-empty serving bowls, dirty dishes, and empty bottles of wine. They were slouched in their chairs, eyes half-shut, talking in inaudible, hoarse voices. To Charlie, it was apparent—there would be no reconnections, no second chances, no renewals or rebirths that would come out of that blurry, wine-soaked haze. But then he looked at Jimmy, who was reaching across the table to touch Mary's hand, and Charlie saw that his mother was leaning in close to his father, as if she expected to hear some profound secret. Mary sat up, and her eyes brightened. She smiled. Jimmy said something to her, and then Charlie saw that his mother was laughing; she was laughing and tossing her hair.

Contributors

DWIGHT ALLEN, author of *The Green Suit* and *Judge*, worked at *The New Yorker* for ten years after receiving his M.F.A. from the University of Iowa Writer's Workshop. His stories have been published in *Georgia Review, Missouri Review, Shenandoah,* and *New Stories from the South,* among other publications. He lives in Madison, Wisconsin.

DEAN BAKOPOULOS was born in Detroit in 1975, attended the University of Michigan, and then earned his M.F.A. from the University of Wisconsin–Madison. His first novel, *Please Don't Come Back from the Moon,* was published in 2005. He is currently the executive director of the Wisconsin Humanities Council.

MARGARET BENBOW's prize-winning stories have been published in *Zoetrope: All Story, The Georgia Review, The Antioch Review,* and elsewhere. She has received a Pushcart nomination, and in 2003 was given a Wisconsin Arts Board grant for fiction. Benbow is presently working on a novel, *Boy into Panther.* Her poems have appeared in *The Kenyon Review, Poetry, The Antioch Review,* and numerous other magazines and anthologies, including *Western Wind* and *Poetry Daily Anthology.* Her collection *Stalking Joy* won the Walt McDonald First Book Award. Benbow has just completed a second book of poems, *Believing Your Eyes.*

ANTHONY BUKOSKI grew up in Superior, Wisconsin. He teaches English at the University of Wisconsin in the port city where his Polish emigré grandparents settled. The author of four story collections, *Time between Trains, Polonaise, Children of Strangers,* and *Twelve Below Zero,* he has been awarded the Creative Arts Award from the Polish American Historical Association and has twice won the Anne Powers Book-Length Fiction Prize from the Council for Wisconsin Writers. In 2002 he was named the R. V. Cassill Fellow in Fiction from the Christopher Isherwood Foundation.

KELLY CHERRY's most recent books are *We Can Still Be Friends,* a novel, and *History, Passion, Freedom, Death, and Hope: Prose about Poetry.* Her collection *The Society of Friends,* from which "As It Is in Heaven" is taken, received the *Dictionary of Literary Biography* Award for a

Distinguished Volume of Short Stories in 2000. Her fiction has been represented in *Best American Short Stories, Prize Stories: The O. Henry Awards, The Pushcart Prize,* and *New Stories from the South.* She also holds the Hanes Prize in poetry. She is Eudora Welty Professor Emerita of English and Evjue-Bascom Professor Emerita in the Humanities at the University of Wisconsin–Madison and sometimes serves as the Visiting Eminent Scholar at the Humanities Center of the University of Alabama–Huntsville.

TENAYA DARLINGTON lives in Madison and writes for *Isthmus.* Her poetry book, *Madame Deluxe,* was winner of the National Poetry Series. She has been previously published in the *Atlanta Review, Chronicle of Higher Education, Beloit Poetry Journal,* and *Southern Poetry Review.* Her work also appears in *Scribner's Best of the Fiction Workshops 1998* and *In Brief: Short Takes on the Personal.* Her first novel, *Maybe Baby,* was published in 2004.

MACK FRIEDMAN is the author of Lambda Literary Award–nominated *Strapped for Cash: A History of American Hustler Culture.* His work has also appeared in the anthologies *Obsessed* and *Wonderlands.* His first novel is scheduled to be published in 2005. He now lives in Pennsylvania.

JANE HAMILTON lives, works, and writes in an orchard farmhouse in Wisconsin. Her short stories have appeared in *Harper's* magazine. Her first novel, *The Book of Ruth,* won the PEN/Ernest Hemingway Foundation Award for best first novel and was a selection of the Oprah Book Club. Her second novel, *A Map of the World,* also a selection of the Oprah Book Club, was an international bestseller. Her novel *The Short History of a Prince* was a *Publishers Weekly* Best Book of 1998, won the Heartland Prize for Fiction, and was short-listed for Britain's Orange Prize. Her most recent novel is *Disobedience.*

JOHN HILDEBRAND is professor of creative writing at the University of Wisconsin–Eau Claire. He is the author of two books, *Mapping the Farm: The Chronicle of a Family* and *Reading the River: A Voyage Down the Yukon.* His work has been anthologized in *Best American Sport Writing 1999, American Nature Writing 1997, The Great Land: Reflections on Alaska,* and *The River Reader.* His articles and essays have appeared in *Harper's, Audubon, Manoa, Outside,* and *The Missouri Review.* He is the recipient of a Bush Artist Fellowship, a Wisconsin Arts Board Fellowship, the BANTA Award from the Wisconsin Library Association, and the Maxwell Schoenfeld Distinguished Professorship.

Contributors

JESSE LEE KERCHEVAL was born in France and raised in Florida. She is the author of six books, including the poetry collection *Dog Angel,* the novel *The Museum of Happiness,* and the writing text *Building Fiction.* She is the Sally Mead Hands Professor of English at the University of Wisconsin, where she directs both the Wisconsin Institute for Creative Writing and the M.F.A. Program in Creative Writing. She lives in Madison with her husband and two children.

J. S. MARCUS was born in Milwaukee and graduated from the University of Wisconsin–Madison. He is the author of a book of stories, *The Art of Cartography,* and a novel, *The Captain's Fire.* His fiction is included in the anthology *Wonderlands.* His nonfiction has appeared in many publications, including the *New York Times* and the *New York Review of Books.* He currently lives in Connecticut, where he is completing his second novel.

JUDITH CLAIRE MITCHELL is a graduate of the Iowa Writers' Workshop and a recipient of a James Michener/Copernicus Society of America Fellowship. She was a James C. McCreight Fellow at the Wisconsin Institute for Creative Writing and currently teaches creative writing at the University of Wisconsin–Madison. Her debut novel, *The Last Day of the War,* was published in 2004 to critical acclaim.

LORRIE MOORE is the author of five books, the most recent of which is the story collection *Birds of America,* which won *The Irish Times* Prize for International Literature. She is currently the Delmore Schwartz Professor in the Humanities at the University of Wisconsin–Madison.

ANN SHAFFER's poems have been published in *Poetry.* Her essays have appeared in *Isthmus,* the *Milwaukee Journal,* and other publications, and her criticism has received a Milwaukee Press Club Award. She is the author of the children's book *The Camel Express* and has published numerous stories and poems for children. Shaffer has also been a commentator on Wisconsin Public Radio's *To the Best of Our Knowledge.* She is currently writing a novel and lives in Madison.

RON WALLACE was born in Cedar Rapids, Iowa, and grew up in St. Louis, Missouri. He is Felix Pollak Professor of Poetry and Halls-Bascom Professor of English at the University of Wisconsin–Madison. He serves as codirector of the Program in Creative Writing, which he began in 1975, and as editor of the University of Wisconsin Press Poetry Series (Pollak and Brittingham Prizes), which he founded in 1985. His most recent poetry books include *Long for This World* and *The Uses of Adversity.* In 2000, he won the "World's Greatest Short Short Story Contest."